THE ART OF KISSING

"Don't tell me you consider yourself qualified to give me instruction on the art of kissing! What an elevated opinion you hold of yourself."

Alysson felt a perverse desire to shatter a little of his arrogant self-assurance. "Well then, you are welcome to try."

He raised an eyebrow, staring at her in disbelief.

She laughed. She had succeeded in rendering him speechless.

Her enjoyment was short-lived; a strange, unfathomable smile tugged at the corner of his mouth. "I am tempted, I admit. If I were to instruct you, I would take you in my arms, like so . . ." Suiting action to his words, he slipped an arm about her waist and drew her fully against his body. He held her thus, with consummate ease, one arm about her waist, while his other hand lifted to brush the vulnerable column of her throat.

Against her will Alysson found herself actually, incredibly, wanting his kiss . . .

"Lord of Desire is a wonderful love story with a spellbinding essence . . .
Alysson and Jafar have my hands-down vote for outstanding hero and heroine of the year."

Affaire de Coeur

Lord of Desire

NICOLE JORDAN

AVON BOOKS ◆ NEW YORK

LORD OF DESIRE is an original publication of Avon Books. This work has never before appeared in book form. This work is a novel. Any similarity to actual persons or events is purely coincidental.

AVON BOOKS
A division of
The Hearst Corporation
1350 Avenue of the Americas
New York, New York 10019

First Avon Books Printing: January 1992

AVON TRADEMARK REG. U.S. PAT. OFF. AND IN OTHER COUNTRIES, MARCA REGISTRADA, HECHO EN U.S.A.

Printed in the U.S.A.

RA 10 9 8 7 6 5 4 3 2 1

To Ann, Sandra, and Irene—for having the immense good taste to fall in love with my valiant desert sheik, and the skill to help me give him life.

When love has pitched his tent in someone's breast,
That man despairs of life and knows no rest.
Love's pain will murder him, then blandly ask
A surgeon's fee for managing the task—
The water that he drinks brings pain, his bread
is turned to blood immediately shed;
Though he is weak, faint, feebler than an ant,
Love forces him to be her combatant;
He cannot take one mouthful unaware
That he is floundering in a sea of care.

FARID UD-DIN ATTAR
Twelfth Century

Prologue

Kent, England
1840

The rawboned Barbary stallion looked out of place standing before the Duke of Moreland's family estate. The august mansion, golden-hued and boasting magnificent proportions, was the epitome of grace and elegance, while the sweeping lawns and topiary yews had been clipped and manicured and cultivated within an inch of their civilized existence.

In contrast, the fiery Barb with its sinewed haunches and overlong mane seemed almost savage. Indeed, it bore scant resemblance to the sleek thoroughbreds in the fabulous ducal stables. This animal had been bred for endurance and speed in the harsh desert climate of the Sahara, and trained for war. Held by a wary, liveried groom, the bay stallion snorted defiance and pawed the ground while awaiting its master.

The horseman who at last came bounding down the wide stone steps of the ducal mansion also contrasted with his noble surroundings—despite his tailored frock coat and starched cravat of black silk, despite even his claim to noble birth. The young gentleman was the duke's grandson, but his bronzed skin and hawklike gaze lent him a hard, ruthless air that the refined British gentleman of his class would never attain. There was nothing refined, either, about the way he leapt on the stallion's back or wheeled his mount as if he'd been born in the saddle.

Muscles quivering in response to its rider's innate restlessness, the horse strained eagerly at the bit, in anticipation of freedom.

Yet Nicholas Sterling kept the Barb tightly reined as they traversed the smooth graveled drive between two rows of stately oaks; for once he checked his impatience to be away. He could afford this last mark of obeisance, this final show of respect for his grandfather. His interview with the duke successfully concluded, he was at last free to pursue his own life. Ten years. Ten long years in this foreign land, enduring what had felt like captivity. But at last he could shed the trappings of his civilized English upbringing, as well as the English name that had been thrust upon him.

The taste of freedom was sharp on his tongue, as sweet as the spice of fall in the air, as vivid as the oaks turning the colors of autumn. The stallion seemed to sense his mood, for the animal began a spirited dance, nostrils flaring, ears pricked forward, as they passed beneath the canopy of the giant oaks.

The horse never flinched as an acorn whistled over its head and fell to earth, a credit to the stallion's training. Nicholas absently murmured a word of praise, his thoughts occupied by his impending departure from England.

The next instant he heard another faint whistling . . . then a small, dull thud as his silk top hat went flying off his head to land in the drive. Scattering gravel as he spun the stallion around, Nicholas reached for the curved dagger at his waist—a habit learned in youth—before remembering he had no reason to carry a weapon in this tame country. He had not expected danger to be lurking in a British tree.

Or a female, either.

But that was precisely what met his astounded gaze as he stared overhead. She was hard to see. If not for the acorns he would have passed her by; her black gown was nearly hidden in the dappled shadows. Even as he peered up at her through branches and leaves, she defiantly flung another acorn at his fallen chapeau, missing it by mere inches.

The bay stallion, taking exception to this aggression, thrust its forehooves squarely on the ground, tossing its proud head and snorting in challenge. Soothingly Nicholas laid a gloved hand on his mount's neck, but his mouth tightened in anger.

"The first acorn," he said softly, "I mistook as an act of nature. Even the second, when you targeted my hat, I excused as an accident. But not the third. Would you care to know the consequences of a fourth?''

When she didn't reply, Nicholas's gaze narrowed. By now his vision had grown accustomed to the shadows, and he could see that the perpetrator perched on the limb overhead was a young girl of perhaps thirteen, with chestnut hair, several shades darker than his own dark gold, styled in ringlets. The hem of her gown was a scant four feet from his head, giving him a glimpse of lace-edged pantalettes. The quality of the material was unmistakable, bespeaking wealth if not current fashion.

Even as he fixed her with a hard stare, the girl tossed her head defiantly, much like his stallion had just done. ''Tuppence for your consequences! You don't frighten me in the least.''

The novelty of her reply gave him pause. He was not accustomed to being challenged by a female, certainly not by a child. Staring at her, Nicholas was torn between amusement and the urge to turn her over his knee. Not that he had ever raised his hand to a woman. But he didn't intend to divulge that particular fact just now. Repressing amusement, he schooled his features into suitable fierceness.

''If you decide to throw another acorn,'' he warned, ''I shall be persuaded to give you the thrashing such willful misbehavior deserves.''

In response, the girl raised her chin another notch. ''You will have to catch me first.''

''Oh, I shall. And I guarantee you won't like it if you put me to the trouble of climbing after you.'' His tone was pleasant, yet carried a hint of something soft and deadly. ''Now, do I disarm you, or will you surrender your weapons without a fight?''

She must have believed his threat. After a moment's hesitation, she let the fistful of acorns drop harmlessly to the ground.

Nicholas was satisfied that she wouldn't again dare hurl one of her missiles at him, but he couldn't leave her to pelt other unsuspecting travelers with acorns. ''You should have considered what might have happened,'' he added more casually. ''Had my horse been any less well-trained, he might have bolted, perhaps even sustained an injury or delivered one to me."

"I wasn't aiming at your horse, only your hat. I would never hit an animal. Besides, he didn't bolt. You didn't have any trouble holding him, for all that he looks so savage."

"You presume to be a judge of horseflesh? I assure you, this beast is far more valuable to me than any of the pampered animals in the duke's possession."

"Will you sell him to me?"

The sudden question, delivered in such a hopeful tone, took him aback.

"I can afford his price," she said quickly when he hesitated. "My papa was exceedingly wealthy."

Several answers immediately came to mind. That his horse was not for sale. That a stallion was not a suitable mount for a young lady. But his curiosity was aroused. "What would you want with him?" Nicholas asked instead.

"I shall need a horse when I run away."

He raised an eyebrow at her. The rebellion was back in her tone, echoing a sentiment that was familiar to him. "Where do you intend to go?"

"India, of course."

A smile tugged at the corner of his mouth. "I'm afraid you cannot ride a horse to India."

"I know that! But if I am to find a ship to take me, I must first travel to a seaport. And I cannot *steal* a horse, you see."

"Ah . . . no, I fear I don't see."

"I am not a thief!" She sounded indignant. "And if I were to steal one, they would discover it missing and come after me sooner. Well," she demanded as he silently pondered her logic, "will you sell him to me or not?"

"This particular horse is not for sale," Nicholas said, managing to keep the laughter from his voice. "And in any case, I expect your parents would be rather concerned if you were to run away."

He expected her to be disappointed, but to his surprise, the girl suddenly swung down from the tree limb with a flurry of skirts to land on the low stone wall beside the drive. There she stood for an instant, staring back at him.

She was an intriguing child, with huge storm-gray eyes

that seemed too big for the rest of her plain features. Eyes that were angry, defiant . . . anguished. He caught the reflection of tears in those haunted eyes, before her defiance crumbled. "I don't have any parents," she whispered in a grief-stricken voice.

The next moment, she leapt down from the wall and fled across the manicured lawn, to the shelter of a copse of willows.

So strong was the impression of a wild young creature in pain that Nicholas had to follow. Reining back his mount, he urged the stallion over the low wall, then cantered across the lawn and skirted the willows. He found her lying face-down on the grass beside an ornamental lake, sobbing as if her world had shattered. Unexpectedly, he felt guilt. Had he caused her tears?

Dismounting, Nicholas sank down beside her and waited. Not moving, not touching her, merely letting her feel his nearness, the way he would one of his horses. She didn't acknowledge his presence in words, yet he knew by the stiffness of her shaking young body that she was aware of him. And after a while, her sobs lessened enough for her to speak.

She didn't want to answer his probing questions, though. Her first reply, when he asked her what was troubling her, was a husky "Go 'way."

"What kind of gentleman would I be if I left a young lady in distress?"

"I am n-not in distress!"

"Then why are you filling the lake with your tears?"

She didn't reply; she only curled her knees up more tightly and buried her face in her arms, in an effort to shut him out.

"Tell me what the trouble is and I will go away." Again no answer. "I can be very patient," Nicholas warned quietly as he settled back for a long wait. "Why do you not have any parents?"

He heard a watery sniffle. "They . . . they died."

"I'm sorry. Was it recent?"

After a moment the girl gave a faint nod.

"And you miss then?"

Her nod was a bit more vigorous this time, but still she didn't volunteer any answers.

"Why don't you tell me about it?" Nicholas prodded. "I would like to hear what happened. Was it an accident?"

It took some time, but by gentle persuasion, he learned the cause of her grief: her parents had died from cholera in India, and she had just been sent back home to England to attend boarding school. That was why she was dressed in mourning. That was why she was sobbing so bitterly.

Nicholas remained silent, understanding now. He had once felt the same anguish, a grief so deep it seemed fathomless. Grief and a fierce hatred. He knew what it was like to be orphaned without warning. To have childhood abruptly ended in one brutal, mind-branding moment.

"I should have died, too!" she cried in a voice muffled by her arms. "Why was I spared? It should have been me. God should have taken me."

Her desolate plea brought the memories crowding in on him. Her death wish was something Nicholas also understood. Guilt for having lived, for having cheated death when loved ones had not escaped. He had seen his father struck down by a French bayonet, his mother brutalized and murdered by soldiers who were no better than ravening jackals.

"I hate England!" the girl exclaimed suddenly, fervently. "I despise everything about it! It's so cold here . . ."

Cold and wet and alien, he thought. The constant chill had bothered him, too, when, against his wishes, he had been sent to live among his mother's people ten years ago. England was so very different from his native country—the vast deserts and rugged mountains of North Africa. Watching the girl shiver, he wanted to console her. He fished in his pocket and found a monogrammed handkerchief, which he pressed into her hand.

"You will grow accustomed to the cold," he said with quiet assurance. "You've only been here . . . what did you say? Two days?"

Ignoring his handkerchief, she sniffed. "I like hot better." Lifting her head then, she turned those huge, gray, glistening eyes on him. "I *shall* run away. They shan't keep me here."

Seeing her mutinous expression, he was struck again by

the passionate nature of her defiance. She was a strong-willed, rebellious child . . . Not so much a child, really. Rather a young girl on the brink of womanhood, a bud beginning to unfold. And just as intriguing as he had first thought. Hers was a plain little face, true. Plain and piquant and rather incongruous. Nothing matched, and yet it was arresting on the whole. Given a few years she might be fascinating. Her heavy, straight brows gave an exotic, almost sultry look to those haunted eyes, while her sharp little chin indicated a stubbornness that boded ill for anyone who tried to control her.

He felt a strange kinship with her, this young English girl who wanted to return to India where she had been raised. He understood her compelling need to defy authority, to lash out at even those who had her best interests at heart.

He knew; he had been there. Leaning back on his hands, Nicholas recalled the half-wild boy that he'd been. He had run away twice before he'd agreed to his grandfather's bargain: he would remain in England to be educated, until he reached his majority. Then if he was still of a mind to return to Barbary, the duke would fund his passage.

Had the bargain been worth it? For ten years he had chafed to return to his homeland, while his grandfather had nearly despaired of turning "a savage little Arab" into a civilized English gentleman.

The transformation, though ultimately successful, had been painful. He was only half English, born to a woman enslaved by a Berber warlord after her ship had been captured by Barbary pirates. He couldn't deny his warlike Berber blood—though his noble English grandfather would have preferred to ignore it altogether. He was considered by some to be a dangerous rebel, by others an infidel. Even though his parents had eventually married, his father had been of a different faith.

But he had mastered to perfection the fine art of acting the aristocrat: boredom, cynicism, hypocrisy, seduction. Not only was he accepted by the fashionable world, he was sought after by the opposite sex with fascination. Despite his mixed blood and questionable legitimacy. Or perhaps because of it. The ladies of his grandfather's class who were first to profess themselves shocked at his background were willing, even eager to invite him to their beds, curious to find out if he was the dangerous savage they conjured up in their ignorant imaginations.

Nicholas's gaze shifted to the young girl beside him. His term in England was ending, while hers was just beginning. She would have to endure the lonely existence, just as he had endured.

His probing gaze surveyed her damp face. Though the flood of warm tears had abated, she was still grieving; her trembling lower lip lent her a vulnerability that was heart-rending. Nicholas longed to comfort her.

"Have you any family here?" he asked gently. "Did your parents have relatives?"

Her young face clouded with pain before she looked away, her fingers clutching the handkerchief he had given her. "I have two uncles . . . three if you count the one in France. But they don't want me. I would just be a burden to them."

At the mention of France, Nicholas felt his stomach muscles tighten, yet he forced himself to reply lightly. "Then I suggest you convince them differently. Perhaps you should contrive to become indispensable to your uncles—give them good reason to want you."

When she turned to stare at him, the thoughtful expression that crept into her eyes almost made him smile. "Wipe your face," he said gently. "You have tearstains on your cheeks."

She obeyed him almost absently. When she was done applying his handkerchief to her damp face, she held it out to him. "I should give this back . . . thank you."

The handkerchief bore the initials of his English name. "You may keep it," Nicholas replied. "I won't be needing it any longer where I am going."

She eyed him quizzically. "Where are you going?"

"Away. To another country."

Sudden hope lit her face as she scrambled to her knees. "Will you take me with you? Please? *Please?* I won't be any trouble to you. I can be a model of decorum if I truly put my mind to it. Truly I can."

The impropriety of asking a perfect stranger to escort her to a foreign land obviously hadn't occurred to her. Yet Nicholas hesitated to correct her. The plea in her voice, in those huge gray eyes, made him suddenly wish he could do what she asked.

Slowly he lifted his hand to her face. Tenderly, with his thumb, he wiped away a tear she had missed. "I'm afraid I can't," he said softly.

Just then the bay stallion which had been standing obediently lifted its head to sniff the wind. Nicholas turned to watch as a small, dark-skinned man appeared from behind the willows. He wore the native dress of India, a white cotton tunic and loose trousers, and a plain turban wrapped around his head.

Seeing him, the girl sat down abruptly, smoothing her rumpled skirts and wiping at her red eyes again with the handkerchief.

The small man approached with a soft tread and bowed low before the girl, his dark forehead nearly touching his knees. "You gave me great fright, missy-sahib. You should not have strayed so far in this strange place. The Erwin Sahib will say I do not take care of you. He will beat me and cast me out—may Allah protect me."

Nicholas expected the girl to take exception to the servant's scolding, but instead her tone was one of fond exasperation, not defiance.

"Uncle Oliver will *not* beat you, Chand. He never blames you when I misbehave."

"You have been hiding yourself from me again." The Indian raised his eyes heavenward. "What have I done to deserve such ingratitude?"

She actually looked contrite. "I am sorry. But you needn't have worried, Chand. I've come to no harm. This gentleman—" She gave Nicholas a quick glance that carried a hint of shyness. "—has been kind enough to lend me his handkerchief."

Protectively, the servant scrutinized Nicholas and his manner of dress, but the dark little man must have been reassured, for he tendered another bow before addressing the girl again. "The Erwin Sahib has requested your presence. May I say you will come, yes?"

She sighed. "Yes, Chand, tell my uncle I shall be there in a moment."

The servant did not appear pleased with her response,

but he bowed again and withdrew, muttering under his breath. Nicholas was left alone with the girl.

"My Uncle Oliver," she said by way of explanation. "He is paying a call on the duke. Uncle Oliver brought me here to England because he feels responsible for me, but I know he will be happy to wash his hands of me."

Nicholas smiled, gently. "Then you had best begin at once to change his mind."

The faint smile she gave in return was tentative, shy, but a smile nonetheless. "Thank you for not telling Chand . . . about the acorns. He would have been ashamed of me." She hesitated, twisting the handkerchief in her fingers. "I owe him my life, you see. In India, when I was a child, he pushed me from the path of a rogue elephant and saved me from being trampled. That was why my papa engaged him—to watch over me and keep me out of mischief."

"Is he ever successful?"

Her eyes widening, she stared at Nicholas a moment before apparently realizing he was teasing her. The rueful smile she gave him this time was genuine. "I suppose I am a sore trial to him sometimes."

Nicholas could well believe it. "Just promise me you won't throw any more acorns. You are dangerous with those things."

"Well . . . all right, I promise."

He rose then, dusting off his buff trousers. Looking down at the girl, he felt strangely lighthearted; she had quit weeping, and the grief had faded from her eyes.

Without another word, he mounted the Barb. But as he rode away, he gave a final glance over his shoulder. The girl was sitting with her arms wrapped around her knees as she stared at the lake—contemplating her future, he guessed.

Satisfied, Nicholas turned his attention to his own future, to the bitter score that needed settling. Today he had turned twenty-one. He was celebrating not his birthday, but his freedom; today he had received the duke's reluctant blessing to return to his country, the land the French had named Algeria.

Freedom! For himself and his father's people. He would return, with but two purposes filling his heart: to drive the French from his homeland, and to seek vengeance against the man who so brutally had claimed the lives of his beloved parents.

Freedom! How sweet it would feel to set foot once more in his native land. To gallop across the hot desert plains, to slake his thirst at a well, to find refuge from the heat in the rugged mountains. How glad he would be to give his back to this cold, damp country with its hypocritical morals and twisted notions of civilization.

A moment later, when he passed his silk hat where it had fallen, he left it lying in the dust. No longer would he have need for that or any other English thing. Not his fashionable clothing, not his name of Nicholas Sterling.

Henceforth he would resume the noble Berber name he had been given at birth. Henceforth he would be known as Jafar el-Saleh.

Part One

Her passion is quite African; her desires are like a tornado in the desert—the desert, whose burning vastness is mirrored in her eyes—the desert, all azure and love, with its unchanging sky and its fresh, starry nights.

HONORÉ DE BALZAC

Chapter 1

Algiers, North Africa
1847

Vengeance had been a long time in coming.

Jafar stood on the darkened terrace outside the brightly lit chamber, calmly watching the man he planned to kill. The arched doors of the reception room, though open to the night, were curtained with a silken gauze. The sheer draperies lent a hazy glow to the glittering soiree within, muting the sounds of gay laughter and conversation. They also served a useful function, letting him see inside while preventing him from being observed by either the crowd of wealthy Europeans or their host, Colonel Gervase de Bourmont.

With one finger, Jafar held the curtain slightly parted. His face was set with cold determination as he silently studied his enemy. The colonel was a tall, dark-haired gentleman in his mid-thirties, a military man of striking good looks and a keen intelligence. Jafar had never met the Frenchman face-to-face, but the name of Bourmont had been branded on his mind for seventeen years.

And now, finally, the moment for revenge was at hand.

During the past few months, since Bourmont's arrival in Algiers, Jafar had become well-acquainted with the colonel's every movement. His spies had been unfailingly thorough. He knew down to the smallest detail every aspect of both the colonel's official and personal habits. What he ate for breakfast. Which route he took to his offices each morning through the narrow, twisting streets of Algiers. What horses he preferred. Which prostitutes he patronized.

15

The colonel's taste in women ran to full-blown, lusty beauties with generous curves and sultry looks. Which was why his choice of a bride was surprising.

Jafar's eyes narrowed as again he shifted his gaze to the young woman standing beside the colonel. She was scarcely average height, with a slender waist that a man could span with his hands. Very definitely a lady, and most likely a virgin.

The moment he'd learned of Alysson Vickery's existence, Jafar had known she would become his means of revenge. Grim excitement filled him as he coolly appraised his quarry. Soon Miss Vickery would be in his power. Very soon. Her innocence would only work to his advantage, he thought with harsh satisfaction. The colonel would be that much more willing to protect her, to preserve her honor.

Tonight's events had merely confirmed the rumors of her impending engagement to Bourmont. The reception this evening had been given in her honor, and during the entire time, the colonel had paid court to her most assiduously, scarcely leaving her side.

Jafar could see how the colonel might be smitten with her. The young lady was obviously wealthy. She wore a gown of shimmering pale silk, delicate and full-skirted, the sculpted bodice encrusted with seed pearls. More lustrous pearls gleamed at her throat and in the rich chestnut hair that was arranged in a loose knot—a style unusual for its lack of ringlets. But it was not her jewels or unconventional coiffure or fashionable Parisian gown that commanded attention.

What drew the eye was her vividness, her restrained energy that he could feel even at a distance. She stood there radiating vitality and life, much like an oasis in the desert. And despite her graceful slenderness, her figure was as enticing as water to a thirsty man.

Unwilling admiration shone in Jafar's eyes as he took in the lush curve of her bare shoulders and firm, high bosom. The gown's décolletage was modest by European standards, allowing little more than a glimpse of pale, silken breasts. But the effect was tantalizing.

His gaze caught by the alluring sight, he wondered how

those soft, ripe swells would feel beneath his palms, would taste against his lips.

A faint smile curled his mouth.

Perhaps before long he would know.

Alysson no longer had any doubt. Her Uncle Honoré was hiding from her.

Her suspicions had been aroused the moment Honoré disappeared from the reception line, leaving her to face the guests at Gervase's side. But only now, when she finally had a moment to herself, had she been afforded the opportunity to look around for her uncle.

There was no sign of the fainthearted, elderly Frenchman.

"You cannot escape the inevitable, *mon oncle*," Alysson murmured to herself, torn between amusement and exasperation. She would find her cowardly relative presently and wring an answer from him. He had postponed the decision as long as possible. Tomorrow would be too late.

Alysson unfurled her painted-silk fan to ply it against the heat, an occupation which helped hide her restlessness, while her searching gaze lingered on the throng of guests. She had arrived in Algiers nearly a full week ago, and as yet she'd seen little of the city that had been the refuge of pirates and a stronghold of Turks. Of the country, she'd seen nothing at all—and she could scarcely contain her impatience.

Not that her staid Uncle Honoré would ever understand her attitude. Her uncle had no conception of what drove her. A heart thirsting for passion, for adventure, was entirely foreign to him. He would never comprehend that this elegant gathering was not what she wanted out of life. This was not why she had come to Algeria.

By conventional standards, she should have been pleased with the soiree given in her honor. This evening she had been presented to royalty, a glittering triumph for a merchant's daughter. But for Alysson, an empty triumph.

With effort she maintained a polite smile as she surveyed the crowd of elegant Europeans. All pomp and glitter and triviality. Odd to think how desperately she had once longed to be a part of all this. There was laughter, but it was the shallow amusement of bored wives and cunning politicians. There was music, but it was the formal refrains of a French orchestra, not the strange, exotic rhythms of the East. The conversation, too, was conducted in French, consisting of meaningless chatter and spiteful gossip. Even the furniture was French, reducing the huge chamber with its Moorish arches and fretted work, delicate as lace, to the appearance of any other European ballroom.

Only the turquoise and scarlet tiles covering the floor in a floral mosaic looked appropriately Eastern. Alysson longed to slip off her elegant shoes and feel the cool tiles against her silk-stockinged feet. But she had promised her uncle to be on her very best behavior. And indeed, she'd kept her word. She had done nothing scandalous or wild in well over a month.

But enough was enough.

Furling her fan, Alysson circled the room in search of her uncle. She found him half-concealed by a potted palm, engaged in conversation with a French couple who had settled here in the new colony. Nearing sixty, Honoré was short of stature and inclined to portliness, with a head of thinning, silver hair, the top of which barely reached Alysson's ear.

Honoré gave a guilty start when he spied his niece.

Her suspicions confirmed, Alysson favored the elderly gentleman with an accusing smile. Actually her great-uncle, Honoré Larousse was the brother of her late French grandmother who, as an emigré, had fled the terror of the French revolution. Of her three uncles, he was her favorite.

"Will you forgive me," Alysson inquired politely of the other guests, "for stealing my uncle away?" Slipping her arm through Honoré's, she drew him aside. "You *have* been hiding from me, haven't you?"

Blustering a denial, he tried to change the subject. "How can it be that you are all alone?" Honoré asked in French. "A moment ago there were a dozen young bucks vying for your attention. Never tell me Gervase has abandoned you."

"I've only been alone for a moment, Uncle," Alysson replied in the same language. Her schoolgirl French had progressively improved over the years, due to the summers she'd spent with Honoré in France, and she found it easy now to respond fluently. "The prince required Gervase's attention on some matter, and his officers went with them. But you know that isn't what I wanted to discuss with you. You promised to give me your answer tonight, remember?"

"So I did." His heavy white brows drew together in a scowl as he tried unsuccessfully to stare her down. Alysson met his gaze calmly, trying not to laugh. It was obvious her uncle wanted to avoid a scolding.

"You look in need of refreshment," he stated, avoiding giving her an answer. Hastily, he retrieved two glasses of champagne from a passing waiter and pressed one on his niece. Lifting his own glass to his lips, Honoré took a swallow and grimaced. *"Merde!"*

Alysson had expected his reaction. A vintner of the highest reputation, her uncle deplored wine that was not of the first quality. And this was both bitter and slightly flat.

"Take heart, Uncle," she soothed. "In only a few years you will be able to savor your own vintages." Honoré meant to expand his Bordeaux vineyards by purchasing property in the French colonial province. Land here was plentiful and cheap, now that the war with the Arabs was virtually over. Later he hoped to build a winery to carry on the tradition of his forebearers.

"If I can survive on this pap till then," he complained.

"The sooner you begin, the sooner your plans will come to fruition."

"Tomorrow is soon enough."

"Ah, yes . . . tomorrow. Shall we discuss our expedition, then?"

Tomorrow they would set out for the fertile coastal plain where her uncle meant to establish his new vineyards. A practical businessman, Honoré insisted on viewing the land before making the final commitment to buy.

Alysson would accompany her uncle only because she refused to be left behind. But the real contention between them was rooted in her determination to travel beyond the settled areas. After visiting the prospective property, Alysson wanted to journey further south, into the interior of the province. She had been eager for such an expedition for years. She'd once seen the works of the painter Delacroix, who had traveled through Algeria. Ever since, she'd longed to explore this rugged country for herself. Her Uncle Honoré, on the other hand, couldn't care less about exploration or adventure.

Alysson didn't understand his attitude, any more than he understood hers. "Don't you wish to know anything about the land you mean to settle?" she asked curiously.

Honoré shook his head with adamance. "No. Absolutely not. I cannot see how it will make the least difference to my vineyards whether or not I see the desert. Very likely such a journey will prove detrimental to my health, and yours, too, my dear. And I am not the least interested if the natives can stand on their heads or dance naked on their camels. They can keep their barbaric customs to themselves."

"Uncle, they don't stand on their heads . . ." Her exasperation nearly got the better of her. Trying another tack, Alysson softened her tone to a plea. "What about our bargain? Come, Uncle, you must give me due credit. I have been a perfect angel for ages. I've allowed Gervase to pay me court, just as you wanted me to—"

"You have not agreed to marry him."

It was Alysson's turn to frown. "That was *not* our bargain."

"Perhaps. But how can you fall in love with the fellow if you do not see him for months on end?"

"We will only be gone for a few short weeks, Uncle. And I've told you before, this journey will have no bearing on my decision to marry Gervase."

Honoré gave her a penetrating look. "If I refuse to go, no doubt you will proceed without me."

"I wouldn't like to act against your wishes, but yes . . . I would consider making the trip alone."

"Well, I suppose I cannot let you travel such a distance by yourself." His dark eyes took on a mischievous gleam. "Perhaps then it is fortunate that I have already made the arrangements."

Alysson stared at her uncle at length. As the truth slowly dawned on her, her lips curved into a smile. "You, *mon oncle*, are a complete fraud. You meant to go all along."

Honoré chuckled, looking pleased with himself. "Do not

tell Gervase, I beg you. He will not be happy that I am abetting this flaw in your character."

"No, of course not. He can blame me for corrupting you." Preferring not to dwell on Gervase's concern, she let her eager thoughts race ahead to the morrow. "We should get an early start in the morning, if you can bear it."

"I have already promised I would, have I not?"

"Yes," Alysson said, "but I wasn't sure you meant it."

"Only for you, my dear, would I drag myself out of bed at an obscene hour to journey into the wilderness."

"It isn't the wilderness, Uncle. The Plain of Algiers is not so different from the farmland in France."

"So you say." Honoré again scowled at her from beneath his heavy brows. "Just do not expect me to chase tigers or elephants or some such thing, the way your Uncle Oliver does."

Honoré's gruffness never fooled her; she leaned forward to kiss his cheek. "I won't, I promise."

"I should never spoil you the way I do."

Not denying the charge, Alysson flashed him a conspiratorial smile. She might have been neglected as a child by her parents, but she'd been spoiled from birth by her army of servants, and later, after her parents' deaths, indulged by her uncles, especially Honoré. He had become the father she'd lost, and she loved him dearly. "You do spoil me most dreadfully, best of my uncles—and you enjoy every minute of it."

He chuckled fondly and patted her hand. "His Highness seemed much taken with you this evening," Honoré observed, a satisfied expression on his face.

Diplomatically Alysson refrained from answering as she recalled the past half hour. Not only had His Royal Highness overlooked the stigma of her mundane birth and the unelevated circles in which she'd been raised, but he had sought her out to discover her opinion of Algeria, and engaged her in conversation for a full ten minutes.

Alysson was well aware of the honor he'd paid her. He was the son of the king of France, the Governor-General of Algeria, while she was a mere bourgeois *Anglaise*. Her father had been a common merchant—but one clever and lucky enough to make a fortune serving with the East India

Company. *That* no doubt was her prime attraction to the prince; he wanted her to invest some of her great wealth here in Algeria.

Skeptical amusement played about Alysson's mouth as she glanced over her shoulder at the tall double doors in the middle of the long room. They were open to the night, but covered with gauzy curtains that trapped in the heat. "I think I will take a turn about the courtyard where it is cooler. Will you come?"

"Not now, my dear. I believe I shall seek out the fellow who was telling us about his vineyards."

"If Gervase inquires, tell him I shall return in a moment."

Honoré allowed her to go, but with an admonition not to forget she was the guest of honor and remain away too long. Giving her champagne glass to a passing waiter, Alysson lifted the hem of her full-skirted evening gown, an airy, silken confection of white mousseline de soie, and made her way out onto the narrow terrace.

Like the house she and her uncle had let for the duration of their stay in Algiers, Gervase's home was built around a central courtyard. Before her, the long flight of stone steps led downward to a profusion of oleanders and palms and lotus trees that were occasionally illuminated by torches set at intervals. For an instant, when one of the shadows stirred, Alysson thought someone might be down there in the garden—one of the guests, perhaps. But when she caught no other sign of movement, she dismissed the idea.

The evening was warm, even though summer had long ended, for Algiers enjoyed a Mediterranean climate. After the heat of the great chamber, the soft breeze was cool on her bare shoulders, the air redolent of lemon blossoms and jasmine and that inexplicable mystery that hung in the African night. Alysson closed her eyes, drinking in the sensations: the smells of the East, the whisper of fountains, the rustle of tall date palms.

How different and yet how similar to the India where she had been raised. And how different it would be to experience a strange new land in the company of Uncle Honoré, rather than her Uncle Oliver.

Older than Oliver by twenty years, for one thing, Honoré

was a staid, middle-class Frenchman who preferred the comforts of home and hearth to wandering the globe. Her British Uncle Oliver, on the other hand, was a world traveler with a passion for adventure, a bachelor who fancied himself a great explorer.

She had seen a good deal of the world with her Uncle Oliver during the past three years. At seventeen, when her schooling had finally ended, Alysson had persuaded Oliver to let her accompany him on his journeys. With him she had visited czars in Russia, hunted tigers in India, penetrated the fascinating deserts of Arabia. He treated her more as a son than a daughter, but she never complained; they were kindred spirits, fellow adventurers at heart. She liked wild places and exotic new cultures as much as he did.

Places like Algeria. Excitement bubbled inside her like champagne at the thought of the morrow. Tomorrow, with Uncle Honoré, she would set out on a new adventure.

A soft footfall behind her interrupted her reverie. Alysson turned to find Gervase de Bourmont regarding her with a quizzical frown.

"Your uncle said I could find you here, my love," he said in French.

Alysson smiled in welcome. "I grew overly warm inside and stepped out to enjoy the breeze."

"I understand you have persuaded Honoré to undertake an expedition into the interior." The disapproval in his tone was unmistakable.

Alysson didn't respond to his comment, not wanting to spoil the pleasurable moment with a dispute. Turning, she gazed down at the garden below. "Your home is very beautiful, Gervase."

He came to stand beside her, his expression grim. "It will be your home as well if we are married. Alysson," he added abruptly, not giving her a chance to reply, "I do not want you to attempt this trip. It is bad enough that you must accompany your uncle to visit his holdings without dragging him all over the province."

"Gervase, do you know how you sound? You are already acting the demanding husband."

"I think I have the right to question your actions."

"To question, perhaps, but not to forbid," she said, trying to keep her tone light. She couldn't be offended by his proprietary attitude. Gervase felt responsible for her, she knew, but his concern stemmed from a desire to protect her, rather than any need to keep her under his thumb.

"I won't forbid you outright, *coquine*, but surely you must see this is foolhardy."

He spoke with the familiarity of long acquaintance, calling her "minx" as he'd done since she was a mere girl. Indeed, they had known each for years, ever since the first summer she'd spent in France with her Uncle Honoré. Though, to be truthful, Gervase had paid little attention to her then, when she was a headstrong hoyden of fourteen.

Alysson glanced up at him. Gervase was an exceptionally attractive man—tall, athletic, dark-haired, with a dashing mustache and blue military uniform that most women found extremely appealing. Alysson thought so, too, and yet . . . He was gallant and handsome and the dearest of friends, but just the least bit staid when it came down to it. She had hoped she would feel differently about him here, where the opportunity for daring exploits and courageous feats was far greater than in France. A colonel in the French army, Gervase had recently been posted to Algeria as head of the *Bureaux Arabes,* the French system of governing the natives.

It was Gervase who had persuaded her Uncle Honoré to consider expanding his enterprises to colonial Algeria—and Honoré who had insisted that Alysson come along on the visit. Uncle Honoré very much wanted to see her safely married. He didn't approve of her traipsing all over the world with her Uncle Oliver, or exposing herself to the dirt and disease of London hospitals with her other uncle, who was a physician.

For Honoré's sake she had agreed to consider seriously Gervase's marriage proposal. She desperately wanted to repay her favorite uncle for his many kindnesses to her. Over the years Honoré had given her so much, providing her a refuge from the lonely confinement of boarding school, treating her as a cherished daughter, making her feel wanted and loved. Loved for herself, not her vast fortune. From her first moment in England, she'd either been fawned over for her wealth or snubbed by her blue-blooded peers.

Her uncles had been her salvation. She'd taken the advice of a stranger and tried to earn their attention and affection. Alysson counted herself immensely fortunate to have managed it, to have found a place in her uncles' hearts. With them she felt a sense of belonging, of family, a feeling of shared hopes and dreams and destinies. Especially with Honoré.

And now he was requesting something in return—for her to consider marriage to a man she had long admired and respected. It was the only thing Uncle Honoré had ever asked of her.

And she did truly care for Gervase.

That he counted on her acceptance of his suit, however, was wishful thinking on his part. More than once she'd told Gervase that she wasn't ready for marriage. She was scarcely twenty, after all. But he was so certain he could change her mind.

Alysson wished she could be as certain. She *wanted* to feel more for Gervase than deep friendship. She *wanted* to fall in love with him. Yet it would be cruel to give him false hope. She had promised her uncle, though, not to refuse Gervase's proposal outright. Still, she would be glad to begin the journey tomorrow and thus put some distance between them. Perhaps the separation would give her the opportunity to examine her feelings and come to a definite conclusion about her future with Gervase.

Gervase was apparently thinking about her departure as well, for he shook his head in protest. "I would accompany you if I could, Alysson, but duty compels me to remain here. I don't care to think about what could happen to you without me to protect you."

"There is no reason for you to be so concerned, Gervase. The escort you intend to provide will surely be adequate."

"I can ensure your safety better here."

"Your men will be armed, as will I. And you know I am an excellent shot."

"Still, I would prefer that you remain in Algiers." He gave her a reproachful glance. "I confess I don't understand why you insist on taking such a grave risk."

Alysson felt a twinge of exasperation. In Gervase's opinion, no woman should have such a fondness for travel as she did. But she couldn't change simply because he held such straightlaced notions about how a woman should behave. "What is the risk? You said yourself that the war is over."

"It won't be entirely over until Abdel Kader surrenders. And even then, some of his followers will no doubt try to carry on his Holy War."

She had no need to ask what Gervase meant. Long before she'd come to Algeria, Alysson had heard of the Berber religious leader, Abdel Kader. Fifteen years ago he had united the Berbers and Arabs in a Holy War against France. Indeed, the handsome, dashing, romantic sheik had once been all the rage in the salons of Paris. But that was before the war had turned so brutal.

Not that the Arabs were the only ones to blame for the savagery. Since invading in 1830, the French had committed their fair share of barbarities in their effort to conquer this proud nation. From what she had gathered, even Gervase's own father had been guilty of unforgivable excesses. General Bourmont had been involved in the initial invasion seventeen years ago, and was reported to have encouraged the most violent actions in putting down the rebellious natives.

Gervase was very different from his father, thankfully. Different from most of his countrymen, for that matter. He was far more sympathetic to the plight of the Arabs. Gervase had arrived in Algeria barely six months ago, but he seemed to have a far more humane understanding of how the French should play their role as conquerors. It was for that reason she thought he would prove to be an admirable administrator of the Arab Bureau.

Still, she felt Gervase was overly concerned about her visit to the interior. Only last year Abdel Kader had been driven into neighboring Morocco with his followers. And the atrocities committed on both sides had finally come to an end. No longer were the French colonists being killed and burned from their homes as in past years; the natives in the northern provinces had finally been subdued by the powerful French army, and the Plain of Algiers was once again safe for Europeans, protected by the *Armée d'Afrique*. Some settlers had even moved further into the interior to carve domains out of swamp and arid wasteland.

No, if she had thought the risk too great, she never would have considered making the journey. She herself would not have minded the danger, but never would she gamble with Uncle Honoré's safety. As it was, she felt guilty enough simply for planning to deprive her uncle of his comfort for the few weeks or so that it would take to visit the outskirts of the Sahara. At least the heat of the desert would not be quite so unbearable now that it was October.

When she didn't agree with Gervase's estimation of the risks, though, he made a gesture of impatience. "Alysson, will you listen to me! There are untold dangers in the interior—bandits and slave traders and hungry nomads, fanatical Arabs who refuse to admit the war is over . . . even deserters from our Foreign Legion."

"Chand will be with us."

"That is not a comfort to me in the least," Gervase said tersely. "Chand is devoted to you, obviously, but he is hardly the appropriate servant for a lady. I cannot like it that you will have no female chaperone or attendant to care for you."

Alysson sent her prospective fiancé a warning glance, unwilling to countenance any criticism of her faithful Indian servant. "Gervase, perhaps you didn't know, but I owe Chand my life—several times over."

Realizing then that her tone had become overly sharp, she softened her next words and gave him a disarming smile; sweetness and logic would be more effective in coaxing Gervase out of his ill humor. "Chand has been my friend as well as my servant. I think you can safely trust him to take good care of me. Besides, you forget that I am an Englishwoman. The English have far less to fear from the Arabs than do the French."

But Gervase wouldn't accept this argument. "The Arabs hate all infidels," he replied, shaking his head. "And I cannot—"

"Gervase, you are worrying needlessly."

The sigh he gave held regret. "Perhaps."

At length he shrugged, his features relaxing their tautness. "It is just that I don't want any harm to come to you. And I am selfish, I suppose. The next month will be unbearable with you gone."

He reached for her hands then. Drawing her near, he gently pressed her fingers to his lips. "Do you realize how very much I love you, *coquine*?"

"Gervase . . ." Alysson started to protest. The desire in his eyes disturbed her, and so did his declaration. She was fearless about most things, but avowals of love had the power to disquiet her, arousing painful memories she would sooner forget. She'd learned from bitter experience to be wary of hucksters and fortune hunters who plied her with sweet words.

Gervase was no fortune hunter, certainly; she was convinced he truly loved her. But she couldn't understand what he saw in her. She wasn't a beauty, admittedly, and her independent nature was hardly a quality a man looked for in a wife. Indeed, she had grave doubts that she could ever make Gervase a good wife.

He was still looking at her ardently, Alysson realized. Still gazing at her with that hot desire that made her feel flustered and unworthy of his adoration. "Gervase . . ." Alysson said uncomfortably. "You promised to give me time . . ."

He sighed softly. "I suppose I am in good company. Honoré tells me you once refused the hand of a rajah."

Relieved that Gervase didn't mean to insist on an answer, she let her mouth curve ruefully. "That isn't quite what happened. A rajah once offered to purchase me as his *third* wife. Uncle Oliver was inclined to haggle over the price, but I didn't relish being relegated to third place."

Gervase's answering smile warmed her. "No, you, my shameless minx, would insist on being first. And as usual you would get your way. No doubt when we are married, you will be able to wrap me around your finger as you do your uncles. Alysson . . ." His voice dropped to a gentle murmur as slowly he drew her into his arms. "Will you kiss me so that I may endure the coming weeks without you?"

She couldn't deny such an earnest plea. Mutely she nodded, wishing with all her heart that she could respond to Gervase the way he wished her to.

At her acquiescence, he tightened his arms around her and bent his head. His lips were warm and loving—but careful, exhibiting the self-restraint expected of a gentleman toward a young lady. His consideration, rather than flattering her, though, left Alysson with a vague sense of frustration. She longed for Gervase to embrace her more purposefully, to sweep her off her feet, to inspire in her the kind of passion and desire that the poets raved about. But it had never happened. Gervase's kisses were always persuasive and skilled, but she felt no thrill in his arms, no rush of excitement that set her heart to pounding, no spark of fire between them. Instead, his caresses always left her feeling somehow . . . disappointed.

Like now. There seemed to be something *vital* missing in his kiss. Her own lips parted in anticipation as she felt his tongue slowly delve into her mouth, but Gervase's gentle coaxing roused in her only a nameless, unfulfilled longing. His accomplished embrace kindled in her nothing more than a feeling of sadness . . . that he wasn't the man she wished him to be. That she wasn't the woman he needed and deserved.

Gervase seemed to be satisfied with her response, though, for when finally he raised his head, it was to gaze longingly at her. "Go quickly, my love," he said in a husky whisper. "Make your journey short, so that we may be married as soon as you return."

Alysson started to protest, but Gervase silenced her by pressing his fingers to her mouth.

Finally releasing her then, he stepped back. "Do you mean to stay here for the rest of the evening? My guests will soon miss you."

"A moment longer only."

"Very well, but only a moment, or you might catch a chill."

Alysson refrained from responding that she had never caught a chill in her life. Instead, she watched silently as Gervase went back inside the house.

Turning then, she gazed down at the shadowed garden. Her conversation with Gervase and his kiss afterward had only renewed her restlessness. Anxious again for the morning to come, Alysson descended the long flight of stone steps into the garden and began wandering along the torchlit path.

She had only taken a few steps, though, when she came to a startled halt; a gentleman in evening clothes stood there in the shadows, one shoulder negligently propped against the thick trunk of a palm tree. Her hand flew to her throat, while she barely managed to stifle a gasp.

He made no move toward her as he spoke in a low voice, in fluent French. "Pardon me for frightening you, mademoiselle."

Alysson willed her heart to settle down as she peered at him in the dim light. His face was half-hidden by the dancing shadows so she couldn't make out his features, but he didn't appear dangerous. He was a tall, lean man, a striking figure in black evening attire. Imposing perhaps, but not frightening.

"Did no one ever tell you," he continued in French as she stared at him, "that it does a young lady's reputation no good to be seen unchaperoned in a darkened garden, kissing a man?"

His tone was amused, yet with a curt edge that sounded almost like scorn. It took her aback.

Hot with embarrassment over being caught kissing Gervase, Alysson couldn't help the blush that rose to her cheeks. To think that this stranger had been watching her . . . "Did no one ever tell *you*, m'sieur," she retorted with irritation, "that it is impolite to eavesdrop on an intimate conversation? You should have made yourself known at once."

"You gave me no opportunity."

That was such a patent falsehood that Alysson didn't deign to reply. Grasping the fan dangling from her wrist, she flicked it open, using the rapid feminine movement to show her displeasure. "I trust you were pleasantly diverted," she said finally, the sweetness of her tone scarcely veiling her own scorn.

"Oh, indeed. It was quite . . . entertaining."

She thought the darkness fortunate, for it hid her heightening color. Vexed by her unaccustomed discomposure—and unwilling to allow this provoking stranger to prolong the moment any longer—Alysson gave him her back as she prepared to follow a different path.

"Have no fear, mademoiselle," he murmured. "Your reputation is safe with me."

The soft mockery in his voice set her nerves on edge. She whirled again to face him. She couldn't see how her reputation or her conduct was any of his business. Not that she had much of a reputation to lose. She'd been called eccentric, scandalous, wild, even fast by stalwart arbiters of society—more critical judges than this presumptuous Frenchman. She should have grown inured to such comments by now, yet this time she was piqued into defending herself.

"In certain circumstances," Alysson said with exaggerated civility, "I believe the young lady may be excused. When she is engaged to be married, for instance. If the gentleman she is kissing is her fiancé, there can be no harm in sharing a simple display of affection."

"So the colonel truly is your fiancé."

It was an odd statement to make, Alysson thought. Even more odd was his quiet tone; it held both satisfaction and a hardness that inexplicably made her want to shiver.

Unable to define why this elegant stranger should suddenly seem dangerous to her, she gave him a quelling stare. "I cannot conceive how our engagement is any of your concern."

"The colonel's father was an old acquaintance of mine. I have since come to know his son."

"You cannot know Gervase well, or he would have presented you to me in the reception line."

"I arrived late."

"And then hid out in the garden?" Alysson asked skeptically.

He shrugged, a casual, eloquent gesture that was as arrogant as his low-pitched voice. "Like you, I wanted to escape the heat." Pushing away from the tree then, he took a step toward her. "But in fact, I was anxious to meet you. I had heard the colonel had offered for the hand of a beautiful heiress."

Beautiful? She wondered where that rumor had started. Servants' gossip, no doubt. Or officers' talk. Wealth often gave the aura of beauty to those who possessed it. But the thought fled as the stranger came nearer. He moved toward her purposefully, as if he intended to inspect her, to judge her beauty—or lack thereof—for himself.

Alysson began seriously to doubt the wisdom of being alone with a man she couldn't identify. Involuntarily, she glanced back at the house, finding it farther than she expected, yet she stood her ground, determined not to be intimidated by this arrogant stranger. As he emerged from the shadows, into the glow of torchlight, she could see that his hair gleamed a dark gold beneath his chapeau. Then the blur of his face became focused. His bronzed features were angular and lean . . . proud, she would have to say. Noble, even. And hard. Alysson experienced a vague feeling of unease at the hawklike expression that dominated his countenance.

He came to a halt directly in front of her, looking down at her critically. She had to crane her neck to meet his gaze. He had long-lashed, hooded eyes, she saw . . . predatory eyes. Eyes that were a dark and disturbing gold, the color of brandy in firelight.

Then suddenly his sharp gaze narrowed. He became very still, staring down at her as if in surprise, as if she was not what he had expected.

His strangeness disturbed her enough to make her demand, "Is something wrong?"

He seemed to recover himself. "No. You remind me of someone I once knew."

He, too, looked oddly familiar, Alysson thought, but she couldn't place where she had seen him. Not recently, that was certain. She would have remembered someone so . . . compelling. He was nothing like the Frenchmen of her acquaintance, with his athletic height and lean, ascetic features. Indeed, the overall effect was almost savage . . . the lean hollows beneath angled cheekbones, the narrow aquiline nose that suggested patrician fineness, the hard, sensual mouth. Together with those hawklike eyes, they gave the impression of ruthlessness, of fearless determination. Alysson couldn't drag her gaze away.

"You should heed the colonel," he said softly.

"I beg your pardon?" His swift change of subject bewildering her, she stared at him in puzzlement.

"Your journey into the interior tomorrow. You should fear the dangers. Bourmont was right. Christian foreigners

will never be safe in Algeria as long as there are Arabs who
refuse to abandon the Holy War.''

Rigid with annoyance, both at the reminder of this man's
eavesdropping, and that he, a perfect stranger, would have
the audacity to question her judgment, Alysson had difficulty managing a cool reply. ''If you overheard my discussion with Gervase, then you also heard my answer. Our
party will be well armed . . . and the leader of the Arabs
has fled to Morocco.''

''Ah, but his lieutenants have not forsaken him. Emir
Abdel Kader might lack a regular army, but his followers
stand ready to foment the spirit of insurrection at the
slightest opportunity.''

Her gray eyes narrowed. She had assumed this gentleman
was French, since they were conversing in that language,
and since he spoke with a fluency that excelled her own.
But his comment made her wonder, for it suggested that on
this issue he didn't side entirely with the French. And again,
there was something in his tone that gave her pause. It
sounded almost as if he was issuing a warning . . . or a
threat.

Controlling the urge to moisten her lips nervously, she
raised her chin to stare him out of countenance. Unyielding,
his gaze captured hers in a long glance.

The air suddenly became charged with inexplicable tension, a tension which Alysson was hard-pressed to understand. He made her feel as though she couldn't take a deep
breath.

''I am not afraid,'' she finally said, her anger returning
at allowing herself to be daunted by this disquieting man.

''Then you are either very brave . . . or very foolish.''

Alysson clamped her lips together to keep from retorting
with an epithet that was quite unladylike, but her simmering
silence, her indignant glare, indeed her very posture, con-
veyed her vexation.

Her ire apparently had no effect on him. ''It would
seem,'' he remarked in that same casual tone, ''that the
colonel is far too indulgent of you.''

What effrontery the man had! ''I repeat,'' Alysson said
through gritted teeth, ''I fail to see how it can be any concern of yours.''

He merely continued to stare down at her, those keen golden eyes regarding her with speculation. "That was not much of a kiss the colonel gave you. You didn't appear to be enjoying yourself."

Her expression turned incredulous. "Don't tell me you consider yourself qualified to give me instruction on the art of kissing! What an elevated opinion you hold of yourself."

"Oh no, *ma belle*. I would never have the patience." A corner of his mouth turned up in faint amusement. "Nor, if I were to instruct you, would I be satisfied with so lukewarm a response from you."

She could hardly believe what she was hearing. Alysson felt a perverse desire to shatter a little of his arrogant self-assurance. Swallowing her outrage, she summoned laughter instead. "Well then, if you think you can do better, you are welcome to try."

There, that would call his bluff. No man with even marginal good sense would want to risk Gervase's anger by stealing a kiss, even an invited one. And even should this stranger dare, he wouldn't be able to make her respond to him, any more than Gervase had. His claim was mere boast.

From his expression, she could see that her challenge had taken him aback. "It would seem, m'sieur, that *you* are the one who is afraid," Alysson said sweetly, her dulcet tone a taunt. "But have no fear, your reputation is quite safe with me."

He raised an eyebrow, staring at her in disbelief.

She laughed again, this time in real amusement. She had succeeded in rendering him speechless.

Her enjoyment was short-lived; a strange, unfathomable smile tugged at the corner of his mouth. "I am tempted, I admit."

His voice had dropped to a mere murmur, and the low sound, velvet-smooth and husky, made her breath catch and her heartbeat quicken.

He moved then, silently, eliminating the distance between them. "If I were to instruct you," was his quiet comment, "I would take you in my arms, like so . . ." Suiting action to words, he slipped an arm about her waist and drew her fully against his body.

The wealth of emotions that swept over Alysson startled

her nearly as much as his unforeseen move. He had been right; he was nothing like Gervase—and neither was her response to him. She was shocked by his boldness, incensed by his insolence, unnerved by his gentle attack, flustered by the unexpected hardness of a masculine body that was all muscle. Yet at the same time, to her great dismay, a part of her felt thrilled and challenged. She had always admired men of action, and she was vaguely curious to see if he would take his arousing embrace further. Some irrational segment of her mind wondered what it would feel like to have that hard mouth on hers . . .

Fortunately, sense won out. She forced her hands up between them, to press furiously against his chest.

But he refused to let her go. He held her thus, with consummate ease, one arm around her waist, while his other hand lifted to brush the vulnerable column of her throat.

Her heart began to race. She could feel his breath whisper intimately over her lips. Against her will Alysson found herself actually, incredibly, wanting his kiss . . .

Then his fingers closed warm and threatening over the fragile, pulsing hollow of her throat.

She went rigid in his arms. Was he going to kiss her or strangle her? Her own fingers tightened around her fan as a shivering fear ran through her.

"You would be making a mistake," he murmured gently, almost inaudibly, "if you married the colonel . . . a man with the tainted blood of a murderer in his veins."

The delicate fan snapped under the pressure of her fingers. The very softness of his tone frightened her. *Murderer?* What was he talking about? Was she being held by a madman?

Frantically, Alysson pushed against the hard wall of his chest. When he suddenly released her, she took a stumbling step backward.

She stood there staring at him, her heart pounding, her breath ragged. He remained motionless, observing her silently, his hard face a savage mask in the dim light.

Slowly, with herculean effort, Alysson edged away from him. Three steps back and she managed to break the seemingly paralyzing force of his deadly gaze.

Lifting the hem of her filmy skirts, Alysson turned and

ran along the path and up the stairs, seeking the safety of
Gervase's house. When she reached the curtained doorway,
she threw an agitated glance over her shoulder, searching
the garden below.

He still stood there, watching her, a sleek shadow in the
night.

Quivering, Alysson made her escape. She, who feared
nothing and no one, fled as if a real murderer were on her
trail.

The man she left behind in the garden court stood there
a long while, shifting through the inchoate emotions assailing him.

First, the unwanted attraction. He'd thought he had shed
any lingering penchant for things European—clothes,
horses, women. When he'd returned home to Barbary and
resumed his name of Jafar el-Saleh, he had eschewed any
trappings not of his own culture. Relentlessly he'd rooted
out all traces of his old life, crushing even the desires he
had learned during his banishment in England, in an effort
to purify his thoughts and deeds and actions, to make himself worthy to lead his tribe. But that determination had
wavered a short while ago as he'd stood outside the reception hall, watching Alysson Vickery through the filmy curtains. And later, when she'd made her way down toward
him in the courtyard, the sight had taken his breath away.
The pale gossamer of her gown shimmered as she floated
down the steps, her bare throat and shoulders gleaming in
the faint light. She was a natural temptress, alluring and
provocative. He had felt the quickening of a raw flame leaping in his loins.

The second unexpected sentiment was surprise. He'd been
startled to recognize her, to realize the vision of loveliness
was the little ruffian who had once pelted him with acorns,
the same girl he had comforted years ago. But it was she,
Jafar had no doubt. He could never have forgotten those
huge, rebellious gray eyes. Here in the garden, they were
no longer filled with pain. Instead, they held pride and a
sharp intelligence that was unusual in a woman. There was
an open, forthright quality about her gaze that contrasted
keenly with the submissive deference of Eastern women.

Yet she still possessed the same defiant spirit he remembered. A defiance that was both intriguing and infuriating. In one stroke, she had managed to rouse both his passion and his male pique. He had never before been treated so dismissively by a woman, but tonight not only had she challenged him to kiss her, she had laughed at him as well. How he had wanted to respond to that challenge! He'd found himself fighting down the insane impulse to bend his head and slowly, endlessly kiss the irreverent laughter from her soft, inviting lips.

Next in his surfeit of unwanted emotions was unease. It disturbed him to realize that *she* was the fiancée of the man he intended to kill. It disturbed him more that she would be his means, the instrument of his revenge. He had done his best to warn her, as had the colonel, but she'd scoffed at the dangers. She meant to go forward with her plans to explore his country, despite the risks. In bemusement, Jafar shook his head. Not only was the young lady courageous but strong-willed. It had been written in every line of her slender body, in the lift of her arrogant, yet surprisingly delicate chin.

And last, regret. He regretted having to involve her in his personal vengeance.

But not enough to forsake his purpose.

A muscle tightened in his jaw as he renewed his resolve. No, he would not change his plans because of her. He had waited too long for this moment.

Quelling his misgivings with ruthless determination, he turned and disappeared into the night shadows.

Chapter 2

C hand was ill.
     The second morning of their journey, Alysson's Indian servant was stricken by a mysterious malady that re-

sulted in an ailing stomach and a low fever. The lieutenant
in charge of their escort, too, suffered the same complaint.
The cause of their illness no one knew, but conjecture was
that they'd eaten something that disagreed with them. No
one else in their party took sick. Not Alysson, nor her uncle, nor their Arab guides, nor any other of the French
troops sent to guard them.

Alysson wanted to cancel the expedition entirely, knowing any enjoyment for her would be spoiled as long as Chand
was ailing. But for once Uncle Honoré overruled her. As
long they had come this far, Honoré declared, they might
as well visit his prospective property before returning to
Algiers.

It was decided that Chand and the lieutenant would remain there at the campsite, with an Arab servant to care for
their needs. If they recovered quickly, they could catch up
to the party; if not, they would all return to Algiers together, and scotch the lengthy trek to the desert.

Alysson had to be content with the new plan. But still
she worried about Chand who, like her, normally was never
ill. His unexpected affliction filled her with a vague foreboding, coming as it did on the heels of that absurd warning
by the savage stranger in Gervase's garden two nights ago.
She managed to repress a shiver at the memory, but as she
said farewell to her faithful servant, she wondered what
more would go wrong during their journey.

Chand clearly shared the same concern, for his strangely
pallid face was contorted more in woe than in pain. "Allah,
forgive me," he breathed. "I have failed you, memsahib."

"Goodness, Chand, you are not to blame for becoming
sick."

"You will take care?"

"Of course I will—if you promise to do the same."

It was nearly noon by the time they broke camp and
started on their way. Alysson rode beside her uncle. The
day had already grown hot, although yesterday morning
when they'd ascended the steep green hills behind Algiers,
it had been quite chilly. They'd made good time then, considering the number of horses and pack mules in their party;
by noon yesterday their procession had descended from the
high, hilly coastal region where evergreen trees predomi-

nated, to the broad and fertile valley that the French colonists had settled.

The Plain of Algiers was precisely what Alysson had been lead to expect—miles of graceful undulating farmland, hemmed in by mountains. Here trees of wild fig and olive grew in abundance. Today, like yesterday, they passed acre after acre of orange groves and well-cultivated fields sown with barley and wheat and millet. Watching the harvest ripening under the African sun, Alysson felt her mood lift somewhat. Her Uncle Honoré's vineyards would prosper here.

As for herself, she would never be content to settle in such a tame region. Her gaze traveled farther south across the rolling landscape. In the distance, she could see the lower slopes of the mountain range known as the Tell Atlas. It was there that she longed to explore. There, and beyond, where the wild country lay, the remote steppes of the High Plateaux, and the barren desert.

She had dressed appropriately for such rugged terrain, in a severely tailored jacket of blue serge, short blue pantaloons, and a stout pair of boots. A wide-brimmed felt hat protected her face from the burning sun and her eyes from the dazzling glare. Her masculine attire was less a matter of convenience than of necessity. In the thick woods and mountain heights she would eventually encounter, the long skirts of a riding habit would be sadly in the way.

Likewise, she rode astride, eschewing a sidesaddle for both comfort and safety. Her mount, a gray Arab mare, had proved a delight—spirited but manageable.

They had been riding only a short while when she first noticed the horseman. He was some distance off the road they traveled, half-hidden by the shadows of a tamarind tree. He wore native dress—black robes and turban—and sat unmoving upon a powerful black horse, watching them. Alysson couldn't help but glance over her shoulder as they passed.

And hour later, her attention was again riveted by the horseman. This time he was poised on the crest of the hill above them, making a dark silhouette against the azure sky.

Both rider and horse were as still and silent as the desert. Alysson felt a prickle of alarm as she noticed the long-barreled rifle slung over the horseman's shoulder. Her apprehension was absurd, of course; Arabs always carried such weapons. Still, her hand surreptitiously sought the double-shot pistol in her saddlebag.

The next instant proved her caution well-founded, for the horseman suddenly unslung his gun. Instinctively her fingers clenched around the pearl handle of her own weapon.

Yet she was given no cause to use it. Whirling, the dark figure set his horse to a gallop, the skirts of his black burnous flying straight out in the wind as he disappeared over the crest of the hill.

A moment later she heard the sharp report of the gun.

When her French escort immediately reached for their rifles, her Arab guide raised a soothing hand. "He hunts for boar," the guide informed them.

The French soldiers relaxed. Alysson did, too, somewhat, while her elderly uncle muttered a Gallic invective, directed at inconsiderate savages who had nothing better to do than frighten peaceful citizens.

It was late afternoon when the road threaded between two high hills covered with a wild tangle of Barbary fig. With her thoughts centered on Chand and his strange, sudden illness, Alysson was unprepared when a volley of rifle shots exploded all around them.

The next moment, a horde of black-robed Arabs burst from the shelter of the trees, galloping in a wild path around them, brandishing swords and muskets.

The chaos was instantaneous, the attack so sudden that the French troops had time only to form a protective circle around Alysson and her uncle. She herself was occupied controlling her mount and imploring Uncle Honoré to keep his head down, trying to make her voice heard over the shouts and gunfire.

It was a moment before the clamor quieted. When the haze of dust and heat finally settled, Alysson found herself, her uncle, and their French escort surrounded, with three dozen Arab muskets pointed at them.

None of her party seemed to be hurt, she saw with relief. Her uncle's face was red with anger and her own breath was too ragged, but they were both unharmed. Assured of Honoré's safety, she focused her attention on her attackers.

They all wore black robes, while their heads and faces were wound in long black scarves. Their eyes glinted through the slits, as did the blades of their long curved swords thrust without scabbards in their belts. Alysson was quite glad she had the protection of the French soldiers. Because of them, she wasn't afraid . . . yet.

Then she spied the dark horseman, the same man she'd seen twice earlier that day. Her heartbeat took on a erratic rhythm. Had he been following them?

He rode a great black beast with a high curved neck and long flowing tail, and like the others, his features were hidden in the wrappings of his scarf.

When he issued an order in a low commanding tone, she couldn't recognize a word. It wasn't Arabic, she was certain. Perhaps it was the Berber language, which she didn't speak at all.

Indeed, these had to be Berbers, Alysson concluded, eyeing the faces of three men who weren't wearing scarves. Unlike her Arab guides who were swarthy Bedouins, these men surrounding her were fair-skinned, with hard, lean, proud features. And they were much taller, their carriages athletic and noble. She had been told about this fierce warrior race that populated the mountains. The Berbers had lived here for centuries before the conquering Arabs had swept over the face of Africa.

She would have inquired as to their intent, but her uncle spoke before her, demanding in French to be told the meaning of this outrage. Alysson had thought the dark horseman was their leader, but it was one of the other Berbers, a red-bearded man, who responded to her uncle.

He smiled benignly, pressing his hands to his mouth. *"Salaam aleikum,"* he greeted them courteously in Arabic, then repeated in French, "May peace be with you."

"What the devil do you mean, accosting us in this manner?" Honoré exclaimed, ignoring Eastern etiquette entirely.

It seemed rather absurd to be exchanging polite salutations while the acrid smoke of the Berbers' musket fire still hung in the air and their horses stamped and blew, but Alysson was both more familiar with and more accepting of other cultures' customs than her uncle.

"Aleikum es-salaam," she replied, repressing her trepidation. "Perhaps you will forgive my uncle," she added in French, "if he is anxious to learn your intent. Your actions just now do not argue for peace—"

The dark horseman interrupted her with another order in that strange tongue.

"Abandon your weapons," the bearded man advised, "and you will not be harmed."

The automatic refusal that sprang to Alysson's lips died unspoken when she glanced around her. All the Arabs in her party looked appropriately terrified, except her chief guide. He looked infinitely satisfied with present events. Rather smug, in fact.

Anger filled her at the realization that this Arab scoundrel had led them into an ambush. Her gray eyes narrowed, her gaze impaling him.

The guide caught her fierce look and, with a start of alarm, immediately set up a very vocal protest in Arabic against the Berbers, denying their right to make such demands. His resistance rang so hollow that Alysson snapped an order for him to be silent. She was furious that she should have been so dim-witted as to ride blindly into this trap, more furious still at their current dilemma. If they fought now, they might very well die. But the alternative—to meekly hand over their only means of protection—was unthinkable. She would have to determine some way to foil these Berber ruffians—and quickly, before her French escort abandoned her. As it was, they were already shifting uneasily in their saddles, their aims wavering as they looked to her, obviously seeking guidance.

Even as Alysson ground her teeth at their cowardice, a single rifle shot rang out, sending Honoré's hat hurtling into the road and making the Europeans' horses shy.

Alysson flinched, staring in horror. The bullet had come so close! It might have killed her beloved uncle. Honoré's mouth had dropped open in shock, while his angry flush had faded to waxen.

Her gaze flew to the dark horseman. He was calmly reloading his weapon, the black stallion beneath him standing rock-steady.

The tense moment drew out, with only the creak of saddle leather and the clank of bridle bits to alleviate the silence. Alysson regarded the black-swathed Berber with every evidence of loathing, but his veiled face, his hooded eyes, gave no indication that he knew or cared about her fury or disdain. As indeed he had no cause. His ease with the long rifle and the accuracy of his shot just now only underscored something else she had been told about the Berbers: they were outstanding marksmen.

The thought filled Alysson with dismay. Her party would have to surrender. If it came to a battle, her spineless French protectors would prove no match for these fierce Berbers. She wouldn't, couldn't, risk her uncle's life.

Just then the bearded spokesman addressed the French troops directly, his tone soothing, almost deferential, as he reasoned with them, appealing to their logic. "Do not be concerned for yourselves. We mean you no harm. We only want the woman."

They meant to single her out? In God's name, why? Alysson wondered. But it was the answer to a prayer. If she could manage to get free of this melee of horses and men, the Berbers would no doubt follow her. She could draw them away, and her uncle would be free to take cover. Moreover, if she fled, she stood a better chance of foiling their plans for her. She was an excellent horsewoman. She might even be able to escape into the shelter of the hills before they caught up with her. Unless they shot her first . . . but if they wanted her, surely they wouldn't shoot her.

This chaos of thoughts whirled through Alysson's mind, even as her Uncle Honoré sputtered in outrage. Despite his close brush with death, he was trying to urge his mount between her and the Berber leaders, evidently in order to protect her. Alysson's heart swelled with love and fear. That he, an aging, comfort-loving gentleman should be the only man with the courage to defend her made her want to weep. She had to get away, now, before another bullet struck a mortal target on her uncle's person, rather than merely his hat.

Letting Honoré's blustering gestures act as a distraction, Alysson edged her gray mare sideways till she glimpsed a clear path between the other horses. Turning the mare's head then, she brought her riding whip down hard on the animal's flank in a single swift motion and dug in her heels. The startled animal let out a squeal, reared on its hind legs, then bolted headlong through the throng of Frenchmen and Berbers.

The mare's rapid flight was all Alysson could have wished. Bending low over the horse's neck, she called out encouragement as she tried to provide some kind of guidance to the frightened animal.

They left the road, surging up a hill covered with prickly shrubs and ancient olive trees. When they came down again, Alysson spied a narrow ravine. She felt the mare gather for the jump . . .

With a flying leap they were clear and racing across a bare, relatively flat stretch of land that offered not even the dubious protection of the trees.

Then she heard the sound of pounding hoofbeats behind her, and dared to look over her shoulder. Only a single rider pursued her.

The dark horseman on his midnight stallion.

Her heart sank. Had her heroics been for naught? Why hadn't the other Berbers followed her? What was happening to her uncle? What would happen to her if her savage pursuer caught her?

Sudden fear gave Alysson renewed determination. Desperately she used her crop again, calling for all the speed her straining mare could muster. Her hat flew off, ripped from its pins, but she ignored the loss. In the distance, some two hundred yards away, she could see a cluster of tall rocks which might provide cover if she could only reach it.

She chanced another glance over her shoulder at the stallion galloping after her. The black beast was strong-boned, long-legged, powerful. He was from Barbary, after all. Such horses could outrun the wind . . .

How absurd her notion of escape had been! But she wouldn't give up. She groped inside her saddlebag for her pistol, grateful for the comfort it gave her.

Her breath came in ragged spurts as she focused her gaze on the boulders ahead. Nearly there. Twenty more yards. Ten. She could hear the echo of savage hooves pounding in her head, could almost feel the stallion's breath hot on her neck.

She reached the rocks with mere seconds to spare. Hauling back on the reins, Alysson used every skill she possessed to halt her plunging mare. Her heart beating frantically, she flung herself from the gray's back, almost stumbling as she took cover behind a boulder. Catching herself, she whirled, prepared to fight back, desperately aiming her pistol at her attacker.

A scant three yards away, the dark horseman reined back fiercely, bringing the stallion almost to its haunches. She started to shoot. Truly she did.

Then she saw his face.

The wide end of the scarf tied about his mouth had worked loose, slipping down. Dear God, she thought, stunned. The stranger from the garden. She recognized that lean, proud face. He was the same man who only two nights ago had frightened her, had nearly kissed her.

Could she kill someone she had conversed with such a short time ago, someone she had exchanged banalities with, however unpleasant? Her mouth went dry, while her mind wildly sought answers to the questions that were assailing her: why had he pursued her, why was he so determined to frighten her?

She raised her wavering pistol.

Amusement flickered across those arrogant features, as if he saw her dilemma and found it humorous. He made no move to retrieve the rifle that was now resting in its scabbard on his saddle. Instead, he leaned forward and spoke in the horse's ear, as if sharing the jest. Alysson clenched her teeth. When he sat up again, she aimed, this time straight at his heart.

He laughed. He actually laughed, the low rich sound daring her to shoot. His teeth flashed strong and white in the bright sunlight, a startling contrast against his desert-bronzed skin. Then he struck. Heedless of the danger he charged directly at her on his powerful mount.

Fury at his contemptuous mirth, terror at her imminent peril, overcame her misgivings. Her finger frantically jerked on the trigger.

But she had hesitated a moment too long; the bullet went wide, only grazing his arm.

She never got another chance to fire. The Berber crowded

his horse against her, compelling her to stumble back, making her trip and lose her grip on the pistol. The next instant he flung himself from the stallion, landing nearly on top of her as she fell, yet somehow sparing her the full force of his weight. Even so, her breath fled her lungs. Alysson found herself on her back, sprawled beneath the hard length of him, her hands manacled above her head by his long lean fingers.

For nearly the first time in her life she was confronted with real fear. Wild, muscle-stiffening fear. His body was taut and dangerous, radiating menace from every muscle. She could feel it through the thickness of his robes, through her own suddenly inadequate layers of clothing. The threat was as palpable as his body's heat.

Alysson whimpered, the frantic sound of an animal entrapped, as she struggled against unyielding masculine strength.

"Be still!" he ordered in that low, fluid French she remembered from the garden. "I won't harm you."

Her panic abated at his promise, at the quiet reassurance in his voice. She ceased fighting so wildly, though she continued to sob for breath as she stared up into golden eyes that gleamed hot and dangerous. What would he do to her? Torture, murder, rape? Oh, God, what would this savage do?

Those eyes were so fierce, so unforgiving. Her heart pounded in her breast as she lay trembling beneath him.

The force of his unblinking, mesmerizing gaze held hers for the longest moment, before he slowly he sat up. Shifting his weight, he released her wrists but kept her thighs pinned beneath his. His mouth was ruthlessly set as he pushed back a fold of his burnous—the voluminous cloak the natives of Barbary wore—and glanced down at his left arm. The sleeve of his black tunic glistened with something dark and wet.

Blood. She had wounded him. Would he punish her for her act of self-defense?

Alysson held her breath as he reached for the scarf about his throat. Frozen, rigid, she watched him struggle to tear off a piece of the cloth.

He only meant to bind his wound, she saw with infinite relief. Holding one end of the cloth with his teeth, he

wrapped the other about his arm and tried to tie a knot. She
had the humanitarian impulse to offer her help with what
should have been an awkward, painful task, yet he obviously didn't require her aid. His swift, practiced movements
held the ease of a man accustomed to caring for himself,
accustomed also to sustaining the injuries of battle.

Which of course he was, Alysson reminded herself. He
was a warrior, a primitive Barbary tribesman to whom fighting and killing was a way of life. She couldn't afford to
cherish any misplaced consideration for a man who, at the
moment, held her totally at his mercy.

Her gaze flickered over his ruthless features. There was
a cruel determination to his mouth that she hadn't noticed
that night in the dim light of the garden. The sight made
her quiver.

"What . . . do you want . . . with me?" she forced herself to ask, hating the way her voice shook.

He didn't answer, but he did look up, directing his fierce
gaze at her again. Those eyes. Those predatory, fathomless
eyes . . . They took on new menace now that she was in
his power, striking fresh fear in her. They were amber-
brown, glittering with flecks of gold, the irises ringed like
a hawk's. She couldn't drag her gaze away.

To her relief, he returned his attention to his wounded
arm. When he had finished securing his bandage, he reached
inside the sash at his waist and pulled out a length of woolen
cord, then proceeded to bind her wrists together in front of
her.

He had been prepared to take her captive, Alysson realized. He had planned it all.

Oh, he was cunning, she thought bitterly, remembering
the way he had singled her out the way she'd once seen a
sheepdog cut out a ewe from a flock. She had apparently
been his target all along. What a fool she had been to leave
the relative safety of Gervase's men! Now she was isolated
her from her party, with little chance of being found. She
could only hope that her flight hadn't been in vain, that her
uncle was safe. She could only hope that she would soon
have an opportunity to escape from this madman.

When her wrists were fettered, he eased his weight from
her and got to his feet. Alysson felt the sweet relief of her

sudden freedom. With an effort she struggled to her knees,
prepared to make what defense she could. But she hadn't
counted on her body's reaction to fear. She couldn't stop
shaking. And her head spun, making his dark form swim in
her vision. He stood over her, tall and lean and fierce in his
black desert robes.

The unaccustomed fear had also made her limbs weak.
She managed to stand, but her legs wouldn't obey her when
she tried to back away.

"Don't try to run," he advised her in that soft, pitiless
voice. "I would only have to chase you."

She recognized the ring of authority in the low tone and
her retreat faltered. Helplessly she watched as he retrieved
her pistol. After removing the remaining bullet with a swift,
practiced motion, he tucked the weapon in his waist sash
beside a jewel-handled dagger, then moved toward her.

Alysson stood paralyzed—until he touched her. Then,
with a soft cry, she went wild, kicking and lashing out,
flailing at him with her bound hands. His hard arms came
around her, crushing her to him, pinning her thrashing arms
in his merciless embrace, holding her immobile.

"No! Let me go!" But her pleas and her efforts to free
herself were to no avail.

Finally exhausted, she ceased her impotent struggles.
Breathless, trembling, she raised her gaze to his. The terrible force of his stare made her quake.

"Do not fight me," he said softly. "You will only hurt
yourself."

She gave in, her body slumping weakly against him in
defeat.

Bending, he lifted her in his arms and carried her to her
mount as if she weighed no more than a child.

She didn't struggle again. Biting her lower lip to hold
back screams and tears, she lay tensely in his arms, accepting his superior strength. She would gain nothing by
fighting him. For the time being she would have to yield.
He was her captor . . . for the moment.

He set her on her horse, though he didn't allow her to
have control of the reins; those he drew over the mare's
head, before leading her to his stallion. After looping the

free end of the reins around a buckle on his own saddle, he mounted the black horse.

When he gave her a brief glance over his shoulder, Alysson roused herself from her daze of shock and fear. "Where . . . are you taking me?" She forced the words past her dry throat and was ashamed at how weak her voice sounded.

He didn't answer, nor had she expected him to. Instead he reached inside one of the leather pouches hanging from the pommel of his high-backed saddle and drew out a length of black cotton cloth.

"Cover your head and face with this," he said, holding it out to her. "You will need protection from the sun."

She wanted to rail at him, to throw his offering back in his arrogant face. What she needed was protection from *him*, not the sun. But she wasn't a fool. Now that she'd had a moment to calm down, she realized that to refuse the protective head-covering would only be spiting herself. She would end up with burned skin or worse, which would only put her at a further disadvantage. She needed all the strength she could muster if she were to save herself from this ruthless villain.

With wary grace, she accepted his gift and tried to do as he bid, but her bonds made her attempts to fashion a headdress awkward. After a moment of watching her wrestle with the scarf, he nudged his stallion abreast of her mare and took the cloth from her.

When he lifted it to her hair, Alysson shut her eyes. If she didn't look at him, his fierce gaze would have no power over her. Still, she felt his eyes roam lightly over her face as he arranged the haik over her head and wound the ends around her neck so that her chin and mouth were buried in the soft folds. Both his scrutiny and his gentle touch so disturbed her that Alysson barely controlled the urge to shudder.

"I won't harm you," he said in that low voice she was learning to associate with fear.

Her only response was to avert her face. She didn't believe him; his reassurances meant nothing to her.

When he completed the task, they set out. Leading her mount by the reins, he nudged the black stallion into a gallop, and the gray mare followed obediently. For an instant

Alysson thought about flinging herself from her horse and trying to flee on foot, but she dismissed that, too, as foolish. If she didn't break an ankle at this speed, he would only catch her, and probably tie her to her saddle; the cord binding her wrists was uncomfortable enough as it was.

She looked around her, trying to determine where they were going. In the same direction her flight had taken her, she decided. South, toward the mountains and high plains. Berber warlords inhabited those rugged mountains, she remembered Gervase telling her. The thought gave her absolutely no comfort.

As she raced further and further away from her uncle and her party, waves of cold rage and fiery anxiety alternately swept over Alysson. Rarely in her life had she felt such helplessness, and never such terror.

But she couldn't give in to her fear. She had to compose her shaken nerves. She had to think! She had to recall what she knew about the Berbers and use her knowledge to her advantage. Much of what she'd heard was good. Gervase respected and admired the Berbers, in part because they could be expected to act more like Europeans—unlike the guileful Moors of the cities or the nomadic Bedouin Arabs of the plains. What was it Gervase had said? That the Berbers were known for their virtues of honesty, hospitality, and good nature . . . None of which, Alysson thought with a bitter glance at her brutal captor, did *he* possess in the slightest.

They also were known for their vast courage. *That* he did have, apparently. He had defied death to capture her, had even been amused by her attempt to shoot him. And in abducting her, he had also risked the wrath of the French government. Not that such wrath meant much. The Berbers in the mountains had resisted all attempts by the French *Armée d'Afrique* to bring them to heel, Gervase had told her. They were laws unto themselves, giving only condescending lip service to the Arab Bureau's efforts to organize their tribal factions into some civilized form of government.

Then there were the accounts of the recent war. Only a few days ago had she overheard an officer of the Foreign Legion speaking of the campaigns and fierce battles in which he'd fought against the Algerines. "It is better," the Legionnaire had said, "to die in the first assault rather than live as hostage. No man survives the unspeakable tortures the Arab army inflicts on its prisoners. That is why we kill our wounded rather than allow them to be taken alive."

Alysson's gaze stole to the black-robed Berber galloping just ahead of her. Would he torture her? He had said he wouldn't harm her. But perhaps her fate would be worse. In Barbary white women were sold as concubines or slaves . . . Could she bear such degradation, such horror? To be the plaything of some strange, savage man? Or many men?

Trembling anew, Alysson clasped the fingers of her bound hands to keep them from shaking. She did not cry easily, but tears would have brought a welcome relief just now. Still, it did not seem wise to show the slightest weakness before her abductor. Aloof and hard, he was a man to be feared. She'd felt the full force of his potential for violence—in the strength of his muscular body, in the glitter of his eyes, in the edge of his voice.

Alysson tore her gaze away, focusing instead on her surroundings. If she was to find her way back to her uncle, she had to concentrate on locating landmarks and committing them to memory. Minute by minute the terrain was becoming more hilly, the mountains growing closer, she realized with dismay. Soon they would leave the Plain of Algiers behind altogether—and civilization as well.

At the thought of her uncle, though, her worries shifted from herself to Honoré. What had happened to him? What had this blackguard done to him?

They rode at a relentless speed for several more miles, before finally Alysson could bear her fearful thoughts no longer. The uncertainty of not knowing was more nerve-racking than the truth.

Marshaling her courage, Alysson urged her racing mare forward, till she rode alongside the galloping stallion. Her captor turned his head slightly, one dark golden eyebrow raised in question. She started to shout at him, but realized it would be too difficult to make herself heard over the pounding hooves. Leaning forward as far as she could reach, she tugged on her mount's bridle, which made the mare swerve into the stallion. Thankfully, the Berber brought the grueling pace to a halt.

"What have you done to my uncle?" Alysson demanded in breathless English, forgetting that all their previous conversations had been in French.

Not a flicker of understanding crossed the carved mask of his features, but he set the horses in motion again, this time at a rapid walk.

"You . . . you savage brute. If you have harmed him, I swear I will see you hanged!"

"Either speak French or don't speak," the Berber answered in a mild tone.

Glaring, she took a breath and tried again in French. "Very well, *what—have—you—done—to—my—uncle?*" she said through gritted teeth.

"Not a thing. He was to be set free as soon as you were safely in my power."

Could she believe him? Alysson wondered, searching his face. His eyes were as bright as topaz, his gaze as intent as the sharp look of a hunting bird—and just as steady. They were not eyes that lied.

The tense set of her shoulders relaxed the slightest degree. At least that was some comfort; he didn't want her uncle. She didn't have to worry about Honoré as well as herself.

But Uncle Honoré would be frantic with worry for *her,* Alysson suddenly realized. She had to extricate herself from this situation before he worked himself into a frenzy.

But first she had to discover why this black-robed devil had abducted her, what he planned to do with her. Perhaps he might even be persuaded to release her, she thought with burgeoning hope. She hadn't yet tried bargaining with him.

"You don't have to go to the trouble of carrying me off," she said, trying to remain calm. "If you mean to hold me for ransom, I can tell you now, my uncle will pay a great deal of money to have me safely returned."

"It isn't money I want." Not a whisper of emotion was evident in his soft tone, or on his hard features.

"What is it then? What *do* you want?"

He didn't reply; his only response was a long, frustrating silence.

"The soldiers of my escort won't allow you to take me

far. I expect they are directly behind us. They will hunt you down and shoot you like a dog.''

''I doubt it.'' He shook his head as if remembering. ''Such brave men your guards were, to give you up without a fight. They had no more discipline than sheep.''

Though she had thought the same thing, his scoffing tone goaded Alysson into defending her French escort. ''They weren't at fault! They had no one to direct them. Their commanding officer became ill—''

Even as she said the words, sick understanding dawned on her. The lieutenant had become ill only that morning. As had Chand . . . Oh, God . . . Chand.

Anguish etched her features as she cast him an imploring glance. ''Chand . . . my servant . . . please, tell me you didn't have him poisoned?''

''No.'' He shook his head abruptly. ''Your servant is unharmed. The right herb sprinkled in his food merely made him ill. In a few days he will recover completely. But it will be too late for him to find you.''

Absorbing the import of her captor's revelation, Alysson stared at him with mingled dismay and contempt. He had planned her abduction down to the last detail. ''You *bastard*,'' she said with soft loathing.

His hard mouth twisted in the semblance of a smile. ''Such language is not becoming to a young lady, *ma belle*.''

Her fingers clenched into fists. ''I should have killed you when I had the chance,'' she muttered.

''Yes, you should have.''

The amiableness of his answer made her glare at him. ''Next time I won't miss!''

Those were brave words, a threat made in a fit of defiance, and he gave them the respect they deserved: he merely shrugged. ''Instead of cursing me, you should be thanking me. I did you a service, taking you away from Bourmont. I assure you, you do not want to wed him. I warned you of it the other night.''

''The other night you were speaking nonsense, raving about murderers.''

''I never rave.'' His hard gaze found hers. ''And it was not nonsense.''

The sudden lethal note in his low voice made Alysson

want to shudder. "Why do you call Gervase a murderer? What has he ever done to you?"

Her Berber captor made no reply.

"You will never succeed with this! Gervase will rescue me—and he'll bring the entire French army with him!"

He regarded her with a chilling smile. "I sincerely hope the French army does come for you, the good colonel most of all. I will be pleased to welcome him."

Whatever courage Alysson had left quailed before that smile. She lapsed into brooding silence, becoming lost in thought as she pondered his words and contemplated her fate.

Beside her, Jafar watched his lovely captive with reluctant admiration. She had not treated him to the display of tears or pleas for mercy he had expected. Instead she had fought him, challenged him, demanded answers to her questions.

And in spite of her silence now, he knew she had not given up. She would defy him at every turn. And she would interrogate him again about his plans, his motives.

He had not yet decided how much he would tell her. She would never understand the cause that drove him. Killing for revenge was not civilized by her standards. But he was no longer the civilized Englishman she had met that day seven years ago. Nicholas Sterling was someone of his past.

Upon his return to the Kingdom of Algiers, he had joined the resistance against French domination as he'd intended. And in the years since, he'd regained the leadership of his father's tribe through tenacity and sheer ironhearted determination. He'd had to fight for his birthright and prove his abilities. Now he was *caid*—chief administrator of his province, a position he had earned. As such, he had sworn allegiance to the Sultan of the Arabs, Abdel Kader.

But his second major goal had been thwarted. Until now he had been denied the opportunity to avenge his parents' deaths. By the time he'd left England and returned home to Barbary, General Louis Auguste de Bourmont, the man he had sworn to kill, was already dead. But his vow of vengeance remained foremost in Jafar's mind. The bitter memories that haunted his dreams would not let him forget.

The details of that terrible day he still remembered vividly. Even now, seventeen years later, he could still recall his helpless rage at seeing his parents taken from him so brutally, still feel his fierce hatred for the general who had ordered their senseless slaughter.

No, never would he forget the name of Bourmont.

Only now, though, had the chance to avenge his parents' murders presented itself. The general's son had come to Barbary.

The moment Colonel Gervase de Bourmont had set foot on African soil, his life was forfeit; the son would pay for the father's sins.

The notion was not at all uncivilized in the Berber culture. To Jafar's people blood vengeance was a duty, the only honorable course for a Berber chieftain to take.

The only question had been deciding how he would carry out his vow. He could, of course, have killed the colonel on the streets of Algiers, or in his offices. It would have been simple to send an assassin to accomplish the task. Yet this job was one he was obligated to perform himself.

He had few qualms at plunging a knife into the heart of his longtime enemy's son, or firing a bullet into the colonel's skull. But there would have been no justice in allowing the Frenchman a swift death. No justice, and no satisfaction, either. He wanted the French jackal to suffer the way his mother had suffered, to know the agony of the blade, to contemplate death as his lifeblood drained away.

And how much more satisfying it would be to draw the French army into an engagement, to strike a blow for the failing Arab cause. To lure Gervase de Bourmont and his soldiers into the desert, where loyal Arab troops would engage them in battle.

He could have taken the colonel prisoner, of course, instead of Miss Vickery; the same end would have been accomplished. But how much more profound the distress for the colonel to know that the woman he loved was in danger, in the power of his mortal enemy.

And now the trap was set, with the colonel's lovely fiancée as bait.

Jafar's gaze again found his captive. He had spoken the truth a moment ago. He'd done her a service by taking her away from Bourmont. Better now, before the marriage could take place, for he would only have made her a widow later.

He'd done her another favor as well, though she would never know it. He had spared her Indian servant's life. Such a devoted follower would have fought to the death to prevent his mistress's capture. It had been a kindness to render the man too ill to travel. That, too, had been accomplished with ease. The Arab guide had been well paid to ensure that both Miss Vickery's servant and the lieutenant in command of her escort would not be in the way.

After that, her abduction had been child's play. All had gone as planned . . . except for the young lady herself, Jafar amended with a grim smile. His throbbing arm testified to the accuracy of her aim. He should have heeded her claim of being a good shot, should never have underestimated her courage. She was full of surprises—nothing like the maidens of Barbary, either Berber or Arab.

No, she was proud, lovely, defiant . . . Defiant even in fear, he thought, remembering the stormclouds in her eyes as she'd railed at him, remembering also the despair when she'd discovered herself his prisoner.

Seven years ago those anguished gray eyes had had the power to move him. Even now they had managed to strike a tender chord in his heart.

He had to guard against the protective instincts she aroused him, Jafar warned himself silently as he again set the horses into a gallop. Already she had made him question the wisdom of using her in his quest for revenge.

She could never persuade him from his purpose, certainly.

But still, he had to take care.

Chapter 3

The pace was grueling, her captor scarcely slowing even when they began to climb the hilly country of the Tell. Alysson's hopes sank with each swift mile, each foot of elevation. Her French escort would never find her in the mountains. There were too many places to hide.

She stole a glance at the black-robed devil who had abducted her. He had changed direction slightly, heading south and east, but his determination never faltered, and he still maintained firm control of her mount's reins.

Continuing to climb, they passed through forests and lighter wooded lands. An hour later the landscape suddenly turned barren. Chalk rock and red sandstone slopes ran between steep precipices and wild narrow ravines that spelled death to the unwary. The horses were forced to slow to a walk then.

Hot and weary, Alysson clung to the saddle as her mount negotiated a dangerous path strewn with loose stones. To think only a few short hours ago she had been eager to explore this fierce country.

A moment later, Alysson shook herself from her morose thoughts. She had to be brave. She had to accept that she was alone with only her instincts of survival to guide her. Rather than wait for an opportunity to escape, she would have to create one. He had allowed her to ride her own horse, that was something. And if she was his hostage, then surely he would not be so imprudent as to harm her.

Not that he seemed at all concerned about her welfare at the moment. Her thirst was mounting rapidly, and the cord that bound her hands had chafed her wrists nearly raw in places.

She was feeling another discomfort as well, but every

ladylike instinct quailed at mentioning it. By the time they
descended into a bare valley surrounded by naked mountains, however, she decided there was no purpose in pro-
longing the torture any longer.

"Please, I have to stop."

At her abrupt announcement after so long a silence, her
captor halted the horses. When his penetrating gaze found
hers, Alysson resisted the urge to look away nervously. "Do
you mean to make me perish from thirst? It has been ages
since I last had anything to drink."

His hard mouth curved in what might have been a rueful
smile. "I forget the pampered life you have led." He
reached down to retrieve the goatskin water bag that was
tied to his saddle and handed it to her. "Forgive me if I
have no tea or chocolate to offer you."

Repressing a retort, Alysson accepted the goatskin from
him. Raising it to her lips, she drank eagerly, finding the
water tepid and strange-tasting but soothing to her parched
throat.

When she finally handed it back to him, the Berber took
a brief swallow himself, then again secured the bag to his
saddle. He was about to proceed when Alysson gathered
her courage.

"Wait!"

He hesitated, looking at her questioningly.

"I would like a moment of privacy," she said stiffly. She
endured his long scrutiny, feeling the warmth of acute embarrassment but refusing to give in to it.

Fortunately he understood without further explanation,
for he gave a brief nod. "In a moment we will stop to water
the horses. You may have your privacy then."

Alysson had to be content with that, although where they
would find water in this godforsaken place, she had no idea.

But he was as good as his word. In less than ten minutes
they came upon a deviation in the barren rocks where the
vegetation grew lush and thick. A shallow but steady stream
of water gushed from a crevice in the rock, Alysson saw
with surprise. An underground spring.

She watched as her captor dismounted and came to her
side. When he raised his hands to her waist, Alysson
flinched from his touch, not liking even this small contact

with this savage. It made her too aware of how vulnerable she was, alone with the man, at his mercy. Worse, it made her too aware of his hard male vitality, of the trembling agitation he made her feel.

The cynical smile that curved his mouth was almost a taunt, as were his murmured words. "Surely you do not fear me? Not the young lady who boasted of her unconcern regarding the dangers of the interior."

Alysson raised her chin in a brave show of defiance. "I had not expected such treachery as you and your fellow scoundrels showed me."

"Now you know better." His fingers closed firmly about her waist. When her body stiffened with resistance, he added in that calm low tone, as if soothing a frightened child or a skittish horse, "You have no need to fear me. Not as long as you obey me."

Obey him? She would sooner scratch his eyes out—which she would, at the first opportunity.

Steeling herself against the disquieting awareness he aroused in her, she suffered him to lift her down from her mare, but she broke away as soon as her feet reached the ground.

She was weaker than she realized, though. She nearly stumbled in her haste to be free. When his fingers tightened on her arm to steady her, Alysson twisted from his grasp, her pulse accelerating in alarm. "Don't touch me!"

He let her go without argument. With a slight shrug, he turned to gather the reins.

Shaken, breathless, Alysson watched warily as he led the horses to the spring so they could drink. Gingerly then, she shook out her weak limbs and stretched her sore muscles, at the same time looking around her, searching for a private place in which to take care of her needs, or better yet, an avenue of escape.

Even as the thought formed, a wild idea occurred to her. She could not hope to elude him on foot, but if she could manage to steal her horse . . . It might be grasping at straws, but she had to do *something*.

She stole a glance at her fierce captor. He seemed to be paying her little attention. Indeed, his whole attitude suggested supreme confidence, even arrogance. No doubt he was certain she wouldn't have the nerve to attempt an escape, or that he could catch her if she did try. Well, she would show him he wasn't dealing with a frail female who fainted at the first sign of adversity.

But first she had to improve the odds.

Forcing herself to adopt a more conciliatory manner, Alysson approached him warily. When he turned, one eyebrow raised in question, she held out her bound hands. "Do you suppose you could release me? I cannot manage . . ." She faltered, avoiding his golden gaze, as if explaining how awkward the fastenings of her breeches would be with her hands tied embarrassed her. Which it did; the blush that rose to her cheeks was not at all fabricated.

He stood looking down at her for a long uncomfortable moment. Alysson refused to look at him directly, but she could feel him taking her measure. To her dismay, she felt like squirming beneath his intent scrutiny. What was it about this man that unnerved her so?

When the silence drew out, she risked a glance up at him. His face, overshadowed by that black turban, showed no indication of what he was thinking.

"Where can I possibly go?" she asked with a helpless little nod that indicated their rugged surroundings.

When he still made no reply, she tried once more. "Please . . . the binding is hurting me."

That at least brought a response; abruptly he caught her arm, holding her wrists up for his inspection. The slight scowl between his brows as he eyed her chafed skin indicated what? Alysson wondered. Suspicion? Anger? Remorse?

Without commenting he reached inside his burnous and drew the curved dagger from his belt. Alysson couldn't manage to stifle a gasp as the wicked blade flashed in the late-afternoon sunlight.

"Be still," he ordered. His tone was harsh, but his face softened minutely as he cut the woolen cord from her wrists, freeing her.

As soon as he was done, Alysson pulled away and rubbed her sore wrists. "Thank you," she said gratefully.

"Make haste, mademoiselle," was all her captor said in return. "We have a long way to go before nightfall."

For once Alysson did as she was bid. Slipping behind a craggy boulder, she attended to her personal needs quickly. He was waiting with the horses when she returned. Like before, he helped her to mount the gray mare, but unlike before, Alysson gave him no resistance—until he turned away to secure the mare's reins to his saddle.

It was the moment she had been waiting for. With a frantic lunge, she grasped the reins and pulled with all her might, ripping them from his hands, startling a low oath from him. The instant they broke free, she used them to lash at the black stallion's hindquarters, trying to drive it away. Even as the animal shied, she spurred her own horse into a gallop. She had difficulty guiding the mare with reins only on one side, but direction seemed far less critical than speed.

For the space of a heartbeat, she tasted the sweet glory of freedom. Then Alysson heard a sharp whistle and glanced frantically behind her. The stallion had whirled and returned obediently to its master, coming to a skidding halt before him.

Scarcely pausing to gather the reins, the Berber leapt into the saddle and came after her, his black robes streaming in the breeze.

Alysson redoubled her efforts, but it was hopeless. In a matter of moments, her pursuer caught up to her. This time, though, he plucked her from her mount with the ease of a hungry thief picking a ripe plum, and dragged her onto his saddle in front of him.

Wildly twisting, she screamed at him, flailing her arms, beating at his face and chest with all the strength she could muster, trying to break free of his grasp. "Vile coward, warring on women!"

Her struggles were to no avail. Abruptly halting the stallion, he wrapped both his hard arms about her, pinning her own at her sides, imprisoning her in an unyielding embrace.

"Devil! Fiend! Monster!" she sobbed against his chest, still refusing to admit defeat.

"All the more reason to do as I say," he hissed in a low, hard voice.

"Let me go!"

"No, mademoiselle. You cannot be trusted with your own mount, so you will ride with me."

"No, never! I won't!"

The pressure of his grip increased, tightening about her ribs until she thought he might crush the very breath from her lungs. "Will you yield?"

What choice did she have? Finally ceasing to struggle, she managed to nod in surrender.

His fierce embrace immediately eased.

Gasping for air, she closed her eyes in defeat. She lay there awkwardly, half-sitting, half-sprawling in her captor's lap, her face and right shoulder pressed against his chest, her heart still pounding. She refused to acknowledge the stinging tears that were running down her cheeks, yet as he urged the stallion into a walk, in pursuit of the mare, Alysson's thoughts gave her no peace. What good had her attempt at escape done her? Not only hadn't she succeeded, but now she was required to suffer the indignity of sharing a mount with this savage brute. Her discomfort was acute. The Berber saddle was not fashioned to accommodate two riders. The high pommel was digging uncomfortably into her left thigh with each step the stallion took.

Gradually Alysson became aware of another sensation—a masculine warmth that brought heat rising to her face. She shifted abruptly, trying to sit up and thus avoid the hardness of the muscled thighs beneath her. But he prevented her from moving by tightening his arm around her waist and snapping a low command for her to be still.

Only when she quieted did he settle her more comfortably in his embrace—turning her slightly so that she faced more forward, drawing her hips back into the cradle of his thighs, cushioning her head in the curve of his shoulder. Despite his consideration, Alysson remained rigid in his arms, tense with anger and defiance and a disquieting physical awareness of his body against hers. Quelling the urge to shudder at the shocking contact, she willed her erratic heartbeat to slow. She might be humiliated but not vanquished. He would not succeed in whatever scheme he had planned, she vowed. She would defy her ruthless captor at every turn, and somehow she would manage to escape.

Cherishing her smoldering thoughts, Alysson endured his

embrace in silence. When they reached the mare, he bent down and gathered the dangling reins, the secured them to his saddle again. Immediately they resumed the swift pace of before, with the galloping stallion leading the now riderless mare.

They climbed once more, and when they topped a rocky hillock, the landscape abruptly changed again. It was no longer barren here, apparently because rainfall was more abundant. Soon they were riding through a cedar forest, the shadows cool after the heat of the afternoon.

Alysson found herself shivering—but not because of the temperature. Evening was fast approaching, and she found it harder and harder to hold on to her courage with the coming darkness.

She would have given her entire fortune to find herself back in Algiers, in the safe and civilized company of her uncle and her prospective fiancé, surrounded by the powerful French army. But money would not help her now; this savage Berber had already said so.

She should have listened to Chand. Hundreds of times her Indian servant had warned that she would land herself in dire trouble, but she hadn't heeded him. And Gervase. Only two nights ago he'd argued and pleaded with her not to undertake this expedition, but she hadn't listened. How she regretted that now!

Biting her trembling lip, Alysson glanced up at the stranger's face, surreptitiously studying him from beneath her lashes. His sun-hardened features gave no clue as to her fate. His expression was impassive and aloof.

As if he sensed her watching him, he looked down. Alysson was hard-pressed to control a shudder as his amber gaze clashed with hers. He seemed so merciless, so savage. What would he do to her, once it grew dark? Tearing her gaze away, she concentrated on keeping her fears at bay.

Jafar, too, looked away. The stains of tears on her pale cheeks had affected him more than he cared to admit. He hadn't wanted to hurt her—and he wouldn't, as long as he could maintain the upper hand without jeopardizing his mission. Steeling his heart against the insidious tenderness, he forced himself as well to ignore the arousing feel of soft woman, the feminine warmth that was proving a supreme test of his willpower.

The sun burned red and gold on the horizon when he finally brought the horses to a halt. "We will stop here for the night," he told her in a quiet voice.

Alysson opened her eyes and looked around her. They were in another valley, this one flat and treeless, and covered with rank shrub and grass. There was no house in sight, nor was there any sign of a tent. He meant to sleep out in the open, under the stars, she concluded. With effort she fought back her rising trepidation.

Even so, she flinched when his encircling arm tightened beneath her breasts.

Abruptly, his movement stilled. "I trust you don't intend to fight me again."

He had only intended to help her dismount, she realized, feeling awkward. Swallowing her apprehension, Alysson shook her head. She was too weary to fight. Her head ached dully and her neck had grown stiff, caught as it had been against the Berber's rock-hard shoulder.

Perhaps he sensed her exhaustion, for his movements were gentle as he eased her down from the stallion. Alysson sank to her knees right there where she landed, yet she kept her attention focused on her captor, watching him with wary unease as he dismounted. But he didn't approach her.

He saw to the horses instead, first hobbling them with woolen cords so they couldn't roam, then removing their bridles, then arranging a feed bag over the mare's nose. The stallion he fed by hand, offering it small portions of barley in the palm of his hand. Surprisingly, the spirited animal ate with dainty bites, displaying exquisite manners that would have been at home at a formal dining table. All the while the Berber spoke to the horse in his strange tongue, in a soft voice that was at odds with his ruthless treatment toward her.

Listening to the soft murmur, Alysson felt herself being lulled against her will. His voice was attractive and low, with a gentleness that was oddly comforting.

He felt a fondness for the noble beast, that was obvious. But the people of Barbary prized their horses, Alysson remembered hearing, cherishing them above any other possession. And the stallion was a magnificent animal, if a bit savage-looking. Its proudly arching neck, long well-shaped head, and fine tapering muzzle bespoke excellent bloodlines, while the liquid, wide-spaced eyes held both intelligence and courage.

Involuntarily her gaze shifted to the stallion's master. He had strong hands, with long slender fingers that possessed an austere beauty. He moved with an easy carriage, his body fluid and graceful beneath his black robes—

Abruptly Alysson jerked her disturbing thoughts to attention. She had to resist totally the compelling attraction this dangerous man held for her. It would never do to relax her guard even for a moment. She had to remain constantly alert.

Forcing her absurd musings back along safer channels, she watched as her captor removed the horses' saddles and accoutrements. As he began the task of grooming, her gaze fell on the long, silver-embossed rifle that he'd left leaning against the pile of saddlery. Hope suddenly flared within her. If she could only manage to reach the weapon and turn it on him before he could carry out whatever heinous plan he had for her . . . Yet she couldn't afford to give him the slightest hint of what she was considering.

She busied herself with the head scarf he had given her, unwinding it to settle around her shoulders. Then she began the task of repinning her hair that had escaped its knot and was wisping around her face. By the time the Berber was done grooming the horses, Alysson had her expression schooled to impassiveness.

She kept her attention fixed on her ruthless captor, instinctively tensing as he shed his burnous.

He spread it on the ground some ten yards from the horses. "You may sit here."

Alysson regarded him warily. Beneath his desert robe he wore a belted, thigh-length tunic, loose trousers, and soft leather boots. "Why?" Her tone was cautions, shaky.

"So you may eat. I don't intend to starve you. You needn't be afraid of me," he added when she remained silent.

"I am not afraid!" But it was a lie. She did fear him. Determinedly, though, Alysson raised her chin to stare at him, hiding her fright behind a brave front of hauteur.

One corner of his mouth curved wryly, but he didn't contradict her. Instead he sat cross-legged on his burnous and unwrapped a packet of food, removing a round, flat cake of what looked like unleavened barley bread and a chunk of what might have been goat's cheese.

"Come here and eat," he said softly.

Alysson felt her mouth watering. Until now she hadn't realized how hungry she was. But she wouldn't give him the satisfaction of knowing it. Disobeying his command, she remained where she was.

He ate in silence, ignoring her stubbornness. But his intent was clear. If she wanted to eat, she would have to go to him.

After a few moments, Alysson reevaluated her decision. It would be foolish to let fear or pride prevent her from assuaging her hunger, especially since she had to keep up her strength if she were to escape.

Swallowing her trepidation, she rose and went to him. Cautiously she knelt beside his burnous, prepared to flee at his slightest move. But he merely handed her a barley cake and a piece of cheese. A moment later he passed her the goatskin water bag.

Alysson chewed on the tough bread and watched him surreptitiously from beneath her lashes. With the onset of evening, his ruthless arrogance was not so noticeable. The waning golden light caressed his lean face, softening the high, proud cheekbones and the slashing grooves carved on either side of his mouth.

They finished the meager meal in silence. When he was done eating, the Berber turned his attention to the wound on his left arm, examining the crude dressing. Even from several paces away, Alysson could see the black bandage was crusted with dried blood.

Unexpectedly he raised his wounded arm, holding it toward her. "Would you untie the knot?"

Startled, Alysson stared at him. Her first reaction was to tell him to go to the devil. But it was obvious he would have difficulty managing on his own.

With poor grace she brushed the crumbs from her fingers and edged closer on her knees so she could attack the knot. Her movements were awkward and tense as she slowly peeled away the bandage. Through the rent in his tunic sleeve, she could see the groove in the flesh made by her bullet. The wound didn't appear dangerously deep, but she knew it had to be painful. When he rolled up his sleeve, though, to expose the bloody gash, he showed no sign of pain.

"It needs cleansing," he observed, his tone emotionless. He held out the goatskin bag to her. "Pour water on it."

Alysson balked at his obvious assumption that he could order her about. She was not his servant, to do his bidding. She stared at the bag, refusing to take it.

"This is your first lesson in obedience." It was said so calmly, with such deliberate blandness that it took her a moment to absorb his words. Her gaze flew to his. He was perfectly serious, she realized.

A dozen scathing remarks tumbled to be the first from her lips. "You . . . you arrogant barbarian! If you think for a moment that I . . . that you . . ." Furiously, she curled her fingers into fists.

"You caused the damage. Therefore you will be responsible for repairing it. It is the law of this land—just reparation for injuries done."

"I don't give a tinker's curse about your laws!"

A muscle in his jaw flexed. "No, you superior Europeans choose to ignore those not of your own making. But you will learn differently."

"The devil I will!"

Alysson's chin came up in determination while her eyes clashed with his in a meeting of wills. The hard gleam in his was almost frightening in its intensity. Yet meekly yielding to such raw audacity was untenable.

"What about the injury you've done to me?" she exclaimed in frustration. "Did I ask you to abduct me?"

"That too is reparation."

"What do you mean? What are you talking about?"

"The wound. I am waiting."

Alysson clenched her teeth. "You will have a long wait. When icicles grow in hell, then perhaps I will consider acceding to your request."

Calmly he continued to hold out the water bag to her. At his commanding look of expectation, her outrage at his arrogance mounted to an explosive level. Defiantly she snatched the water bag from his hand and threw it away with all her might. It landed some twenty feet away, sloshing water over the thirsty earth.

"Foolish woman!" With a low curse, he lunged to his knees, reaching for her. Recoiling in fear, Alysson raised her hands to block the blow. But it never came. The hard fingers of his hand closed about her upper arm, while his other hand half-encircled her throat, pushing her chin up, forcing her to meet his gaze. His eyes were golden and fierce, as unblinking as a hawk's. She quaked at the leashed violence she saw there.

"You cannot have the intelligence I credited you with," he said through gritted teeth, "if you are so stupid as to waste water in this country. It can mean death for a man without water."

Alysson was already regretting her self-destructive act of rebellion, and realized the truth of his words, but she was beyond rational reasoning. She wanted to scream at him, to pound at him with her fists, to force this savage devil to release her. "I don't care!" she cried, her voice shaking. "If I could cause your demise, I would!"

The Berber regarded her coldly, for a long, uncomfortable moment. Then his taut expression softened the slightest degree. "I will make allowances for you," he said finally, "because you are English. But you *will* learn to obey me. For your sake, I hope you learn quickly. From now on, if you wish to drink again, you will ask politely. And you will tend my wound without complaint."

His hold on her eased then. Abruptly Alysson shook off the loose restraint and scrambled to her feet. "Your arm can rot off, for all I care!"

He, too, rose, making Alysson back away warily. But he merely retrieved the water bag and proceeded to cleanse his wound himself. Alysson was surprised and relieved by her momentary reprieve, yet she knew the battle was not over by any means. He had sounded entirely too confident that she would give in—but that only made her all the more determined she would not.

She watched as he completed his task and carried the goatskin to his pile of equipment. Then he surprised her again by removing his turban. In the gathering dusk, Alysson could see that his hair was liberally sun-streaked, with strands of pale burnished gold. It only made her more certain that he was a descendant of the fair-skinned Berber race. The *barbaric* Berber race, she amended, scowling at his back.

"I want you to remove your boots."

His soft command, delivered with the mild interest of someone talking about the weather, took her aback. When he turned, Alysson gave him a look that clearly said he had lost his mind.

"Without footwear, you will be less likely to wander off."

"You can go straight to the—"

"I won't tell you again. If you won't remove them, I will simply do it for you."

She stared at him in impotent fury. He not only was capable of forcing her to obey him, he no doubt would relish the opportunity. Alysson decided to spare herself the humiliation and perform the task on her own. Sitting on the rough grass, she tugged off her boots and tossed them aside, then glared up at him.

"Now, take off your jacket."

"What?" Her incredulous expression turned wary. "Why? What do you intend to do?"

"Nothing."

"Then why? Without my jacket I'm likely to freeze to death. You apparently don't intend to build a campfire."

"You will not be cold, I assure you. You will sleep wrapped in my burnous."

"How considerate of you."

He shrugged. "Merely practical. Now, do as I say."

Grinding her teeth, silently calling him every eptithet she could think of, Alysson did as she was bid, pulling off her jacket and laying it on top of her boots. She shivered as a chill breeze pierced the fine cambric of her shirt; darkness was descending rapidly and the air had already grown cold.

"Now your shirt."

She stared at him, wide-eyed, appalled. "You can't mean it!"

"Oh, but I do."

"Why? So you can rape me?"

Even as the words left her lips she cursed herself in English and in French. It was foolish in the extreme to put such thoughts in his head.

But his response was not what she expected; his hard mouth twisted in scornful amusement. "Your honor is safe with me, *ma belle*. Unlike your race, I have no desire to rape defenseless innocents." His eyebrow rose at the doubtful glance she gave him. "I merely want to ensure that you do not attempt to escape. The standards of decorum you English ladies observe would never allow you to be seen in less than proper attire. Now, take off your shirt, or I will be obliged to remove it myself."

Cold panic seized her. Alysson measured the distance between herself and the rifle, but she was too far away. She would never reach it before he cut her off. Frantic to delay the inevitable, she voiced the first words that came into her head. "How can I be sure that you won't . . . that you . . ."

"That I won't take advantage of you? I give you my word."

"I don't belive you!"

"What you believe is immaterial." The hard edge was back in his voice. "Come now, I am waiting, Miss Vickery."

She couldn't do it. She couldn't bring herself to undress in front of him, even if he had promised not to assault her. It might be cowardly, but she couldn't. Her gaze fell again on the rifle. Reaching it might be impossible, but she had to try.

It *was* impossible. No sooner had she darted after the weapon than her astute captor swiftly blocked her way. Alysson found herself confronted with the hard wall of his chest.

Her panic rising, she went on the attack, flailing and kicking at him with fury. When her fist managed to connect with his wound, she made him grunt in pain, but when she struck his shin with her bare foot, the blow hurt her far more than it could ever hurt him. With his superior strength, it was not long before he subdued her struggles. Swinging her up in his arms then, he carried her writhing body over to his burnous and laid her down.

When he knelt beside her, Alysson tried again to break free, nearly sobbing in frustration and fear. But her efforts were in vain. He merely pinned her arms at her sides until she finally went still.

"It will go easier for you when you accept that it is useless to defy me."

Determinedly, he bent over her and attended to the small buttons that ran down the front of her shirt, brushing her flailing hands away when she tried to resist his efforts. Alysson squeezed her eyes shut, fighting back tears of fear and humiliation.

"I said I wouldn't hurt you," he murmured, his low, controlled voice penetrating her daze. "Not as long as you obey me."

That was the rub. If she obeyed his wishes, if she meekly surrendered, if she allowed him to have his way with her, then he would refrain from beating her or worse. Well, she wouldn't give in to his threats! She would never calmly accept her captivity. She would fight him every step of the way. She would resist him with every ounce of strength she possessed.

For the moment, though, she had to accept defeat.

She remained rigid and unmoving as he lifted her slightly in order to draw off her shirt, clenching her teeth as he bared her upper body to the chill evening air. Beneath her linen chemisette, her nipples puckered against the cold.

Alysson shivered in response, but her captor suddenly went still. When she fearfully glanced up at him, she realized he was staring down at her breasts with hot golden eyes.

Never more aware of herself as a woman, Alysson flushed painfully. Frantically, awkwardly, she wrapped her arms around herself to cover her near-nakedness. "I despise you," she said with all the loathing she could muster.

Wadding up her shirt, he tossed it aside. With a casual shrug, he glanced down the length of her body. "Be glad that I am letting you keep your breeches."

There was a note in his voice that sounded suspiciously like amusement, but when she glared up at him, she could read nothing in his expression. The gathering twilight shrouded his thoughts.

"A woman should not hide her femininity," he remarked casually. "You could learn much from my countrywomen. They would tell you a mere female must yield to the whims of a man."

It *was* amusement she heard in his voice. He was deliberately trying to provoke her. It made her long to do him an injury.

Just then, however, he stretched himself out beside her on the burnous, slowly, like a cat, looking every bit as alert as one. He held himself up on one elbow, his chest almost brushing her left arm, his shadowed face very near hers. Alysson tensed. She was totally at his mercy. If he chose to break his word, she would have little chance of stopping him from ravishing her.

To hide her fear, she took refuge behind a show of contempt. "I have no intention of yielding to your whims," she retorted. "And I am not a *mere* female!"

"No, you are a young lady, a wealthy Englishwoman . . . spoiled and pampered and petted from birth. I doubt if you have ever performed a day's work in your life."

She had no reply for his cool accusation, for it was true. She was accustomed to having her every wish gratified by her servants, her commands obeyed. And she usually managed to get her way with everyone else. The men of her acquaintance especially leapt to do her bidding. She knew instinctively, though, this was one man she could not bend to her will. Dropping her gaze, Alysson helplessly hugged her body with her arms, rubbing her chilled, bare flesh. Never in her life had she been so shaken by a man.

When she shivered, he reached all the way over her, his fingers grasping the far edge of his burnous. Alysson flinched in alarm as his chest pressed against her. "Don't touch me!"

He paused for a moment, looking down at her, his expression enigmatic. Then he continued with his task, drawing the burnous over her bare shoulders, tucking the edge beneath her arm.

He had only been trying to cover her, Alysson realized numbly.

"I know," he said in a soft voice, but this time the scorn

was unmistakable, "you don't want your lily-pure skin to be contaminated by a 'savage Arab.' "

His characterization of her wasn't fair, she thought defensively. It wasn't because of his race that she didn't want him touching her. Unlike most of her fellow Europeans, she didn't consider Arabs automatically inferior because of the color of their skin. Besides, he wasn't even one.

"You may be incredibly savage, but you aren't an Arab," she ground out. "You're a Berber."

Mocking admiration shone in his eyes. "My congratulations. At least you can perceive the difference. That is far more than many of your race can do."

Annoyed by his provoking sarcasm, she averted her face so she wouldn't have to look at him. "Leave me alone."

Any gentleman would have taken her muttered demand as a dismissal. While he was certainly no gentleman, she at least expected him to take the hint and leave her in peace. Yet he made no move to go.

"I am waiting," she said pointedly, echoing his earlier command. "I wish to go to sleep."

"Please, be my guest."

"Not until you leave!"

"I am not going anywhere."

Whipping her head around, Alysson scowled up at him. "You said if I took off my jacket I could have your burnous."

"It is big enough for the both of us. We will share it."

She gaped at him. "You can't mean for us to sleep together!"

"Can I not?"

"It—isn't—proper," Alysson sputtered, embarrassment, frustration, and dread all warring within her. She had never been overly concerned about her reputation before, nor was that her chief concern now, but she had no qualms about claiming modesty if it would help protect her from this heathen.

"I don't even know your name," she protested weakly. "How can I possibly sleep next to you?"

His chuckle, when it came, was soft, amused. "You may call me Jafar. Does that make it more acceptable, now that we have been introduced?"

"It most certainly does not!"

"Just remember that you are my captive and that you have no choice but to accede to my wishes. That will appease your conscience."

As he spoke, he sat up and fished in his sash for something. Alysson abruptly swallowed the retort on her tongue as her gaze dropped to his waist. In the gloom of nightfall she could make out the glittering stones of the jeweled dagger.

Looking up, she caught the flash of white teeth as Jafar smiled. With exaggerated care, he drew the dagger from his belt and placed it on the ground at his other side, as far away from her as he could reach. Alysson pressed her lips together in anger and regret.

Then he reached down and grasped her stockinged ankle.

She nearly yelped. "What do you think you're doing!" she exclaimed, sitting up abruptly.

He brushed her hands away. "Securing you for the night. I told you, I don't want you running off."

In shock she watched as he encircled her left ankle with a length of woolen cord. He meant to hobble her like an animal!

"Damn you . . . you . . ." She faltered, choking on her own words.

But he wasn't tying her feet together. Instead, he was lashing her ankle to his. If she tried to untie the knot in the night, if she so much as stirred, he would feel her movements and prevent her from escaping.

Shaking with thwarted outrage, Alysson clenched her fists so tightly that her nails scored her palms. "I swear to God, you will rue the day you came near me!"

"Allah is more likely to sympathize with your plight than your Christian god."

His blasphemy made her breath catch. Taking advantage of her momentary lapse of hostility, Jafar gently pushed her back down. To her shock and dismay, he gathered her resisting body in his arms and drew the edges of his burnous around them both. Alysson found herself locked in his strong embrace, her head resting on his good arm, her nose pressed against his chest.

She lay there rigidly, cursing him silently, trying not to

quiver. She could feel the imprint of his hard body burning
through her meager clothing, could smell his male scent.
He smelled of horses and the desert wind . . . and something else, musky and pleasant. Something highly disturbing.

Dear God, she couldn't possibly go to sleep this way.
Even as exhausted she was.

"I hope your wound is painful," Alysson declared, recovering her mettle. *"Excruciatingly* painful."

"It is, but I'll survive. Go to sleep, *Ehuresh.*"

She didn't understand the word, but she wasn't about to
ask him what he meant. Still seething, Alysson wearily
closed her eyes. Oh, how she hated him! It especially galled
her that his warmth was so comforting, that he was protecting her from the cold. She didn't want his protection.
She wanted nothing to do with him . . .

Tense and restless, Alysson lay awake for a long while,
stiffening every time she felt the slightest movement from
him. It was nearly an hour before Jafar felt her slender form
relax in his arms. Her breathing was shallow and uneven,
but she had finally fallen asleep.

Jafar permitted his vigilance to slacken while he tried to
force his thoughts on something other than the young woman
in his embrace. In all he was satisfied with the day. He had
accomplished his purpose with little trouble. He had taken
the woman of his enemy. And soon he would realize his
ultimate objective. He had no doubt the colonel would come
to rescue such a treasure.

Yes, a treasure. Jafar smiled in the darkness, remember-
ing her claim that she was not a *mere* female. No, Miss
Alysson Vickery was definitely unique. And unpredictable.
One moment a spitting tigress, the next a frightened dove.

The memory of her terror made his smile fade. He didn't
like her fearing him. He did not want her recoiling from
him in fright. He much preferred her defiance—however
annoying it might be, coming from a female. And *that* she
possessed in full measure.

Ehuresh, he had called her in his language. Defiant one.
She was defiant yet vulnerable. And quite, quite lovely.
There was a wildness, a sense of daring about her, an in-

tensity that was incredibly arousing. What would it be like to have that wildness unleashed in passion, in his bed?

The stallion snorted just then, making Jafar lift his head. Momentarily he searched the darkness with his keen gaze, but found the horses grazing peacefully.

With a sigh, Jafar let his head fall back. His wounded arm was throbbing, but it was nothing that he hadn't experienced a dozen times on the battlefield.

More severe, though, was another discomfort, the pain of having a lovely young woman in his arms—*this* lovely young woman—but not allowing himself to appease his male urges. Yet there was something elementally satisfying about holding her this way.

Without waking her, he shifted his body, nestling her more comfortably in his embrace. A mistake, he thought, feeling her soft, ripe breasts press against his chest, the innocent thrust of one slender knee as it insinuated itself between his thighs.

He closed his eyes as he vainly sought sleep.

Ah, yes, painful but satisfying.

Here, alone, with nothing but the stars and the wind and his defiant young captive.

Chapter 4

The east flushed rose and blue as Alysson stirred awake the next morning. Feeling the chill of dawn, she sleepily drew the burnous more tightly around her, vaguely missing the warmth that had sheltered her during the long night.

The jingle of metal intruded on her hazy, disquieting dreams. A moment later she suddenly became aware that she was alone beneath the burnous. Her eyes flew open. Her Berber captor, the ruthless barbarian who had called himself Jafar, was bridling the horses.

As if he felt her sudden scrutiny, he glanced over his shoulder, meeting her gaze. There was a shadow of golden-brown stubble on his jaw, Alysson noted, that gave his noble features a disreputable air. And he was eyeing her with a calm look that was no less dangerous for its lack of emotion.

Abruptly Alysson tore her gaze away, wanting to bury her head beneath the burnous. The memory of being forced to undress before his eyes brought fierce color to her cheeks and sent her temper surging. She was unaccustomed to having her will thwarted, but this devil had done everything in his power to frustrate her and to show her how helpless she was against him. She was also weary from lack of sleep after the wretched night she had just passed. She had started awake every hour, only to find herself locked in this stranger's embrace, his hard body molded against her soft one. His disturbing proximity had left her shaken, her emotions in a state of turmoil. It alarmed her, the effect this savage barbarian had on her. Never before had she been so unnerved by a man. Never before had she been so acutely aware of a man's maleness, or of her own femaleness.

Trying to forget that awareness and her humiliation—and to ignore the man who had caused both—Alysson rose silently and dressed. To her dismay she couldn't meet Jafar's eyes, although she was grateful when he allowed her, without comment, to move a short distance away for a few moments of privacy. She was less grateful when he offered her a piece of bread for breakfast, for his generosity did not extend to the goatskin water bag that hung from the stallion's saddle.

He was waiting for her to ask for a drink, she knew, but she didn't intend to give in. She would not beg him, nor would she obey his arrogant whims.

She was surprised to learn he intended for her to ride the mare, but decided it was because he wanted to spare his stallion, not because he cherished any newfound feelings of trust for her. When he would have helped her mount, though, Alysson recoiled, eyes flashing her loathing at his touch. "I can manage on my own!"

A muscle flexed in his jaw, but he said nothing.

Her temper simmering, Alysson pulled herself up on the

mare. When he had gained his own saddle, they set out, with Jafar in the lead, in control of her reins. Alysson kept her gaze fixed on anything but him. She was determined to ignore her savage companion and his ridiculous demands that she do his bidding.

Her determination wavered when a few miles later they came upon another spring. Alysson watched with undisguised longing as Jafar watered the horses and filled the goatskin bag.

His penetrating glance, when he saw her licking her dry lips, was a pointed reminder that she had a choice. "You know the terms," he said calmly. "You have only to ask politely for a drink and agree to tend my wound, and you will be allowed to slake your thirst."

"I am not thirsty," Alysson lied.

She tried to make herself believe it as the morning progressed, but soon their climb ended and they left the relative coolness of the mountains. Before them stretched a broad plain rippling with mild undulations. They had reached the High Plateaux.

When the hot yellow sun began to beat down upon her, her lie became a litany: *I'm not thirsty. I am not thirsty.* But by noon Alysson was willing to admit her misery. She was hot and dusty and hungry and perishing from thirst. She wanted a long cool drink. She wanted a bath. She wanted a soft bed. And more than anything, she wanted a weapon that she could use on this barbarian. At the moment she would relish murdering him by slow degrees.

An Arab method of torture came to mind. She would stretch him out, stake him to the ground in the desert sand, pour honey over his body, and allow the ants to devour him, bite by stinging bite.

Her fierce musings had no effect on her merciless captor. They kept up the same grueling speed, hour after hour. Alysson's weariness and craving for water grew, while her hopes of either escape or rescue sank with every endless mile. She could only pray that her uncle would make it safely back to Algiers rather than setting out in search of her. He could never endure these harsh conditions and would do better to leave the task of rescuing her in Gervase's more capable hands.

By mid-afternoon the high tablelands melted into steppes covered with alpha grass. In the distance Alysson occasionally glimpsed flocks of sheep and goats ranging on the grassy plains, but her Berber captor stayed well away from these manifestations of civilization.

They stopped once more, later in the afternoon, to water the horses. Alysson's resentment at Jafar surged anew. He was trying to kill her, yet he took great care of the animals—slowing to a walk and letting them cool off before permitting them to drink, allowing time to pass before resuming the gallop.

When she felt Jafar watching her with his shuttered amber eyes, though, she stiffened her spine. She didn't know how much longer she could hold out with her throat, parched as it was, and her swollen lips, but some last flicker of pride made her determined not to give in.

Her pride waned, however, as her abductor carried her further into the interior. Alysson had to clench her teeth to keep from surrendering. She wanted to scream at him, to pummel him with her fists, to beg him to let her go, but as she had learned yesterday over and over again, struggling against him was useless, as were all her pleas and threats. He would not release her. He was hard and cruel and relentless, a man who tolerated no opposition to his wishes.

Fighting back a wave of angry sobs, Alysson glared at him, hating him with an intensity that left her shaken.

Jafar was undeterred by her malevolent look, partially because he knew how she was suffering. He felt a grudging admiration for her strength of will, despite his frustration at her rebelliousness.

When a short while later he saw her proud shoulders sag with weariness and despair, he abruptly brought the horses to a halt, determined to put an end to this futile battle. He had meant to teach her a lesson; indeed, he had expected her to give in long before now. But he couldn't allow her to continue suffering any longer. He couldn't bear to see her in such distress. He untied the goatskin and held it out to her. "Here, drink."

Alysson gave the water bag a longing look before raising her defiant gaze to Jafar. "I don't want it."

"Don't be foolish." He unplugged the nozzle and held

it to her lips. "You will kill yourself with your stubbornness, and then you will be useless to me."

Alysson wanted to throw the bag in his face, but when she felt a cool trickle of life-sustaining liquid wash over her lips, she was lost. She opened her mouth eagerly, nearly gulping in her haste to satisfy her craving for water.

"Slowly," Jafar warned. He withheld the bag for a moment before letting her drink again, forcing her to take smaller sips. He took it away entirely before her thirst was completely quenched. "You may have more later. You will make yourself sick if you drink too much now."

Her face flushing, Alysson looked away. He had made no reference to her shameful surrender, nor did he repeat his demands that she do his bidding, but she felt the humiliation of her defeat all the same. And it *was* her defeat. He might have been the first to back down, but only because he needed her alive in order to carry out his nefarious plans, whatever they might be. And in doing so, he had forced her to face the reality of her situation—her helplessness, her powerlessness. She needed him in order to survive, and fighting him would only cause her more misery. The sooner she accepted that fact, the less wretched she would be.

They rode for another hour before the sun began to set. To her left, in the far distance, Alysson could see the beginnings of a mountain chain. Just beyond it to the south, where the rugged terrain sloped into a valley, she caught the golden flash of a river. She also glimpsed what might be a village nestled in the protection of the foothills, but her momentary spark of hope was short-lived. Any village here would likely be a Berber stronghold, and she would get no help from its inhabitants.

They stopped for the night beside a thicket of tamarisk shrubs and pistachio trees, where a spring gushed from an outcropping of rock. Like the previous evening Jafar fed the horses, then hobbled and unsaddled them before allowing himself or Alysson to eat. He didn't withhold water from her this time, but only because she finally brought herself to ask for it.

"May I have a drink?" she muttered when the bite of bread she had just swallowed stuck in her dry throat.

Jafar turned to eye her with a curious gaze. "What did you say?"

"I said, may I *please* have a drink of water?"

The words were polite, the tone like acid. Hesitating, he raised an eyebrow. "And my wound?"

"I will see to it."

"Very well," he replied mildly, his tone devoid of the triumph Alysson was certain he felt.

When they were done eating, he returned the remains of their meal to his saddlebag and pulled out various items from its numerous folds, including a cake of soap and a clean cloth. The soap surprised her, for it had to be European.

He meant to wash in the spring, Alysson realized when he carried the items over and set them down beside the bank. Having given her word, she followed Jafar warily, but she came up short when he began to remove his tunic. The unexpectedly virile sight made Alysson catch her breath. His powerful arms were corded with muscles, while his chest was lightly furred with hair made tawny by shades of gold. She couldn't help noticing, either, how the fine hair on his chest tapered to a narrow line at his waist and disappeared beneath the waistband of his loose trousers.

Her reaction alarmed Alysson. She had seen shirtless men before, of course—two of her uncles and Gervase, as well. But none of them had ever before elicited this sudden fluttery feeling in her stomach. Perhaps because none of them were so . . . acutely male.

Alysson averted her gaze as, reluctantly, she forced herself to take the final steps to reach Jafar's side. From the heat that was flooding her cheeks, she knew she was blushing, yet she hoped her discomposure wasn't obvious. When he handed her the soap and cloth, though, she made the mistake of looking up at him. His tawny eyes gleamed bright with amusement.

"You only have to wash my arm, *ma belle*," he said in a tone laced with soft laughter, "not the rest of me."

By gritting her teeth, Alysson managed to repress a retort. But she was none too gentle as she washed away the dried blood that covered the gash on his left arm.

To her regret, the wound did not look as if it were in any

danger of becoming putrid. It had already begun to heal, the edges starting to pucker with fresh pink skin. The wound would leave a scar, certainly, yet one mark more on his torso would hardly be noticeable. His upper body was branded with scars of various shapes and lengths that made Alysson certain she was dealing with a Berber warrior, a warrior who apparently had participated in countless battles.

Both his amusement and his naked chest making her keenly uncomfortable, she hastened to finish her task and bind the wound with a clean length of cloth. As soon as she was able, she retreated to the relative safety of his burnous, which he had again spread on the ground.

There she waited impatiently for Jafar to finish washing and shaving, using the small mirror and razor he had retrieved from his saddlebag. At least his barbaric traits didn't extend to his personal habits, she thought, stealing a glance at her captor.

Looking at him was a mistake. The rays cast by the setting sun lent his half-naked form a rare beauty that she had only seen captured on canvas by masters like Rembrandt. Against her will Alysson found herself watching the play of golden light on Jafar's muscled shoulders and lean torso.

Only when he turned toward her, wiping his smooth-shaven face with a cloth, was the spell broken. Only then did Alysson manage to drag her gaze away. Pretending indifference, she kept her eyes carefully averted from his half-naked form.

"I should like the chance to bathe," she said with more belligerence than she intended. "In *private*," she added in case he hadn't understood.

To her surprise, he nodded his consent. It was his next words that took Alysson aback. "But I will keep your clothing."

She gave him an incredulous stare. "If you expect me to undress in front of you, you are incredibly misguided!"

"If you wish to bathe, you will do as I say. I won't have you trying to escape the moment my back is turned."

"*Will* you turn your back?" Alysson asked hopefully, latching on to the possibility.

He hesitated. "Yes, if you are so determined to preserve

your modesty.'' He held out his hand. ''Your clothing, mademoiselle.''

This was not her idea of how to preserve modesty. Alysson bit her lip, gazing at him in impotent frustration. ''You are certainly no gentleman.''

''Not the kind of gentleman you admire, no. But then, I have no desire to be considered in the same class as your fiancé, the colonel.''

''You could not possibly be considered in the same class as Gervase. *He* is an honorable man.''

''Obviously we disagree on our definitions of honor. But I do not intend to debate the point with you. Come, *chérie,* I am waiting.''

''I hate you,'' Alysson declared in an adamant tone.

''So you have said.''

Knowing he would not back down, Alysson took a deep breath and slowly, reluctantly, complied. She took off her boots first, then her jacket and finally her breeches.

At that point she faltered. Her cheeks flaming scarlet, she stood before him, dressed only in her chemisette and drawers, while his gaze dropped the length of her body in a slow but dispassionate appraisal. She tried to hold her head high, to look scornful and proud, but her knees felt like water.

To her amazement, though, Jafar took pity on her and turned away. Alysson quivered in relief as he disappeared around the thicket. Turning, she quickly stripped off her underwear and knelt in the stream, then used his soap to scrub herself all over. The water was cold, while the evening breeze dancing over her wet body chilled her flesh. Yet not knowing when she would have another opportunity for a bath, she removed the pins from her hair and washed that, too.

On the other side of the thicket, Jafar busied himself sharpening the blade of his dagger. It was all he could do to keep his mind off the young woman behind him. Visions of Alysson at her bath, her slender, wet body glistening in the rosy light, kept intruding into his consciousness. He wondered if she would take advantage of his generosity and attempt to escape, but he forcibly prevented himself from checking on her. If she did try, he would find her soon enough, and he had promised to give her privacy—

Jafar shook his head in disgust. Twice now he had given in to her, against his better judgment. He was growing too soft with her. If he wasn't careful, he would be doing *her* bidding.

Already he'd found himself forgetting the circumstances between them; at least once he'd had to stop himself from speaking to her in English. And that could prove disastrous. If his fiery captive discovered his British background, it would be too easy for her to make the connection between himself and his other identity, Nicholas Sterling—and that knowledge could lead the French army straight to his tribe. As it was, he was fortunate she didn't remember meeting him that long-ago day in England.

When he had allowed her more than enough time to finish, Jafar returned to the camp. He found Alysson dressed again in her meager undergarments, kneeling beside the stream, combing her wet, tangled tresses with her fingers. Falling only partway down her back, her hair was not nearly as long as that of Algerine women.

He stood silently watching her for a moment. Seeing her shiver as an evening breeze blew over her damp skin, he had the fierce urge to warm her—with his body, with his hands and mouth.

"Are you quite finished, ma'amselle?" His voice was low and gruff and husky, not what he intended.

Alysson gave a start. Turning, she looked up at him with wary eyes.

Imperiously, Jafar held down his hand. "Come, it is time to sleep."

She stared at him. "Don't you mean to wear a shirt?" When Jafar raised an eyebrow, she stammered, "I m-mean, you might get cold."

His smile was soft, amused. "How, when I have you to keep me warm?"

The faint blush that rose to her cheeks was charming, Jafar thought, despite the way her narrowed gray eyes were flashing sparks at him. Meeting her defiant gaze, Jafar felt his will clash with hers. "Are you afraid of me?"

That challenge made Alysson lift her chin obstinately. "No, of course not!" she declared.

But she was afraid. She didn't want to sleep with a half-naked savage, especially when she was so meagerly dressed herself. He hadn't returned even her breeches. She felt exposed and altogether too vulnerable as Jafar drew her down beside him on the burnous. Yet her temper rose when, like before, he tied their ankles together. Alysson stiffened in silent resistance as he gathered her in his arms and settled her with her back to him, her head resting on his uninjured arm.

To her surprise, he spread her damp tresses out so they would dry more quickly. The gesture was gentle and considerate, but Alysson lay there tense and rigid, held in the warm curve of his body, her cheek pressed against naked flesh. How she hated this! The man-smell of his skin, clean and pleasantly soap-scented, was highly unnerving.

Still, his embrace was warm and somehow comforting. At her back she could feel his heart beating in slow steady strokes.

Alysson gave a drowsy sigh. She was more fatigued than she thought . . .

It was early the next morning when she opened her eyes to find a pair of topaz ones gazing down into hers. Jafar, she thought groggily, a strange sense of peace and contentment filling her. For a moment, before her mind began to function, she could only wonder at that strange sensation. It was the same feeling of warmth and security that sometimes came to her in her dreams. How very odd. Odder still was the fragmented memory that teased at her brain. She couldn't shake the feeling of having met him before. He looked so familiar, except for the soft light of desire in his eyes. That was new—

Shock and dismay suddenly flooded through Alysson. Jafar was stretched out beside her, his head supported by his elbow as he gazed down at her. Apparently he'd been watching her sleep.

Before she could open her mouth to speak, he lifted a tress of her chestnut hair, now dry and silky, from her breast. "You should let it fall free, instead of pinning it up."

Faster than a frightened rabbit, Alysson pushed aside the edge of his burnous and scrambled to her feet. "I do *not* require your advice on how to arrange my hair!" Flustered, mortified, she stalked over to the stream, searching for the pins she had left there the previous evening.

"At least you don't torture it into ringlets."

"It is too difficult to arrange in ringlets," Alysson said through gritted teeth, trying to regain her composure. "I am frequently without a maid."

He lay there, lazily watching her. His appraisal acutely disturbed Alysson. To her disgust and dismay, her fingers were less than steady as she used them to comb out the tangles in her hair.

"When we reach my camp," Jafar said after a moment, "I will see that you are provided with combs."

Alysson gave him a cautious glance. His generosity didn't interest her as much as where he might be talking her. "Where is your camp?"

"Another day's ride from here, on the fringes of the desert." When she was silent, he raised an eyebrow at her. "You wanted to see the desert, did you not?"

"Not in your company!"

She saw his mouth tighten, but he didn't reply. Apparently the hostilities had resumed between them. Which was perfectly fine with her, Alysson reflected. She didn't like it when he was treating her with gentleness or tender concern. It was far easier to remember how she despised him when he was acting the uncivilized heathen.

To the best of her ability, Alysson finished combing her hair before repinning it into a knot at her nape. Then she went over to the pile of equipment and clothing. Searching for her own garments, she found her jacket and one of her boots.

She started to put them on but was startled when Jafar's hand suddenly closed over her wrist in a grip that was firm but not painful. She hadn't heard him move. Flinching, Alysson stared up at him in bewilderment. Did he mean to refuse to allow her to dress?

"In this country," Jafar said in a warning tone, "you must be more careful. We will soon reach the desert, and you will have to remain alert if you mean to survive. Check your clothing for scorpions and vipers each morning before you dress."

He didn't mean to keep her half-naked, Alysson thought

as a trembling sense of relief surged through her. She would rather face an army of poisonous creatures than be subjected to his hard golden gaze when she was so very vulnerable.

Her relief was short-lived. Despite his generosity in allowing her to keep her clothes and the haik to shield her head and face, Alysson's feeling of vulnerability, of helplessness, only increased the further they traveled.

Shortly the grassy steppes changed to uneven, broken country of sand and stones dotted with camel-thorn and an occasional shrub. Any civilized person would call this barren land the desert, Alysson reflected, yet she knew it was only the forerunner of the Sahara.

A few hours later, when Jafar slowed the horses to a walk, she made herself pay attention to her surroundings. If she could discover where she was, she might be able to determine where he was taking her.

With more curiosity then she'd felt in two days, Alysson glanced around her. In the distance ahead were clumps of rocky plateaus overhanging the arid flats. "Where are we?" she asked, trying to keep her tone casual.

Jafar didn't answer, preferring not to divulge that this was the Jebel Selat. He didn't want her to have any information that she might use to her advantage. "Why do you wish to know?"

She understood quite well the reason for his caution, and the knowledge made her snap an unwise reply. "When the French army rescues me, I want to be able to tell them where to find you."

A muscle in his jaw tightened as he shot her a penetrating look.

Alysson sighed wearily, wishing she had kept silent, wishing it wasn't so hot, wishing she had never decided to come to this godforsaken land in the first place.

At least her savage Berber captor was soon forced by the terrain to keep the pace slow. Carefully he led her mare through barren hills topped with flat tablelike peaks, and down into gullies that had forgotten the taste of rain. Yet Alysson's discomfort only rose as the morning progressed. The glaring sun beat down on her mercilessly, and the rising heat only frayed her already raw temper.

"This is not what I had in mind," Alysson muttered, "when I planned this expedition. I never expected this land would be so unattractive."

Jafar glanced over at her. "You will find it beautiful after the rains, when the desert blooms."

"I won't," she replied adamantly, shaking her head. "I will never again find anything the least appealing about Algeria. It is too hot."

In response, he unstoppered the goatskin and poured a trickle of water over a scrap of cloth. "Wipe your face with this," he commanded, handing her the cloth.

It felt cool and soothing to Alysson's sweating brow, but it didn't mollify her in the least. "If I had to be abducted," she said in a morose undertone, "why couldn't it have been during the rainy season?"

The sudden smile he gave her bordered on beautiful itself. "This *is* the rainy season, *ma belle.*"

Alysson returned a scowl that would have been lethal, could she had made it so.

After that the country grew more fierce, if that were possible. They wound their way through inhospitable hills of red and gray sandstone and negotiated deep gorges studded with dwarfed Aleppo pines. The wind picked up then, bearing a dust that was coarse and gritty.

"Do we never get to stop and rest?" Alysson complained.

"Soon," Jafar said. "Cover your face."

His "soon" stretched out into hours. They left the hills to ride swiftly over a flat, scrub-covered plain of salt-impregnated sand. Ahead of the galloping horses, scorpions and lizards darted for cover.

Under different circumstances Alysson might have been impressed by the savage, pitiless beauty. But the heat and lonely monotony, the grueling pace and windblown grit, all served to drain away her energy. For a time, Alysson even thought her eyes were playing tricks on her, for to the east, beyond the arid plain, she frequently glimpsed a shimmer that looked very much like a huge lake.

It was shortly afterward that Alysson found herself nearly falling asleep in the saddle. She caught herself with her head lolling forward, just as she was about to slide off her mount.

Jafar saw the danger. Plucking her from the mare, he settled her before him on his stallion. Automatically she started to struggle, but he quieted her with a murmured command to be still. "You are tired. This way you can rest."

Alysson gave a weary sigh as her head found a comfortable place in the curve of his shoulder. She must be growing accustomed to sleeping in his arms, she decided with resignation as her eyes fell closed. The thought was disturbing, but it didn't prevent her from seeking refuge in sleep.

The afternoon dust was ripe and hot by the time she awoke, and the air was filled with strange sounds. Realizing the stallion had slowed to a walk, Alysson sat up groggily.

The sight that greeted her made hope leap in her breast. Shielding her eyes against the glare, she feasted her gaze on a cool green forest of feathery date palms, beneath which grew a profusion of oleanders, tamarinds, and pistachio trees. They had reached a small oasis in the barren wilderness.

The oasis was not unoccupied. At one end, near a well, some two dozen camels stood guarded by long-robed nomads.

A hush fell over the crowd as Jafar and Alysson rode in. These were Arabs of the desert, Alysson surmised, returning their curious gazes. These men were thin-boned and glossy-haired, their olive-tinted faces marked by hawklike noses and dark liquid eyes. She wondered what they would say if she threw herself upon their mercy. It was possible they would agree to protect her from her Berber captor. Then again, they might very well ignore her pleas.

The sharp interest of their gazes disturbed her, making her wonder if she had done something wrong. Perhaps sitting on a man's lap wasn't any more proper in their culture than hers. Awkwardly Alysson shifted her weight, striving for as much decorum as the intimate position allowed. Abruptly she felt Jafar's muscles tense—in the arm that was wrapped loosely around her waist, and the hard thighs that supported her own.

Jafar murmured a silent oath, both because of the feminine pressure of Alysson's squirming, and because he recognized the Arab caravan. They were slave merchants, robbers all, noted for their viciousness and greed. Yet these traders were highly successful in their dealings, for they possessed abundant cunning and no scruples to speak of. Jafar had no doubt they coveted his young captive—if not for her slender, almost boyish figure, then for the curiosity she aroused, and for her potential value at market. European women brought a high price in Barbary.

For the moment, however, he was not worried about Alysson's safety. These traders feared him and his position too much to attack him, even if he was alone. But his fingers closed over the hilt of his dagger all the same.

"Don't say a word," Jafar murmured to Alysson. "Keep your eyes downcast as befits a woman."

She bristled at his arrogant command, but she did as she was told, watching only surreptitiously—and a bit fearfully—as Jafar directed his fierce stare at the group of Arabs. She was amazed to see them, one by one, avert their gazes.

Jafar halted the horses in the cool shade of a towering date palm and lowered Alysson to the ground. "Sit down and be quiet." He hoped she would keep her rebellious behavior under control for the moment and afford him proper respect. If she challenged his authority before these Arabs, he would have to bend her to his will. These slavers understood one law: strength. Allowing a woman to defy his wishes would be seen as a weakness . . . a fatal weakness.

He hadn't underestimated Alysson's defiant nature, for even as he dismounted, she planted her hands on her hips and glared at him.

Jafar caught her arm and forced her to her knees. None too soon, either, for just then a short, full-bearded Arab broke away from the caravan and strode toward Jafar. With effusive greetings of welcome, the Arab made a deep salaam, bowing so low that his nose nearly pressed the ground, before touching his forehead to the hem of Jafar's black burnous.

Alysson stared. Jafar replied in Arabic, but she could make out only a word or two.

Their exchange was brief, musically fluid and low. Finally rising, the Arab clapped his hands and immediately three young boys came running at his command, one bearing a bowl of camel's milk, another a golden-ripe cluster of dates resting on a palm leaf, the third a woven rush mat on which to sit. Laying down their offerings before Jafar, the youths prostrated themselves at this feet.

Such obsequious subservience made Alysson give Jafar a sharp glance. He was obviously someone of importance in the Arab world.

"Are you some kind of sheik?" she asked him when the Arabs had withdrawn.

"*Shaykh* is an Arab word," Jafar said, settling himself on the mat, cross-legged, and gesturing for her to join him.

"Well, Berber, then."

"I am a chieftain, yes."

"And just how did you explain my presence to those men?"

An amused smile curved his mouth as he looked over the food. "A Berber warlord is not required to explain his actions except to his sultan."

Warlord? His confirmation of her suspicions gave Alysson pause.

He took the opportunity to press a handful of dates into her hand. "Now you may feed me," Jafar said, watching her carefully.

Alysson's gray eyes widened as she stared at him. "*Feed* you? Why in heaven's name should I?"

"Because I wish it, and because it is expected by our Arab friends."

She cast a glance beyond his shoulder; they were indeed being watched by the Arabs. "Their expectations aren't of the least concern to me."

"They should be. Those men are slavers. They would as soon sell you into bondage as look at you."

"Slavers! Then that makes your suggestion all the more absurd. I will not debase myself simply to indulge the whims of a group of savages who deal in the sale of human flesh."

"Your compliance will not be considered debasement. Here in Barbary dominance of the strongest is a simple fact of nature. You are my captive. I am your master. You will obey me in all things.''

"You can go to the devil!" Alysson declared, rising to her knees.

"Sit down!"

"I won't!"

His gaze captured hers. "It seems you have forgotten your lesson in obedience," he said softly.

Her cheeks flushed with indignation. Provoked beyond endurance by his arrogant superiority, Alysson raised a hand to strike him. He caught it easily and pressed it flat against his chest. "That was not wise, *chérie*," he said in a tone that made her shiver.

He did not remove his hand, nor did he release her from the power of his eyes. She was mesmerized by the intense heat of his unfathomable gaze, by the glittering gold flecks that floated in the brightness of his honey-colored irises.

His voice dropped even lower, but was no less threatening because of its soft intensity. "Take care, captive, before I decide to sell you to them as a slave."

Alysson regarded him with loathing. He was cold and unfeeling, and no doubt capable of unspeakable acts of brutality. Still, she would prefer to take her chances with the devil she knew. But she would not give him the satisfaction of a complete surrender. She raised her chin with a touch of bravado. "I am no man's slave."

"No," he said after a moment. "I think not. But you will do as I say. I am the only thing standing in the way of your being imprisoned for life in an Eastern harem."

A long, quiet silence ensued before Alysson finally nodded.

When Jafar released her hand, she tore a date from the cluster and held it up for him to eat. He waited, however, until she carried it all the way to his lips.

The distinction was not lost on her. It made her grit her teeth.

He ate the fruit then, gracefully spitting out the pit into his palm and tossing it away.

Alysson fed him another, yet she couldn't help but give a fearful glance at the slavers. "You wouldn't sell me to them, would you?"

His answer, so long in coming, was not particularly reassuring. "No, I have need of you myself."

She shoved another date in his mouth before he had finished swallowing the last. She hoped he choked on it.

Jafar responded with merely a casual shrug. "Pity. You would bring a good price, since you are still a virgin."

His frankness elicited a small gasp from Alysson. "How did you—?" She broke off abruptly, having no earthly intention of discussing the status of her innocence with him.

"How did I know?" A smile that could almost be called satisfied played at the corners of his mouth. "A logical assumption, given the expectations of your race regarding unmarried females. Your response just now merely confirmed it."

While she silently fumed, his eyes dropped lower to scrutinize her breasts and hips. He was still speculating on her value as a slave—merely to provoke her, Alysson was sure.

"With rich food to fill out your curves, you might command a high price indeed. That is, if you could ever learn to be docile."

Her fulminating glare was hot enough to boil the camel's milk he was drinking. "You are insane if you think I could ever be as subservient as your Eastern women."

"I expect service as a slave would curb your rebellious nature soon enough. A day's work in a harem would render you more submissive, and would show you what real life is about."

The measured tones of his voice frightened her. "Is that what you intend to do with me? Am I to be imprisoned in your harem?"

"Hareem is also an Arab word."

"Don't debate semantics with me!" she cried, trying to quell her rising panic. "Am I or am I not to become your . . . your concubine?"

"Would you like to become my concubine?"

Alysson stared at him, anguish and confusion warring for expression on her face.

"If I took you into my harem, I would use you for my own pleasure, and show you pleasure in return."

"W-what . . . what do you mean?"

"Surely you have some idea of what goes on between a man and a woman?"

Alysson nervously wet her lips.

"Perhaps you would like me to teach you." His gaze dropped to her mouth. "You challenged me to instruct you in the art of kissing, did you not?"

His fingers gripped her chin lightly. He was staring intently at her mouth now. Alysson felt the savagery of his kiss, though he had not yet claimed it.

It was all she could do to force a reply past the tightness in her throat. "Do you always terrify your prisoners this way? Does it give you some perverse satisfaction to mistreat me so?"

She saw his topaz eyes narrow in warning. "I have not mistreated you, nor will I, if you obey my commands."

Mustering all the courage she possessed, Alysson returned his fierce gaze. "I may be your captive," she said steadily, "but I am not your slave. And I will never be your concubine."

The pressure of his fingers on her chin increased the slightest degree. "Even so, you will call me master."

His voice was so soft that it was scarcely a whisper, yet the lack of volume made it no less dangerous. Alysson felt herself trembling.

His hard expression softened then, and he released her chin. "I have had my fill of the food. Now you may eat."

Alysson bit back the fierce retort that sprang to her lips. At the moment she didn't have the nerve to defy him further, even though his condescension, his air of superiority, his incredible arrogance, made her want to scream. He was acting like he was some kind of grand seigneur, some high and mighty king—

Of course he probably *was* a king in his culture, or close enough. He was a warlord, a chieftain who held the power of life and death over his followers . . . and his captives.

Alysson suffered his scrutiny in simmering silence as she tried to eat. The dates and camel's milk were a welcome change from barley bread and goat's cheese, but she could hardly force them past her dry throat. Her situation was even more dire than she had thought. He didn't want money, if he could be believed, yet he hadn't answered her question about what he intended to do with her. She wanted desperately to know, but after all his talk of concubines and harems, she was afraid of the answer.

Beneath veiling lashes, she eyed Jafar with fresh trepidation. He was a cool, self-possessed man, handsome in a raw, ruthless way. Despite his occasional kindness toward her, his hard mouth held a hint of what might be cruelty, while his hawk-eyes held shrewd intelligence and determination. He was the kind of man who would always manage to get his way, whatever the circumstances. And she very much feared that in this instance, too, he would prove victorious.

"Come, it is time to go."

Jafar's quiet command startled Alysson from her morose thoughts. Seeing that he had risen and was holding out a hand to her, she allowed him to help her to her feet.

"Is it far, to your camp?" she made herself ask.

"A few hours more, only."

Slowly, reluctantly, she followed him over to the horses. She dreaded the upcoming ride, dreaded even more the end of their journey.

Her sickening sense of inevitability only increased the further they traveled, reaching burgeoning proportions when an hour later Alysson found herself truly on the outskirts of the Sahara. All around her stretched a desolate yellow-and-gray expanse, baking beneath a hot azure sky. Summer was long over, and yet the cruel heat was almost unbearable.

Her spirits wilting, Alysson hung her head.

"Not much further," she heard Jafar say. His tone was gently bracing, and for an instant she even thought she saw sympathy in his eyes.

Abruptly she squared her shoulders, determined not to accept any pity from him.

After another hour of riding, though, the hopelessness of her situation began to press down on her like a crushing weight. To the far right she glimpsed the beginning of another high mountain range. To the far left was the same shimmering mirage that looked so much like a lake.

The mirage was bounded to the south by ranges of golden sand hills. Beyond, in the distance, the desert passed into a limitless gloomy waste, broken only now and then by a scraggly clump of broom or thorn.

Some half hour later, they reached what Alysson realized was their destination. When she shielded her eyes from the glare, she could make out scores of black tents pitched beneath banners that fluttered proudly in the wind.

A camp of war, Alysson thought with dismay. It appeared that her fierce Berber warlord had gathered a small army here at the edge of the world. Wretched, despondent, she glanced at Jafar. He was watching her intently from hooded eyes.

The next moment the air was filled with shouts and cries as a throng of robed horsemen galloped out to greet their leader. Alysson couldn't summon the energy to be alarmed, even when the horde of fierce Berbers surged around them, wildly circling and firing muskets into the air, stirring up clouds of desert sand.

She did feel a welcoming spark of renewed anger, however, when she recognized the red-bearded Berber who had acted as spokesman for the group which had ambushed her uncle's party, making it possible for their chieftain to take her captive.

Had it only been two days ago? It seemed like an eternity.

The bearded Berber did not appear interested in her, though. After only a brief glance at Alysson, he launched into a lengthy conversation with Jafar—probably bringing him up to date on what had occurred during his absence, Alysson surmised.

Jafar listened attentively, only occasionally asking a question or making a comment as he accompanied his lieutenant into the encampment. Not once did he look at Alysson, even though he was still leading her mare.

She wondered hopefully if he had forgotten her presence, but she soon realized the futility of such wishful thinking. The moment he brought the horses to a halt before a large, caparisoned tent, his attention shifted back to her.

"Welcome to my camp, Miss Vickery," he said dispassionately.

When she didn't reply, he dropped gracefully off his stallion's back and strode around to her side, reaching up to help her dismount.

For a moment, Alysson's courage failed her entirely. She stayed where was, staring down into Jafar's golden eyes.

When his fingers tightened about her waist, though, she gave herself a fierce mental shake. Taking a deep breath, she swung her leg over the pommel and let herself slide into his waiting arms. He had promised not to hurt her, hadn't he?

But still she couldn't shake the horrible, sinking feeling that her trials were just beginning.

Chapter 5

Hesitating at the doorway of the tent, Alysson glanced cautiously within, noting double walls of black goatskin and a high roof supported by slender wooden poles. The dwelling was large and spacious as befitted a lord, but sparsely furnished, in the manner of a soldier. The thick carpets that covered the sand floor were scattered with cushions and several small, low tables—the effect practical rather than luxurious.

The slight pressure of Jafar's hand at the small of her back made Alysson step inside. As her eyes adjusted to the dimmer light, she could make out the unlit olive oil lamps hanging from the ridgepole overhead. The tall support poles also boasted numerous hooks, upon which hung saddlery and other accoutrements of war.

Spying movement, Alysson came to an abrupt halt. A tall, turbaned Berber had turned to face them, his arms full of swords and daggers, pistols and rifles. The young man managed a graceful salaam to Jafar, despite the armload of weapons he was holding, and when Jafar issued a command in a low voice, he obediently withdrew. Yet Alysson saw a brief flash of curiosity in his blue eyes as he passed.

She was curious about him as well. Watching him carry

the weapons from the tent, she guessed that he'd been ordered to prepare the place for her residency. The thought made her shiver. Was this to be her prison?

She turned to eye Jafar with a quizzical look, but his hard face gave no clue as to his thoughts, or his intentions.

Not meeting her gaze, he strode across the chamber and drew aside a woolen curtain, revealing an inner room. "If you will excuse me, mademoiselle, there are affairs I must attend to," he told her evenly. "You may rest here."

Alysson followed him with great reluctance. Was this Jafar's bedchamber? Here, items of clothing hung on the pole hooks while a striped woolen blanket lay neatly folded upon the woven-straw pallet.

"I will send a servant to see to your needs," he said, turning away.

Torn between pique at being dismissed so summarily, and the shameful desire to plead with him not to leave her here alone in these unfamiliar surroundings, Alysson couldn't manage to reply before Jafar strode from the tent.

Alone, she glanced around the bedchamber uncertainly. In one corner sat an unlit charcoal brazier. In another, on a small table, was a pitcher and washbowl. Beneath the table, to her surprise, rested a glazed, lidded receptacle that was apparently a chamber pot. Was that for her use? Did Jafar intend to keep her here for the duration of her captivity?

Her gaze stole again to the pallet. She was too keyed up to rest as he had suggested, but even if she hadn't been, she couldn't stay here. Not in *his* bed.

Abruptly Alysson retreated to the large front chamber which no doubt served as a reception room and living quarters. Hearing a horse's whinny, she went to the doorway of the tent. There were several horses tethered directly outside, including her gray mare and Jafar's black Barb. But her hope of claiming one and making an escape was dashed at once. The blue-eyed Berber stood guarding both the doorway and the horses.

When he spied Alysson he came immediately to attention and with his musket blocked her way. *"Eskana,"* he said, motioning for her to turn back.

With a sinking heart, she did so. She needed no inter-

preter to understand that it was forbidden for her to leave
the tent.

She spent the next few minutes wandering around the
large room, exploring her surroundings, looking for a
weapon the Berber guard might have missed. There was
none, though in the far corner she discovered Jafar's library.
The knee-high table was strewn with maps and a few leatherbound volumes written in Arabic, and, to her surprise, several French journals.

Wondering what use he had for them, wondering also
what he intended to do with her, Alysson sank down upon
one of the cushions to await Jafar's return. With effort she
even managed to rally her flagging spirits. She should have
expected Jafar to see that she was well guarded, of course,
but she needn't despair just yet. If she used her wits, she
might still contrive an escape. And there was also the chance
that she could bribe someone to carry a message to Gervase
in Algiers. By now, with luck, her Uncle Honoré would
have returned safely to Algiers, and Gervase would be
searching for her. He would find her before too long. She
had to believe that.

Her worried musings were interrupted just then when a
boy of perhaps ten limped into the tent, bearing a tray.
Alysson gave a start when she looked at him directly. Not
only was the child lame, but one side of his face was hor-
ribly scarred beneath his turban, the flesh red and puckered.

The boy was glaring at her fiercely, as if daring her to
pity him. Realizing her staring had given offense, Alysson
schooled her features into a semblance of equanimity, but
he continued to glower as he bent and placed the copper
tray on the table nearest her.

"My lord bade me serve you," the boy said with undisguised hatred.

His words took her aback, not because of his hostility,
but rather because of the language he had used; he had
spoken in clear, fluent French.

"The master orders you to eat," the boy added, before
he turned awkwardly and busied himself lighting the lamps.

Alysson barely glanced at the contents of the tray, for her
thoughts were whirling. If this boy could converse with

her, then perhaps she could befriend him and eventually persuade him to carry a message to Gervase.

Wondering how to begin, Alysson watched the young servant. He certainly showed no inclination to talk. When he had completed his task without saying another word, he turned to leave.

"Wait!" Alysson called after him. "How is it that you speak French?"

"In Algiers I was forced into the employ of the enemy." The boy nearly spat the words. "Brother of vermin," he muttered under his breath in Arabic, a term Alysson recognized as a curse in any language. She had no doubt he was speaking of the French. "They did this to me." He pointed to his face and his crippled right foot.

The compassion she felt must have shown on her face, for he squared his slender shoulders and straightened to his full, unintimidating height. She wished there were something she could say to console the child.

"What is your name?" she asked, her tone gentle.

He eyed her warily. "I am called Mahmoud."

"I am Alysson Vickery. I am an Englishwoman."

Mahmoud looked rather surprised that she had offered her name, yet still unforgiving. "Even so, it is not befitting for a Muslim to serve infidels."

"I am sorry that you are required to serve me. Perhaps it might help if you remember that I did not ask to be brought here."

He seemed to consider that a moment, but then his scowl returned. "The lord wishes you to eat." Turning abruptly, he left the tent with surprising dignity, dragging his right food behind him.

Alysson suppressed a sigh. Directing her attention to the tray, she saw that Mahmoud had brought her an earthen pitcher of water, a goblet of fruit juice, and a wooden bowl of figs, oranges, and dates.

She carried the pitcher to the inner room, where she quickly made use of the water to wash away the dust. It surprised her that one person had been allowed so much water, but perhaps there was a well nearby.

Returning to the main quarters, she drank the pomegranate juice and ate an orange, finding both refreshing. Still

Jafar did not come, even though it was growing dark outside. Wearily she curled up on one of the cushions and closed her eyes for a moment.

That was how Jafar found her a half hour later, her head partly sliding off the pillow, one slender hand tucked beneath her cheek.

He stood looking down at her for a time, marveling at how sweetly innocent she looked in sleep, with the soft golden lamplight spilling over her. Nothing like the spitting tigress who had challenged him every step of the way here.

An unwanted emotion stirred in his chest. It was guilt, he realized. Guilt for using her in his battle against his mortal enemy. But it was too late now to be harboring doubts about the wisdom of his plan. Events had progressed too far.

Carefully Jafar knelt to wake her. Brushing a wisp of hair back from her face, he resisted the urge to press his lips against the vee where her throat pulsed in tiny waves, and gently squeezed her arm, instead.

Alysson came awake with a start. Seeing Jafar so close, she tried to scurry to her feet, but she made the mistake of gripping the table edge for support. That was how she discovered that the table was merely an unattached platform supported by wooden blocks, so it could easily be assembled for transporting when the Berbers broke camp. The empty goblet went flying, while pieces of fruit rolled across the carpets.

A wry smile curved Jafar's mouth as he watched a date take refuge among his maps. "Leave it," he said when Alysson tried to rectify the damage she had done. "Mahmoud will see to it when he serves supper."

Alysson disobeyed, partly because she disliked putting the young servant to further trouble, partly to give herself something to do, and partly in order to defy her captor.

Shaking his head at her stubbornness, Jafar retreated into the bedchamber in order to wash. He returned to the main room a few minutes later, dressed in a short, white, sleeveless tunic, loose white trousers, and boots of soft crimson leather.

Shortly, Mahmoud limped in, bearing the first courses of the evening meal. With only a sullen glance at Alysson, the boy spread a tablecloth on the carpet at their feet and placed the dishes before them. In the presence of his master, Mahmoud was courteous and deferential toward Alysson, calling her *saiyida*—madam—in Arabic. Jafar he called lord.

Watching them together, Alysson realized then that her plan to befriend Mahmoud was probably doomed to failure; the boy obviously worshiped the man.

Supper was a more substantial meal than any she'd previously had with Jafar. First they were served small glasses of mint tea, sweet and sticky and hot. Then came bread and cheese and olives, accompanied by beans boiled in oil and vinegar. Alysson observed Jafar eat the beans as the native Arabs did, gracefully, with the fingers of his right hand, but she chose to use the wooden spoon that had been provided her.

She was halfway through the course when it occurred to her that she should not be eating with him. In Eastern cultures women dined separately from the men, afterward. The bite she was swallowing suddenly stuck in Alysson's throat. Why was Jafar was making an exception for her? Did he have some ulterior motive that she had yet to fathom?

"I confess," she said nervously when Mahmoud had withdrawn, "I am surprised to be dining with you. I didn't think the opposite genders ate together in Barbary."

Jafar gave her a considering look that divulged nothing of his thoughts. "I told you once, I am prepared to make allowances for your European upbringing. As long as your behavior remains obedient and circumspect, I will permit you more freedom than I would allow a woman of my own country."

The arrogance of his reply grated on her nerves. "I suppose you think I should be honored by your condescension."

"Indeed you should," he returned with a slight smile.

The boy reappeared just then, bringing with him bowls of rich lentil soup, and dessert, bread with honey. Alysson broke off her interrogation and maintained a frustrated silence for the duration of the meal, waiting for a moment of privacy to ask Jafar what he intended to do with her. Whenever he happened to glance at her, she regarded him with a touch of disdain, matching coolness with coolness, arrogance with arrogance.

The moment finally came. When Mahmoud had served them each a small cup of thick, black coffee and proffered a bowl of water for them to wash their hands, Jafar dismissed the servant with an imperious wave of his fingers.

Alysson suddenly wished she could call the boy back. Now that she was alone with Jafar, her anxiety returned in full measure. She didn't like what the soft glow of the olive oil lamps did for his features. His hair gleamed like dark burnished gold, while the light reflected the amber of his eyes. His attire, too, was unsettling. His lean, muscular grace was much more obvious without his robes, making her aware of him as a man, and not just as her villainous captor.

Abruptly she decided that going on the offensive was the best course.

"I did not think you would be so willing to waste water on cleanliness here in the desert," she said tersely, thinking of his cruel insistence on making her ask him for a drink. "Yesterday you made me beg for every drop."

Cradling his coffee cup in one hand, Jafar leaned back on a cushion, supporting his weight on one elbow. "Cleanliness is a virtue in my religion. It is our custom to bathe frequently whenever we can spare the water. In this case it is possible, since my camp is supplied by an artesian well." After a short pause, he supplemented with a mocking smile, "Dug by your own Legionnaires, I might add."

The irony was not lost on Alysson. Naturally he would find it amusing that the French military should aid him in his malevolent purposes, however indirectly. The knowledge of a well gave her no comfort, either. He would need a ready source of water if he planned to remain here for any length of time.

"When do you mean to tell me what you intend to do with me?" Alysson demanded.

He hesitated a moment, his gaze contemplating her. "You may consider yourself my guest."

"Your *guest?*" Alysson gave him an incredulous look. "And for how long am I to remain your *guest?*"

"Until I no longer have need of you."

"And just how long is that?"

Jafar shrugged, keeping his expression deliberately impassive. Alysson pressed her lips together to refrain from shouting at him in frustration. "You won't even tell me what it is you want with me?"

"Simply your presence."

Unnerved by his quiet tone, she stared at him. She wanted to demand precisely *why* he required her presence, but it was obvious he didn't intend to give her any complete answers. "Then would you mind telling me just what I am to do here in the meantime?"

"You may enjoy the freedom of my tent." He gestured with his cup, indicating their surroundings. "I apologize for my humble dwelling, and for the meager fare. It is not what a pampered heiress like you is accustomed to, perhaps. But you will not be uncomfortable here. You will have ample servants to see to your needs."

Alysson stiffened. She admitted to being spoiled and pampered, but she was not about to listen to him telling her so. "Your generosity overwhelms me. However, I find the accommodations hardly up to my usual exacting standards. I'm afraid I must respectfully decline your hospitality."

"I'm afraid," he said softly, "it is not your choice, my proud ingrate."

"Ingrate!" Alysson raised her chin, her cheeks tingeing with the rosy blush of anger. "You think I should be grateful that you attacked my uncle's party, forcibly abducted me, dragged me to this godforsaken place, and mean to keep me prisoner from some unspecified time for some unspecified purpose? What kind of man *are* you? Only a coward and a thief would treat a woman in such a despicable fashion!"

For a moment Alysson thought she might have gone too far, calling him a coward. Jafar made no reply, and no movement—indeed, he remained quite still—but there was an animal alertness behind the indolent pose, and he was watching her with a hooded look that warned her she was treading dangerous ground.

"You would do well to remember one thing, mademoiselle," he said evenly. "Here, I am master, and you will do my bidding."

Her palm itched to strike his hard, handsome face, but she didn't quite have the courage. Instead, Alysson sent him a scathing look. "I don't recognize your authority." Her antagonism was not wise, she knew, but it was better than meek subservience. "I won't feed you again, and I won't see to your wound! You can perish from your injury, for all I care."

"Wounds seldom putrefy in the desert, so I am unlikely to perish."

"How lamentable!"

His eyes narrowed, but there was a sudden glitter in the golden depths that looked suspiciously like amusement. "You should count yourself fortunate that I do not require you to wash my feet as Bedouin women do for their men."

"If you think for one minute—" Leaping up, Alysson stood, hands on hips, glaring down at him. Wash his feet, indeed!

Jafar, watching, thought she looked magnificent in her scorn. A half-smile curved his mouth. "Most men of my race prefer sweetness and docility in a female, but I enjoy a woman with spirit."

When she realized he was deliberately provoking her, Alysson nearly sputtered in her outrage. Oh, how she wished she had a weapon to use on this barbarian!

With royal disregard for her fury, Jafar drained the remaining coffee in his cup. Rising then, he went to stand at the doorway to the tent, his back to her as he looked out over his camp. A lord surveying his realm, Alysson thought with derision, silently cursing the arrogance that categorized everything the man did.

Jafar's thoughts were running along similar lines, though his curses concerned Alysson's passionate spirit. He almost would have preferred the weeping and tears or the cries for pity that was expected of a woman. How much easier he would find it then to resist her appeal. As it was, he was entirely too aware of the angry young beauty behind him. He actually felt himself wanting to soothe and comfort her, to yield to her demands that he release her.

Silently he shook his head, knowing himself for a fool. All he needed was to remember four nights ago when he'd stood outside the reception, watching Alysson Vickery surrounded by her personal entourage of admirers. Every male there, young or old, had been drawn to her like a fly to honey. Her uncle particularly doted on her, while Bourmont . . . that devil-spawned gallant had become so enamored of his lovely fiancée that he'd allowed her to oppose his direct wishes, against every instinct that warned of danger.

A muscle in Jafar's jaw tightened. He would not allow himself to follow the same path as those other witless fools. He would not become a fawning slave to the young lady's whims.

"It is time to retire," he said in a low voice, determined to ignore her anger. "I suggest you prepare yourself for bed." Behind him, he felt Alysson tense.

"You can't possibly mean . . ."

Glancing over his shoulder, Jafar met her gaze. She was staring at him, her gray eyes smoldering. He could read every emotion on her expressive face as she came to the realization that he meant for her to share his bed: fury, frustration, defiance, distress.

Jafar raised an eyebrow and waited. They had been through this before, and the outcome would again be the same.

To his surprise, she capitulated without a word. Her fingers curling into fists, she turned abruptly and stalked into the other room.

Jafar sighed. If there had been another alternative, he would have taken it. If Alysson were a more biddable female, he could have put her with the few unmarried serving women in his camp. But he couldn't trust her not to try and escape. She would have to be guarded day and night, and keeping a close eye on her himself was the most practical solution.

Bending, Jafar secured the front flap of the tent for the night. He was not looking forward to the next few weeks. He'd never had a reluctant woman in his bed before, and Miss Vickery, at the moment, was highly reluctant. Sleeping with her was certain to prove an extraordinary exercise in restraint.

He heard no sounds of movement in his sleeping quarters, so he entered. She was standing stock-still, completely dressed, staring at the brazier. During the meal, Mahmoud had prepared the room for the night, lighting the oil lamp and kindling a few coals in the brazier to ward off the chill of the desert night. For Jafar the fire was not necessary, since he had spent a good deal of his life in this harsh climate, but he'd thought his lovely guest would prefer the warmth of the brazier to the warmth of his arms. He had done his best to provide the amenities to which she was accustomed, though she would probably never appreciate the fact.

Alysson stiffened when he entered, turning to look up at him, her eyes shadowed and opaque, like smoke from a wildfire.

"My little tigress," Jafar said gently, "your time here will go easier if you accept your fate."

Alysson felt the familiar panic curling within her. What *would* be her fate? Was this the moment he would ravish her?

He meant for her to remove her clothing, she knew. His eyes were holding hers, issuing a silent command. Silently she screamed in mortification and fury, but she obeyed, slowly removing her jacket, boots, stockings, and breeches.

"Get into bed," he said then.

With great reluctance, she lay down on the pallet and pulled the blanket up to her chin, watching him apprehensively over the edge, vowing he would not make her beg or cry.

To her relief he snuffed the lantern before he undressed. The coals glowing in the brazier, however, betrayed the outline of his masculine form, red-gold light glinting off his bare back and shoulders, highlighting the solid play of muscle.

When he was naked but for his trousers, he came toward her, his body lithe, sleek and menacing in the darkness. Alysson went rigid, watching him with trembling anticipation. She would fight him to the death if he dared touch her . . .

He sat beside her then, reaching down to bare her ankle beneath the blanket. With a gasp, Alysson sat up abruptly.

But he was merely securing her leg to his, as he'd done all the other nights of her captivity, she realized as relief flooded through her. This time the bond was not wool but silk. She could feel the rough-sleek texture of it against her skin.

When he was done, Jafar glanced up at her. His golden eyes captured the firelight, glinting in the darkness. Alysson held her breath, her heart pounding. His hands, which she imagined were so accustomed to violence, were oddly gentle as they gripped her shoulders and pushed her back down onto the pillows.

Oh, God, what did he mean to do? She bit her lip hard, to keep from crying out. She would not plead for her virtue, or for her life.

But he merely stretched his long form beside her on the pallet. Lying on his back, his head pillowed by one arm, he pried the edge of the blanket from her death grip and covered himself. ''Sleep well, captive.''

Shocked by this unexpected deliverance, Alysson turned to stare at Jafar in the darkness. Within her, relief vied with confusion.

Why in the world had he brought her here to his desert camp? If not because he wanted her as his concubine, then why ever had he taken her captive?

Chapter 6

Much to Alysson's relief, Jafar was gone by the time she woke the next morning. Mahmoud brought her water to wash with, then food to break her fast, which Alysson ate with relish.

As she'd expected, breakfast was couscous—the traditional dish of Barbary—made from wheat kernels steamed like rice and kneaded into tiny balls. For the morning meal, the couscous was sweetened with milk and honey, accompanied by dates and almonds, and served with hot, sweet tea infused with mint.

Refreshed both by the food and a decent night's sleep, Alysson felt almost recovered from the grueling journey of the previous few days. She drank her third cup of tea slowly, watching as a sullen Mahmoud performed various chores around the tent—sweeping the carpets, airing the blankets and pallet, refilling lamps with olive oil, and seeing to his master's clothing.

Outside she could hear sounds of camp activity, and through the open doorway, amid the sea of black tents, she glimpsed dozens of Berber warriors attending to their daily tasks. Beyond the camp lay the vast desert, already shimmering as the sun burned away the last vestiges of morning chill.

Directly outside her tent, Alysson spied the tall, blue-eyed Berber she'd seen the previous day. He was still guarding her, it seemed, even while he occupied himself with caring for the horses. Here, as in the more civilized cultures she was familiar with, the horses must be fed and watered and groomed, their bridles and saddles polished.

The man was some kind of equerry, Alysson decided, while Mahmoud was the equivalent of a body servant or valet. She tried engaging Mahmoud in conversation, to discover any information about where she was and why Jafar had brought her to his camp, but all she managed to drag from the boy was that Jafar el-Saleh was a mighty lord who served the Sultan Abdel Kader, Defender of the Faithful.

Mahmoud had just stomped awkwardly from the room when Alysson became aware that she was being watched. Looking up with a start, she saw some half dozen young women loitering outside the doorway to the tent, eyeing her curiously, as if she were some unusual exhibit at a fair. Lifting her chin, Alysson returned their regard with a frank inquisitiveness of her own.

None of the women were veiled, so she could see their noble, proud features. They all possessed fine-shaped eyes, narrow aquiline noses, and light complexions, while two had delicate tattoos marking their foreheads. They were Berbers, Alysson was certain, for Berber women never veiled their faces as the Bedouin Arabs did. All of them wore colorful tunics girdled at the waist, flowing head-cloths, and dozens of silver chains and bangles.

One of the tattooed women, apparently the oldest of the group, stepped forward shyly and bowed to Alysson, then pointed to herself. "Tahar."

Realizing that must be the woman's name, Alysson gave a tentative smile in response. "I am called Alysson. Al-ys-son."

"Ail-son," the Berber woman repeated with a beaming smile, nodding her head.

When the others began to laugh and giggle, Tahar clapped her hands. At once the Berber women swarmed into the tent, bearing armfuls of clothing and accessories. Alysson found herself surrounded and being urged into the bed-chamber.

"Khemee ekkas," Tahar commanded when the curtain had fallen shut behind them all.

Alysson looked at her blankly.

"You will please to?" the woman asked in haltering French.

She seemed very proud of her ability with the strange language, and the others appeared highly admiring, too, for they nodded in excitement. Alysson was impressed, since she could speak absolutely no Berber, but she still couldn't comprehend the woman's French.

She shook her head, gesturing vaguely with her hands. "I'm sorry, but I don't understand. Please to *what?"*

"Esdig," Tahar explained as she began pulling at the foreigner's jacket and breeches.

It was then that Alysson realized they wanted her to undress. Immediately she backed away, eyeing them warily and shaking her head in refusal. "I am *not* taking off my clothes."

"Esdig, esdig," the Berber woman repeated insistently.

But it was only when Tahar grasped a fold of her own robe and made rubbing motions with the fabric that Alysson understood they meant to wash her clothing for her.

With a pleased smile, she nodded. "Thank you! I would be eternally grateful if you would see to my laundry."

And so for the following hour, Alysson gave herself into the care of the Berber women, to be dressed and perfumed and adorned according to their customs.

First came a long chemise of sheer white linen worn next

to the skin, and over this, a long length of blue-and-red striped cloth fashioned into a tunic. The tunic skirt was belted by a waist sash, while the bodice was folded double over the bosom, and secured by shoulder bands. For her feet she was presented with both soft leather sandals as well as a pair of yellow babouches—slippers with upturned toes.

When she was given combs for her hair, Alysson remembered Jafar promising to provide them for her, and grudgingly acknowledged his kindness. Apparently his royal munificence had interrupted his busy schedule long enough to see that she was decently attired and groomed.

After her hair had been braided and twisted up on her head, she was given a twig to chew, which Tahar called *souak*. To sweeten the breath, Alysson realized after some gesturing by the Berber woman. Next came a fragrant herbal cream, to rub into her sunburned skin. Then she was offered small pots and jars, which contained kohl to darken the eyes and eyebrows, and henna, the dark red-brown stain used to make the patterned tattooes on the Berber women's hands and feet and foreheads.

Alysson put her foot down, however, when they tried to beautify her with cosmetics. She would not paint her face or decorate her body with the heathen markings, or rouge her nipples, which to her extreme embarrassment, they seemed to want her to do. But she suffered the Berber women to arrange a colorful blue headdress over her hair— a square of cloth resembling a large handkerchief worn like a mantle.

There were many more garments, some that Alysson wasn't certain how to wear. It was difficult getting instructions, but between Tahar's negligible French, Alysson's inadequate Arabic, and the sign language that they both adopted, Alysson managed generally to comprehend. For courtesy's sake, she tried to learn the Berber word for each item, which caused much good-natured laughter among the Berber women. To her surprise, Alysson actually found herself enjoying the friendly exchange, even going so far as to forget that she was a captive of their fierce lord. When the pleasant interlude ended, she was disappointed to see the women go. She thanked them profusely for their gifts, responding to Tahar's *"Adieu"* with an invitation to visit her whenever they could spare the time.

When they were gone, Alysson began searching through the garments they had left for her. Earlier she had noticed an outfit that seemed more sedate and appropriate for her situation—a pair of loose brocade pantaloons, to be worn with a blouse and a short-waisted, long-sleeved bolero. She would feel more comfortable in those, Alysson decided, since they were quite like her breeches and jacket.

Pulling off the tunic and chemise she was wearing, she donned the baggy pantaloons and smiled at the way they swallowed her slender hips and legs. She was trying to figure out how to belt them with a sash when suddenly Alysson sensed she wasn't alone.

Looking up, she was startled to find Jafar standing there in the doorway, holding the curtain to one side as he made to enter. He was staring at her bare breasts as a hawk stares, his golden eyes glittering and intent.

With a gasp she dropped the sash and covered her naked bosom with her arms.

"Beautiful," he said slowly, and not in French.

Alysson was so shocked to realize he had spoken in English that she momentarily forgot her outrage at his spying and gaped at him. "You speak English!" she exclaimed, staring at him in return.

Although Jafar feigned unconcern, he silently cursed himself for his slip. The last thing he wanted was for his lovely captive to recognize him. He would have to be far more careful. She was too clever to be misled for long, certainly if he continued to make mistakes like this one.

Lifting his gaze to meet her bewildered eyes, he shrugged. "I know a few words of your language," he replied in French.

At the sound of his arrogant tone, Alysson abruptly came to her senses. "How dare you!" she sputtered. "Get out of here this minute!"

"But this is my tent, *ma belle.*" He moved silently toward her then, his body lithe as a cat's, the flowing skirt of his soft gray robe swirling around his long legs. Alysson retreated in panic, taking three frantic steps backward before she came up against the wall of the tent. Trapped, she stared at him, her cheeks flaming, her heart pounding. If he came a step closer, she would fight him . . .

But Jafar would not be denied. Reaching for her, he easily subdued her struggles and foiled her attempts to twist from his grasp. His hands took possession of hers, gently drawing her arms away from her body, till the dainty fullness of her breasts was bared to him.

Alysson stood there frozen, too stunned by his action, too mesmerized by his gaze, too afraid of the hungry, blatant desire she saw there, to move. She felt herself trembling as he studied her with purely masculine appreciation, his eyes narrowed, glittering, spellbound. Abashed, yet strangely thrilled by the heated intensity of his admiration, Alysson shut her eyes so she wouldn't have to see it. She endured his appraisal, tremulous but proud, vulnerable but defiant.

Jafar observed her blush, her innocent confusion, with fascination and a fierce desire. Slowly his gaze traveled down her body, taking in the young glowing skin of palest honey rose, the small but ripe fullness of her breasts, the slender hips and thighs hidden by the brocade pantaloons. She was not built to pleasure a man the way the women of his own country were, yet she possessed enough curves to fill a man's hungry hands. Oddly, though, seeing her wearing the native apparel of his country was nearly as arousing as the sight of silken bare flesh. It diminished her Englishness, making her seem more a part of his life, his traditions. It allowed him to imagine that she belonged here, to him.

"You delight my eyes," he murmured in French, his voice suddenly becoming soft and whispery.

Slowly, against her will, Alysson opened her eyes to meet Jafar's. She was shaken by the look of raw desire on his face, the almost physical possession of his gaze. She wanted to object to his scandalous behavior, to shout at him to get out, to plead with him to leave her alone, but she couldn't force the words past her dry throat. It was only when his fingers glided gently over her bare shoulder that she found the voice to protest.

"Don't . . ." she whispered. "I don't want you to . . ."

"Is that so, *ma belle?*" His soft smile said clearly that

he didn't believe her. "I think you do. Already your body betrays you. Your nipples are eager to feel my touch . . ."

It was as if his velvet voice had reached out to stroke them. Alysson felt a startling, unfamiliar surge of desire coil deep inside her.

Still holding one of her wrists, he raised a hand to the pert curve of her left breast, grazing the tip of it with his forefinger. "See how it springs to attention?"

She gasped, jolted by the throbbing fire even this lightest pressure made her feel, by the warmth and dampness that suddenly pulsed between her thighs.

"I think it time that we continue with your instruction in the art of kissing."

At his soft declaration, her lips parted to argue, but to her dismay, she couldn't form the words. She was powerless to speak, to move. Jafar spread his fingers against her delicate cheekbones, framing her face in the gentle vise of his palms, his eyes moving over her like flickering torches.

She couldn't look away.

Her gaze focused on his sensual, hard mouth as slowly, slowly, he bent his head. She could feel his breath, warm and provocative, caress her lips. And then his mouth closed over hers, capturing, claiming.

With a sharp inhalation, she tried once more to pull away, but Jafar ruthlessly took advantage of her parted lips; his tongue swept inside her mouth in an intimate invasion, sweetly probing, stroking the soft openness.

The taste of him washed over her like an erotic drug. It was a kiss that stamped his possession, that tantalized and promised, that demanded a response. Never in her life had she felt anything like it. Never, not even with Gervase. Indeed, *this* was the kiss, Alysson realized in some dim recess of her mind, that she had yearned for Gervase to give her, one that excited and aroused her body while calling to the wild, nameless longings in her heart. Overwhelmed by the power of it, Alysson gave a small, involuntary whimper.

The soft utterance was all the invitation Jafar needed. With extreme and deliberate seductiveness, he forced his tongue deeper, tasting, licking, twining in a gentle ravishment that compelled her surrender.

Alysson reeled from the shattering assault. A thousand

sensations ravaged her. She wanted to hate him. She wanted
to feel loathing for his intimate mastery, for the ruthless
way he was taking advantage of her vulnerable position. But
what she felt instead was the boldness of his body, hard and
warm and aggressive, imprinting its maleness onto her.
What she felt was his provocative heat, bathing her senses
and arousing an urgent hunger in her that cried out for fulfillment. Helplessly she swayed against him, straining
closer.

His kiss went on and on, giving her no quarter. She
couldn't escape . . . didn't want to escape.

A wild trembling invaded her limbs. Scarcely aware of
what she was doing, Alysson lifted her hands to grasp his
upper arms, clinging to him for support. And when, a dozen
heartbeats later, his sensitive fingers discovered the silken
warmth of her breast, she hardly knew that the faint moan
that came from her throat was hers.

Jafar recognized the trembling pleasure-sound and felt his
own body aching with an answering passion. Slowly he
broke off his kiss and lifted his head to gaze down at her.
Her eyes were half-closed, soft and hazy and bewildered,
the eyes of a woman experiencing the slow unfolding of
desire.

She was on the edge of surrender, he knew, and yet she
was still afraid of him. He could feel the way her heart
fluttered like an imprisoned bird at his touch.

Before she could recover her dazed senses, Jafar bent to
press a barrage of feather-light kisses at the vulnerable hollow of her throat, then followed the slender column with
his lips, to the line of her collarbone, and lower, to the
rising swell of her breast.

While his palm cupped the delicate heaviness, his tongue
found the erect peak and flicked out to tenderly stroke.

His erotic attentions forced another whimper from her.

"You bewitch me," he murmured before his lips closed
gently over the taut bud.

Alysson thought she would die from the incredible sensation. She found herself straining weakly toward his seeking mouth as Jafar sipped at her nipple.

Devastated by the fierce pleasure streaking through her,
she responsively dug her fingers into the hard muscle of his

arms. Her breath had entirely deserted her, along with the significant portion of her will. She knew she ought to make him stop, but incredibly, a traitorous part of her wanted very much for him to continue this exquisite torment.

"You are . . . despicable . . ." she at last managed to gasp, ". . . forcing me this way."

He paused, his movement arrested. *"Forcing?"* The word was a skeptical rasp.

Even so, her allegation had struck an unwelcome chord within him. Jafar took a shuddering breath. His body was throbbing, yet his desire suddenly was not quite so fierce as it had been a moment before.

Willing the savage heat of his blood to cool, he slowly drew his mouth away from her sweet breast. Just as slowly he straighted to stare down at her. "I have never had to force a woman, *chérie*. And I am not forcing you now."

It was true, Alysson thought with shameful comprehension. She had responded to him with a wantonness that was mortifying. "No . . ." she whispered.

His faint smile was humorless. "How ignorant you English ladies are kept. You don't even recognize desire when you feel it."

With a sound that was almost a sob, she pulled out of his arms. Had she been less upset, she might have felt surprise that Jafar let her go so easily, but all she could think of was what she had done, what she had allowed him to do.

How could she have forgotten Gervase? How could she have betrayed him so? She was considering marriage to him, for heaven's sake. Gervase had given her his love, his trust, and here she was welcoming another man's caresses! A savage stranger, no less!

Wanting to flee, to hide, Alysson began desperately searching through the pile of clothing for a robe to cover her nakedness. She found an embroidered caftan and dragged it on, overlapping the front edges and holding it protectively about her. When finally she turned to face Jafar, her bearing was tense, her expression wary.

His features were impassive but for the wry curve of his mouth, the only indication of the frustrated desire he was feeling. "There is no need for you to defend your virtue so ferociously, mademoiselle."

"No? Am I supposed to simply stand here then and calmly accept my ruination?"

He shrugged, an unconcerned gesture. "If you will only think on it, you will realize you have already been ruined in the eyes of your society, simply because you've been abducted by a 'savage Arab.' Your mere presence here in my camp, alone in my tent with me, will condemn you."

"That isn't so," Alysson replied doggedly, her voice shaking.

"Is it not? Do you think me unaware of your people's standards?" His low-pitched voice dropped a register. "Do you truly believe your Frenchman would want you now, after you have known my kisses? That he would still be willing to marry you?"

"It will not matter to Gervase that you have kissed me!" she cried, though she wasn't as certain as her adamant denial implied.

Jafar's look, as well as his tone, became cool. "If I were to take you for my own . . . if I were to lay you down, there on my bed, and settle myself between your sweet thighs . . . he would mind. Very much, I think. No *civilized* European, including the colonel, would marry you after that."

Alysson stared at Jafar in shock. It was a moment before she recovered enough from his implied threat of rape to force a response past her dry throat. "No . . . you're wrong . . . Gervase would not desert me."

"Oh, Bourmont will come for you, certainly. His honor demands it. But if he manages to avenge your capture and attain your freedom, he will toss you away as something soiled."

"You are q-quite mistaken. Gervase loves me. He wouldn't care if you did . . . ruin me."

When Jafar raised an eyebrow in disbelief, Alysson lifted her trembling chin and stared back at him defiantly.

He felt a spark of reluctant admiration for her as she stood there, proud and quivering. She was absurdly brave, Jafar thought, to deny him what he wanted. And he did want her . . . wanted her with a fierceness that surprised him. Yet he was civilized enough to want her willing.

With a cynical twist of his lips, Jafar shook his head. If he were one of his ancestors, he would not have stopped simply because she protested. He would have made her his personal slave, forced her to serve his physical needs, used her beautiful body for his pleasure . . . and hers. He would not have equivocated at rape.

And by his tribal laws, he would have been entirely justified, seeking revenge in that manner on his enemy, the colonel. But raping an innocent hadn't been his intent when he had taken her captive. His vengeance did not extend to debauching quivering virgins. She was a maid, untouched, and no matter how fiercely he wanted revenge on her fianceé, no matter how much he wanted to succumb to the fire in his Berber blood, he wouldn't take her innocence without her consent.

Yet it didn't mean he wouldn't do everything in his power to gain that consent.

"I think," Jafar said mildly, "that you overestimate the colonel's tolerance. If you were my intended bride, I would kill any man who touched you."

"*Your* bride?" Alysson replied scathingly. "Thank God that isn't even a remote possibility."

His smile this time held genuine amusement. "It is obvious no man has awakened your woman's body, *ma belle*. You know nothing of the delights of the flesh, or you would not willingly forgo my caresses."

His audacity astonished her. "You arrogant savage! The only way I would endure the caresses of a barbarian like you would be if you forced me."

"Oh, I will have you, my sweet, but it won't be by force." His tone was casual, speculative even, but Alysson had the terrible conviction he was making her a promise. "You will submit to me of your own free will."

Her fingers curling into fists, she faced him rigidly, nearly shaking with fury. "You are obviously quite mad! I will never submit to you!"

"Indeed you will, *chérie*. You will call me master . . . and lover. You will not return to Bourmont a maiden."

The soft intensity of the statement silenced her.

"And you will know pleasure at my touch," he added softly into the hush.

His gaze held hers with a force that was unbreakable as he slowly closed the brief distance between them. "I intend to tame you with gentleness, my fierce tigress, and you will respond to me with passion, the way I know you are capable of responding." Deliberately he lifted one hand to her breast.

"Don't!" She drew back with a jerk, as if his fingers had burned. "I don't care how gentle you are! You could never make me respond willingly to you."

"You think not?" His eyes swept down her body, coming to rest with arrogant possession on the soft swells of her breasts, now hidden from his gaze by the rich fabric of her robe. "I hold that you are mistaken. The day will come when you beg for my caresses . . ." With bold determination, he reached out again to stroke her nipple beneath the cloth.

Fiercely Alysson clenched her teeth to stifle the gasp he dredged from her, but still she couldn't prevent her flesh from responding to his expert touch, or deny the quiver that shook her body.

He laughed, softly, at her reaction, the husky sound sending a quicksilver flame of excitement rippling up her spine. "Oh, yes, my little tigress, whether or not you believe it now, we shall be lovers."

He spared a final raking glance for her slender form, before he abruptly turned on his heel and quit the room. Alysson stared after him, regretting fervently that she had missed shooting him through the heart when she'd fired her pistol at him that day.

She stood there for a long moment after he had gone, shivering with fear and an icy fire. *We shall be lovers . . . You will not return to Bourmont a maiden.* The threatening words reverberated in her mind, conjuring up vivid, erotic images that she found impossible to banish.

Images of her lying naked in Jafar's arms, their limbs entwined, while he taught her the kind of passion she had never even dreamed of.

Defiantly she closed her eyes to shut out the terrible visions, but she couldn't shut out the musky scent of him that clung to her skin, or the evocative taste of him that lingered on her lips.

With a muttered oath, she hugged her arms to her body,

furious with him, disgusted with herself, yet touched by a shameful excitement she had never before known.

Chapter 7

W̶e shall be lovers.
The bold prediction haunted Alysson, no matter how forcefully she tried to dismiss it. Much to her dismay, the incident with Jafar in his bedchamber had left her badly shaken. No man had ever kissed her like that. No man had ever taken her in his arms and forced a passionate response from her. No man had ever threatened to compel her surrender, or vowed to make her submit freely to his lovemaking, to find pleasure in his touch.

The day will come when you beg for my caresses.
The sheer arrogance of such a statement made Alysson's blood boil, and yet she felt a vague terror as well. It had taken only one kiss for her to discover that Jafar had the power to fulfill his prophecy. He had proven beyond doubt that he could arouse her desire, that he could make her momentarily forget Gervase and what she owed him. And she was very much afraid that given the opportunity, her savage Berber captor would make her willingly respond to him with passion, just as he had promised.

Her only hope, Alysson concluded, was to deny him the opportunity. She had to keep away from him entirely. That, however, presented a problem, given the limitations of the tent's confines and Jafar's insistence that she sleep beside him.

Nevertheless she tried ignoring his presence. During the following week Alysson refused to speak to him or even acknowledge his existence when she was in his company. She even suffered his occasional provocative remarks in silence, determined not to rise to the bait. When he complimented her on her appearance, saying that she wore the robes of his country well, Alysson pointedly turned her back on him, regretting that she had allowed Tahar and the other Berber women to take away her English clothes.

She also did her best to restrain her natural disposition. Her heartless captor had said he enjoyed "a woman with spirit," that she needed "taming," of all the nonsensical things. Contrarily, Alysson decided to become the opposite of a spirited woman. No longer would she defy or confront Jafar. She would try docility for a change, all the while keeping a sharp eye out for her chance to escape.

Escape would be difficult, though, she realized. She was never allowed to leave Jafar's tent, and so was unable to search for weapons or learn the layout of the camp. And although Jafar's horses were tethered outside his tent, they were well-guarded by the blue-eyed equerry whose name, she discovered, was Saful.

Yet somehow Alysson managed to retain her optimism. Her abduction would not go unchallenged. Doubtless Gervase and Uncle Honoré were searching for her at this very moment. They would post a reward for her safe return, and someone in this vast wilderness—perhaps those slavers she had encountered at the oasis—would be greedy enough to betray one of their countrymen. Sooner or later Gervase would learn where she was being held and would give this arrogant Berber baron his due.

She had no hope that Jafar would release her before then. He would show no mercy, she was certain. Everything about the man was hard and unyielding, tempered like the keen edge of the dagger he wore thrust in his sash. More than once Alysson found herself wondering how she could steal that wicked-looking dagger so she could carve out his black heart, but she didn't dare attempt it. If she failed, he was too likely to turn the deadly blade on her.

As the first week of her captivity passed, her days began to assume a pattern. The Berbers were early risers, and went to bed when it grew dark. In between, they worked hard, only pausing to rest at mealtimes: breakfast at nine after the morning chores were completed, the main meal of the day during the heat of mid-afternoon, when work temporarily ceased in the camp, and a light supper in the evening. Jafar sometimes dined with her for the midday meal, and he frequently held council meetings in their tent, but otherwise, she was alone for much of each day.

Except for the solitary confinement, though, Alysson was well-treated—clothed and fed and waited upon like a princess. Mahmoud served her grudgingly, his actions polite, though his underlying hatred of Europeans was always apparent. The afternoon heat and lack of company were the worst of her grievances. But if she thought of complaint, pride alone kept her silent.

Boredom, loneliness, and frustration became her chief companions. And, whether Alysson was willing to admit it or not, fear.

Fear that Jafar might actually make good his threat to become her lover, to make her beg for his caresses.

She was no longer quite so worried that Jafar might rape her. He had said that he'd never had to force a woman, and Alysson could well believe it. He had a savage handsomeness and cool magnetism that she knew most women would find compellingly attractive. And despite her best intentions, she herself was drawn to him.

But even though he wouldn't force her, she was very much afraid of his threat. She could sense his determination in his merest look. And she had little trouble interpreting his vow, though it remained unspoken between them.

He meant to seduce her.

The possibility terrified her, yet kept her in a state of strange physical excitement. She took to pacing the tent floor, driven by an intolerable tension.

The suspense was nerve-racking. In Jafar's company, she constantly had to remain on her guard, and when he was away, she had to be prepared for his return. The animal silence of his footsteps, however, never gave her any warning. She jumped whenever Jafar entered the tent. His presence filled the room, while his hawk-keen eyes searched her out, conveying the silent message, *We shall be lovers.*

His unrelenting intensity gave her no peace. And regardless of her determination to ignore him, Alysson found it nearly impossible.

His gentleness, however, alarmed Alysson most. For when he behaved toward her with kindness and courtesy, his manners were as impeccably civilized as any European gentleman's. At those times he made her forget that he was an unscrupulous savage, and she found herself unwittingly relaxing her guard.

Until nightfall. When night came, she always remembered with a vengeance just who Jafar was, and how vulnerable her position was, for it was then that he made her undress.

That first night after his devastating kiss and outrageous prediction, Alysson had felt herself quaking. They'd retired to the bedchamber to sleep, and Jafar had stretched out on the pallet, reclining on the pillows as regally as some Eastern potentate as he observed her every movement.

"Do you need help removing your clothes?" he asked when she hesitated. His tone was light and teasing, but the flames warming the depths of his eyes told her he would relish the opportunity to undress her.

Unfortunately, his taunt provoked Alysson into breaking her vow to ignore him.

"I wish you had sold me to those Arabs slavers," she retorted through gritted teeth. "Then at least I wouldn't have to endure you watching me."

He made a sweeping gesture that encompassed her. "This is precisely how it would be if you were sold as a slave— except that all your clothing would be forcibly removed, and your naked body would be subjected to many more pairs of eyes. Here you have only to endure mine."

Alysson clenched her teeth, willing herself not to respond, not to curse him or scream at him like she yearned to do.

When she remained silent, Jafar softened his voice to a murmur. "I would never allow any other man to view you. Your charms are meant for my eyes only."

She managed to keep her oath from his hearing, but it gave her no comfort that only he had the privilege to inspect her.

It gave her no comfort, either, when early the following morning, she awoke. To her acute dismay, she found herself curled against Jafar's warm, lean body, one hand resting on his hard chest, her relaxed fingers tangled in his chest hair. To her further dismay, he stirred in his sleep. Rolling toward her, he draped his arm possessively across her rib cage, pressing against the undercurves of her breasts. At the same time he drew his leg up to cover hers, till his knee rode intimately between her thighs. The masculine hardness was a sensual shock against her softness.

Deathly afraid to disturb him, Alysson lay there unmoving. Embarrassed heat flooded through her, along with another, more scandalous sensation. Desire. Against every inclination of common sense or reason, her body felt a shameful longing. For Jafar.

Desire.

She recognized the feeling, for he had aroused it in her the previous day when he'd kissed and caressed her and shown her body how to respond. The result was the same now. Her nipples were taut and aching, her skin sensitive and shivery, her breath shallow and much too fast. And the hidden recesses between her thighs throbbed with a need she couldn't explain.

Lying here remembering the feel of his hot mouth on her breasts only made the throbbing worse. She wanted him to touch her there, now, and ease the urgent ache.

Unable to banish the fierce sensations, Alysson groaned silently. For the first time in her life, she was confronted with the depth of her own sexuality, and she deplored the wicked, helpless way her body was reacting. These wanton, abandoned feelings were startling to her, and quite, quite, humiliating. How could she feel this way toward such a man? How could she so easily dismiss her obligation toward Gervase, her longtime friend and suitor? She owed Gervase her loyalty, at the very least. The treacherous response of her body was a betrayal of him, as well as of herself.

With an effort, Alysson pretended sleep until Jafar stirred awake. It was all she could do not to flinch when he pressed a light kiss on her temple before he rose for the day.

Two mornings afterward, she woke a bit later. When her eyes fluttered open, she was totally unprepared for the shock she received. Jafar stood there naked, with his back toward her.

He seemed unaware of her as he finished his morning ablutions. He had a beautiful body, she thought, dazed, seeing the golden skin marred only by the scars of battle and the healing flesh wound on his arm made by her bullet. His powerful shoulders tapered to lean hips, with tight hard buttocks and a horseman's strong muscular thighs. His long legs were made of well-honed muscle, dusted with gilded hair. Then he turned.

Even as her gaze swept slowly downward, it faltered. Startled, Alysson stared at the shadowy triangle between his naked thighs. His manhood was fully aroused, jutting out proud and hard, startling in its size and power.

As if he sensed her scrutiny, he glanced down at her. Meeting her shocked eyes, he smiled.

"Sleeping with you has its unwanted effects," he said, his tone laced with wry humor.

Alysson wanted to hide her burning face in the pillows, but for the life of her, she couldn't look away. His compelling gaze demanded her attention.

Casually then, without haste, he reached for his tunic and pulled it on. But he was still watching her. Alysson could see the dark light of desire in the sensual, predatory eyes. And though he didn't touch her, she could feel the promise of his touch down the entire length of her body.

Finally managing to pry her gaze away, she gave him her back. She would not surrender to such a man, she vowed again silently. And yet seeing his nakedness made her even more disturbingly aware of the strange, incomprehensible stirrings of her own desire.

The constant state of tension she felt reached a breaking point later that morning. She was trying for the dozenth time to read one of the French journals that had been placed at her disposal, but images of Jafar's nakedness kept returning to haunt her, totally destroying any attempt at concentration. Finally despairing, Alysson lunged to her feet with a soft curse and threw the hapless newspaper across the tent—at the very same moment that Mahmoud came limping through the doorway.

With a frightened whimper, the young boy dropped the water jug he was holding and cringed, his arm raised as if to ward off a blow.

The paper had missed him by a good five feet, but immediately Alysson was all contrition. "Oh, Mahmoud, forgive me! I didn't realize you were there. I'm sorry—"

She took a step toward him, her hand outstretched in apology, but the servant fell to the floor, prostrating his small form on the carpet, his hands covering his turbaned head. Alysson halted in her tracks; his skinny body was actually quaking.

Horrified, she knelt on the carpet beside him and hesitantly touched his shoulder. "Mahmoud, I'm sorry. Do get up, please. I'm sorry I frightened you. I never intended to throw that journal at you, please believe me."

It was a long moment before the boy cautiously lifted his head to look up at her. His complexion was pale in contrast to the savage red scar covering the right side of his face, and Alysson could see fear in his dark eyes, along with wary regard.

"You . . . do not mean to beat me?"

"No, of course not. Why would you think so?"

"But I dropped the jug . . ."

"Only because I startled you." She bent to pick up the clay vessel and held it up for inspection. "See, no damage was done. And even if there had been, the fault would have been entirely mine. I had no right to take my ill humor out on you, even unwittingly. If I do so again, I hope you will take me to task."

Mahmoud's wary look turned to mild shock as slowly he raised himself to his knees. "Never would I dare such a thing, lady. The lord would be severely displeased should I presume to say a word against you."

Alysson gave a smile that held more than a touch of wryness. "You should meet my servant Chand, then. He speaks against me regularly. If he isn't contradicting me, then he's scolding me like a mother hen."

"And you do not beat him?"

"Good heavens, no. Why ever should I?"

"Because it is your right. A master may strike a servant whenever it pleases him, or even kill him if he wishes."

"That may be the custom in your country, but I assure you it isn't in mine. I wouldn't dream of striking Chand."

Mahmoud looked puzzled. "But my French mistress beat me many times."

That sobered Alysson at once. "Not all Europeans are alike, I'm relieved to say. I would not beat you, Mahmoud.

Ever. Not if you broke a hundred water jugs. There is no reason for you to be afraid of me."

"I am not afraid!" At this slur on his honor, the boy bravely puffed out his meager chest and scowled up at her.

"No . . . of course not," she said soothingly, realizing her error.

His scowl easing, Mahmoud climbed to his feet and abruptly lost his balance, nearly falling. When Alysson grasped his bony arm to steady him, he shot her a self-conscious glance, then ducked his head. He was embarrassed by his handicap, she realized, feeling a wave of compassion surge through her.

Pretending unconcern about the incident, Alysson handed him the jug. Mahmoud averted his face as he accepted it with a mumbled word of thanks, then turned and limped toward the rear room.

Following him with her gaze, Alysson rose slowly to her feet. She had never noticed it until now, but whenever he could, Mahmoud kept the scarred side of his face turned away from her. But then how could she have noticed? Ever since her arrival in the Berber camp four days ago, her concern had only been for herself, her every thought focused on either escape or the threat that Jafar presented her.

Wishing she could make amends for her insensitivity, she followed Mahmoud into the bedchamber and found him filling the pitcher with wash water.

"What of your master?" she asked more casually than her interest warranted. "Does Jafar ever beat you?"

Mahmoud gave her a look of disdain before he shook his head vigorously. "No, never has the lord raised his hand to me. Indeed, he saved me from the French when they would have tortured me again."

"Oh, Mahmoud . . ." Alysson felt a tight ache in her throat at the thought of how much this child had suffered in his short life. She wanted very much to console him, to wrap her arms around his skinny body and promise that he would never have to endure such pain again. But even if he would have accepted such a show of concern from a foreign infidel—which was highly doubtful—any promises she made him would be empty. Mahmoud's fate, like her own at present, was entirely beyond her power to control.

"What of your family?" she asked quietly. "Have you no parents?"

The expression on his scarred young face turned a bit wistful. "I have no father. My mother . . . she was taken away by the French. I do not know what became of her."

"So there was no one else to help you."

"I do not need the help of any but my lord Jafar."

The boy's tone was hostile again, and so Alysson gave up the effort to make him talk or accept a concern that was obviously unwanted. Leaving Mahmoud alone to his tasks, she went to the front doorway of the tent and settled herself there on the carpet.

In the distance, beyond the camp, the immense and un-cultivated desert stretched in undulating sweeps—an empty sea of inhospitable yellow sand that appeared harsh and un-forgiving to the civilized eye. Not a breath of wind stirred to cool her face, and already a shimmering haze rose from the hot, dry ground. Overhead a burning sun hung in the cloudless sky.

But oddly, the barren land no longer seemed quite as cruel to Alysson as it had just a few moments ago. After hearing of Mahmoud's suffering, she believed the burden of her captivity would not be quite so hard to bear.

An ache welled up in her throat as she remembered the way the child had cowered before her in fear. Nothing she had ever witnessed had made her feel quite so inadequate, quite so full of shame. And his touching dignity when he declared himself not afraid, even as he tried to hide his crippled leg and horrible scar . . .

Closing her eyes against the memory, Alysson silently made herself another vow. While she was here in this camp, she would do her utmost to make Mahmoud lose his fear of her. Even if she could never hope to win his friendship, she might possibly gain his trust and perhaps alleviate some of his hatred, as well. She could show him that not all Euro-peans were alike. And if she was persistent enough, even-tually she might make Mahmoud lose his hostility toward her. It should not be an impossible task. She had never yet met a male whom she couldn't charm if she tried . . . except his master, that is. But she refused to think about Jafar.

Still, she would have liked to hear the story of how Jafar

had saved Mahmoud from the French. Perhaps, like the
desert, her Berber captor wasn't quite as cruel as he seemed
upon first acquaintance. He evidently cared enough about
the boy to see to his welfare. Yet Jafar had hundreds of
dependents to care for. How much attention could he give
a child who was merely a servant?

How lonely that orphaned child must be, with no family
to call his own. What Mahmoud needed was someone like
her Uncle Honoré, someone who would give him love and
affection simply for himself.

Absently, Alysson found her thoughts drifting to her uncle. She had given him a great deal of trouble over the
years, but nothing like this latest debacle of her abduction.
He would be frantic with worry for her by now. She would
have given anything if she could have spared him that. Anything, even including marrying Gervase and settling down
to a staid home life. If she'd done that as her uncle wished,
she would not be in this fix now.

Her lips curved in a sad smile as she realized where her
thoughts had led her. How delighted her uncle would be to
hear of her change of heart. Honoré had long wanted her to
marry. Indeed, she could almost hear his gruff voice com-
plaining about her refusal to give serious consideration to
any of her suitors, and her propensity to drive them away
with her unconventionality.

"Bon Dieu! Why can you not act as the other young girls
act—simpering and flirting? How shall I ever marry you off
if you never make the effort to curb your wildness?"

And yet for all his bluster, she knew quite well that Honoré only wanted her happiness. He had not pressed her to
encourage someone she could not love, not after her first
disastrous experience with a suitor. The incident might have
left her heart cynically scarred for life, if not for Honoré's
wise counsel.

She'd been pursued by the brother of a schoolmate, a
belted earl, the month she turned sixteen. She'd been so
grateful to be noticed by the handsome young lord, so desperate to conform to his aristocratic world after being
shunned by it for so long, that she'd believed his protesta-
tions of love . . . until she chanced to overhear his comment
to his sister. "Once I have control of her fortune, I will no

longer have to dance attendance on the common little upstart."

Common little upstart. The memory still carried a vicious sting.

She'd had Honoré to run to, at least. Like a father, he had consoled her and mended her wounded heart and sent her back into the world a little wiser and a great deal more careful. "Someday you will find a man you can love," he'd told her then.

He had wanted Gervase to be that man, but had almost despaired that it would ever happen—

Alysson's wistful thoughts were interrupted just then by Mahmoud as he limped past her.

"Mahmoud," she called to him gently.

The boy half-turned, keeping his right cheek averted as he waited.

"Thank you for taking such good care of me."

His dark eyes narrowed in mistrust, but he gave her bow of grudging obeisance. "It is my duty."

"All the same, I thank you. You've made my imprisonment here easier to bear."

The odd look of confusion on the child's face before he turned away almost made Alysson smile.

Her imprisonment *did* seem easier to bear during the next few days. She still refused to speak to Jafar or acknowledge his existence, and the tension she always felt in his presence didn't diminish in the slightest, but remembering what Mahmoud had said about Jafar saving him from torture made Alysson a bit less apprehensive about her own fate. Perhaps Jafar was not the murderous barbarian she had first feared, after all.

Still, there was a purposefulness about him, an unwavering determination that almost frightened her. That, and a savage quality that seemed an inherent Berber trait.

Pride was also a Berber trait, Alysson decided by the end of her first week in the camp. All the warriors she'd observed possessed it in full measure, but even the few women she'd seen bore themselves with a quiet dignity that she could only admire. Yet Jafar had a regal confidence that belonged only to powerful warlords. That he held complete control over his fellow Berbers was most apparent when he administered to his tribe. From the rear chamber, Alysson could view the proceedings through a part in the curtain as Jafar held audience in his reception room. He sat cross-legged in his desert robes, listening intently without reaction, then speaking in sibilant Arabic or the less guttural Berber. He never raised his voice, never lost control of his emotions, yet his authority was unequivocal, his decisions unquestioned. Alysson had no doubt that his every command was obeyed implicitly.

By observing Jafar during these audiences, or noting when he rode away on some business or other, Alysson was able to piece together the daily fabric of his life.

During the day, the demands on his time were endless. If he wasn't holding audience, he was in council with his lieutenants—preparing for some act of defiance against the French, Alysson suspected. She paid particular attention during these sessions, though she understood only one word in twenty.

He also spent a large portion of his time riding, whether for work or pleasure she wasn't certain. Sometimes when she sat at the outer door of the tent, observing the camp, she could glimpse Jafar galloping one of his mounts; for some inexplicable reason she had no trouble distinguishing him from all the other tall, fierce, black-robed Berbers. He was always occupied with training his horses, or participating in wild Berber games that were conducted on horseback, or hunting with falcons, if she could judge by the number of small game birds that she sometimes spied tied to his saddle when he returned.

In the evenings, he read, or studied his maps, or readied his weapons. This last activity did nothing to relieve her concern that he was planning some act of war. And always it brought home the fact that he was a savage warlord, with some sinister purpose in mind.

His ruthless determination was ever-present. The only time he shed it, it seemed to Alysson, was at prayer. He was not an overtly religious man—most Berbers weren't nearly as devout as the Bedouins, in any case, Alysson remembered hearing. But Jafar performed his devotions with a simple sincerity that made her wonder how he could ever wish her harm.

Did he wish her harm? He had not hurt her physically yet, despite his threat to become her lover. But if he didn't plan to ransom her, what then did he intend to do with her?

She was contemplating that question for the hundredth time late one afternoon as she watched Jafar and his Berber warriors exercising their mounts at the outskirts of the camp. From the shelter of Jafar's tent, shielded from the worst of the sun's glare by the tent wall and a haik covering her head, Alysson could see some two score horsemen showing off their skill. Her guard, Saful, was positioned a discreet distance from her, oiling a rifle, but he seemed to be paying her little attention.

In the distance, the mounted warriors tilted at one another with swords, wheeling and evading, exhibiting their mastery. Others rode at a full gallop and scooped up sashes from the ground. The most picturesque feat, however, was when a horse leapt into the air while its rider tossed his musket high overhead and then caught it again.

Witnessing their marvels of horsemanship, Alysson couldn't fail to be impressed by either the warriors or the splendid horses they rode. Superbly trained, the animals would stop short at a full gallop, or stand quiet when the rider simply dropped the reins.

She knew it had taken years of careful training to manage such responsiveness. During the past week, she'd seen for herself the infinite patience and care the Berbers showed their mounts; apparently the Berbers, like the Bedouin Arabs, loved their horses like children.

But it was Jafar who caught her eye time and time again. A magnificent horseman, he seemed to have been born to the saddle. Not only was he a graceful rider, but his superiority was apparent, even to her untrained eye.

She watched with bated breath the astonishing feats he performed. He would place one hand on the stallion's back and vault over to the other side. Or, putting the animal at full speed, he would disengage his feet from the stirrups, stand up in the saddle, and fire at a mark with the utmost precision.

It was at one of these moments that Alysson felt a quiet presence beside her. Mahmoud, to her surprise, had paused in his work and come out to observe the warriors with her. He, too, was watching Jafar's performance with rapt attention.

"I wish I could ride like that," Alysson murmured a short while later, not aware that she'd spoken until she heard Mahmoud's soft scoffing sound.

"Females do not ride war-horses," he pronounced with a masculine certainty that was almost smug.

Alysson couldn't help the wry retort that sprang to her lips. "Females generally don't shoot firearms or engage in swordplay, either, but I am skilled at both."

The boy flashed her a highly skeptical glance, but she merely returned a disarming smile before focusing her gaze on the horses again. What would it be like to race, wild and free, across the desert plains on one of those magnificent Barbary steeds? With the wind in her hair—

"You can fight with swords?" Mahmoud asked in the same tone of wonder he'd shown when she'd claimed she never beat her servants.

"I know how to wield a rapier and can hold my own in a match with many of my male acquaintances, yes. Does that shock you?"

"Yes. You are a very strange lady," Mahmoud said slowly in bemusement.

That brought a ripple of laughter to her lips. "So I've been told."

"Have you killed many men?"

Alysson drew a sharp breath, taken aback by the eagerness of the child's question. "Not a one, I'm afraid. Have you?"

"No," Mahmoud said sadly.

He fell silent then, while Alysson wondered what she might say to draw the boy out. "Can you ride a war-horse?" she asked finally.

That seemed to strike the right note, for Mahmoud's face brightened. "I can ride all the horses of our tribe," he answered with pride. "Even the lord's, though he does not permit me to ride the black. I can do many, many tricks. My leg loses the weakness—" Abruptly the child stopped, as if realizing he'd said too much. "I know how to ride," he continued, his tone suddenly sullen again.

"I would like to see you someday," she said, keeping her tone casual, knowing better than to press.

Mahmoud shrugged his bony shoulders, saying as he turned away, "If the lord permits."

Disatisfied with her slow progress, Alysson regretfully watched him go, while his last comment echoed in her ears. *If the lord permits.* It always came back to that, she thought with a sigh. But the lord evidently did not intend to permit her to do much of anything.

She sat there for a long while, watching the horsemen until they finally disbanded and the usual stillness of the desert was restored. All around her, the camp still bustled with activity as the Berbers prepared for evening, but Alysson ignored it, instead focusing her gaze on the distant horizon.

The red glory of the setting sun was magnificent, awe-inspiring. Seeing the rippling dunes and ridges of golden sand like this, in the fading rosy light, Alysson remembered what had fascinated her so about this region and made her long to explore it. This was a lonely land . . . vicious, cruel . . . yet it possessed a mysterious sensuality that seemed to beckon to everything that was wild and free-spirited in her. She could fall in love with this country so easily . . .

The wistful thought was shattered by the soft plod of a horse's hooves nearby. Glancing up, Alysson saw that Jafar had returned to the tent with his black stallion.

When he was but a yard away, he drew the horse to a halt, yet he sat there unmoving, staring down at her. Alysson froze. His amber eyes were warm and dark as they silently appraised her. She was wearing one of the rich tunics she'd been given, a robe of deep blue-and-red striped linen, with a soft haik of matching blue covering her hair.

His gaze roamed over her headdress, her face, her shoulders . . . then dropped lower. Alysson felt herself trembling. He was staring directly at her breasts, his eyes so intense, so warm, she felt the invading heat through the fabric of her robe to the bare flesh beneath. He was remembering that moment a week ago, she knew. The moment when he'd caressed her breasts with his hot mouth. His eyes were touching her now just as his lips had done then. Her breasts swelled painfully at the memory, the hardening nipples pressing against the soft linen.

Her heart thundering, Alysson helplessly endured his silent scrutiny, unable to turn away. Finally, Jafar's gaze lifted to capture hers. The shock of meeting his hungry, sensual look almost stole her breath away.

It took all the willpower she possessed to force herself to break contact with his heated gaze. Defensively she uncurled her legs and drew her knees to her chest, wrapping her arms around herself, yet she still quivered with the tension that had coiled in her body at his sensual appraisal.

It was then that Alysson remembered they weren't alone. Saful had risen to his feet and was respectfully awaiting his lord's command.

With a creak of saddle leather, Jafar dismounted and turned the reins over to the equerry, while Alysson watched warily. Unbuckling the silver scabbard that sheathed the long sword at his waist, he handed the weapon to Saful, then turned to enter the tent.

Without a word, Alysson pulled back to allow him to pass, keeping her gaze averted. She sensed, rather than saw, Jafar's frown of displeasure, and was relieved when he didn't stop but continued past her, into the tent.

Shaken from the disturbing encounter, she turned her attention back to the distant horizon, staring at the darkening landscape, feeling again the grim loneliness of the desert.

How could she? Alysson berated herself. How could she allow a mere look from Jafar to affect her so? How could her treacherous body react to his merest glance, against her will? How was it possible to be physically attracted to a man who was nothing more than a desert heathen?

She had no right to feel such wanton sensations for such a man. He was her captor, merely that. To even think of Jafar in any other terms was a betrayal of Gervase. Gervase, whose friendship and respect meant so very much to her.

Alysson closed her eyes at the feelings of guilt welling up in her. The elaborately decorated sword Jafar had worn just now had done nothing to quiet her inner turmoil, for seeing it had only roused a memory of Gervase, on one of the many occasions she'd seen him wearing a sword.

It was the first time Gervase had kissed her. The first time he'd looked at her as a woman, instead of a provoking child—just after her disastrous experience with the fortune hunter when she was sixteen, after she'd fled school in humiliation and taken refuge with Honoré in France.

Gervase had been in Paris on furlough and had called at their hotel within hours of their arrival. Alysson had come upon him unawares as he awaited her uncle in their private parlor.

She thought Gervase looked dashing in his dress uniform, a feathered shako on his dark head, a glittering saber at his side, but she couldn't resist the chance to provoke him. While his back was toward her, she tiptoed up behind him and drew his saber from its sheath.

Gervase whirled, his hand clasping the empty scabbard. When he saw Alysson grinning up at him, his startled expression turned into a smile twisted by annoyance. "Alysson, you little wretch! Is this how you greet me after three months?"

Giving him a saucy curtsy, she flourished his saber in the air. "How do you do, Gervase. Thank you for the loan of your sword. I shall return it shortly—I merely want to borrow it for a while."

"Good heavens, why?"

"There is someone I intend to run through."

He laughed. "Is that so, my bloodthirsty minx? And just who is this unfortunate devil who has so earned your displeasure?"

"Merely a scoundrel who coveted my money more than my person," she replied, hiding the raw hurt and bitterness she felt.

"I cannot imagine any gentleman failing to succumb to your feminine charms," Gervase replied with no little irony.

At her sudden scowl, he abandoned his sarcasm and swept her a gallant bow. "Tell me the name of the dastard who has offended you and I will accomplish the task for you."

"I can do it myself, thank you very much!"

"I don't doubt it. Your Uncle Oliver has turned you into a formidable gladiator."

"Uncle Oliver has had little to do with it. I paid for

fencing and shooting lessons myself. As my trustee, he only had to approve.''

"Regardless, with your skill at arms, I would do well to hire you to defend my regiment.''

She managed to laugh at his left-handed compliment, and when he held out his hand commandingly, surrendered the saber to him. "Ah, well, I suppose I can always shoot the villain instead.''

Sheathing the weapon, Gervase ruffled her curls good-naturedly, as he'd done a hundred times before. She made a face at him and was about to pull away when his hand suddenly stilled on her hair.

His smile faded as he stood looking down her with a strange expression, almost as if he had never seen her before. Slowly then, as if against his will, he bent toward her and pressed a light kiss on her lips, the merest brush of pressure.

Shocked, Alysson brought her fingers to her mouth and stared up at him.

"You've grown up, *coquine*,'' Gervase whispered . . .

The tender memory of that long-ago kiss haunted Alysson now as she stared out at the shadowy desert. That first kiss of Gervase's had startled her, flattered her, but it hadn't shaken her. Not the way the unwanted caresses from her Berber captor had done.

What vital element was missing in Gervase's kiss that was not missing in Jafar's? Why had a ruthless stranger been able to arouse her passion so easily, in a way Gervase never had? How could she feel such inappropriate desire for one man and absolutely none for the other?

She sighed, wishing she could banish her disturbing thoughts.

Behind her, within the tent, Jafar heard her sigh but attempted to ignore it. At the moment he was wrestling with his own haunting thoughts.

He understood quite well his own feelings of desire, and the cause: his bewitching captive. The pleasure of seeing her graceful figure draped in the robes of his country . . . the gratification of finding her sitting at the entrance to his tent, as if waiting for his return . . . the pain of sleeping next to her night after night without being able to touch her

. . . the memory of having her melting in his arms for one brief moment.

He couldn't cease remembering the exquisite triumph of his momentary possession, or the delight he'd felt when she had responded to him with passion, or how captivating she'd looked. Her body pale as ice and beautifully mysterious, her nipples rising like jeweled ornaments to his touch . . .

He wanted to taste again the delectable warmth of her breasts on his tongue, to experience the riveting sweetness of her kisses, to absorb the inner fire and spirit of the woman herself.

And his desire was affecting his judgment, Jafar knew. Again and again he found himself wanting to neglect his many duties. From the moment he first woke each morning, he found himself reluctant to leave her side. Watching Alysson sleep, seeing her tumbling chestnut hair flowing across his pillow had a strange, unsolicited effect on him, arousing a protectiveness, a tenderness in him, in addition to the hunger. If not for his responsibilities, he could have spent hours lying there with her, simply to be near.

And when he was away, he looked forward to the end to the day when they could be alone together. Which was rather absurd, Jafar thought dryly, considering the extreme hostility of their relationship. In his company, his lovely young captive either ignored him entirely or treated him to a bout of simmering, mutinous silence.

This was new to him, this overpowering need to be with a woman. Certainly one who did not want him in return, one who belonged to another man.

He had never denied himself for any other woman, either. The mornings were worst. It would be so easy to take her while she slept, to roll over and glide into her slowly, to lose himself in her sweet heaven.

But he wanted her willing. He wanted to effect her surrender without conquering her pride. He wanted to teach her the meaning of pleasure. Most of all, he wanted to make her forget that she had ever been betrothed to Gervase de Bourmont, his hated enemy.

And that last, more than anything else, was very likely an unattainable possibility.

Chapter 8

Humility did not come easily to Alysson, but for the sake of her own sanity, she decided that night to swallow her pride and ask Jafar if she could occasionally be allowed to ride. She chose a moment when they were alone, when she thought he would most likely be amenable to her request. The supper dishes had been been cleared away and Mahmoud had withdrawn for the evening.

Surreptitiously, Alysson sipped her coffee and watched Jafar. He was reading, stretched out lean and catlike on the pillows, his newspaper angled to catch the light from the lamp. He subscribed regularly to the French journals, it seemed; she had read every issue in the tent twice during the past week, simply to keep herself occupied, even though some were outdated by nearly a month.

It surprised her that a Berber warlord was interested in the news from France. But then he was a surprising man, Alysson admitted. She never knew quite what to expect from him—whether she would encounter the savage desert chieftain or the suave, educated gentleman. At the moment he looked almost civilized. He had removed his turban, and a few strands of his hair fell loosely about his face, sunstreaked honey and amber in the lamplight. Except for his sun-darkened complexion, he might pass for European, she decided. Perhaps that was the basis for his seeming oddly familiar to her.

The glow of the lamp softened the lean hardness of his features, creating an effect that was both disturbing and deceptive; it made him look younger, and far more gentle than she knew he was. And yet he *could* be gentle, Alysson reflected, recalling the tenderness of his kisses and the shameful way she had nearly surrendered to him. Abruptly

Alysson shook herself. Thinking of that only pummeled her already raw nerves.

"Why do you read those journals?" she asked suddenly, as much to take her mind off the disquieting man before her as to initiate a conversation.

Jafar looked up, one eyebrow lifted, as if surprised that she had addressed him. It was the first time in days that Alysson had spoken voluntarily to him.

"I like to keep abreast of what is happening in France," he replied after a moment.

"Why?"

"So that I know what the French intend for my country, now that they have become our conquerors."

"Is that how you learned to speak French so fluently? By reading the journals?"

He shrugged. "That and other means. A wise man learns the language of his enemy."

Alysson almost pursued this line of conversation, but decided she didn't want to become involved in his concerns. All she wanted was to be set free . . . and to see him pay for abducting her.

"I have a request," she declared, changing the subject rather abruptly. "I should like to be allowed to ride for an hour or two each day."

He regarded her at length, taking a long while before he answered, "Why?"

"Because I need the distraction. I'm going mad here with nothing to do. I am not accustomed to being idle all day long, nor am I accustomed to having to beg for the least courtesy."

"Has not Mahmoud seen to your needs?"

"Yes, of course, but you haven't permitted me even the slightest freedom! I am never allowed out, never allowed any company but yours—and that hardly constitutes scintillating companionship."

"I will send some of the women in the camp to visit you, perhaps Tahar—"

"Thank you," Alysson muttered grudgingly, "but I need *exercise.*" When he didn't answer, she lost the careful control she'd been keeping on her tongue. "Have you any notion of how excruciating it is to be imprisoned here day after day? To have nothing to do all day long except pace the floor and worry about when you will ever again see your family, your loved ones, your country?''

A muscle flexed in his jaw, but he remained calm in the face of her anger. "I will consider your request," Jafar said finally.

"Why can you not give me an answer now? Are you afraid I will try to escape if you let me ride?"

His smile was brief. "The thought had occurred to me."

The thought had occurred to her, too, but Alysson was not about to admit it. She managed to shake her head scoffingly. "It would be suicide for me to attempt an escape in the middle of the desert. Where could I possibly go?"

"At the moment, you may go to bed. It is time to retire."

She stared at him, her eyes suddenly bright, glistening with frustration. "Damn you . . ."

Forcibly, Alysson bit her lip, clamping back the curses she wanted to throw at him. She would not, *would not,* allow him to infuriate her to the point that she said or did something rash. Nor would she plead with him. She would not humiliate herself by begging, as apparently he meant for her to do.

To her amazement, though, Jafar granted at least part of her request.

The following morning her blue-eyed guard Saful appeared, carrying his long-barreled rifle, and with gestures and some words of Arabic that she knew, he made her understand that she was to accompany him. For several hours then, Saful escorted her all around the city of black tents—the *douar,* as she learned the Berber encampment was called. Savoring her first taste of freedom in over a week, Alysson found it all fascinating, but still she was careful to view her surroundings with an eye for escape.

The tents were generally arranged in a large circle, while the horses and pack animals were kept within the protected boundary. Outside the circle, Alysson saw the artesian well that supplied the camp with fresh water, and the sandy depression that served as a latrine. She had expected as much, for none of the Arab tents she'd ever been in had possessed sanitary facilities. Except Jafar's, Alysson reflected. The presence of the chamber pot in his only confirmed her belief that he'd carefully planned her abduction. He hadn't wanted her to have any reason to leave his tent.

He hadn't wanted her to dress in breeches either, Alysson surmised, for her European clothing had never been returned to her. But despite the fact that she was dressed much like the other women, in a long belted tunic and haik, she drew curious looks from everyone in the camp—looks that she returned.

The Berbers were a handsome people, she decided. Most of the men she saw possessed the same fine aquiline features as Jafar, though many of them wore beards.

Some of the Berber men had wives to see to their needs, she concluded, but there was a cooking tent where the meals for the soldiers and servants were prepared by the women of the camp. When Saful allowed her to pause at the cooking tent, Alysson saw Tahar at work with some dozen other woman.

"Ehla," Tahar said with a shy smile. "Welcome."

Alysson returned her smile with genuine pleasure and watched as the women prepared the main meal. They were cooking over fires fueled by dried camel's dung, delicately roasting desert partridges which Tahar called *ketaa,* and making the customary couscous, the national dish of Barbary. This was not sweet like the couscous at breakfast, however. The steamed wheat semolina was served with pieces of lamb and vegetables.

Alysson was reluctant to leave the women, but later that day, after she had returned to her tent, she was able to ask Mahmoud about his people. Grudgingly he told her something of Jafar's tribe.

There were Arabised Berbers, she learned, who normally lived in the mountains. All of the men and many of the women spoke fluent Arabic. When in the desert they adopted the ways of the Bedouins, but Mahmoud clearly considered himself and his people better than the Bedouins.

"Berbers are *men,"* he said proudly, puffing out his skinny chest so far that Alysson was hard-pressed not to laugh.

Yet she had heard the same thing said admiringly by a French Legionnaire who despised most Arabs. And Gervase had said the Berbers were a proud and fiercely independent people, who enjoyed fighting and who in battle showed magnificent bravery and spirit.

When she pressed Mahmoud to tell her about the women in the camp, she learned that Tahar was second wife to one of the warriors, but served Jafar as chief cook since he had no wives of his own.

"He has no wives?" Alysson repeated curiously, though why that fact should interest her, she would not allow herself to reflect on. She also discovered something else that surprised her.

"The lord has no slaves in his household," the boy told her.

"None? But I thought the chieftains in Barbary usually kept slaves."

"He does not permit it."

"Why not?"

Mahmoud shrugged but could not explain.

But even without slaves, Alysson learned, Jafar had ample followers to serve him. Here, like in other Berber tribes, the members were divided into vassals who did all the manual work, and nobles who were required to do none.

Jafar was very definitely a noble, and yet he was not averse to physical labor, Alysson had to conclude. That very evening, after he had sent his equerry on some errand, he saw to the feeding of his horses himself. She could see him through the open door of the tent, his body a dark, lean silhouette against the lavender sky.

Despite her best intentions, Alysson was drawn to the doorway. Settling herself on the carpet, she wrapped her arms around her knees and pretended interest in the desert.

Eventually darkness fell and a crescent moon came out. The scene was beautiful, she thought, gazing out beyond the *douar* at the silvered landscape. Moonlight rippled over the pale desert sands, pooling in hollows and making the black shadows of ridges stand out in stark relief.

Yet her gaze kept straying from the distant sands to the man who had brought her here against her will, who had turned her life upside-down and stirred her feelings into a turmoil of nervousness and confusion. The night surrounded him, but lamplight from within the tent cast a faint glow over him as he tended to the horses.

Not for the first time since being taken captive, Alysson found herself wondering what kind of man Jafar truly was.

He was a leader, that much she knew. A hard man, certainly. But whether he was cruel and vindictive, she wasn't yet sure. Although he was often surrounded by others, he seemed to hold himself apart. She had never seen him laugh with any of his men. In fact the closest thing to friendship she'd seen him exhibit had been with his horses. He seemed, if not lonely, then alone. But he was a warlord. Perhaps he couldn't allow any of his men to become too close for fear of losing their respect—although that explanation didn't seem to fit. She believed Jafar el-Saleh would command respect, no matter how intimate or distant he became.

At the moment he seemed more approachable than usual, for he was treating his big black stallion like a pet hound. He'd removed the nose bag of barley, and was hand-feeding the noble beast dried dates, one at a time. The stallion apparently was accustomed to this ritual, for it chewed each one before skillfully spitting out the pit.

Alysson watched for a moment, then surprised herself by speaking. "Thank you . . . for allowing me to walk around the camp this morning."

Jafar looked over his shoulder, holding her glance. "I gave you my trust because you had earned it."

His reply stirred both anger and guilt in her. Anger because he'd apparently been giving her another of his "lessons in obedience." Guilt because she hadn't earned his trust. She'd spent much of the time searching, memorizing, plotting her escape.

Lowering her gaze, Alysson restlessly plucked at the skirt of her russet-colored robe. After a while, though, she found herself watching Jafar and the stallion again.

The noble animal obviously had a great fondness for Jafar, playfully nuzzling its intelligent head against him and nibbling at his fingers. The sight was almost amusing, Alysson thought, for the black beast most certainly had been trained as a war-horse. Its lean and vigorous lines were pure Barb, a breed noted throughout the world for speed and endurance.

This animal was rawboned and powerful, with a flowing tail and long thick mane that fell to the right side because

Arabs mounted on the right. The Barb stallion was not, Alysson decided, as handsome as her Arab mare, which possessed a refined head and silky mane. But in this savage land, beauty was relative. Here a man's life often depended on the ability of his mount. The swiftness to pursue or elude an enemy, the stamina to gallop across miles of desert or mountain range, the courage to charge an enemy in battle, all would be considered far more important than mere beauty, and valued far more highly.

She watched in spite of herself as Jafar began grooming the stallion, rubbing its sleek black coat with a woolen cloth. "Your horse," she said after a while. "What is he called?"

"Sherrar. It means 'warrior' in my language."

Alysson nearly smiled. "Warrior" didn't fit a creature with such a gentle disposition. "Just now he doesn't seem to be living up to his name."

"He is a fine warrior," Jafar said softly, with pride. "I bred him myself."

Jafar's youthful reply made Alysson wonder curiously just how old he was. He seemed fairly young, in his late twenties perhaps, but there was no hint of boyishness about him.

"I've heard that your desert horses are the swiftest in the world."

He nodded. "Here in Barbary the horse is called *chareb-er-rehh*—'drinker of the wind.' "

"How beautiful."

"Yes." He murmured something to the stallion, who flicked its ears attentively. "The best horses are found in the mountains of the Sahara, not the plains," Jafar added after a moment.

His voice was low, muted, and sleekly velvet as the night. Alysson felt it reaching out to stroke her. She stirred uncomfortably. "You treat Sherrar so much like a son, I wonder you didn't name him after you, or someone in your family."

"Muslim horses are never named after people. It would be a sacrilege to give a possession a name used by one of our saints."

"A possession? Does that include slaves, too?"

He slanted a glance at her. "Yes, slaves, too."

"So Arabs give the same names to their slaves as their horses." Her tone was dry.

"In part. Only the best horses are given names, whereas every slave has one."

"What an honor."

Jafar flashed her a smile of amusement. Touched by its warmth, Alysson was never more aware of the contradictory feelings he produced in her. When he looked at her so intently, so intimately, she wanted to flee. For it was when her captor was treating her with gentleness and admiration that he was the most dangerous.

You will call me lover. You will respond to me with passion.

Disconcerted by the intrusive memory, Alysson forced herself to maintain her wry tone. "I suppose infidels are not allowed names of people, either."

"Naturally not."

"So to you I am an nonentity. I always knew it."

"You are hardly that." He looked up from his grooming to consider her. "I think if I were to name you, I would call you *Temellal*. It means 'beauty.'"

"But I am not beautiful."

He gave her an odd look.

"I'm not!"

Seeing her startled gray eyes, Jafar realized she actually believed his words were empty flattery. But he'd spoken only the truth. Perhaps she didn't possess the classic beauty that sculptors raved about, or the insipid looks that the English gentry considered fashionable. But there was a fire and intensity about her, a vibrant, restless energy that was indeed beautiful. Such spirit was to be prized in a woman—although some of his countrymen might not agree, Jafar was aware.

Alysson was only aware of the discomfiting way Jafar was regarding her. It brought a flush of warmth to her cheeks. "But you always call me 'Ehuresh,'" she said in distraction. "Is that a Berber word?"

"Yes." Jafar's mouth curved in a brief smile. "It loses something in the translation, but essentially it means 'one who defies.' That, too, fits you well."

This discussion was becoming far too intimate for Alysson's peace of mind. "Why don't you own any slaves?" she asked quickly to change the subject.

"What makes you think I don't?"

"Mahmoud told me."

"Mahmoud has a loose tongue."

"Is it supposed to be a secret?"

"No."

It was only when he remained silent for a long while that Alysson realized he didn't intend to reply to her question. Yet he seemed to be in a relaxed mood. Perhaps she might persuade him to answer some other questions she had, such as why had he abducted her, and what were his plans for her.

"If you won't talk about that," she ventured to ask, "could you possibly tell me how much longer you intend to keep me here?"

"It depends."

"On what?"

"On when your fiancé comes for you."

Startled, bewildered, she fell silent.

"I expect by now the colonel is searching for you," Jafar said, his expression deliberately impassive.

"How could you possibly know what Gervase would or would not do?"

He shrugged. "I have spies in the French government. I pay them well to keep me informed of the colonel's movements."

Spies? That no doubt was how he had managed to arrange her capture so easily. A hollow, sinking feeling suddenly welled in the pit of Alysson's stomach. "Just . . . just what is it you want with me?"

"I told you. Merely your presence."

"But why? What ever good could my presence do you?"

He was silent for so long that at first she thought he didn't mean to answer. When finally he spoke, his tone was quiet and deadly. "It will afford our troops an engagement with the French army."

His reply made Alysson shiver. Was that what he wanted? A battle with the French army? Then she remembered something Jafar had said just after he'd taken her captive. *I sincerely hope the French army does come for you, the good colonel most of all.* Did he mean to lure them into a trap of some kind? If so, then she was the bait. Dear God . . .

She opened her mouth to speak, but the words lodged in her suddenly dry throat. It was a long moment before she could force herself to reply. "You mean to use me to trick the French army into fighting you?"

"I mean to fight the French, yes."

But it doubtless would not be a fair fight. This ruthless Berber warlord would set the terms of the battle to his great advantage. Countless men would die, and it would be *her fault.*

The thought made her quake.

"What you've planned is despicable, vile," Alysson declared in a hoarse voice. "It's the act of a coward, using a woman to carry out your treacherous plot."

He didn't acknowledge her comment as he groomed the stallion's powerful hindquarters.

"What will you do with me when I've served my purpose? Kill me? Sell me as a slave?"

That made Jafar pause. Glancing over his shoulder, he met her gaze, his own eyes narrowed. "Afterward you will be free to return to your uncle. Unlike the French, we do not not make war on women and children."

"No?" She laughed, a scoffing, incredulous sound. "Then what do you call your abduction of me?"

"You have not been harmed. I've given you no cause to complain of your treatment," he replied, his voice nonchalant yet having a sharp thrust. "You haven't been raped or beaten or tortured."

She wanted to protest. She wanted to shout at him: *You kissed me. You assaulted me with your caresses. You promised to take my virginity. You threatened to make me respond to you and want you.* He might not have actually hurt her, but his promise of seduction had unnerved her more than any threat of physical torture could have done. And now that she knew what he planned, she was terrified that he would actually succeed in his aims.

Her voice shook when she demanded, "What about your sultan, Abdel Kader? Does he approve of your barbaric methods, using innocent prisoners as bait in your trap?"

"Abdel Kader shows every consideration for this Chris-

tian prisoners, especially women. It distresses him greatly
that they should become victims of our Holy War.''

"Holy War!'' Alysson's voice throbbed with outrage and
dread. "There is nothing in the least 'holy' about your war!
How can you possibly commit countless atrocities and then
claim you do so in the name of your god?''

"By Allah—'' The soft curse rent the air as abruptly Jafar
whirled. In four strides he reached Alysson's side, his fingers closing over her shoulders as he pulled her to her feet.

Alysson stood frozen, shocked by the swiftness of his
assault, frightened by the fury she saw in his burning amber
eyes. She had finally moved him to anger.

She flinched and tried to take a step backward, to break
away, but his fingers gripped her like steel talons as his
words struck her. "All you rich, pampered Europeans, living in your protected world . . . you know nothing of real
atrocities! You should ask the boy who serves you about
barbaric methods. Mahmoud was tortured by the French
and barely escaped with his life.''

Alysson quivered. Jafar's fierce gaze bored into her, giv-
ing no quarter, while his voice dropped to a savage murmur.
"Shall I tell you about other atrocities committed by the
French? About the custom your Legionnaires have adopted?
They make tobacco pouches from the breasts of murdered
Muslim women and then boast of how fine and soft the
leather is.''

To emphasize his point, his hand rose to cup her breast.
There was nothing remotely sensual in his touch; it was a
threatening gesture, purely hostile.

Her heart pounding, Alysson stared up at him, alarmed
by his burning intensity. At the moment this fierce Berber
chieftain seemed hard and unforgiving enough to retaliate
in kind. When suddenly he released her, she exhaled in
relief. Her knees sagging, she sank to the carpet. Jafar
turned back to the stallion and picked up the cloth he had
thrown to the ground.

Alysson watched him warily, afraid of what he might do.
How had their discussion turned so violent so suddenly?
She wished she had never begun this conversation. But he
wasn't done chastising her by any means.

"You call *us* barbaric,'' Jafar muttered. "Surely even you

don't condone the French army's method of 'pacifying' our tribesmen—asphyxiating hundreds of women and children in caves. You heard of that incident, didn't you, mademoiselle?''

"Y-yes," Alysson replied. She had heard of it. Like many, she had been appalled by the actions of one French colonel who had lighted fires at the mouth of a cave in which some five hundred native men, women, and children had taken refuge. The scandal had shocked even the staunchest supporters of French colonization, and had been denounced in France as an abomination.

"The next time fifteen hundred Muslims died," Jafar said almost absently.

"The . . . next time?"

"Two months later another of your French colonels repeated the tactic. You never learned of it because it was kept out of the French newspapers." Jafar shook his head in disgust. "Don't talk to me of barbaric methods."

Irritated by his accusing tone, Alysson lifted her chin, mustering her courage. "That still doesn't excuse the abominable acts carried out by your side. Only a few years ago your Arab troops massacred the French garrison at Biskra."

The look Jafar gave her was hard and angry. "Those were soldiers, men who chose to fight and die in a war the rapacious French government began. Soldiers who never quailed at murdering entire villages of civilians, I might add."

"What then of all the innocent French settlers who have been slaughtered?"

"*Innocent* settlers who stole our land over the bloody corpses of our people? This is wartime, Miss Vickery. What did you expect us to do, welcome them with open arms?"

Alysson fell silent, thinking of all the senseless carnage that had resulted from the war. No one had been spared, not the innocent, not the women and children. And even they had been guilty of atrocities. Indeed, the women of Barbary were said to be even more fierce and savage than the men.

With a shudder, she remembered a Legion officer discussing with apparent relish the horrible mutilation of captured French soldiers after a particularly bloody battle, how the Arab women enacted unspeakable tortures upon wounded Frenchmen before finally allowing them mercy in death. That was why, the Legionnaire claimed, it was better to die in the first assault than to survive to become hostage to their cruelty.

Alysson might have mentioned that to Jafar, but she saw no point in debating the issue of which side had been more vicious. The humane conventions of war had been ignored on both sides. And, thankfully, at least now the war had ended. If only her Berber captor would come to accept it.

"The war is over," Alysson said finally. "Don't you realize that? You can never win."

Jafar's fingers fisted around the cloth in his hand. "Perhaps. But we will never cease trying to drive back the invaders who conquered our shores."

"But more killing won't solve a thing. Don't you see? It is so pointless!"

Hearing the note of anguish in her voice, he turned and met her troubled gray eyes. "Fighting tyranny is never pointless, mademoiselle."

She stared at him, her expression one of frustrated incomprehension. Seeing her despair, Jafar suddenly wanted her to understand. He wanted her to know what drove him to defy the conquering French against impossible odds, what made him hate this particular enemy so much that it was a festering wound within him.

"Consider for a moment, if you will," he said in a rough whisper, "why we have such a hatred of the French. They swarmed over our country, burning with a love of conquest, and wrought destruction on everything they touched. They polluted our wells, burned our crops, raped and killed our women, orphaned our children, profaned our mosques and graves . . . They surpassed in barbarity the *barbarians* they came to civilize."

He paused, his burning gaze holding hers. "Not satisfied with the pace of acquisition, then, they violated their own treaties of peace and seized private properties without compensation. Then they taxed and exploited our impoverished population to the point of starvation, and forced the weakest of us into servitude. The despoilment is unending. The French are filled with an insatiable greed. They want our plains, our mountains, our inland cities. They covet our horses, tents, camels, women. At the same time they hold in disdain our laws and customs, our religion, and expect us to endure the contempt of their white race, their arrogant sentiments of racial superiority."

Jafar muttered a word in his language that Alysson knew was a curse, but his gaze never left her. "Do you honestly expect me and my people to bow our necks to a foreign yoke without a struggle? To surrender to French domination without a fight?"

The question, soft and savage, echoed in the silence.

"You say the war is over," Jafar declared softly. "I say it will never be over. Not as long there is a single Frenchman residing on African soil. The French will be our enemy, always and forever."

Alysson slowly shook her head, understanding his bitter hostility for the French, but not his particular hatred for Gervase. The French might be his enemy, but it was Gervase he had singled out. "But . . . you don't just plan to make war on the French army, do you? There is more to it. You've planned some sort of revenge against Gervase. That's why you've abducted me."

His golden eyes locked with hers without flinching. "Yes."

The single word was curt, adamant, unrelenting.

The sick dread in Alysson stomach intensified. "And when Gervase does come for me?" Her voice was a hoarse whisper. "What do you intend to do to him then?"

Abruptly Jafar's features became impassive, his gaze unfathomable. Breaking the contact of their gazes, he turned away. "The colonel will get precisely what he deserves."

Alysson felt herself shaking. He meant to kill Gervase, she was certain. And that thought frightened her more than anything that had happened to her since her capture.

Trembling, she rose to her feet. "I hope you burn in hell."

Jafar's tone, when he replied, was cold. "The prospect of your Christian hell holds no terror for me, mademoiselle."

Alysson clenched her fists. She hated him at that moment, with a fierceness she hadn't thought possible. Yet she hated her helplessness even more.

With a sound that was nearly a sob, she turned and fled into the relative safety of the tent.

Watching her go, Jafar gritted his teeth, while the knuckles of his hand turned white from gripping the cloth. Within him, the cold rage of vengeance faded, to be replaced by hollow fury at her despair. It galled him that she cared so deeply for that French jackal, Gervase de Bourmont. Galled and sickened him. Yet even in his fury, Jafar found himself struggling against the urge to follow her and comfort her.

What solace could he offer her, though, when he intended to kill the man she planned to marry?

With a violent curse, Jafar set his jaw and forced himself to return to the task of grooming the Barb.

Chapter 9

The noonday dust swirled ripe and hot as Alysson watched the mounted Berber warriors at play. Their activities looked like sport, yet knowing now what she did about their lord's plans, their games took on an ominous significance.

They were practicing for war and death.

From the shelter of Jafar's tent, she watched numbly, with a kind of horrified fascination, unable to look away. The moment Jafar directed his prancing steed toward his tent, though, Alysson retreated inside. She hadn't spoken a word to him for two days, not since the evening he had told her of his plan to lure Gervase and the French army into battle.

For two days the turmoil had eaten away at her. She couldn't sleep and had little appetite; the churning in her stomach wouldn't go away. Her tension, her fear, her feeling of helplessness, had increased tenfold. For now she knew it wasn't only her life at stake. She had heard it said that the Berbers were unconquerable in war. If Jafar succeeded in carrying out his plan, then scores of French soldiers might perish. And Gervase as well, the man who loved her. And her Uncle Honoré.

With brutal clarity she'd suddenly realized what would happen when her uncle learned where she was being held. Honoré would never allow Gervase to search for her alone. Though ill-suited to withstand the rigors of a desert campaign, he would accompany Gervase into the desert to find her. And he might very well die.

"I won't let it happen!" Alysson murmured defiantly, yet the tight ache in her throat belied her determination.

It would be her fault if they were killed; their blood would be on her hands. She was responsible for this situation. If she'd never insisted on accompanying her uncle, she never would have been taken captive, to be used as bait in Jafar's snare.

If only she could send Honoré a message that she was unharmed, that she was relatively safe and well, that he wasn't to come for her, she might rest more easily. At least Gervase was a soldier, a brave and skilled officer who stood a fighting chance against a warlord of Barbary. Just possibly he could avoid whatever terrible fate her demon captor had planned for him.

Exactly what that fate might be she had lain awake contemplating for two nights now. What manner of revenge did Jafar mean to exact? And what had Gervase done to deserve such enmity? Why had Jafar called him "a man with the tainted blood of a murderer in his veins"?

Revenge implied prior acquaintance, so the two men must know each other; indeed, Jafar had implied as much. And he'd done more than imply that her abduction was only a means to an end. He had told her so.

She was his means for revenge.

She should have suspected as much, given the fact that Jafar had yet to harm her. He hadn't raped her, and that in itself should have been portentous.

She could almost wish he had. If Jafar had simply ruined her in order to shame her fiancé, she could have dealt with that. Her reputation had never concerned her overmuch, for she refused to allow society to dictate her actions. She would gladly have sacrificed her good name if it meant sparing Gervase's life. She would even have surrendered her body to her barbaric captor, as he seemed to want. But she realized now that her surrender alone would not satisfy him.

He wanted Gervase's death. That was crystal clear to her now. And she knew instinctively that nothing she could do or say would change his mind. Jafar was not a man who would be swayed by pleas or tears. Nor could she appeal to his moral conscience or his sense of honor. This was not England. This was the desert, where civilized rules didn't apply, where standards of honor were far different than in her country. Here in Barbary, women were possessions to be bought and sold and used. Here men took what they wanted. Here men like Jafar el-Saleh made their own laws.

"Good afternoon, *ma belle.*"

Alysson tensed at Jafar's greeting as he entered the tent. Deliberately, she turned and gave him her back.

Behind her, Jafar swore silently. For the past two days, his lovely young prisoner had treated him as if he were a viper she had found hidden under a rock. Her disdain annoyed him fiercely. Her smoldering silence, too, irritated him. And this from a woman! Only to his English grandfather had he ever owed deference; only to his sultan did he owe allegiance now—and that only because he chose to. And yet he believed Alysson Vickery deserved an explanation for why he'd involved her in his personal vendettas. He had tried to make her understand his reasons for opposing the French invaders, but she was obviously too stubborn to try and comprehend.

Worse than annoyance, though, was the way his heart wrenched every time he saw the torment in her expressive eyes. Her distress at his revelations was palpable.

It was all he could do to remain unaffected. He hadn't expected to be this moved by her anguish. He wanted to go to her and take her in his arms. He wanted to kiss away the misery on her face. He wanted to drive away her hatred and fill her with passion . . . passion for himself and not his blood enemy.

Determined to ignore such weakness in himself, Jafar crossed his arms over his chest. He could not allow his resolve to be softened by her despair. There was far too much at stake.

"Allah is merciful," he said tauntingly. "He has seen fit to bless me with a model captive."

Her only response was a narrow-eyed glance over her shoulder.

"A silent woman is unique in my experience."

There was mockery in his tone and in his eyes. Alysson stiffened in fury. The scathing look she sent him could have torched wet kindling.

In response, Jafar slowly strode across the tent to her side. When he raised his hand to gently brush her cheek, though, Alysson recoiled from his caress.

"If you touch me, I swear I'll kill you!"

His golden gaze hardened. "You dare defy me?" he asked in a voice that was lethally quiet.

"Yes, I dare defy you, you . . . barbarian."

Deliberately, with careful precision, he reached up and grasped her chin. Alysson cringed.

His eyes surveyed her flushed face, her frightened expression. "That would not be wise, *chérie*. For then I would have to punish your defiance."

Holding her breath, Alysson quivered with outrage and fear and something else that she didn't want to name.

"Perhaps," Jafar added softly, his gaze dropping to her trembling lips, "I should punish you with kisses, since you profess to dislike them so much."

The desire that she had refused to acknowledge made her heart race and her skin turn hot. "N-no . . ." she whispered, but he didn't seem to hear. His fingers shifting, he stroked his thumb slowly over her lower lip, barely grazing the warm moist interior.

"Temellal," he murmured. "My beauty."

I shall be your lover. He hadn't spoken the words, and yet she heard the silent whisper. And, incredibly, she wanted to believe.

Her emotions in turmoil, Alysson stared at Jafar, trying to fathom the bewildering way he made her feel. How could she be so affected by a man she hated? How could she feel this unnerved, this feminine, this shivery? What gave him the power to make her knees so weak, to make her heart hammer so? What gave him the ability to shatter her firmest resolve with merely a look from his hot, amber eyes?

Try as she might, she couldn't prevent what his nearness did to her, or ignore the stunning awareness she felt for this man. All she could do was remember how he had once kissed her—the heat of his mouth, the masculine taste of him, the tender skill of his hands. Jafar overwhelmed her with sensations, made her forget who she was, who he was. He made her own body betray her. She *wanted* him to kiss her again, to touch her, to take her in his arms . . .

"No," she whispered again, desperation giving her the strength to protest.

His expression was gentle, his stroking touch erotic, his tone low and husky as he murmured, "You should thank me, *Temellal,* for taking you away from Bourmont. He is no match for your intelligence or spirit. Nor is he man enough to make a woman of you."

The remembrance of Gervase, of the peril he was in, sent a wave of guilt flooding through Alysson. Guilt for desiring Jafar. Guilt for even momentarily forgetting her responsibility to Gervase, to her uncle, to her country, even. It made her humiliatingly aware of how dangerously close she had been to succumbing to Jafar's sensual caress. With near-panic, she pulled away from his hold. "Don't talk to me of Gervase!" she nearly shouted at him. "You aren't fit to polish his boots!"

A muscle flexed in Jafar's jaw. He stared at her for a long moment before letting his hand fall, and turning, finally, left the tent.

Watching with fervent relief, Alysson set her teeth. She couldn't allow him to bait her like this. She couldn't allow him to use her this way, as his pawn, his instrument of revenge. She couldn't allow his vital male presence to overwhelm her senses.

She had to pull herself together. She had to think, to plan. She had to eat in order to keep up her strength. She had to sleep so she would have the energy to escape this fiend who had abducted her and who threatened the lives of those she loved. She had to discover any information she could about her captors which might give her even the slightest advantage.

With that objective in mind, she questioned Mahmoud later that afternoon about Jafar and his conflict with the French.

The conversation did not go smoothly. The moment she mentioned the French, Mahmoud cursed. "Zfft! May those sons of jackals live in misery and contempt!"

But she did manage to draw from the boy more details about his master. From what she could glean, Jafar was a powerful *amghar*—administrator of a large Berber tribe. He also held the additional title of *caid,* which meant he had been appointed by the Sultan of the Arabs, Abdel Kader, to act as the local official of the loosely organized Arab government.

Mahmoud's prideful disclosures only confirmed what Alysson already suspected. Jafar el-Saleh was a monolith of authority and fearlessness, a Berber chieftain who had taken the field for the freedom and independence of Algeria.

In all honesty, she couldn't blame Jafar for defying his enemy, the French. That she could understand. She even could almost admire his fortitude in the face of such vast odds. He was fighting for what he believed in, against oppression, against his country's conquerors.

It was his unwavering determination to exact revenge that tormented her. She couldn't bear to think that she might be the instrument of Gervase's death, or that of her beloved uncle.

She had to stop Jafar somehow.

But how? His tribe's loyalty to their lord was unquestionable. It would be nearly impossible to bribe any of them, or persuade them to aid her.

After her disheartening discussion with Mahmoud, Alysson began to think she might never succeed in preventing Jafar from carrying out his vile plan. Quite against her normal optimistic nature, she found herself fighting an overwhelming sense of despair.

That, however, was before she stole the dagger.

It was the following afternoon, during her daily walk around the camp. She had spent the morning asking Mahmoud about the Berber language, and convincing him to teach her a few words. If she could learn enough to understand, Alysson hoped, she might be able to overhear some scrap of information that would be of use to her.

An apt pupil, she caught on quickly. By the time her blue-eyed Berber guard came to collect her for her walk, Alysson was able to surprise him by greeting him in his own language. And when during her tour she visited the camp's cooking tent where Tahar was busy with the other woman, she used the opportunity to practice her new skills. Tahar had called on her twice in the past few days, apparently on Jafar's orders, but with his threat against Gervase preying on her mind, Alysson had been too distracted to enjoy her budding friendship with the Berber woman.

Accepting the handful of parched chickpeas Tahar offered her to eat, Alysson asked questions as the women worked, determined to learn the Berber names for various objects. Her efforts at pronunciation earned both good-natured laughter and respect from the ladies, but after a time she could see Saful growing impatient as he waited by the entrance to the tent.

She was just about to leave when she spied the dagger—a small curved blade that had been used to carve the meat—lying on a platter. Her heartbeat burst into a savage rhythm. Was this the chance she had been waiting for?

Pretending to admire a dish, Alysson surreptitiously scooped up the knife and concealed it in a fold of her robe. Her heart still pounding, she shot a glance at her blue-eyed guard. He hadn't seen her.

Masking both her triumph and trepidation, she said farewell to Tahar, then continued her tour of the camp. By the time she returned to Jafar's tent, she was having difficulty controlling her nervousness, an agitation that only increased when Jafar didn't join her for the midday meal. She had managed to arm herself, but had yet to decide how to exploit her advantage.

The dagger could mean her freedom. She could use it to overpower her guard and steal a horse—but her escape no doubt would be immediately detected. No, she would be better off waiting till the camp was asleep for the night. Jafar would be the only one guarding her then.

And then what?

As she sat staring out at the Berber encampment, consid-

ering the answer to that question, a dark shadow suddenly
spread over the camp. Glancing up uneasily, Alysson realized the sun had disappeared behind a stormcloud.

A few moments later she received her first taste of rain
in the desert, a fierce deluge that threatened to wash away
the camp. Then, just as suddenly as it had begun, the down-
pour abated and the sun came out again, drawing the dampness in heavy steam-clouds from the reeking sand. In half
an hour the streams and rivulets created by the storm had
vanished, and the coating of desert mud was dry. After the
earlier heat, though, the afternoon now seemed winter-cold.

Shivering, Alysson absently fingered the sharp blade hidden in her robes.

The real question was, could she bring herself to use it
on another human being?

Could she kill Jafar?

Her opportunity came that evening, when Jafar returned.
By that time, Alysson's nerves were worn to a fine edge,
yet she still had not come to a decision.

She watched Jafar surreptitiously as he read one of his
French journals before supper, her mouth tightening with
annoyance and dismay at the picture he made. He looked
even more attractive than usual tonight. Wearing a sky-blue
djellaba—a long robe of fine wool—Jafar reclined on the
cushions with assured masculine grace, his eyes firelighted
with amber, his tawny hair gleaming in the lamplight.

Alysson studied him without wanting to, noting his lean
features . . . the high cheekbones, the hard line of his jaw
and mouth. They seemed faintly arrogant and savagely noble, and filled with determination. Jafar was quite capable
of carrying out his diabolical plan for revenge, unless she
could prevent him.

Her hand trembled as she touched the knife hidden in her
robe, but she left her fingers lying against the blade, needing the reassurance the cold steel gave her. Could she do
it? Could she use the knife to stop him? Could she kill Jafar?

She was grateful when Mahmoud appeared to serve the
evening meal, but the cold knot of tension in her stomach
destroyed her appetite entirely. She merely toyed with her
supper, all the while conscious of Jafar's intent gaze on her.

"It disturbs me that you are not eating, *ma belle*," he said finally. "You cannot afford to lose much weight."

Alysson was in no mood to suffer his amused taunting. "Why don't you go to the devil and leave me alone?"

He eyed her with calm self-control. "Finish your food. It might improve your disposition."

The food didn't help, however. She managed to choke down a few bites, but they only churned in her stomach.

When she pushed away her plate, Jafar gestured to the servant to clear away the dishes. Mahmoud, salaaming deeply, obeyed and then left for the evening.

"I understand Mahmoud neglected his duties this morning in order to entertain you," Jafar said, sipping his coffee.

The probing note of query in his tone made Alysson eye him warily. Was that an accusation? Was Jafar fishing for details? Or had he already learned from his servant about her vocabulary lesson that morning, the way he seemed to learn of everything else that occurred in his camp?

"It was nothing so enjoyable as entertainment," she replied cautiously. "Mahmoud was only teaching me your language."

"I didn't think you would put yourself to so much trouble."

Alysson shrugged, trying to hide the tension rioting within her. "I was bored."

"Or intent on gaining an advantage over us ignorant savages?"

"Can you blame me if I was? You said a wise man learns the language of his enemy."

"Indeed." Hard golden eyes challenged gray. "It is a wise strategy. But your knowledge of our language will make no difference to the outcome of your captivity. You will not escape me. And you would do better not to try."

His soft warning echoed in the close confines of the tent. Alysson stared at him, her heart pounding. Did he know about the knife?

The uneasy silence stretched between them until Alysson thought her nerves would shatter.

To her bewilderment, then, Jafar shifted his position and returned to reading his journal. He had presented his back to her, leaving himself wholly, carelessly, vulnerable to attack.

She watched him for a long while, indecision warring within her.

Her mouth dry, Alysson reached inside the folds of her robe to grasp the handle of the dagger. If she could get near enough to him, if she could move closer on the pretext of searching for a book, perhaps, it would be relatively simple to drive the blade into his back, deep, between the shoulder blades.

The hand holding the dagger suddenly grew slick with sweat. The thought of how easily that sharp point would slide into his flesh made her sick.

Shutting her eyes, Alysson mentally railed at herself. How could she be such a coward? She had killed wild game before. She had shot tigers in India, wild boars in Russia. Once she had even brought down a rabid wolf.

And this desert chieftain was no better than that wolf. Any capacity for compassion or forgiveness he might once have possessed had been eaten up, destroyed, by his need for revenge.

But even the knowledge of his ruthlessness wasn't enough. With a feeling akin to despair, she realized she couldn't bring herself to do it. She couldn't kill a man this way. Not him. Not in cold blood.

Releasing a ragged breath, she eased her hand away from the dagger. She would have to think of another way. She would have to wait until Jafar was sleeping and then use the dagger to free herself from her bonds. If she were lucky, she could manage to steal from the tent, take one of the horses, and be miles away before Jafar awoke. If she were not . . .

No, she wouldn't consider the consequences of failure.

Slowly, Alysson wiped her palm on the skirt of her robe, ridding it of dampness. She had made her decision—a decision that strangely relieved her.

Now she could only pray.

She lay in the darkness, listening to the soft even sound of Jafar's breathing, and watching the faint red-gold light from the brazier's coals dancing upon the tent walls.

Two hours ago, when Jafar as usual had given her time alone to prepare for bed, she had hidden the dagger beneath the edge of the pallet. It had been all she could do to pretend disinterest as Jafar tied the silken cord around her ankle. It had been even harder to pretend sleep, to lie there beside him as if every nerve in her body was not taut with apprehension. Yet she had to wait until she was certain her movements would not awaken him.

She let another hour pass, each minute seeming like an eternity. Then, finally, she slid her hand stealthily beneath the pallet to retrieve the dagger.

The smooth wooden handle felt cool against her clammy palm as she drew it out. Jafar didn't stir.

She waited another long moment, her heart thrumming an erratic rhythm. Taking a deep breath, then, Alysson slowly eased herself into a sitting position. Furtively, she stole a glance at Jafar. He hadn't stirred. His naked chest rose and fell in a relaxed rhythm.

Not daring to breathe, she leaned forward to cut her bonds, pushing aside the blanket and slipping the blade in the space between their ankles. With infinitely careful strokes, she managed to slice the cord that bound her to Jafar.

Some instinct warned her the instant before he moved; the hairs on the back of her neck stood straight up. Panicking, she tried to bolt, yet her desperate lunge wasn't enough to save her. In a startling swift motion, Jafar snaked an arm around her waist and jerked her backward, into his arms.

The next moment he shifted his weight and rolled over her. Before she could even cry out, Alysson found herself pinned beneath his lean body, his fingers clamped around the hand that held the dagger.

Too shocked to utter a sound, she stared into the feral gold eyes glittering down at her. In the faint light, she could make out the hard, chiseled face, the strong flared nostrils, the glint of white teeth.

And what she read in his savage expression terrified her. So did his gently whispered, "A grave mistake, *chérie.*"

His hand slid to her throat, resting lightly on the vulnerable exposed curve, his fingers capable of tightening to a stranglehold. His other hand pried loose the dagger and tossed it the width of the chamber, out of reach. "You should never have hesitated when you had the chance to kill me."

His tone, so harsh and cold, made her want to tremble. "I w-wasn't . . . going to use the knife on you," she murmured, ashamed of the way her voice quavered.

Jafar's gaze narrowed ominously. "No? Why not, I wonder? I gave you ample opportunity, all evening long. I expected you to strike any time these past few hours."

A breath caught in Alysson's throat. *He had known.* Somehow he had known about the dagger she had stolen. And he had been waiting for her to make her move.

Forcing back her trepidation, she raised her trembling chin. Never would she admit to him that she hadn't had the courage to kill him. "I am not a murderer, like you are!"

It was the wrong thing to say. His grip loosening, Jafar's hand skimmed downward over the sheer white linen of her chemise, coming to rest threateningly on the swell of her breast. "How foolish of you to disregard my warnings." His touch remained gentle, almost a caress, but it raised gooseflesh on her skin; she could feel his simmering anger. "By now you should know better than to challenge your master."

"You are not my master," she hissed through gritted teeth.

"Yes," he replied almost as fiercely, "I am your master, my proud beauty. And it is long past time you were taught that lesson."

Alysson stared at him, a new fear dawning on her. "What . . . do you mean to do?"

His eyes held hers in the darkness. "Aren't you woman enough to know?"

His whisper, harsh yet sensual, sent a strange thrill quivering down her spine. Yet seeing the smoldering coals in his eyes, feeling the masculine arousal of his body that pinned hers down, she could have no doubt as to his meaning. Tonight, he would become her lover. It was to be her punishment for defying him.

Alysson went pale with shock. "No . . ." she pleaded as she began to struggle ineffectually against him.

He caught her flailing arms, pressing his body harder

against hers. "Yes, my fierce tigress. You will learn to obey me. Now. Tonight." Jafar hesitated, gazing down at her. "And before the night is over," he said, lowering his head slowly, "you will learn about pleasure."

"No!" she cried again, just before he covered her defiant lips with his own.

It was a stunning assault. It was a seizure that punished, that dominated her mouth with a dangerous and cruel sensuality. His tongue, like a hot dagger, stabbed past her lips to invade the recesses of her mouth, thrusting deep to overwhelm her resistance.

Shaken, dazed, Alysson could scarcely find the strength to fight him. If a woman could be ravished by a single kiss, that was what Jafar was doing to her. Completely and irrevocably, he claimed her, in an invasion that held such intimacy she found it hard to breathe. With almost practiced detachment he set about subduing her, mastering her. Ruthlessly he learned the taste of her and forced her to learn the taste of him. She could feel the anger making his body taut, yet in some dim recess of her mind, she knew he was using her not only to vent his fury, but also because he desired her.

In turmoil, Alysson whimpered, as much in fear of the fierce sensations he was making her feel as in protest of his harsh treatment. Abruptly Jafar gentled his assault. Tenderly now, as though trying to kiss away the hurt he'd inflicted before, he moved his mouth over hers in a tantalizing display of controlled passion. Coaxing. Careful. Alysson felt the first stirring of a familiar response that she'd learned to deplore, the sweet awakening of desire. *No*, her mind screamed, and yet her body, her traitorous body, reacted so differently.

She was panting for breath by the time Jafar finally lifted his head. When he gazed down at her, she could see the dark light of desire in his jeweled eyes.

"*Ehuresh,*" he whispered. "My lovely defiant one."

Her lips parted in protest as he reached up to loosen the drawstring of her chemise, but he forestalled her by pressing his fingers gently against her lips.

"Don't fight me. You cannot win." His voice was a low

rasp as he slowly drew down the bodice of the garment to bare her breasts.

Alysson closed her eyes, feeling shame, both at the possessive intimacy of his heated gaze, and the traitorous yearning it aroused in her. But she obeyed; she didn't fight him as his hand roamed downward.

Deliberately, with the slowest of seductive movements, he captured her breast. Alysson drew a sharp breath, then went rigid as he caught her nipple between his thumb and forefinger. His bold fondling dredged another gasp from her lips. She hadn't expected the brutal rush of feeling as her nipple tightened unbearably, or the hard, rebellious ache that flared quickly between her shivering thighs.

She should struggle, Alysson told herself as he molded the satin flesh of her breasts with his long fingers. She should resist him with every ounce of strength she possessed. She should try to escape his vengeful lovemaking. Yet she couldn't summon the will. Besides his superior strength and overwhelming masculine vitality, she was also fighting the dazing sense that what would happen between them was inevitable. They were meant to be lovers. He had told her so, and she, God help her, believed.

She remained trembling and still when he divested her of her chemise, not pulling away as he tossed the garment aside. Helplessly, Alysson lay naked to his gaze, to his touch, her heart pounding.

His eyes swept slowly over her body. "Beautiful," he murmured, the French word a husky rasp. Alysson could feel herself quivering at the seductive promise in his tone.

Without leaving her side, he drew back to quickly shed his trousers. In the darkness, she glimpsed the beautiful, sculptured perfection of his male form—his body lithe as a cat's, as sleek and powerful as his favorite stallion's. Then he returned to gather her in his arms.

His naked skin was hot to the touch, Alysson realized with an acute sense of awareness. Every angle of him fit intimately against her, making her feel the thin dusting of his leg hair stroking her own smoothness, the hard wall of his muscled chest meeting the yielding swell of her naked breasts, the shocking evidence of his desire pressing against her abdomen. Alysson stiffened at that hard, vital ridge of flesh. Startled by the enormous size of him, by his very maleness, she shivered with fear and an unaccountable thrill of longing. Dear God, what was happening to her? She couldn't allow him to continue.

"No . . . I can't let you . . ." she whispered.

His eyes glittered with heated promise as he gazed at her. "Yes . . . you can, *ma belle.*" His gentle reply held no margin for negotiation.

She watched the play of light and darkness in his eyes as he began to caress her. His movements were slow, so slow. And incredibly stirring. Caught by the wonder of it, Alysson remained completely still, until his fingers glided between her thighs.

"No!" she gasped again, clutching at his arm to prevent him from proceeding further.

"Yes." Jafar bent his head to kiss the corner of her mouth. "Open for me, *Ehuresh.* Let me take you to paradise." His fingers threading in the curls hiding her femininity, he lowered his mouth to hers again, its warmth moving hotly over her lips.

She made one last frantic attempt to break away, but his mouth kept hers captive. He wouldn't let her go. His kiss was hot and deep and long, his hands hard and skilled on her body, arousing her in ways she had never dreamed possible. Desperately, she fought the tightening of her body, trying to hold herself aloof, but it was no defense against his warm mastery. She found herself clutching at his shoulders, even as she opened her mouth further to his thrusting tongue and arched her spine to meet his caressing fingers.

Feeling her involuntary yielding, Jafar slowly parted her thighs, opening her to his caress. When his fingers touched a dewy warmth, Alysson inhaled a sharp breath.

"See, your honey flows for me," Jafar murmured, his voice stroking her as his rough fingers were doing. A soft shock of shameful pleasure rippled through Alysson.

She wanted desperately to pull away, but she could only tighten her grip, feeling the muscles of his powerful shoulders coil and slide under the satiny skin. In a dim corner of her mind, she was aware of the tension thrumming through Jafar, the iron control keeping his body rigid, but the hungry plundering of his mouth, the drugging heat of his body, was making her senseless. She was a willing captive.

She shuddered under the intoxicating influence of his lips and hands. For long minutes, he never let up, his tongue pressing into her mouth in an erotic mimicry of his finger's rubbing, thrusting rhythm. In response, she could manage only small, sultry cries of shock and confusion as she writhed against her will, in rhythm with his passion.

A moment later she tensed, suddenly afraid of the white-hot heat building inside her. "No . . ." she gasped in English.

"Yes," Jafar replied harshly in the same language, relentlessly driving her on.

And then the unbelievable things he was doing with his hands and mouth pushed her to the brink of insanity. A scream of pleasure and shame ripped upward through Alysson's throat. Fire streaked through her body, followed by a moment when reality splintered into a thousand sensual fragments of sensation.

Reveling in her heated response, Jafar held her shaking form and whispered her name triumphantly against her mouth. Her intense climax had brought him fierce satisfaction. Her body had surrendered to his, overwhelmed by blind desire. He had brought her to a state of sweet sexual arousal, had given her pleasure, whether she willed it or no.

As her cries faded away, he held himself still, his forehead pressed to hers, his face contorted with pleasure and pain. He wanted to bury himself in her silken heat, to drive into her endlessly. But while he might claim her innocence, while he might make her a woman and teach her the delights of her own body, he wouldn't take her maidenhead.

Forcing himself to move, Jafar eased away from Alysson's shaking body. Frustration screamed through him. He ached with need. Yet he wouldn't take her. It had become a matter of pride. She must come to him willingly.

Willingly.

The image of Alysson giving herself to him, lying beneath him wild and willing, was more than he could withstand. No longer able to control his need, Jafar gave a growl, raw and primitive. "Merciful Allah . . ." he gasped as his body tightened and convulsed. Twisting his hips, he spilled his seed onto the bedcovering.

When it was over, he lay there, his breath coming in harsh pants, his skin covered with a fine sheen of sweat.

Next to him, Alysson lay curled on her side, her face averted, her body weak and spent and throbbing. She was still trying to comprehend what had happened to her—and still unwilling to face herself for what she had allowed Jafar to do. She would have liked to forget it entirely, to obliterate all memory of the past half hour. Yet she couldn't disregard the hard, vital man lying beside her, or the naked awareness of intimacy that pulsed between them. Nor could she dismiss the fact that she had failed in her attempt at escape.

She doubted Jafar would dismiss it either.

"How did you know?" she asked finally, in a tone so low he could barely hear.

He realized without asking that she was speaking of the dagger. Jafar gave a sigh of regret for the intrusion of reality into the sensual moment.

"You are not good at hiding your feelings, *chérie*. Every time you dared look at me this evening, I could see you measuring your chances. I have fought too many men to misunderstand that look."

When Alysson didn't respond, Jafar suspected she was cursing herself for not taking more care to disguise her intentions. But it was not only her assessing glances earlier, or her nervousness, that had aroused his suspicions, but his sharply honed instincts for danger. He had spent half a lifetime guarding against attack and the threat of assassination. In this ruthless country, a man who was not prepared for treachery and violence did not live long.

As for his young captive's actions this evening, he wasn't sure he believed her claim that she hadn't intended to use the knife to kill him. He had expected her to try. Certainly he would have done the same had their positions been reversed, had he been the captive. But then he was not as softhearted as a woman. His heart had hardened to stone seventeen years ago.

Still, Jafar was surprised to realize he didn't blame her for trying to escape. Indeed, he would have admired her less had she not.

Slowly he shifted his weight, rolling onto his side to face her. His anger had cooled, though his blood was still fever-hot. His searing release had left him temporarily sated but totally unfulfilled.

But the night was not over yet.

Before it ended, she would learn what he had always known. The attraction between them could not be denied or banished simply by willing it so. He would teach her a lesson in desire.

Deliberately he reached out to stroke her bare shoulder. Alysson flinched, but Jafar didn't draw back, instead running his hand over her silken skin with a skilled sensitivity. In only a moment she was quivering.

With gentle insistence, Jafar turned her to face him. His eyes glowed with a molten intensity as he drew her full and tight against him, his manhood intimately knowing the cradle of her femininity. His boldness drew a startled gasp from her.

"No . . . don't," Alysson said in a breathless plea.

"No? But I won't do anything you don't wish me to do, *ma belle.*" His gleaming golden eyes held amusement, as if he knew he could make her want him.

You will call me master. The day will come when you beg for my caresses.

The promise echoed in Alysson's mind as Jafar bent to her breasts and began a dizzying, lazy seduction.

"I mean to kiss you here," he murmured against her skin, . . . and here . . . and taste you with my tongue . . ." His hot mouth moved in deliberate provocation, teasing, coaxing, arousing. "Don't deny me this pleasure, *chérie.* Don't deny yourself . . ."

Alysson trembled. With acute dismay, she realized she didn't want him to stop. She wanted him to touch her this way, to kiss her again with tender savagery . . .

Surrendering, she closed her eyes. And when his fingers found that point of hot pleasure that had driven her wild before, she gave a hushed moan and let her head fall back.

That, however, was before he trailed a path of searing kisses down her body and let his mouth replace his hand.

His scandalous action startled a cry of shock and embarrassment from Alysson; her cheeks flamed scarlet as her body gave a sudden jerk, trying to escape.

"Be still, my sweet tigress," Jafar commanded in a husky voice as he caught her flailing hands. He held them at her sides, while his probing kiss invaded her, exploring the yielding, feminine flesh with sure mastery. In only a moment he forced a shuddering moan from her. Then, very slowly, he thrust his tongue into her waiting, honeyed warmth.

Alysson thought she might die of the exquisite pleasure. "No . . ." she whimpered once more, with the last vestiges of reason. "I . . . don't . . . want . . ."

Jafar didn't seem to hear. Instead he laughed. Softly. In arrogant satisfaction. As if he knew her protest was merely to save her pride.

Part Two

Love distills desire upon the eyes, love brings bewitching grace into the heart of those he would destroy. I pray that love may never come to me with murderous intent, in rhythms measureless and wild.

EURIPIDES

Chapter 10

⟨⟐⟩

S unlight filtered beneath the edges of the tent, scattering dreams and flooding consciousness with harsh reality. Alysson groaned and buried her head beneath her pillow. She didn't want to face the morning, yet memories of the scandalous events of last night assaulted her, stimulating emotions that were too humiliating to contemplate.

She had challenged Jafar and lost.

Yet that didn't explain her capitulation. How could she have submitted to Jafar so wantonly? How could she have failed to put up the least resistance? How could she have dishonored Gervase so? She felt self-disgust and shame—because she had surrendered so easily, and, more damningly, because she had felt such profound pleasure in Jafar's arms. She wished now that she had never tried to escape, had never given him reason to force the issue of his power over her. She wished . . .

The thought shriveled abruptly as Alysson became aware of a lean finger stroking her bare shoulder. Raising her head, she looked directly into a pair of lazy-lidded golden eyes. They were calmly watching her, glinting, catlike in the gray light.

"Good morning, *ma belle*," Jafar murmured in a husky voice, the same voice she'd heard whispering endearments and bold persuasions in her ear much of the night.

Alysson shut her eyes tightly. She hadn't dreamed last night. She was lying here naked beneath the blanket, next to Jafar, who was just as naked. Her pride was in tatters, her composure shredded. She wanted to flee, to hide. And yet she couldn't even force herself to move as Jafar trailed his finger languidly along the line of her collarbone.

"There is no need for you to feel shy with me," Jafar

said calmly. "Or to blame yourself. What happened between us was natural . . . and inevitable, as I've told you before."

A flush of hot color rose to her cheeks. He knew exactly how she felt—which made him all the more dangerous. If he could read her mind and predict her reactions, then how much more easily could he bend her to his will?

"I don't blame myself in the least," Alysson retorted stiffly. "You are entirely responsible for what happened last night."

He raised a skeptical eyebrow. "If it comforts you to pretend that I forced you against your will, then do so, but we both know differently."

Deliberately, then, he bent his head. Alysson lay rigid and unmoving as he pressed his lips against the corner of her mouth, then lower, along her throat, brushing aside the hair that tumbled over her naked shoulders to allow him better access. She didn't respond until he drew the blanket down, exposing her breasts to his warm breath.

"No," she whispered then, an echo of the hundred denials she had given him the night before.

"Yes," Jafar contradicted pleasantly. "I want to kiss you here . . . and here . . . I want to ravish you with pleasure . . ."

Shifting his weight, he rolled toward her, pinning her beneath him, gently pressing her down. Alysson felt his masculine hardness, rigid and needing, felt the warm, rough man-thigh that separated hers.

"No!" she protested again, more frantically, more forcefully this time.

"No? Is that all you can say, obstinate one?"

"Damn you . . ."

He chuckled softly. "At least that is an improvement." Despite her protests, though, his mouth lowered to nuzzle her right nipple.

Alysson quivered. How could she fight him when he overwhelmed her this way? He emanated a raw sensuality that was impossible to fight or resist. She felt like a fool for lying here desiring him, and yet she was powerless to do more than demand weakly, "Let me up!"

"Not yet," Jafar murmured as he feasted on her sweet flesh. "Not until you give me what I want."

Frantically Alysson squeezed her hands between their bodies and gripped Jafar's shoulders, pushing with all her strength. To her surprise, she succeeded in making him lift his head. "What more could you possibly want from me?" she cried, panting from the exertion. "You took everything last night."

"Not everything." His mouth curved in an amused smile as he reached up to spread her gleaming chestnut hair over the pillows. "Not nearly everything."

Her gaze dropping, Alysson stared at his hard, beautiful mouth. Did he expect her to kiss him? Was that what he wanted?

"I will allow you up," Jafar said lazily, "but first I expect a polite greeting."

"Go to the devil!"

He raised his hand to catch her chin with his fingers. "That will not suffice, my sweet tigress. A courteous good morning is what I wish from you."

Alysson fumed. This was another of his lessons in obedience, she was certain. "Or what? If I refuse, what will you do?"

"Then I will keep you here in my bed. I can think of a dozen satisfying ways to pass the time."

All of which left her at a vast disadvantage, Alysson thought with barely repressed rancor. "*Good morning*, then," she said through gritted teeth.

"Politely, *ma belle*. Not as if you would like to carve out my heart with the dagger you stole."

He waited, his mouth poised above hers, while she debated defying him. But she knew she would lose this battle, too. Alysson sighed in disgust. "Good morning," she murmured, succeeding in keeping the fury out of her voice.

With an approving smile, Jafar bent to kiss her. Alysson tried to avert her face, but his mouth covered hers, warm and coaxing. When still she resisted, he nipped her bottom lip.

"Don't!"

A laugh, soft, indulgent, was his reply. But he rolled away, allowing her to scramble to her feet. Frantically,

Alysson reached for her clothes. She was pulling on her chemise when Jafar spoke again.

"Last night you were surprised and frightened by the pleasures that a woman can feel, but you will grow accustomed to them—and to me."

"I will *not!*" Alysson retorted stiffly.

"You will. And you will lose your anger at yourself, as well."

"I am not angry at myself! It's you—"

"You are, *chérie.* You are angry because you submitted to me so easily. Your entire posture speaks most eloquently of injured pride."

It was all Alysson could do to repress a retort. She gritted her teeth as she dragged a tunic of white cotton on over her head, entertaining satisfying thoughts about what it would be like to bring this insufferable Berber baron to his knees. He was so arrogant, so secure in his practiced power with women—

Jafar interrupted her thoughts as he chuckled to himself in satisfaction. "Last night, the spitting tigress became a cooing dove."

Driven beyond endurance, Alysson turned to glare at him—a mistake, she realized at once. Reclining on the pillows with his arms behind his head, Jafar looked like some royal Eastern potentate in all his naked splendor. The light of day highlighted the magnificence of his lean, virile body, making her breath catch in her throat.

Alysson knew she should look away, but before she could avert her gaze, Jafar spoke. "You won't find me such a hard master," he said softly, his eyes touching her more intimately than even his hands had done.

Discomfited by his tender look, Alysson turned to fumble with her sash. "I won't find you *any* kind of master," she said tightly. "Your wits have gone begging if you think for one minute I'll allow you to add me to your harem. I refuse to become one of your concubines."

"I have no concubines, *chérie,*" Jafar remarked blandly.

She didn't believe him, not in the slightest. No Eastern lord of his power and wealth would be without dozens of female odalisques to satisfy his needs.

But the thought fled her mind when she heard Jafar rise

from the bed and approach her. Tensing in alarm, she moved away. But he kept coming with the deceptively lazy grace of a stalking cat. Soon there was nowhere to run.

Fighting a burning awareness of his sheer physical nearness, Alysson flinched when Jafar reached out to catch her wrist. Glancing down, she could see the honey-gold hairs gleaming on his arm as he turned her to face him.

"Don't run from me, lover."

Startled by what he had called her, she looked up to find amusement glittering in his eyes. "I am not your lover!"

"Yes, you are, O, donkey ears," he replied, teasing her for her stubbornness. As if to prove his point, he reached up to cup her breast. It was a gesture of possession, gentle but determined.

Alysson's spine went rigid, even as blood rushed to every place in her body that he had taught to feel pleasure. "Don't!" she exclaimed, her voice shaking with intensity, the erratic beat of her heart making a mockery of her thought to escape.

He paid no attention. The fingers of his other hand threading in her hair, Jafar cradled the back of her head with commanding tenderness.

"Don't . . . please," Alysson pleaded, reduced to begging.

He laughed throatily. Pulling her close, he lowered his head.

His kiss was long and deep and hot, arousing her just as he had done last night—effortlessly. Trembling, powerless, Alysson submitted to her new devil master.

A score of pounding heartbeats later, Jafar's mouth slowly pulled away, leaving hers wet and wanting, her body throbbing with unfulfilled longing.

"You must learn how a woman kisses a man," he whispered. "It is an art that will bring us both pleasure."

Alysson swallowed hard as she gazed helplessly at him, her eyes shimmering with the moistness of pride. His arrogant presumption that in time she would beg him to take her seemed all too inevitable. Already he could control her body with his skilled caresses. Already she was beginning to yearn for the spiraling tendrils of desire that assailed her whenever he touched her.

Struggling against the overpowering emotions of shame and despair, she raised her chin and forced a note of loathing into her voice. "Can you even imagine how much I hate you?"

"Yes, my dove, you hate me. So much that your sweet body quivers with desire when I touch you . . ."

Briefly he bent again to brush her lips, his breath warm and moist and scented with the taste of her mouth. Then, reluctantly, he released her.

Alysson fled to the other room, not waiting to comb her tangled hair or even put on sandals.

She did hate him, she thought furiously, wiping her lips to erase the taste and feel of him. She hated him desperately, even while acknowledging his mastery of the art of seduction. And even though she had managed to escape Jafar's presence for the moment, she couldn't escape her chaotic thoughts, or the contemplation of what had happened to her last night.

She was far less sheltered than other young women her age. She hadn't yet grown into womanhood before she'd learned what occurred during the physical mating between a man and a woman. Her ayah—her Indian nurse—had spoken quite freely about the human body and the duties of a woman toward her husband. Hindu texts, the words of gods and sages, taught the science of pleasure and love, and elevated the act of sexual intercourse to a religious ritual. Moreover, India abounded with statues and relics that depicted sexual acts. Alysson would have had to be blind not to notice, and dull-witted not to be curious.

What had happened to her last night had not been the complete act, she knew. Last night she had learned what it meant to be a woman, what it meant to be the object of a man's passion, but Jafar had not gone so far as to claim her virginity. He had held back for some reason. His restraint puzzled her. Especially since he had made it clear he intended to become her lover—

Lover.

Shame flooded her cheeks with hot color as she recalled how easily he had made his promise come true.

Alysson shook her head, her shoulders slumping wearily. There was no denying it; she had surrendered herself to her ruthless captor, to a savage barbarian who intended to murder the man to whom she was practically betrothed. Against her will, her body had betrayed her. And in turn she had betrayed Gervase. She was a traitor both to him and to her own principles. It was unbelievable, unforgivable.

But she wouldn't allow it to continue. She wouldn't permit Jafar to use her as a pawn in his deadly game.

She had to fight him more ardently. She had to strive harder to escape. Gervase's life was at stake, as was her beloved uncle's.

Bringing herself up short, Alysson moved to the door of the tent. Shielding her eyes from the brilliance of the sun, she stared at the sprinkling of color that met her delighted gaze. *Flowers,* she thought with surprise. As a result of the rain yesterday, the sparse desert vista around the camp had suddenly burst into bloom.

There was no sign of her blue-eyed guard, Saful, she realized, glancing around her. But a saddled chestnut horse stood unattended beside the adjacent tent. Alysson was about to turn away when her attention was caught by an object leaning against the tent wall. The long-barreled musket flashed in the sunlight, beckoning to her.

Her gaze arrested, Alysson stared at the weapon. Her eyes shifted once more to the horse.

Did she dare?

She couldn't take the time to consider further; her hesitation last night had ended in disaster. It was a slim chance now that she would both be able to ride the chestnut out of the camp and elude pursuit, but she had to take it.

Girding her courage, she left the shelter of Jafar's tent and ran barefoot across the sandy distance. Scooping up the rifle, she turned to the chestnut.

Arab horses were taught never to run when their reins trailed the ground; they would stand obediently for hours, even days. This animal was no exception. It didn't move as she gathered the reins, although it began to dance skittishly when she tried to mount from the left.

"By the sword of the Prophet!"

Jafar's soft curse made Alysson jump. Reflexively she turned to look over her shoulder, and her heart sank. Jafar stood some three yards away, the expression on his face fierce and dangerous.

"What in the name of Allah do you think you are doing?"

Forcing back her fear, Alysson abruptly swung the musket around, pointing it at Jafar. He might have prevented her from taking the horse as she'd hoped, but he wouldn't disarm her this time the way he had last night with the dagger. She would shoot him first.

"Keep away from me!" she warned, aiming the muzzle at his heart.

Jafar glanced at the weapon, his face becoming cold and impassive. Yet he didn't laugh as he had the last time she'd trained a gun on him.

"You dare much, woman," he said instead—softly, his tone far more threatening than if he had shouted. He took a step toward her.

"Don't move! Or I swear I'll kill you."

"Then do it."

Alysson stared at hard-faced man before her. It seemed to her that his eyes had turned to golden stones. "I will, I swear it! I won't let you use me as bait for your treacherous trap."

"You can't prevent it." Jafar took another step. "Go ahead, *chérie*. Kill me. My men will simply carry on the fight without me."

It was true, she reflected with dismay. Things had gone too far to be turned back, even with his death.

Slowly, with her finger still on the trigger, Alysson rotated the rifle in her hand, till the muzzle pressed against her breast. "You can't use me if I kill myself."

Jafar halted abruptly, his skin growing sharply taut over his high cheekbones. She thought his complexion looked a shade more pale, too, but she couldn't be certain.

He held her gaze as he shook his head slowly. "Your death, too, would be in vain. It will make no difference to my plan. The colonel won't know you are dead. He and the French army will still come."

He was no doubt right about that, too, Alysson thought, nearly despairing.

"Give up the weapon," Jafar said sharply, his tone harsh and uncompromising.

She stared at him, loath to admit defeat, unwilling to concede yet another victory to him.

Before she could decide whether to flout his direct order, however, the choice was taken from her. Jafar snapped his fingers, a sudden hard imperious sound, and Alysson felt the musket being stripped from her grasp. Stunned, she looked around to find Saful scowling down at her, his expression one of fierce disappointment and disapproval.

Another black-robed Berber, apparently the owner of the rifle and the horse, ran up to Jafar and fell prostrate before him.

Interrupting the man's abject apologies, Jafar issued an order that Alysson interpreted to mean "Keep your weapons away from the woman!"

"You have spoken, *saiyid*," the cowering man replied, before he half-crawled away, looking relieved that he was to go unscathed for his negligence.

Alysson did not think she would get off so lightly. The look in Jafar's eyes as he strode toward her with suppressed savagery struck cold terror in her heart. She had finally goaded him past the point of acquired civilities, she knew.

He caught her by the wrist and pulled her after him, exercising a violence that was even more menacing for being so carefully controlled. Alysson tried unsuccessfully to keep up with his swift strides as he forcibly escorted her back to his tent, stumbling more than once. One glance at his furious expression, however, and she bit back the oath she wanted to fling at this son of darkness. His eyes seemed savage and brilliant, and all too frightening.

She pulled back then, trying to slow the pace and delay whatever punishment he had planned for her. But her efforts failed utterly. When they reached the interior of his tent, Jafar dragged her through the main chamber to the sleeping quarters. Then he released her so suddenly, she nearly fell.

'When I look at you," he said through gritted teeth, "I swear I see intelligence in your eyes, but I am wrong. That was a *stupid* thing do!"

With a flimsy courage at best, Alysson raised her chin as

she rubbed her aching wrist. "It wasn't stupid to try and escape!"

"I don't mean your attempt at escape! I was speaking of your threat to kill yourself."

"If I thought it would do the least good, I wouldn't hesitate," Alysson vowed. "I won't be used to lure the men I love to their deaths! I would rather die myself!"

A flare of some brilliant harsh light shone in Jafar's eyes. Slowly he clenched his hands into fists, then just as slowly released them. "You should know by now that I won't allow you to act against my wishes."

When Alysson didn't reply, he waved his hand in a gesture of frustration. "Why do you persist in underestimating me? You constantly try to fight me, ignoring my orders even though you know I will make you obey them . . ." He paused, then took a calming breath. "I want your word that you won't try to appropriate any more horses or weapons."

Her chin trembling, Alysson returned a scathing look. "Or else what?"

"Or else I will be obliged to curb your freedom."

"Then do it!" she cried, echoing his own words of a moment ago. "I'm sick of your threats and your inhuman schemes of vengeance. I won't give my word to a savage fiend who has no honor! I won't stay here willingly, to be used as your pawn. And I won't ever stop trying to escape!"

Abruptly, without further argument, Jafar turned to retrieve one of the silken cords he used to bind her to him each night. His hard face intent, unsmiling, he caught her arm and drew his defiant captive toward the pallet.

Fearing a repeat of last night, Alysson resisted with all her strength, but as usual she was no match for Jafar's determination. With ease, he pushed her down on the pallet and proceeded to tie both her hands and feet.

Alysson nearly wept in frustration, yet she held back her tears. She wouldn't give him the satisfaction of seeing her cry.

His fingers were impersonal but gentle as he completed the task. When he brushed the bare skin of her ankle, Alysson tried not to remember the last time he had touched her that way. Yet without warning, the memory of his hands and his mouth and his muscular body assaulted her, flooding her senses with warmth.

Suddenly his hands stilled. Jafar looked down at her, his gaze locking with hers. He was remembering, too, Alysson realized.

"Let me go," she whispered, and didn't know if she meant from her captivity, or from the depths of his gaze.

"No," he said finally, slowly rising to his feet. "I will never let you go. Not until my mission is fulfilled."

With that, he rose to his feet and stalked from the room, dropping the curtain behind him, enclosing her in semi-darkness.

Alysson gazed helplessly after him, tears of fury and despair gliding down her cheeks. How she hated him! How stupid she had been in hesitating to kill him! Next time she *would* shoot him, regardless of the consequences. How gratifying it would be to put a bullet straight through his black heart!

Yet underlying her professed hatred, she was conscious of a plaguing thought that taunted and bewildered her. Jafar's fury hadn't resulted because she had tried to escape. Or even because she'd threatened to kill him.

Inexplicably, it was because she had threatened to take her own life.

Chapter 11

For the remainder of the day, neither her rage nor despair diminished. When Jafar returned to the tent for the midday meal, Alysson gave him a look that held all the contempt and loathing that she could muster. She swore to herself she would never forgive him for tying her up again or foiling her best chance of escape, or for his diabolical schemes to destroy Gervase and the French army.

Jafar wouldn't relent either. He allowed her the freedom of her hands for the meal, but then bound them again before he left.

Her face was still stormy when he returned for the evening. Supper was a grim affair, with Alysson picking at her food and treating Jafar to smoldering silence. As she prepared for bed, however, her thoughts turned violent. If he dared lay one hand on her, if he dared subject her to his despicable lusts, or tried to arouse her fledgling passion the way he had managed so successfully the previous night, she would scratch his tawny eyes out.

Except for binding her wrists and ankles again, though, Jafar made no move to touch her. Alysson was left alone to fume in restless agitation; she couldn't sleep, and she prevented him from sleeping as well.

"Be still!" Jafar growled finally in irritation, after two hours of lying beside her thrashing form. "You are like a flopping fish."

Alysson smiled grimly in the darkness. She was glad she had disturbed his sleep. Indeed, she would enjoy disturbing him a great deal more.

"Why do you hate Gervase so much?" she asked suddenly, intent on making him as uncomfortable as she could—as well as learning the answer to a question that had plagued her for days.

"It does not concern you. Now go to sleep."

"Not concern me! How can you possibly say that when you mean to lure him into the desert and kill him, using me as bait?"

"Matters of war are not the realm of a woman."

Alysson bristled. "You should have thought of that before you involved me! Beside, this is far more than a matter of war. This is some kind of personal vendetta against Gervase."

"My business is with the French army. Colonel Bourmont is a commander in that army. My meeting with him will be a military engagement, nothing more."

"It isn't just the French army you are after! It is Gervase himself. Revenge against him was your reason for abducting me—you implied as much the other day."

When he didn't reply, she turned her head on the pillow

to look at Jafar, searching his face in the faint light from the brazier. His eyes were closed, his arms resting on his stomach, as if he was determined to sleep despite her insistent questions. But Alysson was just as determined to force him to talk. "You must hate him for some reason. The other day you said 'the colonel will get precisely what he deserves.' What did you mean by that?"

Silence met her probing query.

"You intend to kill him, don't you?"

It was a long moment before Jafar finally answered. "Yes, I intend to kill him."

"Why?" The word was a hoarse whisper. "What did he ever do to you?"

Jafar sighed in irritation. It was becoming obvious that his thorny captive was not about to let the subject drop. But perhaps it would be better if she knew the reasons behind his hatred for Bourmont. At least then she would see why he could not be swayed from his course of vengeance. And it might prevent her from threatening to end her life as she had done so foolishly today, to his everlasting dismay. Involuntarily Jafar clenched his jaw, remembering that chilling moment when she had turned the rifle on herself. His heart had stopped beating for those endless moments before the weapon had been taken from her. It was odd that he should have been so terrified for her, especially when he didn't fear death for himself.

Pushing away the thought, he forced his mind back to the issue at hand—explaining to Alysson Vickery the reasons for his quest for vengeance.

"To understand," he said in a quiet voice, "you must first know what occurred seventeen years ago when the French invaded this country. Even after subjugating Algiers and then driving out her ruler, the French jackals were not satisfied with the wealth and plunder they seized. Determined to conquer the entire kingdom, the French army pressed south into the interior, led by a powerful general.

"At that time there was a great *amghar*—a Berber chieftain similar to that of an Arab sheik—who lived in the mountains. Unaware of the invasion, the *amghar* was traveling with his wife and young son to Algiers when their caravan was attacked by French troops led by the general.

"The *amghar* fought valiantly to defend his family but he was badly wounded. Even then he might have survived, but the general ordered that the *amghar* be put to death. When the lady pleaded for her husband's life, the general gave her to his soldiers for their sport. Their *sport.*"

Jafar's quiet vehemence made the word into an obscenity. Alysson listened with growing dismay, having little trouble envisioning what might have happened to the lady. It was a moment before Jafar continued.

"The *amghar* lived long enough to see the woman he cherished and revered above all others defiled and slain by the French troops. The *amghar* himself was subjected to tortures that you—" He turned his head to look directly at Alysson. "—would call savagely hideous. There was one man—one only, of all those involved . . . a priest, who urged mercy and begged for the slaughter to stop, but the general paid no heed."

She started to say something, but Jafar raised a hand, cutting her off. "The boy, who was eleven years of age at the time, attempted to save his parents, but he was no match for the soldiers. He was subdued and forced to watch."

Alysson gave a soft exclamation of horror. Hearing the hushed agony in Jafar's voice, she understood then what he was trying to say to her. She could feel his pain, as well as the rigid control he held over himself as he lay beside her.

"You were that boy," she whispered.

"Yes." His reply was barely a breath. "I was that boy. The *amghar* was my father, the lady, my mother."

Jafar shut his eyes, remembering the horror. He had wanted to kill that day. And he would have, had he not been half-dead already, with his limbs bound to prevent movement. Had he been free, he would have slain the French general Bourmont with his bare hands.

He had also wanted to die. He'd actually been grateful that the general had ordered his own death after those of his parents. Only the intervention of the compassionate French priest had spared him. It was only later that he'd seen the priest's interference as fortuitous; he had to remain alive in order to seek retribution.

"I vowed then to avenge their murders," Jafar said softly, "if it took the rest of my life."

Alysson was silent, not knowing what to say.

Restlessly Jafar raised an arm, draping it across his forehead as he remembered the events following the murders, events that had changed his life forever. When the priest had learned of his mother's noble English blood, Jafar had been sent to her previous home in England, to his ducal grandfather. That had given Jafar yet another cause to hate the French. They had invaded his country, murdered his parents and members of his tribe, and banished him to a cold, foreign country. But he had vowed to return one day and kill the French general who had ordered the slaughter of his beloved parents.

After a moment of bitter reflection, he spoke quietly into the silence. "The general's name was Louis Auguste de Bourmont."

Alysson's gasp was audible. She stared at Jafar, searching his face, but his shadowed features were an impenetrable mask, his eyes glittering and cold. "Gervase is the general's son," she said hoarsely.

"Yes, Gervase de Bourmont is his son. The general himself died in his bed, of some paltry illness or other." The contempt in Jafar's tone was apparent.

"But . . ." Alysson said slowly, trying unsuccessfully to follow his savage logic, "Gervase had nothing to do with your parents' deaths."

"His treacherous father's blood runs in his veins. It is enough."

The tainted blood of a murderer. She remembered Jafar saying as much that night in the garden. But still that did not justify another murder. "Is it fair to kill one man for what another did?" Alysson cried.

"Yes, it is fair. In my people's customs, blood vengeance is not only just, but imperative. It is my obligation, my duty. Even had I not made my vow, I am bound by my tribe's laws to seek out my father's murderer."

In dismay, Alysson stared back at him, into amber eyes that were hard as nuggets of gold.

"Console yourself, *ma belle.* Colonel Bourmont is a soldier, and I will give him a soldier's chance to comport himself honorably. It will be a fair fight, in battle—which is more than his father gave mine. And who knows? The colonel may best me yet, if Allah wills it so. Now go to sleep.''

Turning over then, he gave Alysson his back, leaving her to ponder what he had told her, to struggle alone with her conflicting emotions. Distress was her chief feeling. Her heart went out to the young boy who had been forced to witness his parents' brutal deaths. She could even understand why Jafar was so intent on vengeance. But she couldn't accept his ruthless condemnation of Gervase. It was barbaric, savage, to kill a man for what his father had done years before.

Her mind in turmoil, Alysson stared up at the tent ceiling. If she hadn't been able to sleep before, now she was doubly wide awake.

It was well into the night before she drifted into a troubled slumber.

The next thing she was aware of was Mahmoud shouting through the curtain at her.

''Awake, lady! The lord bids you dress! We must make preparations to receive the Khalifa Ben Hamadi!''

Too groggy to be alarmed, Alysson shook herself awake. The excitement in Mahmoud's voice made her wonder if perhaps the camp was being attacked. But she soon learned that it was something quite different. One of the sultan's own generals—a powerful Arab *khalifa*—was expected to arrive at the camp at any moment. According to the young servant, Ben Hamadi was the right hand of Abdel Kader himself.

''Hurry!'' Mahmoud urged her for the third time as he struggled to untie her bindings. ''He is coming.''

Alysson swallowed her disappointment; her intention to ask Mahmoud about Jafar's past would have to wait. She hastened to wash and dress, only because she didn't want to be caught at a disadvantage in front of an Arab general. Donning her blue-and-red tunic, she draped the blue haik over her head and shoulders and joined Jafar a few moments later at the entrance to the tent.

He said not a word as he briefly surveyed her appearance. Seeing the cool fire of his eyes as he met her gaze, Alysson remembered the terrible tale of murder and vengeance he had told her last night in the darkness. She was startled to feel a sudden well of sympathy and compassion for the boy he had once been.

She also wondered if Jafar had refrained from binding her hands and feet again because of the expected visitor, but there was no time to ask. In the distance, a large column of Arabs was galloping toward the encampment.

In a only moment the racing column came to a flourishing halt before Jafar's tent. The leader, who sat a powerful white horse, was a small man, and definitely an Arab. He had obsidian-dark eyes, an olive complexion, and lean hawklike features that were half-hidden by a full black beard, and he was dressed much like the wealthy sheiks she had seen in Arabia. He wore an Arab *kaffiyeh*—a head cloth held in place by a braided gold band around the forehead. His djel-laba was rich crimson wool, over which flowed a brilliant white burnous.

The Arab chieftain let his horse fret and stamp a moment as he surveyed the camp with obvious approval. When finally he dismounted, Jafar strode up to him.

Pressing his right hand over his heart, Jafar salaamed deeply. "Peace be with you, Hamadi Bey. May Allah glorify you . . ."

Listening intently, Alysson understood the first part of Jafar's flowery greeting, but the rest of the exchange, Mahmoud had to translate for her:

"And you, Sidi Jafar el-Saleh. May Allah recompense you with His highest rewards, and make your portion exceedingly rich and full in everlasting felicity."

After more words of welcome, Jafar then stepped aside, allowing other members of his tribe to greet the high-ranking Arab official. The Berber men approached the *khalifa* eagerly, with respect and reverence, going down on their knees and kissing the hem of his garments. Alysson wasn't surprised when Ben Hamadi spoke to each man with familiarity, calling them by such intimate terms as *ya aini*—my eye—and *ya akhi*—my brother. She had once heard it said that to an Arab, every other Arab is his brother. She supposed that was somewhat true of Berbers, as well, since the two cultures were united by their religion.

Alysson was a bit startled when Jafar interrupted her

thoughts by beckoning to her. When she obeyed warily, he drew her forward to present her to the khalif.

"This is Miss Alysson Vickery, Excellency," Jafar said in French—so that she could understand, Alysson presumed.

"Ah, yes, the Englishwoman," Ben Hamadi acknowledged, switching with some difficulty to the French language. "It is an honor to meet you, Miss Vickery. I trust you are being well-treated."

Alysson gazed into the general's fathomless dark eyes, not quite knowing how to respond to this bit of politeness. Certainly he would not want to hear about the trials of her captivity, nor would it do her cause any good to curse or revile Jafar before this powerful man. Especially since he might very well hold her fate his hands. Keenly aware that Jafar's hand rested possessively at her waist, she forced a civil reply. "As well as can be expected under the circumstances, Excellency."

He gave her a gallant smile. "I shall look forward to becoming better acquainted with you later." Then, dismissing her with a wave of his hand, he reverted to Arabic to discuss with Jafar the arrangements for his forces.

Alysson gritted her teeth at this imperious treatment, thinking that the *khalifa*'s obsequiousness resembled Jafar's at his most obnoxious. Mahmoud, however, seemed quite impressed that the general had spoken to her at all. Khalifa Sidi Ould Ben Hamadi was one of the leaders of the Holy War against the French, and it was a highlight of Mahmoud's short life to have touched the robe of the mighty man. The young servant sang Ben Hamadi's praises all morning long, until Alysson was ready to consign both Mahmoud and his precious *khalifa* to perdition, along with His Royal Munificence, Jafar el-Saleh.

Indeed, not only was she not pleased by Ben Hamadi's arrival, but the appearance of an Arab general in Jafar's camp disturbed her greatly. She could only assume his presence had something to do with Jafar's plan to lure the French army into battle. Why else would the khalif have brought so many forces bristling with arms? Mahmoud either did not know, or would not tell her.

She would have liked to ask Jafar, but he was occupied

elsewhere—accommodating his guests, Alysson supposed. The entire camp was busy making preparations for a banquet to be held that evening in the khalif's honor. A hunting party that was sent out returned with the bounty of several gazelles, and a whole sheep was spitted and roasted for the occasion. All this Alysson learned from Mahmoud, for she was not allowed to leave Jafar's tent, or even look out the entrance. Saful was guarding her as if his life depended on it. Which perhaps it did, she thought wryly, remembering Jafar's lethal expression when she had tried to escape yesterday.

To her surprise, Mahmoud kept her company the entire day. Possibly because he felt sorry for her, Alysson suspected, though he didn't once mention his lord's fury at her yesterday, or how Jafar had tied her up after her attempted escape. Mahmoud was more forthcoming than usual, though, and he voluntarily gave her another lesson in the Berber language.

He also kept giving her odd glances, as if trying to determine the answer to a puzzle. Finally he came right out and voiced the thought that apparently had been bothering him.

"Why do you not turn away when you view my face, mademoiselle? The highborn ladies of the French look upon me with fright and disgust when I show myself."

The question caught Alysson off guard and filled her with dismay; Mahmoud's disfigurement obviously troubled him deeply.

She regarded him solemnly, longing to console him. "My uncle in London is a doctor," she answered truthfully, "and I sometimes visited him at his hospital. I saw countless victims of smallpox there, many whose faces were disfigured worse than yours."

"Worse? Did they not frighten you, either?"

"At first, perhaps, but I grew accustomed to seeing them."

"I did not think it possible to grow accustomed to such ugliness."

The note of quiet despair in the young Berber's voice tore at her heart. And oddly, it made her think of Jafar. But there was a similarity between them, she realized. Mahmoud was much like Jafar must have been as a boy, his soul branded by bitterness and hatred. His scars were more visible, that was all.

Swallowing the tightness in her throat, she chose her words carefully. "There are more important things than appearance, Mahmoud. Your scars don't make you a better or worse person. It is who you are inside that matters. Courage and compassion, kindness—those are a test of man's worth, not how attractive he is."

Mahmoud gazed at her wide-eyed for a moment, then ducked his head. "But with my face, I will never find a bride. No female would wish to marry a man who looks as I do."

"I don't agree in the least," Alysson said, trying to keep her tone light. "Why, your scar might even prove to be an advantage. When your bride marries you, you can be sure it is because she loves you for yourself, not for any other reason. Trust me, I know about such things. All my life I've had to beware of suitors who only wanted me for my fortune. You won't have to deal with that uncertainty at least." She paused, reaching out to touch his hand gently. "Someday you will find a woman worthy of you, Mahmoud. I'm sure of it."

The boy looked away then, coloring with sudden embarrassment. Out of consideration, Alysson changed the subject and resumed the language lesson, but she knew she had comforted him, at least to a small degree. She wished she could do more.

Mahmoud's concerns momentarily made Alysson forget the magnitude of her own problems, but they shortly came back to her in a rush. She was not invited to dine at the banquet, but to her surprise, she was asked beforehand—or rather, ordered politely—to the *khalifa's* tent.

It was apparently an important occasion, for Tahar not only interrupted her many duties to help Alysson dress, but insisted that she wear the finest garment in her wardrobe, a caftan of rich forest-green brocade, with a haik of ivory silk to cover her hair.

Jafar was already present when she arrived at the large, ceremonial tent, but his enigmatic expression told her nothing. Flustered more by his cool look than by his illustrious companion's formal reception, Alysson did her best to ignore Jafar entirely. When Ben Hamadi honored her by offering her a cup of the sweet mint tea, she accepted with a gracious smile.

She had hoped she might question the general about his reasons for coming here, but he evaded all her leading queries with the skill of an experienced diplomat and proceeded in his far-from-perfect French to tell her about the Sultan of the Arabs, Abdel Kader.

"It has been fifteen years, Miss Vickery, since Abdel Kader was proclaimed Commander of the Believers. There was no one better suited to champion Islam against the infidels. His family were sherifs, descendants of Mohammed. His father, a marabout—a holy man. In only a short time, Abdel Kader rallied to his standard all the tribes of the kingdom."

Alysson murmured some polite reply, remembering the first time she had heard of Abdel Kader. The valiant Berber chieftain had been viewed then with awe and admiration in the salons of Paris. But that was before the *Armée d'Afrique* had nearly gone down in defeat. Before whole divisions of French troops had been annihilated by the fierce Berbers and Arabs. Afterward society hostesses no longer had raved about the handsome, dashing, romantic sheik.

But she didn't want to hear about Abdel Kader. She wanted to know what military strategy Jafar and Ben Hamadi were planning to use against Gervase.

Unable to help herself, Alysson gazed across the low table at Jafar, aware that her anguish was written on her face for him to see. Jafar, in turn, was uncomfortably aware that her large, lustrous, troubled eyes were turned upon him.

"We pray Allah to smooth and prosper our affairs," Ben Hamadi droned on. "Just as you Christians pray to the prophet *Aissa* . . . Christ, as you call him . . ."

Not listening, Alysson gave a start when Ben Hamadi interrupted her thoughts.

"I trust I have not bored you, Miss Vickery," the khalif said solemnly. "To have discomfited so lovely a young lady would be a shame to my beard."

Dragging her gaze away from Jafar, Alysson managed a faint smile. "Forgive me, Excellency. I am honored that

you would share your confidences with me. It has been a
long day, though, and I find I am exceedingly weary. If you
will please excuse me, I will seek my bed.''

She suspected she had violated proper etiquette by asking
to be excused, but with the throbbing headache that had
developed behind her eyes, she couldn't bear to listen a
moment longer to the khalif's effusive exultation of his sultan.

Fortunately he did not take offense, but instead nodded
his dismissal. Not looking at Jafar, Alysson escaped into
the cool night air with a feeling of relief.

As usual, Saful escorted her back to her tent, then settled
himself at the entrance. Alysson wandered around the tent
disconsolately, a black depression weighing her down, along
with a desperation near panic. She had to act soon, but what
could she do? The only way to protect Gervase and her
uncle Honoré was to escape in time to warn them of the
treachery Jafar planned. But all her attempts at escape had
been inept and disastrously unsuccessful. She was guarded
day and night, and after her last aborted effort, Jafar probably would keep her bound in future, as well. If she did
manage to leave the tent and find a horse, there would be a
dozen pairs of eyes watching her—

Except now. Now, when most of the camp was at the
banquet. Now, when her nemesis Berber captor Jafar was
occupied.

Her hopeful gaze flew to where Saful sat just outside the
tent. He had his back to her as he carved on a piece of
wood. At the moment, he was the only one who would
prevent her from leaving. If she could render him senseless . . .

Slipping into the bedchamber, Alysson changed her
clothing as quickly as she could, donning pantaloons,
blouse, long-sleeved bolero, and her riding boots. She was
shaking with anxiety and hope, she realized. Willing her
heart to stop pounding so erratically, she retrieved the earth-
enware wash pitcher and hid it behind her back as she cautiously approached Saful.

She didn't want to hurt him, for he had been kind to her
in his way. Yet she had to do it. Never would she have a

better opportunity. She raised the pitcher high above his head.

Some sound must have alerted him at the last moment, for he started to turn. Closing her eyes and biting her lip, Alysson brought the pitcher down on his head, flinching at the dull, sickening thud the weapon made. Saful collapsed without a sound.

She stared down at him for a startled moment, her stomach roiling. Slowly, forcibly, she bent down to check on him. She hadn't killed him, Alysson realized with a ragged sense of relief. He was still breathing.

Making herself back away, she collected a hooded black burnous from the bedchamber. In the darkness perhaps she could pass for a Berber woman. Now she had to find water and food for her journey. In the next tent, she came upon a full goatskin bag of that precious liquid. Several tents over, her search revealed both bread and fruit, which she wrapped in a cloth. What she thought would be the hardest task, however, proved the easiest. Tethered in front of the very next tent, she found a small, friendly mare who wore a halter of hemp.

Trying the water bag and cloth filled with food together, Alysson draped the bundle over the mare's back like a saddlebag. Then, untethering the horse, she led it quietly from the camp. She wouldn't dare risk trying to mount just now.

She could hear sounds of music and revelry behind her, yet her heartbeat seemed incredibly loud in her ears. Any instant now she expected to hear the cry that would alert the camp to her escape.

None came.

Tensely, with bated breath, she kept going, struggling to keep her footing in the deep sand, her short prayer for deliverance a litany, *please, please, please* . . .

When she had covered the distance of several hundred yards, she brought the mare to a halt. Slowly, carefully, murmuring soothing and meaningless sounds, Alysson hauled herself up on the mare's back.

Gathering the lead rope like reins, she nudged the animal forward. Then heading north and east, her way lit by a sliver of moon, she set out across the desert.

Chapter 12

❧❧❧

Alysson traveled through the night, across the lonely wastes made lonelier by the eerie cries of the jackals, never stopping. Stars blazed like diamonds overhead in the heavens, while the endless sands stretched before her, pale, mysterious, infinite.

It was the most solitary place of all, the desert. The vast emptiness made her feel insignificant, and yet strangely a part of it. The silence was so deep she could hear the beating of her heart in concert with the soft, rhythmic plodding of the horse's hooves.

The air was clear and cold, the shadowed darkness soothing. For long moments at a time she could almost forget her anxiety, her desperate need to escape. Then fear would return, and she would glance over her shoulder, expecting to see Jafar pursuing her on his powerful black Barb, his burnous streaming in the wind.

The silent hours wore on, enveloping her in weariness. She jerked herself awake whenever she started to nod off, counting the stars and reciting proverbs and childhood poems to keep herself alert. Occasionally she was required to discipline the mare, who wanted to unseat its unfamiliar rider and return to camp.

Near dawn, the mare suddenly swerved and reared, spooked by some unseen phantom. The next instant found Alysson sprawled in the sand, gasping for the breath that had been jolted from her body.

The return of her senses brought a staggering awareness of her new plight. With acute dismay, she listened to the sound of retreating hoofbeats as the mare galloped off into the darkness, back in the direction of the camp. *She had no horse.* Here, in this arid wilderness, where life depended on the stamina of a man's mount and the availability of water.

Water.

The thought sent her frantically groping for the goatskin bag. Ragged relief flooded through her when her fingers touched the soft leather. At least she still had that.

Her gaze lifted to the eastern horizon that was beginning to lighten over a great, golden stretch of sand. She had no choice but to press on across the desert flats. She couldn't, wouldn't return to her savage captor.

Pushing herself up, Alysson slung the water bag and sack of food over her shoulder and struck out. The sand was no longer so deep and shifting as it had been, but it was coarse and gritty—and rough beneath her palms when sometimes she stumbled and fell. Shortly the sun rose to a great sphere of flame in the sky, the early-morning glare and the heat a portent of the difficulties to come. Though sweltering beneath her layers of clothing, Alysson was grateful for the protection of her burnous. She drew the hood close around her face to screen her skin from the harsh sun and wind-blown grit, and plodded on.

Against her will, she had to be careful to ration her water. Perishing of thirst would be a painful way to die, so she could allow herself only a trickle every half hour or so. If she were lucky enough to find a well or a spring, then she could drink her fill.

There was no well in sight. There was only vacant sky, empty sand, and the pitiless sea of the desert. She met no one, saw nothing but scurrying lizards.

Soon sand gave way to clay, broom to thorn and scrub. The cruel white haze blinded her, and heat drugged the air she took into her lungs, leaving her light-headed and fighting a terrible thirst. Each minute became an eternity as she struggled to stay on her feet, to keep going.

By early afternoon, the foolishness of her endeavor became apparent. She was utterly alone in this desolate emptiness, her water nearly gone, while the savage sun beat down mercilessly.

Her lips were caked, her tongue swollen, her throat on fire. A threatening blackness reeled before her eyes. And when she glanced up, she could see the scavenging birds already beginning to wheel high above her head, searching the flat, scrub-covered plain for prey. For her.

As the burning day dragged on, she lost all sense of time or distance, everything except the desperate need to drive on. In her weakest moments, she thought she might have welcomed death.

The mirage shimmering in the distance brought a sob from her throat. Water! The lake she had seen when Jafar had first brought her to this godforsaken end of the world.

She tried to run toward the precious, life-giving liquid, but she staggered and fell. Yet hope gave her new energy. Pushing herself up, Alysson forced her feet to move. She wouldn't be defeated. She *would* survive.

That was how Jafar found her—weaving between clumps of camel-thorn and Jericho rose, cursing the lake that never seemed to come closer.

"Blessed Allah . . . Alysson!"

She froze, praying she had dreamed the harsh shout, that she had imagined the galloping hoofbeats of his black stallion.

But she hadn't imagined it. The stallion was real, Jafar was real, and the ragged note of relief in his voice had been real.

When Jafar reached her, he brought the horse to a plunging halt. For the span of several heartbeats, he simply sat there, gazing down at her dazed, sunburned face, drinking in the sight. Half his tribe was out combing the desert in search of her, but they'd been forced to wait until dawn to begin. In the daylight the mare's hoofprints had been easy to track, but then they had abruptly ended. Realizing Alysson had lost her mount, Jafar had to fight to control the fear that rioted within him. The odds of her survival were slim, the odds of locating her before she perished from heat and thirst almost nonexistent.

Praying to his god and hers, Jafar had followed the footprints Alysson had left in the sand, footprints that later had disappeared on the hard earth. Only a miracle or the will of Allah had led him to her. That, and the dark flecks overhead that dipped and swung—the birds of prey tracking her.

Now that he had found her alive, his heart's erratic

pounding settled back to something resembling normalcy; the coil of fear twisting in his gut slowly unraveled.

Urging the stallion close to her, Jafar tried to take Alysson up with him on his horse, but she backed away.

"No! Keep away from me!" The words croaked from her parched throat. She was too weak to continue standing, yet too proud to collapse, too stubborn to admit defeat.

Jafar glared at her. She would have died had he not discovered her. The stark relief that he'd felt upon finding her splintered into slow-burning rage that she had endangered herself this way—and guilt that he had driven her to make the attempt.

But when she turned away to continue her toiling march, he didn't stop her. He would allow her this measure of pride. She would have to admit defeat soon. She couldn't go on much further.

Jafar followed slowly on his horse, riding alongside her. In only a few moments, however, his exasperation got the better of him. "It is foolish to be so stubborn, *Ehuresh*. You will die of thirst if you don't allow me to help you."

Alysson's chin came up as she forced a reply in a cracking voice, "Not . . . if I reach . . . the lake."

Jafar's gaze rose to the shimmering waves of heat on the horizon. He knew what she meant, what she hoped for. The burning sunlight reflecting from the blue-green shrub and giant patch of mud frosted with salt gave the appearance of a lake—but it was not.

"I am reluctant to disappoint you, *chérie,* but Chott al Hodna is not a true lake. It is a salt pan. It only appears that way from a distance. At this season, you will find water in the very center, but that is not for miles and miles."

Alysson stumbled to a halt, dismay stabbing her, making the heat and weariness too great to bear. Hopeless tears began to seep from her eyes. She caught one of them with her tongue, but it did nothing to quench her terrible thirst; it only teased her cruelly.

She staggered forward, but the hard ground grabbed at her, tripping her and yanking her down. The fall knocked the breath from her. For a moment she just lay there, dazed, defeated, surrounded by her fractured pride and an overwhelming hopelessness.

Venting a low oath, Jafar started to dismount in order to help her, but just then Alysson gave a sharp cry. Jafar caught a glimpse of a small crablike animal with a forked tail as it scurried away from her.

Dread filled him. The scorpion was not the harmless variety that inhabited the coastal plains. This had been larger and much darker—the deadly species that lived in the Saharan sands.

"Alysson!" The word was a hoarse whisper as he flung himself from the stallion's back and ran to her side. "Were you stung?"

Gasping in pain, she clutched her right leg as he knelt beside her. "Y-yes . . . on my . . . thigh."

She tried helplessly to rise, but he forced her to lie back. Rolling her over, Jafar ripped the material of her pantaloons to expose a red mark on her inner thigh that already was beginning to spread. His heart stopped beating. She would die unless he acted quickly.

Drawing his curved dagger from his waist-sash, Jafar ignored her gasp of alarm and issued a brusque order to her to be still. "This will cause you more pain, but I must suck out the venom."

"A . . . tourniquet first," she said through dry lips. "Uncle Cedric . . . a doctor. He would . . . prescribe a tourniquet . . . tie . . . above the wound."

Praying it would help, Jafar pulled the sash from around her waist and tied it tightly around her thigh. Without giving her further time to protest, he made a shallow incision in her flesh, then another, forming an X over the wound. Alysson clenched her teeth to hold back a cry. The pain obscured the indelicacy of being tossed on her back, her leg bared to this man. She tried weakly to direct her thoughts elsewhere as Jafar bent and closed his mouth over the wound, but the effort was too much.

For a long moment, he drew on the poison, then spat it out, repeating the process again and again. He tried to shut out her sobs of pain and the desperate way her fingers clutched his shoulders. He would have given his eyes if he could have spared her this, but it was the only way to save her life.

Finally there was nothing more he could do. He drew

away, gazing helplessly down at her. She lay unmoving, her eyes closed, her face pale.

Haltingly he slipped his arm beneath her shoulders and gathered her against him. Her lack of resistance attested to her fading strength of will.

"Alysson," he said in a voice that was low and fierce and yet trembled, "we have to return to my camp. We have to find you medicine to counteract the poison."

To his surprise and relief, she didn't protest. At her weak nod, he lifted her in his arms carefully, holding her as if she were a precious piece of porcelain.

"Jafar . . ." She grasped weakly at a fold of his burnous, but he had to bend his head to hear her. "I had . . . to try . . . to escape."

"Yes. I know. Now sleep, *Temellal.* Save your strength."

He wasn't sure she heard, for she had fainted in his arms.

He never knew how he made it back to camp that day. Afterward, he could only remember snatches of time, the agonizing miles, the pounding hoofbeats, the blood thrumming in his ears, the chill, mind-numbing fear that it would be too late to save her.

Yet the cold determination that had ruled his life for the past seventeen years would not let him give up. He drove the stallion relentlessly, calling on the courageous animal to give its last ounce of strength. The shiny black coat was sweat-streaked and flecked with foam, the powerful, churning legs beginning to labor, by the time they reached his camp. And Alysson was burning up with fever. Barking orders right and left to his men, Jafar carried her unconscious form into his tent, laying her gently down on his bed. Then needlessly he repeated his sharp command to summon an old Berber woman with her healing herbs.

The woman, whose name was Gastar, came, but Jafar never left Alysson's side.

"Dhereth," Gastar proclaimed when she examined her patient, her wizened face drawing into a scowl. *Very bad.*

"Save her," Jafar said simply, his hoarse voice almost a plea.

"If Allah wills."

Gastar packed the wound with powder of *alhenna,* and forced a tincture of opium down Alysson's throat, but Jafar could not put his trust only in the desert remedies that had been used by his tribe for centuries, or even his fervent prayers. Late that evening, he also resorted to a European cure to bring down the fever, a phial of sulfuric ether that he had saved from one of his trips to Algiers. With trembling hands, he forced Alysson to drink a spoonful.

He nursed Alysson himself, even though Gastar was more than willing. He poured liquids between her lips and made her swallow by stroking her throat. He bathed her nude body with cool water over and over again. When she shook with chills, he gathered her tightly against his nakedness, trying by sheer nearness to infuse her with his own strength. When she writhed in pain, Jafar soothed her, murmuring gentle words of encouragement in English as well as French and Arabic and Berber.

His heart contracted in pain every time he looked down at her pale face, her bloodless lips as she barely breathed. She was so ill, her skin so scalding hot to the touch. The *thoula*—the fever—was burning her alive. He was responsible for this. If he had never taken her captive to use for his own single-minded purposes, she would not be lying here now, in this critical condition, fighting for her life.

By the third day the ether was gone, but her life still hung in the balance. Jafar was conducting his vigil by her bedside when his forgotten guest, the Khalifa Ben Hamadi, asked permission to enter.

Jafar raised his head sharply, his thoughts abruptly interrupted. Carefully, he drew the blankets up to Alysson's chin, covering her slender body that was so wasted by the fever. Then he bid the khalif enter.

Ben Hamadi glanced briefly at the sick woman, then averted his gazed politely as he tendered the appropriate flowery greetings to Jafar in Arabic. In turn, Jafar offered him the hospitality of his humble abode and wishes for peace and the blessings of Allah, for once experiencing impatience with the customs of his people. Although Alysson's fever had lessened, her life was still in jeopardy, and until the danger had passed, he had no time to waste engaging in meaningless chatter.

The keen-witted Arab general must have sensed the tension in him, however, for he settled himself cross-legged on the carpeted floor, his gaze resting intently on Jafar.

"I would not dared have been so rude as to intrude into your privacy, my brother, but we must discuss our affairs. The prisoner has been occupying your time of late, and, I suspect, your thoughts."

It was a subtle rebuke, Jafar was aware. For the past four days he had totally neglected his duties, yet he couldn't bring himself to care overmuch. And at the term "prisoner," a surge of anger joined his impatience. The word was so cold, so indifferent, and came nowhere close to describing the relationship he had with his defiant young captive—or what he felt for her.

Aware of the need to curb both anger and impatience, Jafar forced his reply to remain even. "I could not leave the Englishwoman's side while she is barely alive, Excellency. I do not want her death on my conscience. It would be a stain to my honor, and that of my tribe, if I did not see to the safety of a captive. Moreover, she is an innocent in this affair. If I can help her survive, I will."

"Her death—or life—is in the hands of Allah."

"Sometimes it is wise," Jafar said with deliberate enunciation, "for men on earth to aid Allah, in order that His will be carried out."

The khalif's dark eyes narrowed, but Jafar returned his gaze steadily. What he'd just said was close to blasphemy in their religion, but he meant every word. He blamed himself for allowing harm to come to his captive. Because of his laxness in letting her escape, Alysson had nearly died—and still might. He could not let it happen.

Ben Hamadi must have realized his determination, for he shrugged gracefully and changed the subject. "Your plan is working, *sidi*. The rumors you planted in the ears of the French have been fruitful. Colonel Bourmont has left Algiers for the desert with a large force."

Jafar simply stared, aware of a feeling of vague surprise. His longtime enemy the colonel had not even crossed his mind during Alysson's illness—which was unique. Until now, not a day passed since the murder of his family that he had not cursed the name of Bourmont.

"The French troops will reach us within the week," the Arab noted, "perhaps less."

A week. Perhaps less. In only that short while he would have the revenge he had sought for seventeen years. Why then could he not summon the anticipation, the sweet satisfaction, that should have accompanied such a revelation? Jafar glanced down at Alysson, at her ravaged form so still and unmoving . . . and he knew the answer.

"I will take the young woman with me," Ben Hamadi added, "if she lives."

If she lives. Jafar clenched his teeth, refusing to consider the possibility that she might not. But like it or not, he was obliged to discuss his English captive's fate with his guest, a discussion they had already begun the evening of Alysson's escape.

Ben Hamadi had never intended to remain in Jafar's camp. Shortly before the French army arrived, they would separate their forces and wait for the right moment to strike. For that battle, Jafar would lead the attack, while the Arab general's troops circled around to assault the French flanks and prevent escape.

As for Alysson, Ben Hamadi had proposed they transfer the English prisoner to his own large encampment, where she would be kept with his women until she could be escorted back to Algiers. Despite his instinctive objections, Jafar had not dismissed the suggestion out of hand. Alysson's safety might be better assured were she well away from the battleground. But the most pressing reason, the overwhelming one, was his growing awareness that he was losing objectivity where Alysson was concerned. More than once he had let his fierce desire for her affect his judgment, had let his heart rule his head. He would do better to sever this dangerous attraction at once, before he found himself making decisions based not on what was best for his people or his country, but on what a fiery English captive asked of him.

Now, however, with Alysson so near death's door, he scotched the khalif's plan entirely. Ben Hamadi would protest, but Jafar would not turn her over to be cared for by anyone but himself. Not now, when he owed her his most valiant efforts.

"She cannot be moved, Excellency. Even if . . . she survives, she will be too weak to travel in the near future. I will see to her welfare here."

"You need have no fear, my brother. While in my charge, she will receive the best of care."

"I will not give her up."

There was a long silence, while the general scrutinized Jafar with his keen black eyes. "It will not do to become overly fond of the foreign woman," Ben Hamadi said finally, a gentle warning.

Jafar glanced down at the young woman they spoke of. *Foreign?* But she was not foreign to him. The same English blood that ran through her veins ran through his, though he often tried to forget that truth. And they had been lovers. After the intimacies he had shared with her during that long passion-filled night, intimacies known only between a man and a woman, she was as familiar to him as the desert, as the mountains that he called home. Alysson, with her defiant, smoke-hued eyes. Alysson, with her passion and vitality and indomitable spirit, a spirit that called to him and touched something wild within him. Somehow, in the past few weeks, she had managed to make all the other elements of his life pale to insignificance. And for the mind-numbing eternity of the past days, all his hopes and wishes for the future had converged, centering on the single fervent desire that she would survive her battle with death.

Just then Alysson stirred, muttering some unintelligible phrase. Bending over her, Jafar smoothed a tousled tress back from her hot forehead. "Be still, little tigress," he murmured in English.

The endearment drew a sharp look from the khalif; Jafar could feel Ben Hamadi watching him speculatively.

"Perhaps it is not wise to speak to her in her own tongue," the Arab suggested uneasily.

Within Jafar the slow heat of anger uncurled itself. Not hesitating, he raised his golden gaze in challenge. "It calms her to hear her own language."

Ben Hamadi was the first to break contact with that fierce gaze. After a long moment, the Arab let his hawklike features relax beneath his beard. But when he rose to withdraw, he added one last caution. "Take care, my friend, that you do not put her welfare above the lives of your own people.''

It was perhaps two hours later that Alysson slowly opened her eyes to find Jafar sitting beside her, his chin resting on his fist.

How strange, was her first foggy thought. She had been dreaming of that long-ago day in England, of her arrival at the elegant estate of an English duke. She had climbed an oak tree and thrown acorns at a fair-haired stranger. But then she had cried and he had comforted her.

Alysson blinked and squinted her eyes at the black-robed man beside her. This was Jafar, a fierce Berber warlord, not the fair-haired English stranger of her dreams.

But something was wrong about him. His head bowed, he appeared deep in contemplation, while his shoulders slumped as if under the burden of some great weight.

Slowly, weakly, she reached out to touch him on the knee. Jafar reacted the instant she moved. Startled, he caught her hand and pressed it between his own as he stared at her.

"Thank you, Allah," he said a long moment later, his voice a hoarse rasp.

Alysson watched him in puzzlement. He looked terrible. Deep lines of weariness etched his face which was covered by several days' growth of beard. She had never seen him so unkempt.

Something else was different about him as well. His expression of gratitude to Allah had been in English. Why would he speak to his God in her language? But the elusive thought faded under the effort of having to think.

"I . . . didn't die . . ." she whispered, her own voice sounding like the croak of a frog.

A slow smile, beautiful in its sheer happiness, curved his mouth. "No, you didn't." Still holding her hand in his, he reached out to touch her damp forehead. "The fever has finally broken. How do you feel?"

"Thirsty . . ."

Immediately he reached for a cup of opium-laced water. Slipping his arm beneath her shoulders, he held the cup to her lips. "Here, drink this."

Strange, Alysson thought again. Was their conversation

really in English? She sipped weakly from the cup, watching Jafar, staring into his golden eyes. "Did I . . . hit you?"

His brows drew together in a frown at the odd question. Alysson wanted to ask if she had thrown acorns at him, but she couldn't find the energy to form the words.

"No, you didn't hit me, *Ehuresh*. Now, drink again."

Obediently, Alysson complied. His order had been in French, of that she was certain. But a fragment of a thought, interposed with the fading memory of her dream, swirled in her hazy mind. Jafar looked so much like the fair-haired English stranger in her dream. And she had heard him use English before. At least once, when he'd unexpectedly come upon her half-naked, he had called her beautiful. And again when he had made love to her that shameful night, some of his passionate words had been in perfect English.

Jafar had said he knew some words of her language, but it seemed he was more familiar with English than he had admitted. Of course, it was not beyond possibility that he should have learned English as well as French, the language of his enemies . . .

The unfocused thought brought back all the painful memories of the past few weeks in a fierce rush. His plan to lure Gervase into the desert, her attempted escape . . .

Nothing had changed. He still intended to kill Gervase, still planned to endanger her beloved uncle with his schemes for revenge. And it was her fault. If she had managed to escape . . .

Alysson closed her eyes, feeling tears forming beneath her lids. She was too weak to face the horrible future, the guilt of failure.

"Sleep, little tigress."

Jafar again, his voice low and gentle. She felt his soothing hand stroke her forehead and didn't fight it. Praying for the oblivion of sleep, she let herself be drawn down into the swirling blackness. But one last puzzling thought prodded her before she drifted into unconsciousness. Had Jafar spoken to her in English?

Chapter 13

S he had failed. That was the bleak, never-changing truth that haunted Alysson during the slow days of her convalescence.

The knowledge of her failure, even more than the fever, left her shaken and withdrawn. Tears came easily now, and she was thirsty all the time. Her body ached, but her spirit ached more. The guilt was crushing, and so was the fear. Gervase would die because of her. Her Uncle Honoré would come in search of her and would be shot by a Berber bullet or mown down by an Arab scimitar.

She couldn't face it, and so she retreated into numbness. Day turned into night, then back into day, but Alysson could find no reason to fight the awful flood of emptiness and defeat that oppressed her spirit. The entire interlude of her attempted escape and Jafar's rescue seemed dreamlike, unreal, as did the past few days.

Jafar cared for her, she knew that. When she needed to eat to regain her strength, he fed her the choicest bites from his own plate, and made her drink nourishing fruit juices. When she was hot and fretful and ached for coolness, he bathed her body with cool water. When she was too weak to move her limbs, he dressed her with as much gentleness as if she were an infant.

Her utter helplessness and dependence only added to her despair. Her life had been saved by a man she professed to despise, and yet she couldn't be glad.

She couldn't be glad, either, about the various visitors who attended her sickbed. Tahar sat with her for several hours each day, keeping her company, but the gentle Berber woman's attempts at conversation drew little response from Alysson.

The blue-eyed Saful expressed Alysson's own sentiments precisely when he was shown in to see her. She had not hurt him badly when she'd crowned him with the wash pitcher—at least not physically. His pride and honor had both suffered much more from the blow, for Jafar had released him from his guard duties and set three other men in his place. The fact that his lord would not trust him again to act as her guard was a bitter, shameful pill for Saful to swallow.

"My soul is dark and gloomy," he told her in Berber, his feelings translated by young Mahmoud.

Wearily Alysson closed her eyes, too wretched to be concerned about anyone's soul, even her own. Especially her own.

To his credit, Mahmoud tried to cheer her up. For her entertainment the boy brought his pet lizard in to visit her, a black-striped reptile that he called a "fish of the sand."

"See, lady, I make him dance!"

The lizard did indeed seem to be dancing for its supper. In other circumstances, Alysson might have asked Mahmoud to set the poor thing free, for it was cruel to keep a wild desert creature in captivity. But Mahmoud obviously had formed a bond with the ugly little reptile, perhaps because it, unlike people, did not notice the boy's scarred face or awkward limp. Even so, she could not even summon the energy to be concerned for the boy's pain. Her own pain was too great, her hopelessness too overwhelming.

Her listlessness disturbed Jafar most of all. She was recovering her health slowly, but the luster had gone out of her eyes, the fire out of her spirit. The only time he had seen an inkling of the same passionate defiance Alysson possessed in such great measure before her illness was the first time he bathed her after she regained consciousness. In a pitifully weak gesture, she had tried to cover her nakedness and ordered him from the room, but the rebellion had cost her every ounce of energy she had. He had won the battle, but the victory gave him no satisfaction.

Still he wouldn't abdicate his responsibilities. He continued to change the dressing on her wound regularly, carefully massaging the muscles of her thigh around the scorpion's bite to keep the flesh supple. He continued to feed her, even though she might have managed it on her own, for she would not have eaten one tenth of the food that he persuaded her to swallow by sheer persistence. And he continued to bathe her.

Four days after the fever had broken, Alysson lay quiescent and unmoving as Jafar bared her body for his ministrations. For one brief moment, as he peeled away the gauze to expose the wound on her thigh, she tried to close her legs to him, but Jafar scowled down at her, a glimmer of something protective and fiercely intimate in his eyes.

Subdued, she looked away, her moment of rebellion over.

"The flesh is no longer so swollen and red," he pronounced as he gently washed the lacerated area.

Indifferently, her shoulders moved in the barest of shrugs. "You said wounds heal quickly in the desert."

Physical wounds, yes, Jafar thought, but not the despondency that was consuming her. He wanted to shake her, to breathe life into her, to erase the stamp of defeat in her new manner. He wanted to see a return of the courage and indomitable spirit that had first attracted him to her. He wanted to revive the passion that was so much a part of her, to feel once more the heat and honey between her thighs.

Deliberately, he moved the damp cloth upward, to the vee between her legs. After a brief, startled look, Alysson closed her eyes, not caring what he did to her.

Tempering a surge of impatience, Jafar slowly trailed the cloth upward, over the silken skin of her abdomen. When still she didn't respond, he covered a small, lush breast with his hand.

How fragile her nipple felt against his palm. He was suddenly filled with a tension that had little to do with desire: tenderness, possessiveness, a need to care for and protect that was at sharpest odds with his fighting instincts. What was it about her that aroused such protective feelings in him? He had never been particularly kind to women, yet he found himself wanting—no, *needing*—to comfort and console her, to lend her his strength.

Reluctantly he withdrew his hand, no longer willing to press her, hoping that somehow he would soon overcome her indifference.

* * *

The following day Jafar had more success. When he parted her robe, leaving her naked and open to his gaze, Alysson roused herself enough to protest again. It did no good. Jafar ignored her muttered imprecation entirely as he proceeded to bathe her.

Alysson felt her fingers curl into fists. "I can do this myself," she said tightly.

"No you can't. You are still as weak as a newborn lamb."

"But it isn't seemly for you to be taking care of me this way!"

Wry amusement curved his lips. "Allah deliver me from the prudery of women. My eyes have already seen your nakedness, *chérie*. My lips have tasted every inch of you. You have nothing to hide from me."

The faint blush that stained her cheeks was the first real sign of life he had seen from her in days. Jafar gazed down at her, a wash of tender emotion, alien and strong, sweeping over him. "I enjoy helping you, *Ehuresh*."

"You enjoy provoking me."

"Yes." The word held a hint of smug laughter. "And you, in turn, take delight in defying me. I swear you are as stubborn as the offspring of a cross-eyed she-goat."

His gentle teasing had the desired effect; Alysson glared at him with a trace of her former spirit. Now that he had managed to a provoke a response, however, he would not give up his methods. When he had finished with her bath, Jafar casually announced that he would wash her hair.

Alysson balked, but in the end she was forced to submit to his ministrations. To her dismay, the simple task of washing and combing out her wet tresses seemed even more personal and intimate than bathing her naked body. The light touch of Jafar's fingers in her hair was tranquilizing and incredibly sensual. Alysson closed her eyes, both fatigue and listlessness slowly draining away. She was awed that the cold, ruthless man she knew him to be could show such infinite tenderness.

Lulled by his quiet efficiency, Alysson allowed him to dress her in a soft robe of white cotton, making no protest until, to her surprise and alarm, Jafar lifted her in his arms.

"Where are you taking me?" she demanded as he cradled her against his chest.

"For some fresh air, my dove. You have been confined here for too long."

Striding with her through the main room, he set her down at the entrance of the tent. The late-afternoon sunlight was bright and glaring after her long convalescence, even though it was the beginning of November, but the rays were welcoming and warm on her face.

Jafar spread her damp hair with his fingers, arranging it over her shoulders so it would dry. Then, settling himself behind her, he drew Alysson back against his hard chest. She couldn't find the will to resist him; his sheltering arms were warm around her, his presence intimate and soothing. For a moment, his nearness seemed even to banish the chill in her soul. She could almost forget the terrible truth that divided them.

Allowing herself to grow limp, Alysson stared out past the encampment, at the vast desert. Even after her brush with death, the arid wilderness beckoned to her. That surprised her. After all that had happened to her, she should have been terrified by the danger the desert presented. Yet she felt almost as if she belonged here . . . in this hard land . . . with this savage Berber warlord who had brought her here.

The thought was absurd, of course. And so was the rich languidness that stole over her, one of peace and contentment. Alysson wouldn't let herself wonder about it, though, or the strange longing that kept her, for just this small length of time, a willing captive in Jafar's arms. She refused to think about it.

She couldn't dismiss Jafar so easily. His thumb stroked her inner wrist absently, but Alysson was aware of every caress, and of the quivery sensations he sent racing along her skin. As much as she wanted to, she could never be indifferent to his touch. She shivered.

"Are you cold?" Even the low resonance of his voice was capable of causing her pulse to quicken.

"No," she replied swiftly, but his arms tightened about her. She felt the warmth of his breath on her cheek, which did nothing for her equanimity.

"How is it that you know about tying a tourniquet for a poisoned wound?"

She sighed in defeat. If Jafar was intent on making her talk to him, as she suspected, she had best answer him. He would prod and pester her until she obeyed from sheer frustration. She had never met a man more determined to have his way. "My Uncle Cedric is a physician in London. I visited him sometimes at his hospital."

"This uncle . . . he is familiar with the sting of scorpions?"

"No, but he once had a patient who was was bitten by a venomous snake. Uncle managed to save the man's life, in spite of the vast odds against him. You can't imagine the sordid conditions of the hospitals in London . . . the filth . . . the slovenly, drunken women who nurse the patients."

"I can't imagine that a wealthy heiress would want to expose herself to such conditions."

Alysson gave a slight shrug. She had contrived to make herself useful to her uncle, so that he would have a reason to want her. "Uncle Cedric has a theory about cleanliness being the best way to prevent disease. When he could not convince the directors to adopt his methods, I donated the funds to build a hospital of his own."

"A noble gesture."

Alysson shook her head. "A selfish gesture, actually. I have more money than I could spend in a lifetime, and he could put it to better use than I. But mainly I wanted to see him succeed with his dream. He has spent the past seven years searching for a cure to cholera. My parents died of cholera, you see . . ."

Suddenly, she turned to gaze up at Jafar, searching his face. She was struck by the oddest feeling that she had told him this story before. It wasn't possible, and yet . . .

Had she merely dreamed of meeting him in England? The similarities between her Berber captor and the fair-haired Englishman of her dreams were striking, especially now, when the waning sun highlighted the gold of Jafar's hair and set his sherry-colored eyes aglow with amber fire.

"Have you ever been to England?" she asked, holding her breath as his gaze locked with hers.

He didn't answer at once, yet neither did he look away.

"Yes," he said finally. "Four years ago my sultan sent an embassy to your Queen Victoria to gain support for our cause against the French, and to press for England's acknowledgment of our national independence. I was a member of that delegation."

Alysson stared at him. "I never heard that my government was considering acknowledging yours."

It was Jafar's turn to shrug. "Because our efforts were unfruitful. We were never granted an interview. Your queen was more interested in maintaining relations with the French jackals than with championing justice."

Alysson knew better than to pick up that gauntlet, even if she'd had the energy. "Is that," Alysson asked in her native language, "when you learned to speak English?"

Jafar understood her, she was certain, but still he answered in French. "No, I learned before then."

"Then why do you pretend not to know it?"

"I am uncomfortable with your language. Just as you would be uncomfortable speaking Berber or even Arabic."

Alysson wasn't sure if she could believe him, but she turned back around, again leaning against him and falling silent as she pondered his answer.

Jafar was relieved that she had dropped the subject. He didn't want to lie to her if it could be helped, yet he couldn't afford to have her divulge his identity later to the French government. I would mean death and persecution for his tribe.

Gently shifting his weight, he rested his chin on the top of Alysson's head, staring out at the desert, listening to the familiar sounds as the camp made preparations for the evening, savoring the moment. This was the best time of day in the desert, when the scorching heat had ended, when the sun set the horizon aflame with red and gold. His mother had loved this time best, as well.

The reminiscence brought to mind an errant memory during one of his family's yearly treks to Algiers, a childhood memory of peace and serenity: his noble father sitting before their tent . . . his mother gazing at her lord with love and adoration. Recalling that innocent time could set him dreaming—

Jafar gave a soft sigh. A rare indulgence, his dreams. They had no place here, when his country was torn by war, when his heart was filled with vengeance.

Alysson must have been thinking along similar lines, for she broke into his musings with a thoughtful comment. "If your sultan named you to his delegation, then you must be one of his trusted lieutenants."

"It was my duty to serve him."

"And to fight for him against the French?"

Jafar nodded. "To Muslims, war against the Christians is a religious obligation."

"It seems absurd to me to kill people in the name of religion. It is bad enough to die for it."

"But Muslims look upon their death, if it occurs, as a new life," he replied softly. "And in Barbary, religion is the only political sentiment which unites the population. Abdel Kader is the incarnation of that sentiment. His campaigns, his mode of administration, principles of government, plans for reform, all have been directed at one simple and majestic idea of Arab nationality, under Allah."

Alysson shook her head slowly. "Does he truly think that God will help you vanquish the French?"

"Abdel Kader believes that God is on our side, yes."

"And you? What do you believe?"

It was a long moment before Jafar replied. "He is fighting a Holy War. I am fighting a foreign oppressor. The French conquerors are like the *simoon*—the fierce desert wind that destroys and kills. They must be resisted, even to our last dying breath, our last drop of blood."

Alysson fell silent, her thoughts occupied. Did Jafar's admission mean his religious beliefs were secondary to his hatred for the French? But yes, he had already said that vengeance was his motive for seeking Gervase's death, she remembered with a return of some of her former frustration. Yet for the first time since she had learned of Jafar's plan, she was filled with a measure of hope. Jafar wasn't as ruthless and as black-hearted as she had once thought him. Not only had he remained by her side when she lay so near death, but she'd seen kindness in his eyes these past few days when he'd cared for her. And now for once, they were discussing the war in a civilized fashion. Perhaps, if she could talk to him about Gervase, if she used logic and reason, she could persuade Jafar to turn away from his compulsive revenge.

"But Gervase is not the oppressor," Alysson said, her tone low but insistent. "He has done nothing to harm you."

"I beg to differ, *ma belle*. The colonel is the archetype of French tyranny. Not only is he a high-ranking military commander, but he is the head of the bureau which, by its very nature, is intent on subjugating my people."

She bit her lip, wondering how she could convince him. She knew Gervase didn't condone the violence of his predecessors, nor did he support the harsher measures of the French government, such as prescribed confiscation of Arab lands for minor infractions of French rules. In fact, to her, privately, Gervase had decried the official "scorched-earth" policy during the French occupation—the burning of crops and homes to prevent the native population from giving support to Abdel Kader. She could only admire Gervase's commitment to improve the lot of the vanquished Arabs and Berbers.

"I think you are condemning him unjustly. Since his arrival, Gervase has only used his office to help better the conditions of your people. He has provided a voice of reason within the army, against the settlers who would force all the Muslims off their land."

At her back, she could feel Jafar's muscles tense in an effort at control. "Even if that were so, it would make no difference. My dispute with the colonel is personal."

"Your dispute was with his father, who is no longer even alive. Besides, I doubt the late general would have been pleased with his son now. Gervase is nothing like him, in temperament or principles."

Jafar was silent.

Alysson turned to look up at him. "You spoke of your religion. Well, mine teaches that love and forgiveness are to be valued above war, above revenge. What his father did to yours was terrible, I know, but killing Gervase will not bring your parents back to life. Could you not learn to forgive the past?"

Gravely, Jafar returned her gaze. Her eyes were wide and still and heartrendingly vulnerable. "Do you love him so very much, then?" Jafar asked quietly, the involuntary question dredged out of him.

Surprise flickered in the gray depths of her eyes, yet he

did not withdraw the question. Instead, he waited anxiously, searching her face, not wanting to admit how important her answer was to him.

"Would it matter?" she replied, her voice almost a whisper.

Yes, yes, it would matter, Jafar wanted to shout. The thought of this woman giving all her love to his blood enemy sent a cold knot of raw jealousy and despair coiling in the pit of his stomach. She couldn't love another man that deeply. She belonged to *him*.

The vehemence of his possessiveness took him aback. He had never before found a woman whom he had wanted for his own. For the past seven years, his time had been consumed with fighting and fulfilling his tribal duties. He'd seldom had the leisure to indulge his sensual nature, and never the inclination to pursue the business of getting sons to follow him and inherit the leadership of his tribe. Against tradition, he had not established any concubines in his harem or acquired any wives. He'd taken his pleasure among the sultry courtesans of the neighboring Beni Ammer tribe or the Arab beauties of the wandering Ouled Nail nomads, never keeping one long enough to bore him or plague him with the jealousies and cunning stratagems for attention that females so often engaged in.

Alysson Vickery was the only woman he had ever wanted to possess. Not possess in the Eastern sense. Though Berber society was far less restrictive than Arab regarding the female sex, in Eastern cultures women were considered merely the instruments of a man's pleasure, the bearer of his children. But Alysson would mean more to him than that. He sensed that she might touch him, fulfill him, satisfy him in some way he'd never been satisfied before.

Jafar reached up to fondle a lock of her hair, his fingers caressing it. Nearly dry now, it was fragrant with the sweet-smelling herbs that he had used in the rinse, and it stirred his senses.

Indeed, just looking at her now made him ache to kiss her, to take her. She would be wild as a hawk in her love-making if she ever came to give herself to him freely. *Freely*. He wanted that more than anything except his vengeance. He wanted to see the same love and devotion on Alysson's face that his English mother had felt for his Berber father, the same desire. He wanted Alysson's eyes smoky with passion, her slender body swollen with his child . . .

A tight band suddenly wrapped around Jafar's chest at the breathtaking vision. His child. His sons, who would possess their mother's fiery courage. His daughters, who would have her passion and independence—

Abruptly his fantasies came crashing back to earth with a violence that shook him. There could never be children between them. His vow of revenge must be fulfilled. He would have to kill the colonel, her fiancé. And in doing so he would destroy any chance that Alysson would yield to him willingly.

She was still watching him, Jafar realized, and with a questioning plea in her eyes. Suddenly he no longer wanted to know how deep her feelings for Bourmont ran, or how intense the love she felt for the colonel was.

"No, it would not matter how much you loved him," Jafar said, his voice low and hoarse.

When her pleading look turned to anguish, the torment in her eyes was nearly more than he could bear. His hand moved to her cheek, a gentle touch grazing the flesh. "I cannot forsake my duty, even for you."

His own eyes were dark with regret and a glaze of passion that Alysson didn't want to recognize. She stared at Jafar numbly. "And I cannot," she whispered, "sit by and do nothing while you plan to murder the people I love."

Unable to hold her gaze any longer, he looked away.

The bleak chill of despair came seeping back into Alysson's soul once more in full force. Turning, she shivered.

At her trembling, Jafar became aware that the shadows were lengthening and the temperature rapidly dropping as the sun slipped behind the horizon.

"Come," he said quietly. "It grows cool."

Lifting her in his arms, he carried her back inside—but not to the bedchamber. Instead, he settled her among the silken cushions in the main room, then busied himself retrieving a blanket with which to cover her, lighting an oil lamp, closing the tent flap against the evening air.

Not for the first time, Alysson was struck by the consideration and care he showed her, the extreme tenderness that contrasted so dramatically with the determined, ruthless man she knew him to be. Just now, the lamplight shone on his gilded head and muted the hard lines of his face, disarming and softening.

Against her will, she lay there watching Jafar, studying his austerely handsome features, as if she might find the key to the enigma. It was almost as if he were two different men. One forbidding, hard, dangerous. The other gentle and compassionate . . . and almost vulnerable, in a way she couldn't begin to fathom. There was something lonely about him. More than that, there was a sadness in his soul, as if it held dark secrets that he could share with no one else.

Then she remembered the tale of his childhood. What would it be like to watch one's parents murdered so hideously? To be forced to watch their brutal tortures, unable to raise a finger to aid them? How could someone as proud and authoritative as Jafar endure such helplessness?

She couldn't hate him for wanting to avenge their murders, or for wanting to protect his people from the rapacious French. She couldn't hate him at all . . .

Alysson closed her eyes, deliberately shutting out this softer image of Jafar, yet unable to dispel her intense awareness of his nearness. A desolate smile of irony touched her lips. Sometime during the past days of pain and fear and despair, she had given up her futile attempt to despise him. And she very much feared that in the end, she would learn to want him, just as he had predicted.

Chapter 14

"**T**hey come! They come!" Mahmoud exclaimed as he rushed into Jafar's tent the following morning. "The French troops—they come!"

Struggling to sit up on the cushions where she'd been resting, Alysson stared at the boy in alarm. She had thought that when the time came for battle, her concern would only be for Gervase and her Uncle Honoré. But at Mahmoud's shouted revelation that the French army was on the march, the first thing that entered Alysson's mind was fear. Fear for Jafar. She had never before considered that Jafar might be wounded or even killed in the fighting. As a Berber warlord, he seemed so powerful, so invincible. And yet he was mortal. Bullets and sharp steel would penetrate his flesh as they would any other man's.

Raising a calming hand, Alysson momentarily pushed aside her disturbing reflections about Jafar and tried to question Mahmoud. He was nearly dancing with excitement, despite his crippled foot.

"Allah be praised! We will make a *razzia* on the French jackals!"

A *razzia* was an attack, Alysson eventually managed to learn. The Berber scouts that had been sent out to observe the enemy's movements had returned with a comprehensive report. A column of French cavalry had been sighted nearing the mountains to the west. The force consisted of hundreds of mounted troops and an artillery train with at least two cannons. Alysson wondered if those guns were meant for a siege—a reasonable precaution if they expected her to be held hostage in the mountains.

Mahmoud did not know much else about the French army's intentions, or about his lord's plans. He thought it was a French general who led the column, but Alysson was certain Gervase had come as well.

"Those son of swine! Blacksmith's blood!" the boy cried, raising his fists in the air.

Knowing she would get little more useful information from the impassioned youth, Alysson made her way on shaky legs to the tent entrance, where she met a scene of bustling activity. The Berbers were making preparations for the battle to come, outfitting their mounts with weapons and food. Already tall saddles were bristling with arms and other accoutrements, while the horses' caparisoned bridles sported blinders, which would prevent the animals from being distracted by surrounding objects.

Alysson stood watching silently, her heart in her throat. The peaceful Berber camp had instantly become an instrument of war.

Yet how could she blame them? War was the only thing these sons of the desert understood. To them, war was survival. And total loyalty to their lord was a duty. They would live or die for him, as he commanded.

Saful, particularly, was a loyal servant, Alysson knew. Directly in front of her, the blue-eyed equerry was saddling several mounts, one of which was Jafar's favorite black stallion. It appeared that Saful would accompany the Berbers into battle. Naturally he would be anxious for war. Not just for glory, Alysson suspected, but rather to redeem himself for his failure to guard her.

Just then she saw Jafar striding rapidly across the camp toward his tent. Not wanting to face him, she retreated inside to a far corner.

Her precaution was wasted. Jafar entered the tent, his eyes searching the shadows, and Alysson knew he was looking for her.

Spying her, he came to a halt. His face was taut as he stared at her, his eyes restless.

She thought he meant to say something, but without a word, he crossed the room and went into the bedchamber. In a few moments, he returned, dressed completely in black—full trousers, soft boots, tunic, burnous and turban.

"I will leave twenty of my men here in the camp for your protection, and that of the other women," Jafar said as he finished buckling the scabbard of a jeweled sword around his waist.

Alysson didn't contradict him, though she felt certain his men would not be for her protection, but rather to guard her. Jafar's next words took her aback.

"They have orders to escort you to Algiers, if it should happen that I don't return."

She stared at him in shock, startled more by hearing him voice her unspoken fear than his promise of safe escort. The stark realization that she might never see him again filled her with dread.

If he didn't return . . .

Her throat tightened. She couldn't bear to think of such

a possibility. Despairingly, she averted her face, not wanting him to see the fear in her eyes. She had wanted to plead with him to spare Gervase, but the words were overshadowed now by the absurd desire to beg Jafar not to die himself.

For a long moment she felt his gaze on her, searching and intent, while a keen tension filled the silence between them.

Finally Jafar crossed to her side. She stood frozen, immobile, as slowly, hesitantly, he took her hands in his. "Alysson . . ."

She wouldn't look at him.

Again she thought he intended to say something, perhaps to repeat his reasons for seeking vengeance against Gervase. But he couldn't justify his violence to her, any more than she would be able to accept Jafar's death. There was nothing more to be said.

In the end, he gave a sigh and released her hands. Murmuring a brief farewell, Jafar turned slowly on his heel and left the tent.

The ache caught Alysson unaware. Could she bear to let him go away thinking that she hated him, that she didn't care whether he lived or died?

She tried to run after him, but her weak legs wouldn't allow her. Instead, she stumbled to the entrance, where she came to a sudden halt.

It was a sight to behold—nearly two hundred Berber warriors on their prancing steeds, their highly burnished weapons flashing and sparkling in the noonday sun. They looked as fierce and indomitable as the land they lived upon. In the faint breeze fluttered the green banner of the Holy War, alongside Jafar's own standard of red and black.

Jafar was already mounted on his magnificent black charger, his demeanor commanding and as intent as a desert hawk.

Please, she begged silently. *Please take care.*

He had started to turn the stallion when he caught sight of Alysson standing there, looking up at him with mute wretchedness. Jafar tensed, dreading to hear the words on her lips. She would ask him to spare her fiancé's life, and that he could not do. He waited, while the grit churned up by the horses' hooves swirled around him.

"Please . . ." she whispered, her voice so low that he strained to hear. But the words choked in her throat, and the remainder of her plea was lost as tears welled in her lustrous eyes. Faltering, she pressed a hand to her quivering mouth.

Jafar felt his heart wrench with a bitter emotion more powerful than anything he'd ever felt. He didn't need to hear the words; she was pleading for Bourmont's life, he could see it in her eyes.

Abruptly, he whirled his mount.

He didn't look at her again as he took his place at the head of his troops. With effort, Jafar managed to pretend that he hadn't seen the despair on her pale features, hadn't noticed the heartrending trembling of her mouth. With grim determination, he even attempted to dismiss her from his thoughts as he focused on the battle ahead.

But as he rode out of camp with his army of warriors, he was aware that Alysson's haunted gaze followed him all the while.

Against all inclination, despite his most determined efforts, her gaze continued to haunt him. Even on the eve of battle, Jafar couldn't forget the wrenching pain of leaving her behind.

It tormented his thoughts some twenty hours later, when he was ensconced with his men on a plateau of the Ouled Nail mountains. Jafar lay on his stomach, overlooking the narrow gorge below, a field glass pressed to his eye. His Berber warriors were scattered among the mountain ridges and crevices, waiting eagerly for the engagement to come. Beside him was his chief lieutenant, Farhat il Taib—the same red-bearded Berber who had acted as interpreter when they'd first accosted Alysson Vickery and her party nearly a month ago.

Alysson . . . his vibrant, defiant captive. She would never forgive him for what he was about to do. She would—

"They come, lord?" Farhat questioned softly.

Jafar was grateful for the interruption of his tortured

thoughts. "Yes." A quarter hour more, perhaps, and the enemy would appear blow.

He passed the glass to his lieutenant, then glanced over the heights, searching the shadows made by the glaring sun. The black burnouses of the Berbers blended well with the shadows as they waited under ledges and behind rocks. Like himself, his men were seasoned fighters who had seen several campaigns, but Jafar's strategy now was very different from the first battles Abdel Kader had fought against the French.

In the early years of the war, the Arab forces had proved victorious in driving back the rapacious French. Abdel Kader's army had exceeded 40,000 troops, while his cannon foundry and manufactories had supplies his Berbers and Arabs with the munitions of war.

But that was before they'd had to fight the likes of General Thomas-Robert Bugeaud, a marshal of France and commander of the French forces in Barbary. Bugeaud had revolutionized French warfare by mounting his infantry troops. With vastly superior numbers, he'd dealt Abdel Kader several stunning defeats, then set about the ruthless, wholesale destruction of the Kingdom of Algiers and the widespread massacres of her peoples. Abdel Kader's once-powerful army was reduced to partisan resistance, confining themselves to harassing the enemy, cutting off communications, executing sudden and unexpected sallies.

Jafar had developed his current battle plan along these lines. He commanded a smaller force by half than Gervase de Bourmont, but he had the element of surprise on his side, and a keen knowledge of the mountains. He and his men occupied the principle pass of the Nail, a narrow defile through which one could emerge from the High Plateau into the Sahara.

With great care, Jafar had planted the rumors that Alysson was being held captive here in the district of the Ouled Nail tribe. His plan was to oblige the colonel to enter the mountains by the gorge, where the constricted space would preclude the possibility of cavalry movements. Once Bourmont had passed below, Jafar's men would send an avalanche of scree and boulders into the gorge, cutting off the colonel's retreat. When the battle started, the Frenchmen would be entangled among ravines, trapped amidst precipices.

As for the vast remainder of the French troops, Khalifa Ben Hamadi would keep them occupied by falling on the enemy's flank. Here in the gorge, the Berbers would be led by Jafar's chief lieutenant, Farhat. Jafar wanted to be entirely free to meet his longtime enemy the colonel face-to-face.

"It is as you said, lord," Farhat murmured, handing the spyglass back to Jafar. "The colonel is in the lead."

Jafar held the glass to his eye, running it over the French troops as they filed through the mouth of the gorge. There were some eight hundred men, all mounted, most wearing lightweight blue uniforms and kepis with neckcloths. At the rear rode a detachment of men dressed like the native Bedouins—a crack cavalry unit of Arab spahis employed by the French army.

The column was armed with two howitzers, yet the colonel's forces would never have the chance to fire their cannon; Jafar's warriors would prevent it. They stood ready to fire at his signal on the slender column as it wound through the rocky pass.

Jafar's glass swept nearer, over the leaders, and his jaw muscles clenched as he found the face he was seeking.

Bourmont. The name whispered like a demon through his mind.

Yet, oddly, he couldn't summon the fierce hatred that had always accompanied the thought of his blood enemy. Rather he felt numb, except for the tight knot in the pit of his stomach, and a dull ache in the vicinity where his heart should be.

How could that be so? For seventeen years he had waited for this moment. For seventeen years vengeance had driven him. Vengeance for the torturous murders of his parents.

Forcibly Jafar tried to dredge up the brutal memories of that day when he had been forced to become a man, to remember the crimson blood draining from his father's body, the screams of his mother. Yet all he could see was Alysson, the image of her pale face and the sadness in her lustrous eyes.

With a silent oath, Jafar dragged the glass's focus from

Bourmont and aimed it further along the column. The knot
in his stomach twisted as he found another familiar face,
this one ruddy and round.

Alysson's French uncle. And beside him, her Indian servant.

He had expected as much, though he'd hoped fervently
they would remain behind. It was a foolish, futile gesture
to accompany the colonel. They had no experience with
war, with death. But he couldn't blame either of them for
making the attempt. If Alysson had belonged to him, he too
would have tried to save her.

Beside him, he felt Farhat tense. When the Berber
pointed, Jafar followed the direction of his gaze. To the
north, in the distance, rode Ben Hamadi's calvary, moving
like a swift cloud over the plain, spurring storms of sand.
In the wind streamed Abdel Kader's standard, white with
an open hand in the center. The Arabs charged toward the
enemy, a great sweep of them, though they had not yet been
seen by the French.

Jafar nodded. "The time has come."

*The time for vengeance. The time for ending the blood
feud.*

He forced thoughts of Alysson from his mind, welcoming
the chilling calm that settled over him.

Backing carefully away from the ledge, Jafar murmured
his final orders to the men who would remain above. Then
he and Farhat climbed down the steep slope, into the chasm
where the horses stood. They mounted silently.

Then they waited.

In a few moments, the tension of silence was broken by
the sound of steel-shod hooves echoing off rock.

Jafar raised his hand.

Presently a low rumbling noise filled the air as an avalanche of rock and earth tumbled into the pass, followed by
startled French oaths and shouts of alarm.

Jafar's arm dropped sharply.

Immediately the Berbers commenced firing at the oncom-
ing enemy . . . not directly at the Frenchmen but all around
them, so as not to hit the colonel. The pleasure of killing
Bourmont belonged strictly to their lord.

The Frenchmen were disciplined troops, however.

Warned by the noise and tumult of the avalanche, they reacted well to the ambush and brought their rearing mounts under control.

"Aux armes! Aux armes!" came the cry from several of the leaders. In response, the cavalry troops regrouped in the crowded gorge, their column drawn up in a square, facing outward with rifles and bayonets, equally defended on all sides so as to resist a vigorous attack.

And it was vigorous. The Berbers charged with hoarse shouts, urging their mounts along the rocky pass, while those who had been concealed by the rocks rose up before them, swarming over the rugged ground, brandishing glistening swords and firing to shake the steadiness of the French column.

The gorge became closely packed with horses and men. Jafar preceded his warriors to the attack, plowing through the clustering files of French soldiers on his plunging charger, sweeping bayonets aside with his long blade. He felt at ease, cool even in the midst of battle, fearing neither bullet nor saber nor lance. His entire attention, his every nerve, was focused on finding the son of the man who had been his blood enemy for so many years.

Some five yards away, he saw Bourmont putting up a courageous effort amidst the flash of steel blades and the peal of the musketry. Beside the colonel, a volley caught a blue-uniformed man in the chest, while another fell, pierced by sharp metal. Jafar, surrounded by the screams of wounded horses, smoke wreathing around his head, pressed forward, deftly deflecting slashing enemy sabers and thrusting bayonets.

In the next moment the skirmish turned desperate for the French forces. They tried ineffectually to repulse the savage Berbers, who, incredibly, rode directly into their midst. Bewildered by the tactic, the French troops made a straggling and futile defense. Before the onslaught, their line was swept away, their formation broken.

"Alez! Alez!" Bourmont shouted. Obeying the order, his men leapt off their horses and gained cover to try to ward off the attack while they reloaded their weapons.

The Berbers reacted with cries of triumph. Their main goal had been to drive the enemy into the hills while their lord engaged the French commander in combat. Jafar took full advantage of the opportunity. Finally having a clear path, he charged the colonel, sword drawn.

Bourmont swung up his rifle to deflect the blow, but it never came. Instead, Jafar sent his stallion crashing into the colonel's mount. Suddenly unhorsed, the colonel leapt to his feet, drawing his own saber.

Jafar smiled in grim satisfaction. He sprang down from his stallion and attacked, vengeance driving him. The gleaming blades came together with a clash.

They fought hand to hand, violently, each straining for supremacy, both knowing this would be a fight to the death.

For a long moment neither man could gain the advantage. Bourmont proved to be a courageous adversary, but Jafar had the greater skill. That, and the knowledge that justice was on his side. He fought with all the fierce determination inside him—seventeen years of unassuaged rage and bitterness. His heart pounded with hatred, while blood lust surged in his veins, rivaling the explosion of gunshots.

Then abruptly the frequency of shots lessened, reduced to scattered fire. In one corner of his mind, Jafar was aware of the sudden lull in the fighting. He could sense his men watching, and knew the battle was over. By now his warriors would have taken many of the French troops prisoner, and followed the others who had retreated in confusion.

Over the clanging of swords, he could hear another welcome sound. Beyond the avalanche of earth and boulders, shouts of joy resounded along the gorge. They came from Ben Hamadi's troops as the major contingent of French troops wavered, broke ranks, and fled from the victorious Arabs.

Jafar redoubled his efforts. With a fierce thrust of his arm, he sent the colonel's saber flying and Bourmont stumbling to the ground. The colonel lay there frozen, his chest heaving with exertion as he stared up at the savage black-robed Berber above him.

Jafar raised his sword to deliver the fatal blow. "Know you that I avenge the blood of my father!" he called out in French, his voice a harsh cry that echoed off the rocky walls of the gorge.

Gervase de Bourmont stared up at him, unmoving. Jafar's

arm hung poised in the air as he met his enemy's dark gaze. There was resignation but not fear in the eyes riveted on him. A man who sees his own death with regret but not trembling.

Perhaps it was trick of light, but the image before Jafar wavered and changed. Masculine features became feminine. Dark eyes faded to gray. Lustrous gray, filled with despair.

For the briefest moment, Jafar shut his own eyes tightly. But Alysson's haunting image remained; the memory of her anguish smote him.

Alysson.

Her tears.

Her torment.

Her love for this Frenchman.

With a cry akin to agony, Jafar brought the blade crashing down. Yet at the last possible instant his aim swerved. He made no contact with human flesh. Instead, the sword point thrust deep into the earth, a scant four inches from the colonel's head.

Chapter 15

The commotion startled Alysson from a restless sleep. Was that rifle fire she heard?

Groggy and disoriented, she glanced in alarm around the darkened tent, only to realize it was the dead of night. So why did the bustling sounds of activity make it seem that the camp was awake and stirring? *Jafar.* Had he returned? Her heart began a slow, painful pounding.

Abruptly Alysson struggled to her feet and groped for a garment to pull over her chemise. Then she hastened to the tent entrance. Within her, fear vied with weariness for supremacy. She hadn't slept at all two nights ago after Jafar had ridden off to battle with his warriors, and tonight she had only managed to nod off from sheer exhaustion. Nor had she entirely recovered her strength from her nearly fatal bout with fever.

When she raised the tent flap, her gaze swept the chaotic scene: horses and men returning from battle. Women and retainers rushing out to greet them. Some firing muskets in welcome, some waving flaming torches, all chattering excitedly. Had the Berbers been victorious?

Alysson dug her fingernails into her palms, her breath arrested as she searched the crowd for the man who held her fate in his hands. Jafar, her captor. Had he survived the battle? Had he succeeded in carrying out his blood vengeance?

Then she spied him, moving toward her on his black stallion, accepting as his due the rejoicing and the glad cries of his people. On some vague level of consciousness, Alysson was aware that the slow, painful strokes of her heartbeat eased the slightest measure. He was alive. He had returned to her unharmed.

Her throat aching with unshed tears of relief, she focused her gaze on Jafar, on his lean, proud face, a face that against all expectations of reason and prudence had become dear to her.

A silence seemed to descend over the camp as he drew his mount to a halt before his tent. Alysson couldn't speak. She simply stared at him. Jafar, too, was silent. He sat looking down at her, his expression hard and remote in the torchlight, and totally unreadable.

She desperately wanted to know about Gervase, about the outcome of the battle, but she couldn't force herself to ask and hear the dreaded answer. She couldn't face knowing he was dead, any more than she could face knowing Jafar was his killer.

Suddenly, Alysson caught the weak sound of a snarled oath from a short distance away. An oath that was delivered in French.

For an instant she swayed on her feet, not daring to believe. But that cursing, plaintive voice came again out of the darkness, a voice as dear to her as Jafar's.

"Sweet heaven . . ." she whispered through a mist of mingled hope and fear. "Uncle Honoré."

She moved blindly across the camp, tripping and stumbling over the long skirts of her burnous until in a gesture of impatience she jerked them up. She saw her favorite uncle through a haze of tears, recognizing the thinning silver hair shining in the torchlight. Honoré was lying on a stretcher, one end of which was drawn by a horse, the other dragging the ground. It was the kind of device appropriate for an invalid, or a wounded man. And his voice was feeble, even though he was busy swearing in pithy French that these heathens were trying to kill him.

Alysson halted in confusion. A whimper of miserable joy hung in the back of her throat as slowly she knelt beside his stretcher. *"Mon oncle,"* she murmured, her own voice a hoarse rasp.

He left off cursing to stare at her. *"Sacre Dieu . . .* Alysson! My beloved child . . ."

She flung her arms around him just as he reached for her, and for a long moment, they clung to each other, both weeping with relief to see the other alive. Finally, with a groan of pain, Honoré held her away, grimacing as he searched her face. "I was sick with worry for you, my dear. You are unharmed?"

Tears streaming down her cheeks, Alysson nodded, drinking in the sight of his beloved face. "Yes, I am fine—"

Before she could complete the sentence and ask about her uncle's health, a small dark man stepped forward from the shadows and made a deep salaam. "Memsahib? My heart is filled with gladness to find you."

"Chand!"

Leaping to her feet, Alysson launched herself at her Indian servant, wrapping her arms around him in a stranglehold, laughing through her tears as she drew comfort from Chand's dear, familiar presence.

"Memsahib! This is not seemly!" Chand exclaimed. He gave a dignified sniff as he pried himself loose, but she caught the sheen of tears in his dark eyes before his expression sobered.

"Memsahib, I beg you to heed me. Your uncle is gravely wounded."

Alysson's heart leaped again with dread as her gaze flew to Honoré. Gravely wounded? But he did not look as if he were at death's door. Pale, perhaps. And disgruntled. But not dying. Her pulse regained a more normal rhythm. Most likely, Chand was exaggerating as usual.

When she eyed him anxiously, the Indian hastened to speak in heavily accented French. "Is there a place where we may take the sahib so that I may attend to him?"

"Yes, my dear," Honoré put in, resuming his querulous tone, "have you any influence over these barbarians? They have strapped me into this contraption and won't let me out. I vow I am bleeding to death. One of those Arab fiends stuck a sword blade in my ribs, skewered me as if I were a pig to be roasted."

Influence? Alysson thought with desperation. She had no power of persuasion over these Berbers, especially the one whose opinion mattered most, the lord whose word was law here in this wild land. Helplessly she glanced around her, only to have her gaze arrested. Jafar had come to stand behind her and was silently observing her.

She guessed that he had overheard her conversation, for all she had to do was say, "Please . . ." in a soft, pleading whisper, before he gestured to someone in the shadows.

"Gastar will aid you," he said abruptly, almost angrily, before turning toward his tent.

Alysson watched in bewilderment as he strode away. She didn't know what he was thinking, or why he was treating her so brusquely now, after the infinite tenderness he had shown her during her illness. But then the old Berber woman who had helped nurse her through her fever came shuffling forward. Seeing Gastar, Alysson felt a twinge of guilt. She had never even thanked the woman for saving her life. For that matter she had never thanked Jafar, either.

Her gaze followed his tall, black-cloaked figure for another moment, before she managed to drag her thoughts to attention. She had to see to her uncle before she could consider Jafar's actions or his cold treatment of her.

She listened anxiously as Gastar issued incomprehensible orders to several Berber men, then followed as her uncle was carried into a nearby tent. After Honoré was released from the bindings of the stretcher and transferred to a comfortable pallet, though, all Alysson could do was wait. Both she and Chand were left with nothing to do as Gastar worked with swift efficiency over her patient.

That in itself became a problem. Chand was insulted by the old woman's assumption of his duties, not liking to be relegated to the role of spectator, but Alysson prevented him from making a scene with reassurances of Gastar's competence in healing. Even so, Alysson held her breath as the bloodstained bandage covering Honoré's chest was peeled away.

She was eminently grateful to discover that her uncle's wounds weren't as terrible as she feared. The right side of his chest was slashed by a bloody gash, and at least two ribs were broken, but the wound was clean, and the torn flesh easily sutured. She held her uncle's hand as Gastar performed the necessary operation and bound his ribs once again.

It was only when Honoré had been given a potion and was sleeping soundly, however, that Alysson had the time and opportunity to question Chand about what had happened. The French forces had been routed with little effort, she learned.

"At the battle's end, I was engaged in seeing to the Larousse Sahib's wound when the Berber lord discovered us." Chand shuddered, his fear at reliving the moment becoming evident. "I thought he would murder us! I prayed to Allah for mercy, and my prayers were answered, for the Berber lord commanded his men to aid us."

"But why?" Alysson asked, puzzled that Jafar should offer comfort to his hated adversaries. "Did he give you a reason?"

Chand shook his turbaned head. "Only that the Larousse Sahib should not be allowed to die. It was not my place to question the Berber's wishes."

"No, of course not. But what happened then?"

"The lord's men saw to all the wounded, even those of the French army, and buried the dead. Then they brought us here . . . only us. There were others taken prisoner but I know not what became of them." His gloomy tone held a hint of fear. "Now we have found you, memsahib, praise Allah, but we are prisoners with you. What does it mean? Does the Berber lord wish to torture us?"

Alysson was quick with her denial. "I am certain he would never consider such a thing!" She couldn't vouch for Jafar's benign intentions toward the French, but she couldn't believe he would torture a wounded man and an innocent servant.

A frown knitting her brow, she glanced down at her beloved uncle, whose limp hand she still held. She was infinitely grateful to Jafar for bringing her wounded uncle to her, but why had he done it? Simple charity? In the nomad tradition, offering hospitality even to an enemy was a sacred duty. To refuse asylum was a stain upon the Arab character. Perhaps this was so with the Berbers as well. Yet that didn't explain his singling out her uncle . . . unless Jafar intended to use Honoré as another political hostage. That was the only explanation that made sense.

But there were many other aspects of this situation that did not make sense. Why, for example had Jafar taken the time to care for the wounded and bury the dead of his enemies—

The thought made Alysson's throat tighten. Men had died because of her. Her uncle had nearly lost his life, and her devoted servant had sacrificed his freedom, all because of her. "I'm sorry, Chand," she murmured, her voice quivering.

Chand must have understood her guilt, for his dark eyes were full of sympathy. "You have not to blame yourself, memsahib. These peoples of Barbary have been fighting the French foreigners before you came to this country, and they will continue to do so when you have gone."

She took comfort from his logic. And perhaps he was right. She was not to blame for every battle between the Algerines and their French conquerors, and not this battle, either. The deep-rooted animosity and bitterness had been festering for years. Jafar would have used any excuse to fight the French, if not on this occasion, then another. His quest for vengeance had demanded restitution. His hatred of Gervase . . .

Alysson drew a ragged breath, trying to summon her

courage. She dreaded hearing about Gervase, but she had
to ask. "And Gervase . . . Colonel Bourmont? Do you
know what became of him?"

"No, I regret that I do not know. We were cut off from
those troops under the Bourmont Sahib's command."

She closed her eyes, relieved he hadn't said that Gervase
was dead. While there was uncertainty, there was still hope.

"You are weary, memsahib," Chand admonished in his
sternest tone. "Why do you not seek your bed? I will see
to your uncle."

Again Chand was right. There was little more she could
do here at the moment. Besides, she had to see Jafar.

Nodding agreement, she bent and lightly kissed her uncle's ruddy cheek, then did the same to Chand's, much to
his embarrassment. "You must try to get some sleep, too,"
she ordered. "I will return first thing in the morning to
relieve you."

"Where is it that you will stay?"

Alysson hesitated. Naturally Chand would be concerned
about the sleeping arrangements—and not only because he
needed to know where to find her if Honoré took a turn for
the worse. Rather because it was Chand's custom to curl up
each night before her door. She had long ago given up trying to prevent what he believed was his duty; her father had
commissioned him to protect her, and protect her he would.
And guard her virtue, as well.

A blush momentarily touched her cheeks. How could she
confess to Chand, who had looked after her since she was
a child, indeed had cherished her like his own child, that
she slept in her captor's tent, that she had shared intimacies
with Jafar which only a wife or mistress shared with a man?

"I have been given the use of a tent," she prevaricated.

"You will be safe, memsahib?"

The worried note in her servant's voice was a familiar
sound. In reassurance, Alysson forced a smile. "Yes, I will
be quite safe. And so will you, I promise." And she would
do everything in her power to keep that promise, she vowed.

The victory celebrations had died down as she crossed
the encampment, so her progress was unimpeded. There
was no guard, either, to hover over her or prevent her escape. But there was no need, Alysson realized. She would

never leave Jafar's camp now, not as long as her uncle was held prisoner, too. Perhaps that was precisely what Jafar had planned by bringing Honoré here, after all.

She found Jafar alone in his tent, standing at the far corner of the room. A single oil lamp burned overhead, wrapping the room in a soft welcoming glow, but Alysson hesitated at the doorway. For a moment she simply drank in the sight of him. She shouldn't feel so relieved by Jafar's safe return, she knew. Not when she had no idea what terrible fate had befallen Gervase. Not when Jafar might very well be a cold-blooded killer. Yet she couldn't dispel the warmth stealing into her heart.

Even so, she was unsure how to approach Jafar just now. He stood with his back to her, his golden head bowed—in the attitude not so much of a man in deep thought, but of a man suffering some heavy burden.

Indeed, Jafar was suffering . . . his thoughts tormented as he grappled with painful emotions. Unbidden images haunted him as he reflected on his actions of the previous day.

After the battle, he'd searched for Alysson's uncle among the dead and injured, and found him seriously wounded, enough to warrant immediate care. Coming to a swift decision, Jafar had given the order for the elderly gentleman and the Indian servant to be escorted back to the encampment. He had seen the questioning looks on the faces of his men at his decision; they were puzzled and disgruntled by the command to welcome a Frenchman into their midst. But they would not dare to dispute him.

It was perhaps not the wisest action to have taken, but he would make the same decision again. The old man's life would have been gravely endangered on the long march back to Algiers, without rest and proper care.

"Accursed fool," Jafar swore at himself softly, bleakly. Two months ago he would not have regretted the death of one more Frenchman. But that was before he had met Alysson Vickery. The aid he had rendered to her wounded uncle he had given for her sake. He knew enough about her to be aware of the deep love she bore for her uncle. And after all the pain and despair he had brought her, he was determined to give her this much.

Alysson.

Resolutely, Jafar closed his eyes, trying to banish the haunting images of his young captive. Yet he couldn't forget his first sight of her tonight . . . all sleep-tousled and arousingly beautiful, despite the lines of fear on her pale face. Had any of that fear been for him? Had she been even the least bit anxious about him? Or was he only imagining the relief in her eyes when she'd looked at him through a mist of tears.

He hadn't imagined her concern for her uncle, though. Her distress over the elderly man's injury was palpable. Seeing it, Jafar had found himself fighting a fierce yearning, the wish that she would care that much for *him*. When he'd seen the tears streaming down her face, all he'd wanted was to take her in his arms and soothe her pain. Pain he had caused.

Those tears had scalded his conscience, a fiercely unwelcome emotion considering how he'd already flayed himself with guilt and disgust for turning his blade aside at the final moment. For not having the will to carry out his plan of vengeance.

Why, *why* had he abandoned his vow?

There was only one answer. Alysson. That, too, he had done for her sake. Because of her, he had spared the life of the man she loved. Because of her, he had dishonored his Berber name, his birthright.

Jafar's fists clenched convulsively. It was what he had always feared, what he had struggled against for years, his English blood taking preeminence over his Berber heritage. Never, though, had he dreamed he would break the blood oath he'd held as dear as his own life.

And now, Jafar thought bitterly, now he was left to face the enormity of his failure. He had betrayed both his vow and his tribe. Most of all he had betrayed his father's memory. And he would have to pay the price.

Despite his current position as his tribe's overlord, he would be required to answer for his actions. His was a democratic society, but Berber warriors followed only a man they respected or feared. It was not his way to inspire through fear, though. He was not some petty despot, to force obedience by might of arms. If he could not command the loyalty of his tribe by merit, then he did not want to rule.

But then, perhaps he did not deserve to rule now, after letting his blood enemy live—

"Jafar?"

His head came up abruptly; he hadn't heard Alysson's soft tread.

When he swung around and locked gazes with her, she was startled by the dark emotion shadowing his features. His lean face bore the marks of suffering.

"What is it?" she asked in alarm, moving quickly across the chamber to his side.

Immediately his expression became shuttered, his eyes lidded, withdrawn, secretive.

Her own eyes bright with concern, Alysson reached up to touch his stubbled cheek, wanting to comfort him.

It was the first spontaneous caress she had ever given him. It was a gesture of simple compassion.

Jafar abruptly drew back, as if her touch might wound him.

Alysson slowly let her hand drop, feeling dread return to curl in her stomach. When she searched Jafar's hard face, she could find no trace of the gentleness she'd once seen there. She knew she should demand at once to be told what had happened to Gervase, but it was a subject she couldn't bring herself to broach. The truth was she was afraid. Afraid to face the possibility that Gervase was dead, that Jafar was responsible. And so cravenly she continued to put off the question.

A tense silence stretched between them . . . . Alysson not knowing what to say to the hard, enigmatic man standing before her, Jafar waiting for her to ask about the fate of her fiancé. He could read the unasked question in her eyes: *What of Gervase? What have you done to him?*

Jafar's fingers slowly clenched into fists as he fought the onslaught of stinging jealousy. He should tell her, of course. He should allay her fears at once and let her know that her beloved Gervase was unharmed. But he couldn't bring himself to say the words, for then he would see her love for his archenemy confirmed in her eyes.

But her question, when it finally came, was not about Gervase de Bourmont.

"Why have you brought my uncle here?" Alysson asked quietly.

It provided only marginal relief to Jafar that she hadn't voiced her fears about Bourmont. He did not want to discuss her uncle, either, or his reason for bringing the elderly Frenchman here. For doing so would be to expose his weakness, his vulnerability. Alysson herself.

Fortunately, as a Berber warlord, he was not compelled to give her his reasons. He was still her captor; she was still his to command.

Jafar turned away abruptly, impatiently striding across the carpets to the bedchamber.

Alysson followed. At the curtain, she paused, watching as he began unbuckling his elaborately embossed sword and scabbard. "Why, Jafar?"

"Because it was my wish." The words were harsh, gritted out between his teeth.

She hesitated, struggling to fathom his anger. "Jafar, please . . . my uncle is an old man . . . and now he's severely wounded. Have you no pity?"

He cursed softly, while his fierce gaze sliced to hers. "I showed him pity, *Ehuresh*. Would you rather I had left him to die on the battlefield?"

"No . . . of course not."

Alysson twisted her fingers together in agitation. She was immensely grateful for the care Jafar had shown her uncle, but that couldn't ease her fears about how Honoré would fare as his prisoner.

She took a deep breath. She would not plead for herself, but she would pay any price to spare her uncle the ordeal of captivity. Yet she had only one thing to offer that Jafar might want. She swallowed hard. Could she humble herself to become the consort, the concubine of this vengeful Berber lord, a man she didn't know— But she did know Jafar. She knew that sometimes he could be tender and caring. She knew he could be fierce and unforgiving. She hoped he could be merciful . . .

"You once wanted me in your bed," she whispered, her voice so low he could barely hear. "You said you wanted me to submit to you. Very well, then. I will yield to you. I will call you master, whatever you wish . . . if you will only let my uncle go free.''

Even in the faint light, she could tell she had struck a nerve, for Jafar's jaw suddenly hardened. But although he turned to stare at her, he still remained silent.

Alysson's gaze probed his anxiously, trying to read his granite expression. Did he no longer want her as his lover? The hardships of the past weeks could not have enhanced her physical charms, but Jafar's sexual desire for her once had seemed ardent enough to overlook her recent loss of weight now.

"Do you want me to beg, is that it?" Moving closer, Alysson came to stand directly before him. "Should I go down on my knees? I am not above begging you for my uncle's freedom, or that of my servant.''

Startled by her offer, furious that she would consider humbling herself so, Jafar gazed down at her with glittering eyes. "My answer is no.''

His face had darkened ominously, in a way that was almost frightening, but she wouldn't give up.

"Don't you understand? I am willing to bargain with you. Their freedom in return for mine. Release them and I will surrender to you of my own accord.''

"A Berber warlord does not bargain with women!" he ground out, taking refuge in his position.

"In your culture, perhaps women have no power to bargain, but in mine it is done all the time! I mean it, I swear to you. It will be just as you wanted. I'll bow to your will. I won't defy you any longer.''

His expression was no longer shuttered now. There was raw emotion in his eyes; his stance was rigid, his face drawn as though in pain.

And it was pain. Pain and guilt. He should release her, Jafar knew. An honorable man would have done so at once. Yet he couldn't bring himself to let Alysson go—for reasons he didn't want to admit even to himself.

Certainly, he had ample justification for continuing to hold her captive. Keeping Alysson and her uncle in his power would strengthen his bargaining position with the French. Yesterday at the battle's end, he'd taken the defeated

Bourmont prisoner, to be exchanged later for Arab prisoners of war. But until the negotiations were final, he couldn't afford to give up the slightest advantage. Moreover, his tribe would never sanction setting his European captives free without recompense. Not now. Not after his failure to carry out his blood oath.

They were flimsy rationalizations, Jafar knew, but they were preferable to acknowledging another, far more damning reason he had to keep Alysson here.

He couldn't bear to let her return to the arms of another man.

Especially one man, his blood enemy.

Jafar closed his eyes, his lips twisting at the bitter irony. He wanted to laugh at this trap he had devised for himself, but he couldn't find the remotest humor in his present circumstance. It was a situation he himself had made possible—by betraying his oath of vengeance. If he had carried out his vow as he should have, he would not now be facing this bitter dilemma.

Yet there was really no decision to be made. The one thing he was not capable of doing was letting Alysson leave him. She was his, by Allah, *his*.

But she wasn't his. That was the hell of it. Because he had let his mortal enemy live, the young woman standing so anxiously before him could never belong to him.

Fury and despair welled up inside Jafar, making him want to lash out at her, to punish her for causing such weakness in him. "Are you so anxious to share my bed that you would *sell* yourself to me?" he demanded caustically.

Her chin came up abruptly at that. Her gaze was direct, defiant, in direct contradiction to the promise she had just made about no longer defying him. "I am anxious to spare my uncle any more hardship. If that means selling myself, then yes, I am willing."

Willing. That was what he had wanted, Jafar reflected. He had wanted her complete surrender, and now she was offering it to him. Her body for her uncle's freedom.

What kind of man accepted terms like that? What kind of man could walk away from such an offer? He didn't know if he had the strength of will to resist what she proposed.

Dragging in a deep breath, he managed to maintain a

semblance of control as he forced a reply. "The fate of your uncle does not rest in your hands."

"Jafar, please—"

"No! I will not discuss it! I won't bargain with you this way."

She was silent for a long moment. Jafar stared down at her pale, beautiful face, feeling the pain in her questioning, pleading gaze, yet unable, unwilling, to end it.

"You wouldn't . . . hurt them, would you?" she asked finally.

The tremble in her voice smote Jafar with guilt. "No," he answered gruffly. "Of course I wouldn't hurt them."

"But you won't let them go?"

"No."

"Why? Because you need them here? Because you need *me* here? Do you still require my presence here to have your revenge?"

It had nothing to do with revenge, Jafar thought with vehemence—and was surprised by his conviction. When had he stopped thinking of using Alysson in terms of revenge? The moment she had threatened to take her own life with a Berber rifle? When she'd lain so near death from the venomous scorpion's bite?

He stared down at her, recalling with agonized clarity the lament of a Berber love poem he had heard years ago, about how terrible it was to desire and not possess. He had scoffed at such sentiments then. But that was before he knew Alysson, before he knew this burning need to take her and make her his, to brand her with his possession.

Alysson watched his silent struggle, trying to comprehend what it meant. "Will you at least tell me what you intend to do with us?"

Taking a step back, Jafar abruptly turned away. "You will accompany me to my home, where you will remain until your uncle's wounds heal."

"I . . . I don't understand."

"Your uncle will recuperate more comfortably in the coolness of the mountains. And there I can provide the amenities he and you are accustomed to." He hesitated before adding, "You will be my honored guests."

Alysson shook her head bitterly. How like Jafar to couch

his command in terms of a polite invitation. "We will be your prisoners, you mean."

"As you wish."

She bit her lip. "You said when this was over, you would allow me to return to Algiers. You said when you accomplished your mission, you would let me go free."

At her quiet words she saw his entire body tense. "I have not accomplished my mission."

Alysson's heart suddenly seemed to stop beating. "What . . . did you say?"

The glance Jafar threw over his shoulder at her was filled with savage fury. "I said, I have *failed*. I did not kill your precious fiancé."

Stunned, Alysson stared at him. "Gervase is alive?" she whispered hoarsely.

Jafar didn't answer; he only stood there, violently clenching his fists.

Abruptly, Alysson's legs folded beneath her and she sank to her knees. She could hardly credit what he'd said. Dear heaven! Gervase was alive?

"What . . . happened?" she managed to ask. "Was Gervase injured? Did you take him prisoner?"

The brilliance of Jafar's gold eyes impaled her. "I did not kill him. You will have to be satisfied with that."

"Jafar . . . please." Her tear-filled eyes begged him. "I have to know."

Jafar clenched his teeth at her beseeching look. He could have told her that by now Colonel Bourmont and the other French officers would be safely interned in Ben Hamadi's camp; although he'd spared his enemy's life, he had no intention of allowing Bourmont anywhere near Alysson Vickery. Nor did he intend ever to let her know just how much power she had over him.

Yet he could not deny her the simple reassurance she was pleading for. "He is my prisoner," Jafar said finally, "but he is unharmed."

Alysson closed her eyes. Gervase was a prisoner, but he was alive. He was *alive!*

A joyous feeling of deliverance welled in her heart, lightening the burden of despair she'd carried with her for so many days. Jafar had spared his blood enemy. He was not the cruel barbarian she'd feared. He was not a coldhearted murderer. He was noble and merciful and wonderful . . .

She buried her face in her hands, savoring the sensation. Jafar cursed.

Such profound relief for his enemy was something he couldn't bear to see from her. In two strides he was across the room, grasping Alysson's arms and dragging her to her feet. "You will not weep for him!"

Only then did Alysson become aware of the scalding tears streaming down her face. They were tears of joy, of exultation. She gazed at Jafar mutely, her throat too clogged to speak.

When she didn't answer, his fingers tightened painfully on her arms, as if he might shake her. "Stop this, do you hear me?"

She swallowed hard, trying to control her emotions. "And now? What will become of Gervase?"

Jafar's grip only tightened further. "Enough! I forbid you to speak his name in my hearing, do you understand?"

Slowly Alysson nodded. Even Jafar's unreasonable demands could not dim the joy she was feeling at this moment. She was free, free of the dark, insidious fear that had haunted her during the past terrible weeks, free of the crushing guilt.

Through fading tears, she looked up at him without speaking. His eyes blazed with a savage fury that should have frightened her, yet strangely, that burning gaze only reassured her.

More than that, it brought back memories of a night not so long ago, a night sensual and dark with desire, when Jafar had taught her what it meant to be a woman. She had tried desperately to forget that night, to forget the wicked, erotic things he had done to her and with her, the way he'd dominated her senses and made her body shake with passion. But now her pulse, nerves, skin, heart suddenly remembered everything he'd made her feel then.

Inexplicably, uncontrollably, she found herself trembling. She wanted to touch him—with such primal urgency that it gave her the courage to raise her hand and twine her fingers around his nape.

Jafar stiffened abruptly, as if he couldn't bear the contact, but he didn't draw away.

Alysson stepped closer, pressing her body against his. He wanted her, she knew it. Jafar himself had stripped her of her innocence and taught her to recognize the signs of a man's passion. She could not mistake his tenseness, could not doubt the way his body had heated and hardened against hers, the swelling of his masculinity. He was as aroused as a man could be.

And she wanted him in return. She wanted to know the exquisite promise of his body; she wanted the hot pressure of his mouth on hers.

Staring into his burnt-honey eyes, she raised her mouth for his kiss.

"Alysson, don't!" It was a savage growl, a command, a plea. But she didn't obey.

Powerless to move away, Jafar closed his eyes, shutting out the sight of her beautiful face. Yet the first velvet caress of her warm breath on his lips demolished his tenuous control.

His hard mouth came down hers, hungry and hurtful, a raw act of possession as an instinct stronger than reason drove him. He wanted to mark Alysson as his. He wanted to drive all thought of Gervase de Bourmont from her head, from her heart. He wanted to hear her whisper *his* name, to plead in incoherent words against his lips, to cry out in joy as she reached incredible heights of pleasure with him.

The cruel fierceness of his kiss startled Alysson, not because of the unrelenting anger she tasted in his mouth, in his thrusting tongue, but because within that brutal kiss there was pain. His pain. An aching vulnerability that touched her soul in a way nothing else ever had. She made a soft, answering whimper of need deep in her throat and opened to him.

At her surrender, Jafar sank his fingers roughly into her hair, anger and arousal making his blood surge hot. Anger at himself for betraying his blood oath; anger at Alysson for being the cause. Fury that she should love another man. Rage that she was responding now because she was grateful to him for sparing her fiancé's life.

It was gratitude, only that.

The terrible realization was like salt on a raw wound, dragging Jafar suddenly, painfully, back to his senses. He could not, *would* not, allow her to give herself to him out of gratitude. Nor could he take her with the ghost of Bourmont in his bed, lying between them. He would never be able to stomach himself afterward.

Bitterly, with a superhuman effort at control, he tore his mouth from hers, his fingers digging painfully into her arms as he held Alysson away from him.

Startled, she gazed at him in incomprehension. His face was shadowed, his jaw clenched with determination, though his breath came unnaturally fast.

"I won't have you this way, *Ehuresh.*"

His harsh rasp was like a dash of icewater on her burning skin. All she could do was stare at him.

Even more abruptly, he released her and began to gather up his sword and burnous, his movements rapid yet unsteady.

"Jafar . . . what . . . ?"

He made no reply, merely flung his burnous over his shoulders.

Alysson watched in bewilderment as he turned and strode quickly from the chamber. "You're not leaving!"

"Yes!"

She took a faltering step after his retreating form. "But where are you going?"

"To sleep with my men! I find I have a conscience after all!"

Chapter 16

"**G**uests! That barbarian says we are to consider ourselves his guests!" the elderly Frenchman railed at his niece from his sickbed.

"Uncle, please, lie still. Don't upset yourself so." Anxiously, Alysson put a hand to Honoré's forehead, again checking for fever. But his skin was still cool to the touch. He didn't seem to have suffered unduly from his wounds. In fact, he'd professed to having passed a comfortable night.

Unlike her. She'd spent the remainder of the night restlessly tossing and turning, unable to find respite from the storm of reflections and emotions assailing her. So much had happened in the past few hours. Her uncle's captivity. Gervase's deliverance from death. Jafar's clemency. His rejection of her kiss . . .

Incredibly, Jafar had left his tent solely to her; she'd slept alone for nearly the first time since meeting her demon captor. And to her profound dismay, Alysson had found herself missing his warmth, his vital, comforting presence. She felt so alone without him.

Disturbed by the inexplicable yearnings of her heart and body, Alysson had at last fallen into an exhausted slumber. She'd risen at dawn, in no less turmoil than when Jafar had stalked out of his tent a few hours before. Trying to forget her agitation, she'd gone directly to her uncle's tent and found him awake.

Honoré had been appropriately elated when she shared the joyous news about Gervase, but even that had not mollified his outrage at his own treatment. It seemed that Jafar had already paid her uncle a visit this morning to extend an invitation to accompany him to his mountain home. Honoré's reaction had been one of indignation.

"But of course I accepted," Honoré blustered now. "I was hardly in a position to refuse, after all. I am not so foolish as to challenge that savage warlord when I am injured this way—" He waved a hand at his bandaged ribs. "—or at any time. It is wiser not to argue with a man like that."

"Certainly it is," Alysson said soothingly, but Honoré was too worked up to notice.

"We are to leave at once, this very morning. He said it is for our own protection, since this area is no longer safe from attack. *Peste!* That I do not believe."

Alysson was not so quick to dismiss Jafar's reasoning, though she doubted protecting his captives was his major consideration in moving his camp so quickly. He might have been the victor of the recent battle, but he could hardly keep his tribe in the area to become easy targets if the French forces decided to pursue. "I suppose there is some truth to what he said, Uncle. If there is another battle, we could very well be in danger from artillery fire."

Honoré harrumphed loudly. "Perhaps, but is the height of hypocrisy for that . . . that devil to call us his guests."

"I know." She patted his shoulder. "But that is better than being his prisoners. We haven't been treated badly, especially considering that we are his enemy. He could have kept us in chains or even killed us."

Realizing what she'd just said, Alysson shook her head wryly. How ironic that she should be defending Jafar's actions and even his right to hold them hostage. But she couldn't bring herself to condemn him at the moment; her relief over his magnanimity overwhelmed any outrage she might have felt at his continuing to hold her here. Indeed, rather than protest, she was more inclined to go down on her knees and thank him for sparing Gervase.

Besides, by now she knew how futile it was to struggle against Jafar. As usual, she had little choice but to obey him. If he had decreed they were to accompany him, then they would accompany him.

"At any rate," she told her uncle, "you will be more comfortable in the mountains, away from the desert heat."

"Bah! I would be many times more comfortable if I were safe on the soil of France," Honoré retorted in an aggrieved tone.

Suddenly he stopped, his heavy silver brows drawing together in a frown. "What am I saying?" Slowly Honoré turned his head on the pillow to look at her. "What right do I have to complain when you have suffered this captivity for weeks?" Awkwardly, he reached for her hand. "I am not so indifferent as it seems, my dear. When you were taken from me that day, I thought . . . For so long there was no word." Honoré faltered, anxiously surveying her face. "You told me the truth? You were not mistreated? He did not harm you in any way?"

The haunted expression in her uncle's dark eyes told her better than words how deeply he cared for her, how worried he had been for her safety, while the tremble in his voice told her of his need of reassurance. The reassurance that he had not failed her.

Her throat suddenly tight, Alysson shook her head. "He did not harm me, Uncle."

"But you are far too pale, to my mind. And there are circles beneath your eyes."

"I had the misfortune to be stung by a scorpion. I was ill for a time, but I am fine now."

A clatter from outside the tent made Alysson glance over her shoulder. All the while she'd been talking to her uncle, the sounds of activity had been on the rise.

Just then Chand appeared at the entrance to the tent. As enterprising as usual, he had been scouting out the camp to discover what he could about their situation.

The Indian servant salaamed to his mistress, before reporting the information he had gleaned about their impending departure. "Memsahib, the Berber lord bid me tell you that you are to make the necessary preparations for travel. We are to leave within the hour. I was also commanded to say that all arrangements will be made for the Larousse Sahib's comfort."

Honoré grunted at that, but Alysson nodded in acknowledgment, trusting Jafar to keep his word.

Drawing the blanket up to cover her uncle's shoulders, she kissed his cheek. "Uncle, I must go, but I'll return as soon as I can. Chand, would you see to him?"

"As you wish, memsahib."

She rose to leave, anxious to question Mahmoud and discover what the boy knew about yesterday's battle and Gervase's fate—all the details that Jafar had refused to tell her last night.

When she stepped outside, the scene was one of bustling activity as the Berbers broke camp. There was no immediate sign of Jafar, but outside his tent, she found Saful readying the horses. Within, Mahmoud was gathering Jafar's personal effects and amassing the furnishings.

To her surprise and bewilderment, Mahmoud responded to her greeting with a sullen look. Not since before her illness had he shown that hostile face to her.

"Do you wish me still to serve you, lady?" the boy asked without warning.

Alysson eyed him blankly. "Yes . . . is there some reason why I should not?"

"Your servant is with you now."

"Chand?"

"I do not know his name."

Mahmoud turned away, his limp pronounced. Alysson stared after him. Could the child actually be jealous of Chand? "I still need you to look after me, Mahmoud. Chand cannot care for me the way you do, especially now when he will be busy seeing to my uncle."

Mahmoud shrugged his skinny shoulders, but she thought she might have mollified him.

Following him into the rear room, she began to collect the native garments she'd been given to wear and contemplated how to approach Mahmoud with her questions. Beside her, the boy muttered to himself in Arabic as he went about his duties. ". . . blacksmith's blood . . . the devil Bourmont . . ."

Understanding those last words, Alysson felt her heart skip a beat. She let another minute go by before remarking casually, "Last night Jafar told me that Colonel Bourmont is his prisoner."

"Yes, lady."

When the boy shot her a suspicious glance, Alysson resumed her packing, not wanting to appear too obvious. "I must admit I was shocked to learn that the colonel is still alive. Your master left here with every intention of killing him."

Mahmoud's scarred face puckered in a frown. "This is true. There was a fight with swords, but the lord did not strike the fatal blow. Saful saw it with his own eyes. It was the cause of much talk among our people." The boy shook his head in puzzlement. "I do not understand my lord's reasoning. They were enemies of blood. But he must have had good cause," Mahmoud declared, staunchly loyal as always. "Surely it is the will of Allah."

Alysson's fingers tightened involuntarily on the fabric she was folding. "Can you tell me where the colonel is now? Do you know what Jafar means to do with him?"

"The lord does not share his confidences with me," Mahmoud said guardedly. At Alysson's worried look, however, he offered an explanation. "Sidi Farhat has escorted the French prisoners to the camp of the Khalifa Ben Hamadi. Saful told me the colonel and his officers will be exchanged for other prisoners of war."

Alysson nodded and returned to her task, relief flooding through her. A few minutes later she was surprised by Mahmoud's voice.

"Why do you cry, lady?" he asked curiously.

Suddenly aware of the tears on her cheeks, Alysson wiped at them awkwardly and flashed Mahmoud a brilliant smile, the first true smile that had crossed her lips in weeks. "They are happy tears, Mahmoud."

Happy indeed, Alysson thought. Gervase was safe and soon he would be free.

When she had finished securing the clothing in bundles, Alysson helped Mahmoud strike the huge tent, willingly doing whatever she was told. By the time that was done, the hot sun had begun a shimmering trek across the sky, beating down on the Berbers who were forming a caravan of horses and goods. Covering her head with a haik for protection, Alysson went to join her uncle.

She found Honoré somewhere in the middle of the column, with Chand hovering over him. It made her smile to see the luxurious mode of travel her wounded uncle would enjoy. Jafar had shown Honoré every courtesy, even going so far as to have a curtained litter built for his use. Both she and Chand had been provided with horses to ride.

She told her uncle and servant what she'd learned about Gervase, but afterward, Alysson lapsed into silence. As she stood waiting for the caravan to finish forming, she found herself growing impatient. Where was Jafar?

It was nearly twenty minutes later that she caught a glimpse of him, moving on foot toward her. She watched his approach with a new-felt tenderness in her eyes and an eagerness in her heart that caught her off guard.

And yet she shouldn't have been surprised by the depth of her feelings for him. For some time now she'd been increasingly aware of a truth she didn't want to acknowledge.

She couldn't deny the longing she felt for Jafar. The desire. The love—

Abruptly, Alysson drew a labored breath. She didn't love Jafar. She couldn't. It was impossible. He was the man who held her captive, who had taken her uncle and Gervase prisoner.

And certainly he didn't cherish any such tender feelings for her. Color tinged her cheeks as the disturbing events of last evening came back to haunt her. She had humbled herself before Jafar last night, offering to submit to him willingly, to give him the use of her body. Not only had he refused, but when later she'd tried to kiss him, he had rejected her entirely, storming out of the tent as if he couldn't even bear to touch her. The memory made her acutely self-conscious. Biting her lip, Alysson wondered how she would find the courage to face him now.

When Jafar reached her, though, the sight of him startled her. His face was smooth-shaven now but carved by lines of weariness that made her want to take him in her arms and soothe away the pain. Apparently he had not passed a very restful night, either.

His hard golden gaze swept over her briefly, then moved to her uncle, who was lounging comfortably in the curtained litter. "You are ready to leave?"

"Yes," Alysson replied.

His gaze swung back to her. "I will help you mount."

His terse statement was a command that held no warmth. He gave her no time to protest, either, but caught Alysson around the waist and lifted her into the saddle.

Yet when Jafar had set her on her horse, she couldn't help reaching out to touch his lean cheek in a tender gesture. "Thank you . . ." she murmured, her throat tight with emotion.

He looked at her with a slight wariness. "For what, mademoiselle?"

"For sparing Gervase's life."

Abruptly Jafar's expression turned savage. "I do not want your gratitude!"

The words were nearly a snarl as he spun on his heel and stalked off, toward the head of the column.

Startled by his vehemence and abrupt departure, Alysson

watched Jafar's retreating figure with bewilderment. Belat-
edly, she remembered his express command not to mention
Gervase's name in his hearing, and yet she didn't think that
alone explained his anger toward her.

Beside her, Chand, who had not yet mounted, also gazed
after Jafar. "I do not know why the Berber lord did this
thing . . . sparing the Bourmont Sahib."

Helplessly Alysson shook her head. She did not know
why either. In truth, she didn't understand anything about
Jafar anymore.

"I do not believe the Jafar Sahib is as savage as I have
judged him," Chand remarked thoughtfully.

"No," she answered, her expression softening. "I suppose not."

The traveling conditions for the caravan shortly became
very difficult. The limitless sand deepened into shifting
dunes that formed high ridges, broken occasionally by thorn-
scrub. The shimmering panorama of the desert abruptly
ended to the west, however, where gaunt masses of cliff
rose steeply and dipped away to the south. According to
Mahmoud, who rode beside Alysson, this rugged and torn
range was the Ouled Nail mountains.

As the morning progressed, Alysson began to wonder if
she was seeing things, for nestled at the foot of the mountains was a mirage of dark groves and white minarets. It
was with a sense of shock when, an hour later, she realized
the vision was no mirage, but rather an oasis. During her
captivity she had been only a few hours' ride from civilization! If she had known, she might have made good her
escape, instead of nearly perishing in the desert.

Dismayed by the injustice of it, Alysson pressed her lips
together and called herself a hundred kinds of fool for cherishing such tender feelings toward Jafar.

She could not sustain her ill humor, though, once they
arrived. It was a huge oasis, boasting thousands of palms.
Among the towering trees glistened white cupolas and the
slim turrets of mosques, while higher up, on a yellow, rocky
plain, stood a citadel overlooking the terraced mud-houses
and narrow lanes of the town.

The beautiful oasis was called Bou Saada, Mahmoud informed her. "It bears the name 'Abode of Happiness,' " the boy said. Perhaps, Alysson suspected, because of the profusion of lush greenery and obviously productive land. The forests of date palms, crowned by dark green feathery leaves, were still partially laden with golden and coral clusters of dates. Prickly pears and oleanders also abounded, along with apricot, fig, and other fruit trees. Along the way, Alysson caught a glimpse of a riverbed, in which flowed a quiet stream, with thickets of tamarisk bushes lining the high bank.

Their caravan skirted the edge of the oasis, but Alysson was close enough to see that it bustled with activity and swarmed with people: Berbers, Jews, and Bedouin nomads. Merchants, peasants, sheiks. Women, veiled and unveiled.

"Do not look, lady!" Mahmoud exclaimed when Alysson found herself staring curiously at an old Berber woman who was chanting some strange song. "She is a *kahina*, a witch. It will bring grave misfortune to you and your kin to look so closely upon her."

Alysson smiled but refrained from comment, for Mahmoud obviously believed in the power of sorcery. Apparently it was true, as she'd been told, that the Berbers were even more superstitious than the Arabs.

"Is Bou Saada always this crowded?" she asked instead.

"It is possible, I do not know. I have visited here only once. Currently there is a festival in progress."

Intrigued by the prospect of a festival, Alysson feasted on the exotic sights and smells and sounds. Shortly, her attention was caught by shouts and the noise of bargaining, which she recognized as coming from a bazaar—a *suq*, as it was called in Arabic. Every village and oasis had one.

It was at this market, according to Mahmoud, that they would purchase provisions for the long journey to Jafar's mountain home.

Alysson would have enjoyed exploring the *suq*, but she was still weak and her energy was depleted after the long ride. She made no protest when they set up camp on the outskirts of the oasis.

Alysson saw to her uncle first. Honoré was in more than a little pain from the jostling he had received, even in his comfortable litter. She made certain Gastar gave him another sleeping potion, then returned to Jafar's tent to rest for the remainder of the afternoon. She immediately fell into a deep sleep.

She woke several hours later, feeling more refreshed than she had in days. By the time she was fully awake, though, her energy had returned in the guise of acute restlessness.

With no other way to dispel it, Alysson began pacing the tent floor, her thoughts chafing again at her captivity. It chagrined her to think how near to escape she'd been. Just as it frustrated her to still be so helpless . . . more helpless than ever, now that she had to worry about her uncle and Chand as well. This tent, this camp was still her prison.

Alysson interrupted her pacing to pause at the entrance of the tent and look longingly toward the exciting, vivid, thriving community of Bou Saada. The sight filled her with a fiery, restless need. The mounting pressure built till she felt ready to explode, and she turned to pace again—until she suddenly sensed Jafar's presence.

She came to a halt, trying to quell the sudden pounding of her heart, and slowly turned to face him. She'd seen no sign of him for hours. Uncertainly, she regarded him with questioning eyes. Was he still inexplicably angry with her?

"I thought perhaps you might like to see something of the town." His low tone was even, his expression enigmatic as usual.

Alysson let out her breath slowly. She would have given half her fortune to be allowed a moment's freedom.

"Yes, I would love to see the town," she replied, not bothering to keep the eagerness from her tone.

His gaze traveled down her body, which was clad in only in a blouse and pantaloons. "Wear your good robes. I will return for you in one hour."

Alysson didn't need to be told twice. She wasted no time in washing and then dressing in the second-finest outfit she had, a rose silk tunic and haik, with a burnous of soft blue wool as an overwrap. Even after checking again on her sleeping uncle, though, she was ready half an hour early.

She caught her breath when Jafar finally arrived. He was dressed magnificently in a flowing white djellaba and a scarlet burnous that was fit for a king.

Drinking in the sight of him, she realized that he was

also staring at her. The light in his tawny eyes that was so harsh and unreadable suddenly softened with warmth, leaving no doubt in her mind that he was pleased with her appearance, that perhaps he even thought her beautiful.

"Come, *Temellal*."

The husky scrape of his voice surprised and disturbed her, and so did the way he offered her his arm, just as any European gentleman would have done. How could she maintain an impersonal aloofness toward him when he acted in such a provocative, civilized fashion?

The sun was beginning to set as they crossed the short distance from the encampment and delved into the town. Their progress along the busy streets soon became impeded, for Alysson stopped every few minutes, observing everything around her with unfeigned delight and asking questions that tumbled over one another. Her enthusiasm brought a smile to Jafar's lips more than once.

Alysson ignored his amusement, for she was enjoying herself immensely. Even if she hadn't been told of the festival in progress, she would have known from the hint of expectation and excitement that filled the air along with the noise. People of all descriptions crowded the narrow streets, while scores had gathered on the flat rooftops and were leaning from the open verandas and galleries. When over the throng she heard music coming from a distance—the rhythmic sound of drums and trumpets and tambourines—she tugged at Jafar's arm like an eager child.

Shortly they came to a square that was lit by smoking torches. In one corner a juggler performed his act, showing an uncanny dexterity in throwing knives into thin boards. In another corner, beside a huge bonfire, were some dozen musicians.

She could tell they were Berbers by their lean ascetic features. Clad in white burnouses tied at the waist with thick hemp ropes, they were otherwise barefooted and bareheaded. Half of the men were engaged in chanting a solemn prayer, while the others blew on their trumpets and pounded on their drums and tambourines.

In a third corner, an old beggar in tattered rags sat beside two baskets wrapped with strips of linen.

"A snake charmer," Jafar responded to Alysson's questioning glance. He tossed the old man a silver coin and ordered a performance, and almost immediately a crowd gathered around.

Alysson was accustomed to the snake charmers in India, but they were nothing like this. From one basket the old man drew a giant lizard—a varan, she thought. The reptile had a leather strap tied tightly around its neck, which the charmer used to tease it, first letting it scurry around, then yanking on the leash. Alysson winced with every pull.

Finally, from the second basket, the man drew a dark yellow serpent with brown spots and little horns protruding just behind the eyes. The deadly horned viper raised its head threateningly at the crowd, opening its jaws to display venomous fangs.

Remembering the deadly poison of the scorpion that had stung her, Alysson instinctively edged closer to Jafar, and was comforted to feel the strength of his muscular arm come to rest at her waist.

The next moment the two reptiles spied each other. The small viper froze for an instant, then attacked. Alysson gasped. As large as it was, the lizard would have no defense against the deadly fangs.

The battle, however, was not one-sided at all. The lizard whirled and smote the viper with its powerful tail, then caught the serpent in its mouth, as if to crush the small skull. Swiftly, the old man yanked on the leash once more, rescuing the viper. Then calmly he replaced the two reptiles in their baskets, signaling the end of the performance.

"How cruel to keep them imprisoned so," Alysson murmured to no one in particular.

Beside her, Jafar went still. He stared down at her for a long moment until she became aware of his scrutiny and looked up.

"Come," he said finally. "I'm sure you are hungry."

Lifted from her momentary depression, Alysson laughed, surprised to notice that for the first time since her illness, her appetite had returned. "I could devour an elephant."

They walked on through the gathering darkness, up the climbing streets, till they came to the heart of the town. Here the celebration was more circumspect.

When Jafar finally stopped before a house, Alysson could

hear the music of violins and native guitars and the plaintive tones of a flute issuing from within. The place seemed to be the equivalent of an English tavern, she decided as they entered. A blue haze of smoke hung like a veil over the huge room, while dozens of gaily robed customers sat cross-legged on the floor, drinking coffee and smoking the pipes of Barbary.

A small man met them at the door—the proprietor, Alysson assumed. With an obsequious bow, he escorted them up a narrow flight of stairs to the open rooftop. There, oil lamps glowed at discreet intervals, giving the scene an exotic golden cast.

They followed their host across the roof to an area decorated by thick carpets, where a low table waited. As Alysson settled herself upon a cushion beside Jafar, she glanced curiously at the group of musicians who sat off to one side. Besides the drums and tambourines she had seen earlier, she noticed two reed flutes, a double-stringed lute, an instrument similar to a violin, and one resembling a bagpipe. With a flourish, they struck up a tune.

It was only then that Alysson realized she and Jafar were the only guests present. Suspecting Jafar had bought the entertainment for the evening, she glanced at the tall, savagely handsome, enigmatic man beside her. Had he done it for her? In Barbary it was not the custom to allow women to eat with men or enjoy the same entertainments. It warmed her to think that Jafar had gone out of his way to ensure her pleasure.

Their host served them himself. Watching Jafar in order to emulate him, Alysson took a sip of the drink she had been given, and promptly gave a gasp. She hadn't expected it to burn her throat so.

"It is called arrack," Jafar said. "The honey of the date tree. Do you not care for it?"

"Yes, it is fine. I just wasn't prepared."

Warned now, she took another cautious sip of the fiery native drink. It was both sweet and tart, and highly potent. "I did not think Muslims drank spirits," she commented.

Jafar smiled. "The strict rules of Islam are relaxed on the borders of the Sahara. Moreover, Berbers are not as religious as Arabs in general." When she appeared interested, he expounded. "We think nothing of eating wild boar's flesh or other animals branded as impure by the Koran. The wearing of tattoos is expressly forbidden by the Koran, yet it is a custom which prevails among our tribes. Indeed, we have many customs that are not shared by Arabs. We drink arrack and fig brandy . . . we break our fast at Ramadan . . . we are more superstitious . . . we pay our Saints more reverence . . . we do not despise Jews . . . our celebrations are far wilder."

Though fascinated, Alysson regarded Jafar curiously, wondering why he was telling her about his people and their customs. "Mahmoud said a festival was in progress today."

"Yes, a traditional Muslim observance—the Feast of Bairam. It honors Abraham's obedience to God in sending his son Ishmael into the desert."

The first courses of the meal came then, and they truly were a feast. With the lamb and chicken was served an incredible array of vegetables—roasted eggplant, turnips, carrots, and hazelnuts, to name a few. Then came a delicious couscous, eaten with chunks of lamb cooked in chopped onion and nuts. For dessert there was fruit, dates and melons and tangerines, followed by rich strong coffee.

Then came the dancers, women with tattooed foreheads, painted cheeks, and henna-red palms.

The first to perform had jet-black hair and proud beautiful features, with a light, slightly olive complexion and enigmatic eyes. Her regal robes were accented by a golden crown of peacock feathers, while broad bracelets, chains of gold, and heavy earrings adorned her arms, neck, and ears.

When the music struck up, she began to dance in a slow sinuous rhythm, all the while throwing Jafar languorous looks from half-closed eyes. The come-hither glances held a familiarity that Alysson could not misinterpret.

"Do you know her?" she asked Jafar, surprised at the sharp emotion she felt; it was jealousy, hot and stinging and unmistakable.

"Her name is Fatum."

His oblique answer did not at all satisfy Alysson. She slanted Jafar a glance, her eyebrow raised expectantly.

"The women of the Ouled Nail tribe range all over Barbary," he explained. "Their dances are famous in every city."

"I would not have thought their men would approve of them dancing in public," Alysson murmured, recalling how protective the Arabs were of the female gender.

"Their men not only approve, but encourage them." Jafar smiled when Alysson's eyes widened. "These women are courtesans, *Ehuresh*. They make their living dancing and selling their . . . ah, charms to the other tribes of the kingdom for a handsome price. In fact, their men think nothing of selling their wives and daughters for the money they bring."

They were prostitutes, Alysson thought weakly. "How barbaric," she managed to reply.

"On the contrary. It is all quite civilized. They provide a valuable service, and in exchange, earn money to bring home to their husbands, or collect enough for a dowry so they may marry."

Disturbed, Alysson turned back to watch Fatum dance, yet as the slow expressive movements changed into a flaming, sensual frenzy, she couldn't help but wonder precisely what the dancer's relationship was to Jafar. She was grateful when Fatum finally finished.

Fatum was replaced by a second woman with the same thin aquiline nose and fiery eyes, the same jet-black hair. This dancer, however, wore *chalwar*—full pantaloons of scarlet satin brocade—along with a fringed sash and a black velvet bolero embroidered with gold thread. On her head was a small black cap, and on her feet were red suede slippers. She also sported gold anklets in addition to the excessive amount of heavy gold jewelry similar to that which Fatum had worn.

The new dancer's long black hair swirled around her body as she twisted her ample curves in an age-old pantomime of desire, showing to advantage her savagely beautiful and graceful figure.

"I suppose you know her as well," Alysson murmured, unable to keep the waspish note from her voice.

Turning, Jafar raised an eyebrow at her, observing her curiously. There might also have been a hint of amusement in his eyes as he replied, "Her name is Barca."

He deftly changed the subject then, explaining the meanings of the various ritual dances. While Fatum had performed the Dance of the Handkerchief, this was the Dance of the Sword. Next an entire group of half-wild women of the Ouled Nail tribe came out to dance and sing of heroism and love.

Then Fatum and Barca returned to dance more of the burning dances of the desert, sinuously undulating their firm young bodies, emitting a violent and savage sensuality. That, as well as their alluring glances at Jafar, Alysson found profoundly disturbing. If they had not yet known the ecstasy of Jafar's bed, they were certainly amenable now.

Perhaps, Alysson thought, pressing her lips together, Jafar hadn't been lying when he claimed to have no concubines. With beauties like these at his beck and call, Jafar would have little need for a permanent stable of mistresses.

Other than an appreciative interest in the artistry of the dance, however, Jafar paid little attention to the women posturing and swaying before him. And he paid no attention at all to the alluring glances cast by Fatum and Barca. Whatever erotic thoughts he had were solely focused on the young woman sitting beside him. Whatever arousal he felt was due entirely to Alysson Vickery.

And he did feel arousal. Her nearness, her very presence, was like an elixir in his blood. Even now, although sitting quite still, she was so intensely alive that other women seemed tame in contrast.

Involuntarily, Jafar shifted his glance to Alysson, letting his gaze caress her. She was so different from the women of his country, yet she didn't suffer in comparison. Not only was she as fiery as any impassioned daughter of the desert, she possessed the proud and courageous spirit of the Atlas highlands. Her very vitality inflamed his senses. That, and his own vivid recollections.

He felt his blood heat as the image of her lying naked beneath him raced through his memory . . . her slender, flushed body, so shapely and supple and sweet-breasted. He wanted to have her that way again. He wanted her passionate. He wanted to pleasure her, to please her . . .

Alysson chose that moment to meet his gaze. A mistake, she realized at once. In Jafar's eyes she saw an unsettling, smoldering possession that roused as acutely as a touch. Her breathing shallowed. The blatant desire in his golden hawk's gaze was too provocative, too naked. She had to look away.

It startled her that desire could be born so quickly from just a simple glimpse, yet she couldn't deny the savage spark of feeling that flared between them—a fierce, primitive feeling of lust, of need, of want. She wanted him. With a desperation that was totally inexplicable, entirely reprehensible. Which only added further confusion to the tangled, bittersweet, complicated emotions she felt for Jafar.

For the remainder of the performance, Alysson sat in tense, unappreciative silence, trying unsuccessfully to dismiss such disquieting thoughts of him from her mind. She was grateful when the entertainment concluded, for she thought surely the dancers would leave. Much her dismay, though, both Fatum and Barca sauntered over to kneel before Jafar in order to hear his praise.

Alysson forced herself to murmur a polite compliment about their dancing, which Jafar then translated. For a full minute she even endured the sly glances and the not-so-subtle enmity of the other two women while they conversed with Jafar in his language, which she couldn't understand. Then abruptly Alysson rose and crossed the rooftop to the far parapet wall. She knew it was rude of her, but she couldn't bear to remain another minute while those two sultry beauties flirted with Jafar and made arrangements to share his bed.

She was staring restlessly at the crowded streets below when she felt his presence beside her. Behind her there was silence; apparently he had dismissed both the dancers and the musicians. But the noise from below was no less diminished. It only served to scrape her already lacerated nerves.

"Is this an example of your wild celebrations?" Alysson asked finally when Jafar didn't speak.

"Yes. Often dances are held in the open air. Afterward the performances are followed by the ritual of *Leilat el Gholta*. The Night of Error."

"Error? What does that mean?"

"No one knows. *Leilat el Gholta* is a Berber custom which springs from mystic beliefs. The participants choose a partner for the evening and surrender themselves to debauchery for the night.''

Alysson felt shock coloring her cheekbones as she turned to look up at Jafar. "Do you mean to tell me your festival is little more than an orgy?"

He stared down at her for the space of several heartbeats, his gaze dark and intent. But his smile, when it came, was the epitome of masculine beauty. "It is very much an orgy, *chérie.*"

Alysson caught her breath, diverted not so much by the implications of what he had just said, as by the wild and daring notion that had just entered her head.

In fact, she was surprised to feel herself trembling. But it was quite cold, after all. As usual in the desert, the temperature had fallen dramatically with the setting sun. She tensed as Jafar reached around her to draw the folds of her burnous more snugly around her shoulders.

"Come, you are shivering. I will take you . . ."

His hesitation struck her in an odd way. *Home,* was what he had meant to say, she was sure. But she couldn't quell the erotic images his unfinished statement conjured up. *He would take her.*

Mentally Alysson shook herself. Making love to her was not at all what Jafar had meant. Instead, he would escort her back to his tent, but like the previous night, he wouldn't stay. He would leave her to sleep alone, to bear the unbearable ache of physical frustration and unfulfilled desire. Then no doubt he would return here to enjoy the "valuable services" the exotic Ouled Nail courtesans were all too willing to provide.

Unless she stopped him.

The thought made Alysson clench her fingers till the nails scored her palms. Yet she had to acknowledge the truth. In one respect, she was actually no different from those courtesans. She *wanted* Jafar, wanted to give herself to him, to experience fully the passion that she'd only tasted in his arms that night long ago.

Just then she heard shouting in the street. Alysson turned to peer over the wall, deliberately not looking at Jafar. "Are infidels allowed to participate in this Night of Error?"

"I suppose so. Why do you ask?"

She took a deep breath. This would not be the first time she had let herself be ruled by her wild and reckless heart. "Because," Alysson replied, keeping her tone light, "I find the thought of an orgy fascinating. Are participants allowed to choose any partner they wish?"

She could feel Jafar's penetrating gaze boring into her. "Yes. There are no rules governing the choice. It makes no difference whether they are married or are strangers."

"Does it matter who does the choosing, the man or the woman?"

There was a long hesitation, before Jafar answered slowly. "No."

"Well then," Alysson said, somehow managing to keep her voice steady, despite the excitement and sweet arousal that was flooding her veins, "if it makes no difference, I choose you."

Chapter 17

The din of the celebration increased as Alysson and Jafar made their way back to camp through the crowded streets. The noise was a direct contrast to the silence between them. Jafar had not replied to her claim. Indeed, he had not spoken a word since she'd made her abrupt announcement.

Alysson had no idea what he was thinking. When she glanced at Jafar, his face was a collection of harsh shadows. He was not indifferent to her, though, that much she could tell. He had placed an arm around her shoulders to protect her from being jostled, while his other hand rested on the jeweled dagger at his waist. With him so near, she could feel his muscles coiled with a vital, dangerous energy.

She herself felt calm, yet alight with a cold flame of excitement. Tonight would be different from the last. This night she would not sleep alone.

The noise had abated by the time they finally reached Jafar's tent, so much that Alysson could almost hear the erratic beating of her heart. The oil lamp which had been left burning cast a welcome glow over the luxurious interior of the tent. Jafar escorted her inside, but then paused.

Without a word, he turned back toward the entrance.

Alysson felt her stomach twist into knots. "Jafar . . . wait!"

He halted abruptly, his stance rigid, expectant.

Alysson clenched her hands. All she could think about was that he would return to those women, that he would make love to those other women and not her. "Please . . . don't leave."

An eternity passed before he turned slowly again to face her. Meeting his gaze, she could see a hard and beautiful vibrancy deep in his golden eyes. "I told you before, *Ehuresh*, that I don't want your gratitude."

She didn't misunderstand him; Jafar thought she was offering herself because he had spared her fiancé's life. But it wasn't gratitude she was feeling at the moment. She hadn't even thought of Gervase in hours, which was perhaps shameful.

"No." Alysson shook her head. She was immensely grateful that he hadn't killed Gervase, but the powerful emotions she felt for this man standing before her had nothing remotely to do with gratitude. "No," she repeated in a stronger voice. "It's not gratitude. I want you for myself . . . for my lover."

How could he not believe her? Alysson wondered a bit desperately as she stood waiting for his answer. She held her breath while her fate hung in the balance.

Finally, in response, Jafar reached behind him to loosen the tent flap. He let it fall, shutting out the rest of the world. "I wasn't leaving," he said quietly.

Her heart began beating again; her breathing resumed.

Both took up an erratic rhythm when Jafar slowly moved toward her. Standing directly before her, he brushed the hood of her burnous back from her face. With almost a kind of reverence, he buried his hands in her hair, savoring the silky texture. But his eyes were fastened intently on her mouth.

Then he bent his head.

His kiss was not gentle; in it she tasted heat, danger, darkness . . . a hunger that matched her own. Though Jafar held her head still so he could ravish her mouth, she offered no resistance. Instead, her lips yielded under his in lush invitation, while blindly her arms came up to encircle his neck.

His teeth bit her bottom lip, gnawing gently, impatiently, provocatively, pulling the sensitive flesh into his mouth where he sucked it. A soft wild sound tore from her throat.

Jafar reacted to that arousing little sound like a man gone mad. Dragging his mouth away, he frenziedly kissed her slender throat, which arched gracefully, then bent her back over his arm. Feverishly seeking, his mouth moved downward over her robes, to close possessively over the ripe peak of her breast.

Alysson sucked in her breath. Even beneath layers of silk, she could feel the shocking warmth of his mouth and the immediate impact on her body; her nipple budded tightly, while a stabbing pleasure flooded her mind.

For a single moment she let herself ponder how Jafar's other women had managed to survive such incredible sensations. Then she banished the thought. It was useless to wonder how many women had found paradise in his arms before her. For tonight she would simply cherish the extraordinary feeling of being the woman who inspired his desire.

Careless of his headdress, she clutched at his turban, knocking it to the floor. Her grasping fingers twined in his tawny gold hair as she gave herself up with total abandon to the fierce delight of his embrace, to the sensual arousal of his caresses.

It was a long moment before Jafar finally drew a ragged breath and raised his head.

Dazed, awed, captivated, Alysson lifted her gaze to his. There was no pretense of charm within those amber depths, only smoldering fire.

"Undress me." The harsh, throaty texture of his voice ran over her raw nerve endings like a sensual fire. "Not

here," Jafar amended when she reached for the sash at his
waist.

Almost trembling, Alysson obeyed his command. Taking
his hand, she led Jafar into the darkened bedchamber, where
unsteadily she removed the jeweled dagger and let it fall to
the floor, then unwound his sash. Her shaking fingers tangled in the length of cloth because she paid so little attention to her task. All she could do was watch Jafar. With his
hair wild from her fingers, he looked rugged, barbarous,
and so blatantly sensual that she thought she might die if
he didn't kiss her again soon.

But still she was too slow. When she struggled to remove
his djellaba, Jafar took control. Impatiently he tugged it
over his head, exposing his bare chest to her fascinated view.
Awed by his masculine beauty, Alysson raised an inquisitive
hand. She could no more have denied herself the need to
touch him than she could have disavowed her next breath.

Her fingers, tentative yet strangely brazen, spread across
his chest, exploring contours and planes and textures. His
silken skin, hot as fire, rippled over steel-honed muscles,
making her ache with need.

Her wondering touch affected Jafar similarly. When she
made brief shy contact with his hard, flat nipples, the muscles in his jaw tightened as if he were in pain. Murmuring
a soft oath, he stepped back, out of reach, to shed his remaining garments.

When he was done, the sight of his virile nudity stole her
breath away. Dazed, weak, Alysson remained completely
still; she could only stare at his magnificent male form, at
the blatant evidence of his desire.

"Now, you." His voice was deeply husky now and edged
with desire.

Hardly knowing what she was doing, Alysson bent and
removed her slippers, then her own sash. But when it came
to removing her robes, she hesitated, instinctively shying
away from exposing her nakedness.

Jafar wouldn't let her desist, though. He kept his hot,
glittering gaze fixed steadily on her, as if he would seek out
all her secrets and destroy them.

Trembling, Alysson complied with his silent command.
This was not a night for secrets, after all.

She heard his sharp inhalation as her slender body was bared to his gaze. When somehow she found the courage to meet his eyes, the boldness of his scrutiny nearly unnerved her. His eyes made a thorough sweep of her body, roaming over her nakedness, touching her more intimately than his hands had done.

Those golden eyes were unmistakably hungry, yet they hazed with a possessive look as he reached for her, the predator's gaze softened by need.

Surprisingly, he didn't take her in his arms. Instead, his hand lightly feathered across her abdomen, then lower, to the lush riot of silky chestnut hair between her thighs.

"Oh . . . God . . ." Alysson gasped as a shaft of pleasure streaked through her, a pleasure so intense that her weak legs nearly buckled beneath her. Helplessly she grasped Jafar's muscular shoulders to keep from falling.

Yet he didn't stop his skillful, mind-destroying caresses. His features grew heavy with sensual pleasure as he watched her quivering response. Wondering if she could bear another moment of such exquisite torment, Alysson drew a shuddering breath into her lungs and closed her eyes.

Numerous pounding heartbeats later, she heard Jafar's hoarse command as if from a great distance. "Touch me, *Ehuresh* . . ."

With dazed obedience, she let her hands slide down his powerful chest, his tautly muscled stomach, his lean hips, till she found the essence of his maleness. His desire flowed against her fingers, silky and warm, and so potent it stirred an ache in her that was actually painful. And Jafar was experiencing a similar pain, Alysson realized. The soft groan that sounded deep in his throat told her just how agonizing he found the gentleness of her touch.

His arms came around her then. His urgent hands ran down the silky contours of her back, cupped her bottom, and hauled her fiercely close, making her feel the naked heat and strength of him.

"I want you, *Ehuresh*," he whispered harshly. "I want to do everything to you that a man has ever done to a woman . . ."

His lips claimed hers then, and there were no more words. His mouth mated with hers, their tongues meeting in hot, deep, writhing kisses. Passion flowed between them, dark and sweet, with a fierceness that was almost shocking. She felt the near-desperation of Jafar's lips, felt the seeking, the need, the wildness, and it touched an answering need deep within her. The sensual fire that burned in him, burned in her also.

Hardly aware of anything but that fire, Alysson submitted with yielding acquiescence, to the ungentle, prompting pressure that guided her backward. Lost in the dark honey of his kisses, she clung to him as he urged her toward the pallet. Then he was pressing her down among the soft pillows, following her, covering her, the heat from his body bathing her heightened senses.

"Jafar . . ." She only had time to whisper his name before he captured her mouth again with his, kissing her with such fierce demand that she was giddy. At his savage tenderness, she felt something wild and primitive wrench free inside her, like moorings ripped loose by a dark desert wind. It liberated an unknown, unexplored side of her, the side that was tempestuous, eager, not guided by reason, the deepest side of her, a wild and restless and questing Alysson Vickery. Feeling as if her spirit were soaring, she whimpered and strained against him, trying to absorb his body into hers.

Jafar responded with answering frenzy, his fingers delving into the riotous tangle of her hair, while his tongue plunged deeply into her mouth.

His mouth ate hers greedily, with a raw savage hunger that called to her. Warmth spread to her blood with a fierce, unbearable intensity, creating a wonderful, moist, aching weakness that pulsed in her most secret places. When an eternity later he allowed her to take a breath, she moaned, flinging her head back, instinctively offering him her throat and her breasts.

Without hesitation, he accommodated her, his lips moving over her silken skin. His tongue was a pagan lash of fire, leaving her hot and wanting. Her breasts hurt, swelled to his touch. Her body became taut and flushed.

And Jafar shamelessly encouraged her restless ardor. Hoarsely he whispered to her, disjointed words and phrases that made her quiver in response. She heard his murmured endearments as if from a great distance. Want had become craving. Craving had become need. Driving, desperate, mind-blotting.

Her hands roamed blindly over his hard-muscled body. She had never ached to touch a man this way, to be touched so intimately. She craved his possession, yearned for it, a yearning that would have shocked her if she could have thought beyond this moment. Once, the thought of such complete surrender would have appalled her. She had been afraid, perhaps even terrified, to lose herself in him. But his sensual, urgent caresses took away any possibility of fear.

She welcomed him eagerly, twisting her hips, arching upward as his fingers found the secrets of her femininity, stroking the hot, slick dampness, readying her for his taking.

Her eyes closed helplessly; her head thrashed from side to side in tortured longing. Yet the more feverish she became, the more he gentled his touch. Impossibly, he seemed to regain control as hers melted away.

Still, his need was as great as hers, she was certain. She felt his unchecked trembling as he gently parted her legs with his muscular thighs and prepared to claim her innocence. His hard body was shaking, throbbing with the passion he felt. She knew it, yet she could scarcely credit the realization that this proud, hard, ruthless man could be brought to his knees by desire for her.

In one dim, desire-hazed corner of her mind, Alysson felt strangely humbled. The ability to create such vulnerability in Jafar awed her, yet filled her with an overwhelming sense of invincible power. When he settled lower, between her thighs, she found herself responding with her whole heart, without shame or nervousness, straining toward him, lifting her hips to receive him, to join with him in a way that was elemental, natural.

Even so, his slowly thrusting entrance took her unaware, making her suddenly stiffen. She was breathless for a moment, from the sharp pain and from the impact of his invasion.

Jafar went still, gazing down at Alysson with such tenderness that she felt her heart swell with aching emotion.

"Do you want me to stop?" he murmured in unmistakable English. But she was beyond comprehending that strange fact.

"No . . . no, please . . . don't stop!" Her soft gasp was a throaty imperative, a plea.

He smiled . . . a smile of such sensual brilliance that it warmed her all over again. "Never, *Ehuresh.*"

Then slowly, with infinite care, he began to move again, scattering impassioned kisses over her face and throat and shoulders, pressing slowly deeper until her body yielded and took him completely.

Alysson exhaled slowly on a whimper of pleasure. She had not known how empty she was until he filled her. Had not known what rapture was until he became part of her. She felt an amazing sense of completeness that only Jafar could give her. The pain was gone now, leaving only throbbing, pulsing joy.

"Look at me," Jafar murmured hoarsely, but it was an unnecessary command. She couldn't have turned away if her life had depended on it.

He surveyed her flushed, love-drugged face as his hips withdrew and began another slow full thrust.

It was a measured, maddeningly gentle possession that nearly drove Alysson wild. Hot and feverish beneath him, she watched the light and darkness moving in his eyes as his body played skillfully against hers, teasing and tormenting, deliberately arousing her to a heated pitch. Presently, though, Jafar was caught up in the same sensual need he had created in her. Laboring for breath, he gave up his lover's games and increased the tempo. Abandoning gentleness for mastery, he arched over her, his hips moving in and out in a hot urgent rhythm.

"My sweet tigress . . ." Jafar rasped as he surged into her with a fierce, tantalizing thrust. Her whimper of pleasure became a sob of joy. Gasping, she strained against him with frenzied abandon, moving in wild, joyous response to his possession, withholding nothing. For her this joining was a celebration of Jafar's safe deliverance from battle, a celebration of life itself. For him it was a reverent consecration of her surrender.

"You are mine," he whispered harshly, hissing his ownership against her ear.

Yes! She wanted to cry in answer, but her breath was stolen from her as the spiraling ecstasy swept her up in its vortex. All she could do was give herself up to the glorious world of heat and light and sensation Jafar had created for her, as in his arms she became fully a woman.

"Alysson . . ." Jafar rasped her name in a fractured whisper of passion as he joined with her in paradise.

The slow return to consciousness long, long moments later was a cautious affair for Jafar. He felt as though his body and soul had shattered in a million fragments, and he wasn't certain if they could be mended.

For a long while he lay there completely still, his body cradled by hers, not daring to move except for the slight effort to spare Alysson the bulk of his weight. His breath was coming in ragged gasps, his limbs felt hot and heavy and languorous, while the tenderness welling within him made his heart feel near to bursting.

At last he chanced movement, his lips brushing her damp temple, her soft cheek, the curve of her throat, as he waited for the pounding rhythm of his heart to calm.

The imprecise thought that came floating into his mind then was more a vague comprehension than any conscious reflection: the surrender he had demanded of her had been given freely. And in accepting the gift, he had surrendered part of himself in return.

He had possessed and been possessed.

An imprecise notion, perhaps, but he sensed that for a precious moment in time, they had bonded together completely—physically, emotionally, spiritually. Had Alysson experienced that same soul-shattering union as well? Jafar was as certain as he was of his next heartbeat that she had felt at least physical pleasure. But had it been anything more for her?

Her soft sigh, part contentment, part exhaustion, wafting against his lips, didn't provide the answer he needed.

Jafar's own sigh was far heavier as tenderly he gathered Alysson's unresisting body in his arms. For the moment she had surrendered to him. For the moment she had yielded. But as he held her limp and sweetly sated form tightly against him, he had to acknowledge an irrefutable truth.

The mere act of possession did not make Alysson his.

Part Three

Let it be known to all that
The storm of love can kill!
By Allah! if this be so, I have
Not long to live. The sun will
Never shine again upon me!

BERBER POET

Chapter 18

Alysson awoke to the bustling morning sounds of the camp, alone but not lonely. How could she be lonely when she had the incredible memories of last night to warm her?

Reluctant to move, she buried herself more deeply in the blankets, missing the delicious heat of Jafar's body, the arousing sensuality of his caresses.

Jafar had left before dawn. With a soft endearment and a final kiss, he'd extricated himself from the drape of her sleepy body, whispering, at her murmured protest, some low explanation that she'd only half-understood about protecting her reputation and her uncle's sensibilities.

Now, as she stretched carefully, gingerly testing the sweetly aching muscles of her naked body, Alysson realized what Jafar had meant. It would be impossible to maintain appearances if he was found in her bed.

The thought made her smile. That a savage Berber warlord would be concerned about the sentiments of one aging, wounded Frenchman seemed totally incongruous. Yet she'd known for some time now that Jafar wasn't as savage and ruthless as she'd once believed. And she was immensely grateful now that he'd wanted to shield her uncle from the knowledge that they had become lovers.

Lovers.

Her smile softened with remembered pleasure. She had taken a lover. An incredibly sensual man who had carried her to the heights of fulfillment she'd never dreamed possible. A vitally masculine man who had made her feel richer as a woman than she'd ever felt in her life. The knowledge brought no shame, only contentment. She was a woman now; Jafar had made her one. All during the long night he had shown her what it was like for a woman to be properly loved by a man.

He wasn't a gentle lover, except for the first time. He was fiercely tender, exotic, wildly exciting, as ruthless in his lovemaking as he was in war. He had possessed her thoroughly, asserting a mastery that had claimed her heart as well as her body.

Her smile abruptly faded. She could no longer doubt she was in love with Jafar, but those feelings were too new and fragile to bear full examination just yet. And the guilt that accompanied those feelings was too disturbing to dwell on. She had betrayed Gervase. Willingly, by her own choice. With the barbarian who had taken him prisoner, who had taken *her* prisoner, who had the power of life and death over them both. It was not something she could be proud of.

Suddenly restless, Alysson flung off the covers and promptly winced at the tender ache between her thighs. More carefully, she rose from the pallet and hurried to wash and dress, then helped Mahmoud pack up the furnishings and tent in preparation for the long journey ahead. All the while, she tried to discipline her thoughts, but vivid recollections of the warm pulsing rapture that Jafar had created with her last night were never far from her awareness. And when she went to find her uncle and Chand, there was a fresh sparkle in her eyes that belied the dark smudges beneath them.

Still, she managed to act normally until the caravan was nearly ready to depart and Jafar rode up on his black stallion. She hadn't counted on what the sight of him would do to her.

His eyes were like heated golden velvet as they gazed down at her, while the tender curve of his lips, as he smiled softly at her in greeting, made her suddenly remember the taste of his mouth and skin. Her pulse went wild.

Jafar had to be conscious of it, she thought breathlessly. The sexual awareness that arced between them was so powerful, so tangible, that Alysson had the impression the very air crackled around them. When his gaze riveted on her own mouth that was a soft bruised red, she knew without a doubt Jafar was contemplating very seriously kissing her right then and there. She found herself experiencing a flutter of emotions so new, so strong, so upsetting to her usual self-possession that she could hardly think.

"Good morning, Mademoiselle Vickery," he said evenly.

Only the hint of a husky rasp in his voice made his proper, conventional greeting at all palatable. How could he sound so formal when she could almost feel again the bold thrust of him between her thighs?

She must have answered, but she hardly heard his polite inquiry about her uncle's comfort. And when he asked about her own health, she murmured some vague reply that she only hoped was coherent.

"Are you able to ride?" Jafar finally said in a voice too low to be overheard by her uncle or servant.

Alysson gave him a blank look. "Yes, of course. Why shouldn't I be?"

His answering smile was both wry and intimate as his gaze slowly dropped to peruse her body. "I would imagine that mounting a horse just now could only add to any discomfort you might be feeling."

Comprehending at last, Alysson felt a scarlet blush rise to her cheeks. "N-no, I'm quite all right," she stammered, much to her chagrin.

"Very well. But you have only to ask and I will make other arrangements."

"Yes . . . of course . . . thank you."

He didn't kiss her, to her immense regret. When finally he rode away, toward the head of the column, Alysson stood there watching him, feeling wanton longing and a fierce disappointment, her body throbbing with unfulfilled desire.

She mounted her horse gingerly, with those same overwhelming feelings hammering at her thoughts, at her senses. She should be pondering what fate had in store for her, she knew—or more precisely, what Jafar had in store for her. But as she set out on the long journey, her mind was filled to the exclusion of all else with the memories of passion and the sensual, magical prowess of her savage Berber lover.

It took three full days of hard riding to reach Jafar's mountain home. To Alysson's surprise they traveled north and east, almost retracing their steps to the place where she'd spent the first weeks of her captivity. Leaving the desert behind, they entered the arid wastes of the High Plateau and passed the salt lake she had seen during her near-fatal attempt at escape. They were headed, it seemed, toward the distant blue mountains dotted with scrub. The first night they camped near the range of foothills.

Alysson slept alone, which only increased her frustration and longing. She was a jumble of nerves, being so near to Jafar without being able to touch him or kiss him or feel his hard body moving against hers. And yet she didn't dare show such interest in him, not with her uncle so near and with Chand hovering at her side like a mother hen. Chand had taken to scowling at her in silent disapproval, as if he somehow suspected her of harboring unchaste proclivities toward their Berber host.

The journey was just as tortuous for Jafar. He thought of her a hundred times a day; he wanted to touch her no less often.

For the sake of appearances, he kept his distance; he would not shame her before her uncle. Yet he watched Alysson from afar. Seeing her with the elderly Frenchman and her Indian servant, Jafar found himself envious of the easy playfulness in her manner, the loving familiarity between them.

He wanted that same familiarity for himself. Merely possessing her sweet body had not been enough. Even her willing surrender had not been enough. For while taking her body had satisfied him completely, it had only left him craving more. He wanted Alysson with a single-mindedness that was nearly obsession.

And he would have her, for a time. He would keep her by his side until her uncle's wounds healed. Then he would force himself to let her go.

His selfishness was not honorable, certainly. Nor was it something he could justify to her. He'd seen the shimmering questions in her eyes, questions that he couldn't, wouldn't answer truthfully. The excuse of her uncle's health would have to suffice.

Yet that wasn't entirely spurious as excuses went, Jafar thought defiantly. He *did* care about what happened to the elderly gentleman, if only because he didn't want to cause Alysson further pain.

And delaying her release at least would give him time to try and protect her name. He owed her that much. He knew quite well what her prudish, privileged English race would think of an unmarried young female who had spent the better part of a month as the captive of a Berber sheik. A fallen woman. A *whore*. Despite her wealth, she would be shunned and despised, the way his mother had been. The hypocrisy galled Jafar, even now.

No, he could not send Alysson back to endure that fate among her people. He cared too much. He *cared*. He wanted to protect her from such viciousness if he could. Perhaps it was possible. He wasn't without influence in her society, thanks to his noble grandfather. If he could manage to find some elderly European matron of unquestionable reputation who would be willing to swear Alysson had been properly chaperoned the entire time, then she might hope to dodge the vicious arrows that would be aimed at her by her hypocritical society. But it would take time and planning. Time that she would have to remain with him.

Of course, the best protection by far would be marriage—

Jafar grimaced as his conscience smote him yet once again. An honorable man would make reparations by marrying a young lady he had compromised. But making Alysson an offer of marriage was out of the question. He'd spent the last seven years of his life trying to rid himself of the taint of his English heritage, to put that part of his past behind him, and wedding an Englishwoman would destroy any hope of succeeding.

But of far greater moment was his duty. As *amghar*, he was obliged to put the interests of his tribe first. When eventually he did marry, it would be to the noble daughter of a neighboring tribe, in order to strengthen his alliances against his enemies, most particularly the French.

Fulfilling that duty was even more imperative now, after his betrayal on the battlefield. Jafar's jaw hardened at the remembrance. When he arrived home, he would be called to account for his actions before the tribal council. But even if he were somehow vindicated for forsaking his blood oath, he could never forgive himself for his failure. And he *would not* allow himself to betray his tribe again.

No, he knew where his duty lay. He could never consider taking a foreign wife.

But if Alysson married someone else, immediately upon her return . . .

The thought made his stomach churn, yet Jafar forced himself to consider the possibility. Would his archenemy the colonel still be willing to marry a young woman of sullied reputation? But yes. No man in his right mind would give up Alysson Vickery for so paltry a reason. Certainly *he* wouldn't. After he killed the bastard who'd defiled her, he would never consider it again.

But then perhaps he was no longer in his right mind—at least not where Alysson was concerned. For her he had broken a sacred vow, had dishonored his name and his people. And when the decisive moment had come, he'd behaved just like the savage barbarian Alysson had accused him of being. Look at him now. He was carrying her off to his mountain stronghold, where he meant to keep her until he could make himself give her up.

Even that would not be enough, but it would have to do.

He would use the time wisely. His duty permitting, he would do everything in his power to make her feel at home among his people. More than that, he would spare no effort in making her forget her love for his blood enemy, Gervase de Bourmont.

With grim determination, then, Jafar dismissed his morose contemplations. Still, one cynical question persisted in nagging at the edge of his thoughts.

Was Alysson his captive, or was he hers?

On the second day of the journey, in the afternoon, the caravan entered the mountains. On the far side of the first peak lay a rich plain, then another mountain, then another fertile valley, alternating until the rugged ridges and masses became dominant.

The sun remained just as glaringly bright, but as they climbed in altitude, the desert heat fell away. The low scrub of juniper and brambles was succeeded by a primeval forest of holm oak—evergreens which resembled huge hollies. By

the afternoon of the third day that prickly foliage gave way
to venerable cedars.

Staring up at the feathery tops of the ancient giants, Alysson took a deep breath, drinking in the pure clean air of the
highlands. Her spirit felt lighter than it had in weeks. Yet
how could it be otherwise, with magnificent mountains,
jagged and purple, towering around her, with larks and
swallows soaring high overhead? She dismissed the danger
of the mountain path beneath her horse's hooves; it could
hardly be called a road.

An hour later, as they passed through a narrow winding
defile bounded on both sides by high precipices, Mahmoud
found her.

"The lord bids you ride with him," the boy said.

Alysson's heart skipped several beats. With a glance at
the curtained litter where her uncle was sleeping, and an
apologetic smile for the now-scowling Chand, she rode to
the head of the column.

Jafar, his expression strangely sober, waited for her. She
hadn't spoken intimately with him in nearly three days, not
since the night of passion they had shared, but he didn't
seem inclined to talk now. His silence puzzled her, but even
that couldn't spoil Alysson's high spirits. She was content
merely to be near to him.

It was late in the day when she forgot herself long enough
to comment. At the moment the steep assent snaked along
a narrow ridge, while to the left was a sheer drop of some
three hundred feet.

"I suppose it's fortunate that I don't suffer a fear of
heights," Alysson remarked with a cautious glance beyond
Jafar.

"Is there anything from which you do suffer fear, *ma
belle?*"

Her eyes came up quickly at his curious question, but she
couldn't read his enigmatic look. "Oh, indeed," she answered lightly. "In the past month, I've learned to treat
scorpions with a very healthy respect."

He smiled at that.

"These mountains," Alysson said, wishing he would
keep smiling at her like that, as if she were clever and a bit
precious, "are barely accessible. I should think it impos-

sible for anyone to get in or out unless he were invited. An enemy wouldn't stand a chance of passing through here unchallenged.''

Jafar nodded. ''The Biban Range provides a natural defense. In every successive invasion of this province, the Berbers have abandoned the plains but successfully defended their homes in the hills.''

''Is that where we are, the Biban mountains?''

''Yes.''

She waited for him to volunteer more information, but when he didn't Alysson fell silent again. It was a comfortable, companionable silence, though, not one that she felt obliged to break.

The sun was sinking below the horizon when they rounded a peak that overlooked a broad valley. Below lay acres and acres of already harvested fields—or rather terraces—quilted with barley and wheat stubble. Above the mountain farmland, hugging the rugged slope, stood a town. There looked to be several hundred houses, built on ledges rising one above the other, Alysson noted, while the whole was surrounded by thick walls flanked with massive watchtowers and an abundance of trees. Strongly fortified and gleaming golden in the setting rays of the sun, the settlement presented a forbidding and splendid sight.

''These are the lands of the Beni Abess,'' Jafar said in a low voice.

Hearing the taut note in his tone, Alysson turned her head to find him watching her intently. He seemed tense, almost as if he were waiting for her approval. She thought back over what he had just said, wondering if it had some special significance that she'd missed. ''It's magnificent,'' she said finally. ''The lands look very prosperous.'' Oddly, he seemed to relax.

She had only spoken the truth, Alysson reflected. As she rode closer, she could make out the groves of walnut, apricot, and fig that surrounded the walled town. Below, where a thin river roared in its narrow channel down the mountainside, a waterwheel churned—obviously a mill where grain was ground. Above, she could see wreaths of gray smoke curling upward from stone chimneys on the flat roofs of the houses.

No doubt it was suppertime, Alysson thought, and yet suddenly people began to pour from the town in great numbers, to greet the returning lord. In short order a large crowd had formed—men, women, children, dogs—and the excited shouts and laughter created a din that was deafening.

The crowd was also colorful. The men wore vivid woolen djellabas and burnouses, the women dark robes with brightly hued girdles and haiks attractively arranged to cover their hair and shoulders—and of course an excess of silver ornaments.

Alysson had no doubt, looking at the proud, sometimes austere features surrounding her, that these people were Berbers. The unveiled women possessed white skin tattooed with elaborate henna patterns, while among the men she spied a variety of blue and gray eyes, flaxen hair, and red mustaches and beards. As the caravan passed, they greeted their lord with an eager respect, their bearing dignified yet deferential.

Their reception of her, however, was much different. Alysson noted a few bright-eyed and curious looks, but in the main, the Berbers' expressions were solemn, suspicious, or narrowed in what might actually be hatred. It made her uncomfortably aware that she was not welcome here.

Feeling suddenly isolated and alone, she unconsciously edged her horse closer to Jafar's—until she realized he was watching her. Abruptly she flashed him a brave smile that hid her discomfiture. "You should have told me I was to be on display," she murmured sotto voce. "I would have endeavored to dress like a model captive."

She couldn't tell from the wry twist of his lips if he was annoyed or amused by her subtle thrust, but at least it had the desired effect of getting him to look elsewhere.

Shortly they arrived at the town wall, which was built from uncut blocks of stone set in mortar. Stone watchtowers covered every approach, including this one which also boasted a massive gate with huge iron-studded doors. Within the gate was a wide flat area lined by trees, which in England would have been called the village green. No grass grew here, though, for the ground consisted of hard-packed earth.

Reaching the middle of the arena, Jafar brought the column to a halt and spoke a few words in Berber to the gathered crowd, repeating, Alysson presumed, the announcement of his warriors' victory over the French. They no doubt had already heard the triumphant news, but the resultant cheers echoed over the mountain range.

Alysson could not share in the excitement. When finally Jafar turned his horse to lead hers off to the left, she felt relieved. They passed several doorways and dozens of passages that seemed more like cool dark tunnels than streets. Beyond these, on the far side of the village, set slightly apart from the others, stood a huge stone structure that resembled a Moorish castle more than a house. It had to belong to some wealthy lord, Alysson surmised, for it boasted its own water supply. A sparkling stream ran in cascades down the rock cliff beside it, to disappear behind the high walls of the house.

Jafar drew his stallion to a halt before a large, intricately carved door and met Alysson's gaze. "Welcome to my home, Miss Vickery."

She didn't know whether to thank him or make some offhand remark about being his guest against her will. Before she could do either, however, the door was flung open and a blonde-haired woman danced into the street. Laughing in delight, she ran up to Jafar and began kissing his hands.

Tall and full-figured, the woman wore a long haik of blue silk, clasped at the waist in a blouselike fashion by a gold belt and jeweled buckle. Her arms and ears and neck were decorated with not silver but gold. She was beautiful enough to take Alysson's breath away. Far worse, though, was the way the lush beauty reminded her of the exotic courtesans she had seen at the oasis of Bou Saada.

Dismayed, Alysson tore her gaze away to stare at Jafar. Mahmoud had told her that Jafar had no wife, but this possessive female was definitely no sister. Her behavior was too familiar, too bold, too brazen.

This woman was Jafar's concubine, Alysson was certain.

Her heart sank to the vicinity of her knees, while the fragile happiness she'd felt during the past few days of loving Jafar abruptly crumbled to dust.

Chapter 19

Her name was Zohra, and Alysson disliked her on sight. With her fawning intimacy toward Jafar, the Berber beauty managed to communicate quite clearly her privileged relationship to the lord.

The antagonism was mutual. The moment Zohra spotted the English newcomer, her blue eyes flashed instant animosity and disdain.

Fortunately for the sake of peace, Zohra did not make her home in Jafar's house.

"She belongs to another tribe," Jafar explained after the blonde beauty had been dismissed. "Zohra bides with a cousin whenever she visits this village."

Alysson managed to hide her misery and sharp jealousy behind a cool smile, but she was relieved to learn of the living arrangements. She could not—would not—have borne Jafar blatantly flaunting his mistress in front of her, not without making her sentiments clearly known, and likely making a fool of herself in the process . . . a bigger fool than she already was.

How naive she'd been to think she was the only woman in Jafar's life. And how disgraceful her recent behavior toward him had been. It made Alysson flush with shame to recall her wantonness. And made her humiliatingly aware of how docile and accommodating she'd become as well. Suddenly Alysson felt very much the prisoner again, although Jafar did not act as that were so.

"This is your home," he told her as they entered his fortress, and he meant it. Alysson soon learned that Berber hospitality was similar to the famed hospitality in the rest of the Islamic world; a guest had only to admire an object and it would be given to him.

And there was a good deal to admire. The exterior might be plain and painfully rugged, but passing through the arched portal was like entering a different world—an Eastern world of mosaic tiled pavements, arabesque plaster fretwork, and flights of marble stairs. Jafar himself gave her a tour of the house after her wounded uncle had been comfortably settled.

Jafar's mountain fortress, Alysson discovered, was built around a huge central courtyard, with work areas below, living quarters above, and wide flat roofs where dining and socializing took place in good weather. The front wing boasted a dozen guest chambers; the lord's private apartments and offices occupied the right side wing; while the servants' and women's quarters—the latter was called the harem in this part of the world—took up the remaining two sides. Another arched passageway, she was told, led to an adjacent courtyard that was devoted entirely to long ranges of stabling. Along the corridor she could see two of Jafar's warriors standing guard.

"Are they posted there to keep me from trying to escape," Alysson asked Jafar in a dry voice, "or to prevent someone from stealing your horses?"

Jafar gave her a level look. "You, *Ehuresh*, are the only one to develop the annoying habit of making off with my horses." When she glanced at him sharply, the corner of his mouth curled in a very male smile. "To be truthful, theft is not a problem in our society, for the punishment is too severe. But a man in my position must be alert for assassins."

Disturbed by the thought that some treacherous deed might end this vital man's life, Alysson fell silent.

"For that reason," he added, "I must ask that you accept an escort whenever you leave the house. Mahmoud will make the arrangements."

"I may leave the house?"

"Certainly. You are a guest here."

She regarded him with disbelief. "You mean to tell me I may go anywhere I wish, do anything I wish?"

Jafar smiled faintly. "Yes, *Ehuresh*. You will have an armed escort to keep you safe, but you may do as you wish. You have only to ask."

"Thank you."

He bowed slightly in acknowledgment. "My greatest regret is that for a time my duties will prevent me from personally seeing to your enjoyment. There are numerous matters which have arisen during my absence that I now must resolve."

Jafar continued the tour then. In nearly every room she entered, Alysson could smell the fragrance of cedar pitch from the ancient ceiling beams. The only disappointment she found was the scarcity of light. The arched windows were built small to keep out the heat and bitter mountain cold—although there was an abundance of pottery lamps, as well as braziers for the chill nights. The interior walls were whitewashed, while draping silk fabrics and tapestries provided rich ornamentation. As for furniture, it was basic and rare. Thick carpets and painted rush mats strewed the floors, along with an occasional divan or a low wooden table here or there.

Alysson found the accommodations for her uncle simple but luxurious. Upstairs in the front wing, a paved hall set with an intricate pattern of colored tiles was surrounded by some half a dozen guest chambers, accessed by large folding doors.

"This will be your room," Jafar told her as he paused before one of the doors.

Alysson greeted the knowledge with surprise. "You don't mean to keep me incarcerated in the women's quarters?"

This time his smile was indulgent as well as sensual. "I have said I intend to make allowances for your English upbringing, *chérie*. And I assumed you would wish to remain near your uncle. If you prefer, though, you may of course sleep in my harem."

She couldn't mistake the husky, sexual note in his voice. It made Alysson blush and hastily proclaim, "No, this is quite satisfactory."

"Very well. I will leave you now to refresh yourself. Will you join me for dinner in an hour? Your uncle as well, if he feels able."

When Jafar had gone, Alysson glanced around the chamber and noted a bed mat of painted rushes covered by several carpets, on top of which lay finely woven blankets and quilts of colorful silk. The room also contained the requisite number of pillows and carpets on the floor and convenient pegs to hang clothing, but Alysson's gaze kept returning to the bed. At night, when she lay there, she would be able to hear the whisper of fountains from the courtyard below. The disturbing question was, would she lie there alone?

Her servant, however, greatly influenced the decision, for Chand refused to abandon his mistress. As was his custom, he slept before her door, as if he were determined never again to let Alysson out of his sight.

The thought that he might be protecting her honor both warmed and relieved Alysson. If Jafar *had* wanted to visit her bed, he would have found it impossible without alerting the entire household. And she needed the time to sort out her tangled feelings for him before continuing the intimacies they had shared at his encampment. She was too vulnerable to Jafar just now to make any intelligent decision about the future of their relationship.

Alysson saw no indication that he tried to come to her, however. Indeed, except for evenings at supper, she saw little of Jafar during the first days after their arrival. As he'd warned, he spent his time seeing to the affairs of his tribe which had suffered during his long absence.

To her dismay, Alysson found herself missing him. In the beginning her Uncle Honoré slept a great deal, and Chand apparently was not speaking to her at the moment.

Having time on her hands made her all the more grateful for Mahmoud's company. The young servant became her frequent attendant during the daytime, answering her questions about Jafar and his fierce tribe of Berbers and resuming her lessons in the Berber language.

Actually, though, her life was far different here than it had been in the camp. She had the freedom of the village, for example—although she gave up after one attempt to explore the narrow, winding streets. Without Jafar by her side, Alysson felt uncomfortable having to endure the intent, sometimes hostile stares of the Berbers she encountered.

Not everyone was so unamicable, at least. Tahar, the young woman who'd befriended her during the early days of her captivity, was still as gentle and helpful as always.

Drawn by the lure of feminine companionship, Alysson began spending a few hours each day in the lord's kitchen where Tahar worked—a long room divided by low partitions, with stuccoed recesses and cupboards built into the wall. And perhaps she was also acting out of defiance, Alysson admitted privately to herself. Jafar had once called her spoiled and pampered, accusing her of never having done a day's work in her life, and she was determined to show him she wasn't afraid of menial tasks.

To her surprise, Alysson greatly enjoyed the challenge. And the company was certainly welcome. Between Tahar's few words of French, and her own increasing store of Berber and Arabic, the two of them managed to converse, and were soon on their way to becoming friends.

Even so, Alysson found herself looking forward to the end of the day when she could see Jafar. Each evening at supper, he played the considerate host to her and her uncle, seeing to their comfort, engaging them in discussions, and providing for their entertainment. Oddly, Jafar seemed intent on charming her Uncle Honoré. And yet watching him closely, Alysson could tell that Jafar looked weary and at times distracted. She could only suppose that the long hours he kept were taking their toll.

From dawn to dusk the reception hall where he held audience was always filled with a steady stream of people who demanded his attention. The room was downstairs off the court, and Alysson could observe the constant activity whenever she chose.

The courtyard, she discovered, was the most enjoyable spot in the house. The huge quadrangle boasted several flowing fountains and marble basins, surrounded by oleanders and almond trees. In the afternoons Alysson liked to wrap up warmly against the chill fall air and stroll beneath the trees, or sit in the sun on one of the marble benches.

It was there in the courtyard that she discovered a new friend. Jafar owned several Nubian greyhounds, and one of those tall, slender dogs—a young bitch—began to follow Alysson around.

The courtyard also was where she encountered Zohra a few days after her arrival, and where she learned the necessity of keeping up her guard. The beautiful Berber woman might look harmless with her fair skin and pale blonde hair, but her feminine softness hid the disposition of a scorpion.

Zohra spoke French fairly well, and her tone was pleasant enough when she first addressed Alysson. But after the preliminary flowery greetings, Zohra immediately turned to the subject of Jafar.

"You should be honored by the lord's attention," she said with a sly, even hard edge to her voice. "He looks upon you with favor."

Startled by such frankness, Alysson raised a cool eyebrow.

When she didn't answer, the Berber woman tried another tack. "The *saiyid* is a magnificent lover, no? Do you not find him pleasing?"

The pain that observation aroused in Alysson was sharp and twisting. Jafar *was* a magnificent lover, but the confirmation that Zohra had been the lucky recipient of his passion filled Alysson with dismay—a reaction that was absurd and entirely unjustified, considering her own uncertain position in Jafar's life. She had to forcibly refrain from snapping a reply.

"Where I come from," she answered curtly, "ladies do not discuss their lovers in public, or converse on such personal subjects with persons who are virtual strangers."

Zohra shrugged her graceful shoulders, setting her gold chains and bracelets to jingling. Her mouth curved in a sneer. "The women of my country are not so prudish or self-righteous. Nor are we as cold in love. Very young, we learn the art of pleasing a man, how to win his heart."

"The women of *my* country are too proud to share the heart of a man."

"Too proud? But you have no right to pride any longer. You are only the lord's captive."

Alysson set her teeth. "If you will excuse me, I have more important concerns that require my attention."

Rising, she walked away, her shoulders erect, her head high. But when she had sought the safety of her bedchamber, her shoulders sagged. Her throat was tight with an unwanted ache, while at the same time she felt the most barbaric urge to scratch the beautiful Zohra's blue eyes out.

Realizing the significance of that urge, Alysson mentally

flogged herself. Never in her life had she been jealous of another woman, and she was not about to start now. Nor would she demean herself by fighting that blonde witch for Jafar's affections.

Even so, she had no trouble agreeing with Mahmoud's muttered denunciations when he referred to Zohra as "that she-devil" and "the daughter of an obstinate she-camel." Zohra was not in Mahmoud's good graces, it seemed, for quite cruelly she had never let the boy forget his scarred face or his pitiful limp. Alysson found it only a slight consolation when Mahmoud respectfully began to address herself as *lallah,* which was considered a lady of position in Arabic.

Zohra, Alysson learned from Mahmoud, came from the neighboring Beni Ammer tribe and was a courtesan of the first order, like the dancers of the Ouled Nail whom Alysson had seen in Bou Saada. The blonde woman was evidently plying her trade in Jafar's bed.

That no doubt was the reason he hadn't once come to her own bed, Alysson realized miserably. If he could enjoy the services of such a beautiful, accomplished courtesan, why would he possibly want *her?* She was merely Jafar's captive, after all. And a foreign one, at that.

That remembrance sent a new wave of despair rushing through Alysson. She had no real place in Jafar's life, and no future either. She must have been mad to let herself forget that reality, to let her heart rule her head. During the long weeks of her captivity, she'd obviously lost any sense of judgment, any regard for right or wrong. It had been utter folly for her to fall in love with Jafar, and totally wrong of her to surrender her body to him. She should have known better.

Alysson was struggling with those distressing thoughts that same evening before supper as she strolled on the terrace at one end of Jafar's reception hall. She was alone, for the tribal business was finished for the day, and Chand was aiding her uncle in dressing for dinner.

A masterpiece of construction, the terrace was formed by a projecting cliff and sheltered from rain and wind by a granite overhang. Above and beside the terrace, a stream dashed in a foaming torrent to create a lovely waterfall, which could be viewed from stone benches carved from the living rock. Below lay the entire magnificent valley of the Beni Abess, Jafar's tribe.

The sun was setting on the beautiful scene by the time Alysson reluctantly rose to go inside. When she turned, though, it was to find Jafar standing in the doorway, watching her. Her breath caught in her throat at the way his presence immediately filled the terrace and brought it to life.

He wore a lightly flowing white robe of sheer silk that enhanced the lean masculinity of his features, but he had left off any turban. When he stepped onto the terrace, his sunstruck mane seemed ablaze with red-gold light. Gazing at him in near-awe, Alysson felt the insistent sting of her own desire.

It was only when he came closer that she saw the lines of strain on his face, around his eyes and mouth. He was troubled about something, she was certain—though when he came to a halt before her and raised her fingers to his lips, his greeting was pleasant enough.

"I fear I have been neglecting you these past few days, *chérie*, for my far more onerous duties. I hope you can find it in your heart to forgive me."

Alysson had indeed been feeling neglected by him, but she would never have admitted it. "Mahmoud has been looking after me," she said instead.

"Zohra will perform tonight for you and your uncle. I hope you will enjoy it. She is an excellent dancer."

Praise of the courtesan was not at all what Alysson wanted to hear just then, and she replied without even intending to. "I seem to recall you told me you had no concubines."

"So I did." Jafar smiled briefly, his amber eyes holding hers. "Are you jealous of Zohra, my defiant tigress? Shall I send her away?"

There was amusement, even satisfaction, in his voice that grated fiercely on Alysson's nerves. It irked her that he could read her thoughts so easily, and that he could tease her about such a subject. "Are you sleeping with her?" she demanded, unable to bite back the question even though she dreaded the answer.

"No, *Ehuresh.*" His response was swift and unequivocal.

"But you have done so before this."

Gently, to Alysson's consternation, Jafar raised a hand to her cheek. With a long lean finger he stroked the delicate line of her jaw, while his eyes took on a glint of passion. "Would it matter?"

The question was a mere breath of a murmur, a quiet, sensual whisper that sent Alysson's pulse rate soaring. Furious at herself for her uncontrollable reaction, she pulled back with an abrupt "No, of course not!" Less violently, then, she turned to look out over the valley. "It is a matter of supreme indifference to me what you do with her. I was simply curious, that is all."

Yet she wasn't simply curious, that was precisely the problem. She craved Jafar's touch, his possession—she who cherished freedom and independence. It frightened her at times, this powerful need she felt for him.

Even as the thought formed, she sensed his presence behind her, felt his warmth at her back as his hard arms caressingly encircled her waist. When he pressed a gentle kiss against her temple, the simple act of desire drove the breath from Alysson's lungs.

"I have missed having you in my arms at night, *ma belle*, sharing my bed."

She wet her suddenly dry lips. She had missed sleeping with him, too, more than she would ever have imagined.

"Come to me tonight, *Ehuresh*."

"You . . ." She stopped to clear her throat. "You want me to come to your apartments?"

"Consider, *chérie*. If we mean to observe the proprieties, I cannot go to you. Not with your uncle so near, and your servant acting the valiant watchdog."

He was inviting her to his rooms, to his bed? Summoning her for his pleasure, the way he might summon one of his concubines? The way he would summon Zohra?

Riddled with agonizing fresh doubt, Alysson shut her eyes. Did Jafar see her only as another of his concubines? Did she mean nothing to him but physical gratification? The painful thought rekindled a fierce debate within her. How could she desire a man who kept her here against her will? How could she love a savage warlord who despised all foreigners? A man who had nearly caused Gervase's death, who still held him prisoner?

The remembrance sent a cold chill racing over her heated senses. How could she surrender to the ecstasy of Jafar's embrace when Gervase's fate was still so uncertain? And how could she leave herself so vulnerable? Jafar was a highly sensual man who found delight and gratification in a woman's body. He would take his pleasure of her and give her rapture in return—and leave her with more heartache than she could bear.

She had to put an end to their intimacy now, before she succumbed entirely to the hollow promise of passion. Before she totally lost the will to resist him. Before her heart became his captive, just as her physical self was.

"Have you forgotten that I have a fiancé?" she whispered, almost as much to herself as to him.

She felt Jafar stiffen as if he'd been struck. Slowly, then, his arms fell away. He took a careful step back, releasing her.

Alysson could sense from the dangerous silence that he was struggling for control. By the time she found the courage to turn and glance up at him, a hard mask had descended over his features. And yet she knew she had to drive the knife deeper, if she was to have any hope of maintain her resolve.

"How much longer," she forced herself to ask, "will my uncle and I be your guests? Do you mean to keep us here indefinitely?"

She thought she must have imagined the dark flash of pain in Jafar's eyes, for a muscle worked violently in his jaw before he moved to the stone parapet, to stand looking out over his valley.

"I cannot release you just yet," Jafar said finally, in a voice that was barely audible over the rush of the waterfall.

"Why . . . why not?"

He gave a short, weary sigh. "Because at present I am engaged in negotiations with the French government for an exchange of war prisoners. Your being here allows me to deal from a greater position of strength. If I surrender that advantage, it could cost lives."

It was Alysson's turn to feel the knife. Jafar was using

her, just as he had from the very first. He'd used her to lure
the French army into battle, and now he was using her to
strengthen his bargaining power with his enemies. That was
all she meant to him, an advantage to be exploited.

Alysson dug her nails into her palms, till the pain in her
hands overshadowed the pain she felt in her heart. She had
made the right decision in refusing Jafar's invitation to share
his bed. She might be wretchedly in love with him, but she
was not yet so far gone as to allow him the use of her body
in addition to everything else.

"Is Gervase one of the prisoners to be exchanged?" she
asked finally.

There was a long pause before he nodded.

"Well then," Alysson said with an attempt at a smile,
"I suppose I can endure being your 'guest' for a while
longer. May we go in to dinner now?"

Zohra *was* an excellent dancer, just as Jafar claimed; her
performance that evening for his guests was exquisite.

A Frenchman to the core, Honoré Larousse greatly ap-
preciated the display of flashing blue eyes, swirling golden
hair, and an enticing, full-breasted figure. Alysson, however, watched the exhibition of sensual agility and provocative grace with little enthusiasm, and more than a little
distress. The thought of Jafar making love to this wild Berber beauty made her heart ache.

Against her will, she found her gaze drawn to him. Oddly,
his attention was focused not on the beautiful courtesan,
but on herself, his expression intent and brooding.

When the performance was over, though, Jafar roused
himself to become the charming host again. And during the
week that followed, no one could have shown his guests
more consideration.

His courtesies and deference to her wishes didn't help
one whit Alysson's resolve to free her heart from his control. When she admitted to him that she'd seen little of the
village, Jafar himself escorted her around his town, informing her about his tribe and his culture with a quiet pride
that he didn't try to hide.

Both the men and women of the Beni Abess were hard
workers, Alysson saw. The men primarily farmed and raised

horses, while the women were highly skilled at making pottery and woven cloth. There was little time for leisure, especially for the women. If they weren't cooking or cleaning, they were drawing water from wells or making the trek to the river to wash clothes. But their lot was not as arduous or as restrictive as that of their Arab counterparts, Alysson learned. Berber women were not required to remain quiet around men or keep their eyes downcast like Arab women. In fact, if Jafar's casual remarks could be believed, it was Berber wives who ruled their households, not husbands.

It was Jafar who first took Alysson up to the roof to observe his magnificent horses being trained in the village arena. Alysson found it a pleasure to watch the high-mettled steeds as they were taught to charge and wheel and charge again.

It was Jafar, also, who escorted Alysson through his stables, an event which resulted from a taunting comment she made at supper one evening after listening to the conversation he was having with her Uncle Honoré about the difficulties the French had encountered in conducting a military campaign in the rugged Algerian terrain.

"What do you and your savage warriors do when you are not engaged in fighting?" she asked dryly, wishing she could stem Jafar's growing influence over her uncle.

Jafar sent her a cool look. "Besides war, *Ehuresh,* we enjoy the chase, love, and horses. Tomorrow, if you wish, I will show you my horses."

Alysson inclined her head regally, pretending indifference, but the next morning, as they toured Jafar's stables, she couldn't maintain her reserve when near such excellent horseflesh. She listened attentively and with growing admiration as Jafar explained, without exaggeration, that his tribe raised some of the best horses in the country.

When she particularly admired a snowy white mare, Jafar gave it to her outright, not listening to her objections.

Finally conceding with a gracious thank-you, Alysson moved on to the other stalls, till she came to one that held a lean and sharp-boned bay stallion. The horse seemed rather savage as it snorted and pawed the ground—until it scented Jafar. Then it spun and trotted up to him, as docile as a lamb.

For some strange reason the stallion looked familiar, yet Alysson was almost certain it hadn't been one of the mounts Jafar had taken to the desert. "Does this fierce-looking fellow have a name?" she murmured as the stallion affectionately nuzzled Jafar's chest.

"Atoo. It means 'wind.' " She caught the odd look Jafar was giving her, but she had no idea how to interpret it. Moments later, though, she forgot the Barbary steed in her immense delight, for Jafar ordered her new mare saddled and took her riding. For two wonderful hours she explored the rugged countryside and reveled in the long-denied freedom, afterward returning with her cheeks flushed from the chill and the exercise, her eyes glowing with enjoyment.

The following morning, however, her glow faded. When Mahmoud brought her breakfast, the boy seemed more dour than usual, and Alysson asked what was troubling him.

"The council is to meet twelve days hence."

"So?"

A worried frown shadowed Mahmoud's scarred brow. "So the council may vote to remove the lord as *amghar el-barood*. He has been charged with betrayal of his duty and disregard of the law, and thus must prove his innocence."

Alysson felt an icy knot coil in her stomach. Upon questioning Mahmoud, she discovered that *amghar el-barood* meant something like "chief of war." This elected position of supreme commander was filled only in wartime by one of the tribal *amghars* from all the surrounding tribes. Currently Jafar held the position, but it seemed that he stood to be impeached for his action that day on the battlefield, when he had spared Gervase's life and allowed his blood enemy to go free.

"Do you mean to tell me Jafar could be *punished* for showing mercy to an enemy?" Alysson asked incredulously.

Mahmoud nodded sadly. "I do not know what will happen. It is in the hands of Allah."

When she pressed the boy to explain about Berber law, Alysson began to understand why Jafar had so little time for leisure. Besides chief of war and chief of his own tribe, Jafar also held the position of *caid*, which was appointed by the sultan. Only *caids* were allowed to wear scarlet burnouses, Alysson learned, but that was the only simple rule she could discover. The Berber system of government was a tremendously complicated network of inter-lineage blood feuds and interclan warfare—which certainly wasn't made any easier by the independent and warlike Berber spirit.

Alysson thought Jafar's possible dethronement preposterous. During his reign, Jafar had united and led a people whose very instincts drove them to faction and discord, against a superior force of foreign invaders. It seemed almost ludicrous now that he would be required to fight not only the French but his own people.

The threat of impeachment was what had been troubling Jafar, Alysson was certain. She wanted to ask him about it, but could find no opportunity for privacy with him during that entire day. And the next afternoon she was subjected to another encounter with Zohra.

The beautiful blonde woman was waiting for her in the courtyard, much like a watchful spider. Having no intention of becoming Zohra's prey, Alysson started to pass, but Zohra's hissed warning gave her pause.

"You should leave here, lady, before something evil befalls you."

Halting, Alysson turned slowly, her eyes narrowing. "Something evil? Are you daring to *threaten* me, Zohra? I imagine the lord might have something to say about such treatment of a guest."

Zohra's blue eyes showed an instant of worry before the animosity returned in full force. "You have bewitched him, but he will never take you to wife, no matter how you try to lure him with your great wealth! You are an infidel, a foreigner. He will wed one of his own kind, one who can bring honor to his name and favor to his tribe. You have only brought him dishonor! You are nothing to him, less than nothing!"

Having delivered her scornful denouncement, Zohra swept away with a jingle of gold chains, leaving a startled Alysson to stare after her. Take her to wife? The thought of marriage to Jafar had never crossed her mind—at least not seriously. She was his captive, nothing more. And despite Zohra's warning to leave, she had no choice but to remain his captive.

Damn the woman! Alysson fumed, clenching her fists. The Berber witch not only had cut up her peace, but had actually dared threaten her!

The more Alysson thought about it, the angrier she became. After a few more moments of seething, she turned abruptly on her heel and marched across the courtyard, directly into Jafar's crowded reception hall.

He looked up in surprise, as did every other man in the room. The sudden silence in the great chamber told her more than words that her behavior was unorthodox to say the least, but Alysson was too annoyed at the moment to care what Jafar's tribe thought of her.

"I should like to request an audience," she said tightly, coming to a halt just inside the doorway. "If you can manage to spare a few moments."

The concern in Jafar's expression was evident as he dismissed the crowd with a swift wave of his hand.

The hall was cleared almost immediately, the crowd filing out into the courtyard, but the interval gave Alysson enough time to realize her mistake. A flush of embarrassment tinged her cheeks. She had Jafar's undivided attention now, just as she had demanded, but if she complained of Zohra, he would only think her jealous.

When he invited her to join him, she slowly settled herself on the carpet beside him, her mind racing to think of some plausible excuse for her interruption.

"Mahmoud says you may be impeached by your tribal council because you allowed Gervase to live," she said finally.

Jafar seemed to misunderstand the reason for her comment, for his expression became shuttered. "Don't be concerned, mademoiselle, that my disagreement with the council will affect your colonel's release. I have given my word that no harm will come to Bourmont and that will not change, even if I no longer rule."

"That wasn't my concern," Alysson protested. "I just think it immensely unfair that you could be so harshly punished simply for showing clemency to an enemy."

Jafar gave her a sharp glance, as if surprised that her indignation could be for him.

But it *was* for him. She couldn't bear to think his sparing a man's life could cost him so dearly.

Shaking his head slowly, Jafar looked away. "You measure fairness by your Western standards, *Ehuresh*. The council sees my action in a different light . . . a weakness at best, a betrayal at worst. A weak leader is not fit to rule. A traitorous one is not fit to live."

"You are not a traitor!" Alysson exclaimed in outrage, squeezing her hands into fists.

"No?" His smile was faint, bleak. "I swore to avenge the deaths of my parents, but I failed. I broke an oath of blood."

He returned his gaze to hers and Alysson drew a sharp breath at the pain and the unguarded need in his eyes. It was a need for understanding.

That she could give him. She might not comprehend many of his people's customs and laws, but she had lain with this man. She knew the grief he was feeling now in his soul. The sorrow, the regret. She knew because she could feel it herself. His failure had shaken Jafar profoundly. Not just because he might lose the vast power and position he held, but on a far deeper level. Because he had dishonored his beliefs, himself.

And he had done it for Gervase. Because of Gervase, Jafar's entire life might be shattered.

The injustice made her ache. She wished desperately there were something she could say to ease his pain. "You spared a man's life!" she murmured fiercely. "That can't be wrong."

He averted his gaze, staring off at the distance.

"It can't!"

Jafar wanted to wince at her quiet vehemence. Her defense of him had taken him aback, had touched him as nothing else had in a long while, but he could not accept the consolation she was trying to offer.

The silence lengthened.

"Well . . ." she said helplessly. After another long moment she added, "I should go. Forgive me, please, for interrupting you."

Alysson got slowly to her feet. At the door, however, she paused and looked back. "Jafar?" she said, her voice echoing softly across the empty hall. "What will happen afterward . . . after the prisoners are exchanged?"

Jafar did not want to face that question, or the others it raised. What would be Alysson's response when her fiancé was freed? Would she demand her own freedom? A freedom Jafar did not want to grant?

And yet hearing the troubled note in her voice, he knew he had to give her some kind of answer. "I told you, your precious Gervase will not be harmed," Jafar said grimly, forcing himself to look at her.

Oddly, she didn't seem entirely relieved. Instead, she regarded him searchingly. "Do you still mean to seek revenge for what his father did to yours?"

Her persistent fear for his blood enemy infuriated Jafar, but he forced himself to let out a breath. "No . . . I no longer seek revenge."

"But you will never stop fighting, will you?"

Jafar shook his head. As long as he breathed the war would never be over for him. Even if he was stripped of power, he would never give up his quest to rid his country of the foreign oppressors. This interlude, here in his mountain fortress with Alysson, was only a brief respite. Someday soon he would return to the struggle.

"A traitor would not be so dedicated to a cause," she said softly before turning away, leaving him alone.

Her quiet words whispered though his mind, grasping with seductive fingers at his conscience. He couldn't accept her reasoning, but truthfully, he wished he could.

Alysson wished she could convince his tribal council to reconsider their absurd allegations. What Jafar had done was not traitorous; it was right and good. He had not betrayed his countrymen by letting an enemy live. He was still totally committed to his beliefs. He was still determined to fight against the French, in a war he could never win. That should have been proof enough to vindicate him, she thought.

Alysson was still dwelling on the unfairness of it two days later when she was confronted with a discovery that sent her reeling.

Jafar had been gone all morning long, hunting for boar

with his men—an invitation which had not been extended to her, even though she would have liked to participate. Women did not hunt in Barbary, it seemed.

After her recent long ride, however, Alysson wasn't overly distressed at being left out. Not only was she still recovering her health, but the day had turned wet and wretchedly cold, with rain clouds hovering over the mountains much like in the Scottish Highlands—a reminder that the snows would soon come.

Instead, she spent the morning reading aloud to her uncle. After finishing the French text, she wandered disconsolately over to the other second-floor wing that held Jafar's private apartments, intending to search his library for another book.

The library was furnished even more comfortably than the rest of the magnificent house, with dozens of leatherbound volumes filling the wooden shelves and recesses in the walls. Much to Alysson's surprise, she found among the writings of Arabic and French a book of English poetry penned by Lord Byron, the brooding romantic British aristocrat who some twenty-odd years ago had fought alongside Greek freedom-fighters against the bloody Turks.

Curious, Alysson sat down on one of the divans to thumb through the slim volume. When she opened the front cover, though, her hand froze. There on the front leaf, written in a bold flowing hand, the name *Nicholas Sterling* had been inscribed. The words seemed to leap up at her, while her heartbeat surged erratically.

Sterling was the family name of the dukes of Moreland.

Seven years ago she had visited the duke's estate and had been comforted by a fair-haired stranger.

During her terrible illness she had dreamed about that stranger—a comforting image that had somehow become entangled with Jafar's.

Dazed, confused, Alysson stared at the name, trying to fit the pieces of the puzzle together. Just then, she heard a soft, familiar footfall. When she looked up, it was to find Jafar standing in the doorway, his golden eyes focused intently on her, his features shrouded in a look that was both wary and shuttered.

Chapter 20

"**I**t was *you* that day," she accused, her voice barely a whisper.

"Yes," Jafar replied, meeting her questioning gaze.

"I don't understand . . ."

"My mother was British. Her father—my grandfather—is Robert Sterling, Duke of Moreland."

Alysson simply stared. Jafar had spoken in English. Impeccable, clipped, cultured English that could not have been learned with only casual study.

"Then . . . however did you come to be here . . . in this position . . . your tribe?" she said in confusion.

Jafar sighed. After a moment, he moved to sit beside her on the divan. "It is not so strange a story. Years ago, when my mother was young, she disagreed with the marriage her father had arranged for her. In defiance, she took passage on a ship bound for Sicily, where she planned to remain until her father capitulated. But she never reached her destination. The ship was captured by Barbary pirates. My mother was taken to Algiers, where she was sold as a slave."

Enslaved, Alysson thought with a shudder. "How horrible," she said aloud, thinking of the terrible tales she'd heard about Western women imprisoned in Eastern harems.

"Actually she was quite fortunate. She was young and beautiful and brought a great price," Jafar responded. "She was purchased by a Berber warlord, who carried her to his home in the mountains. There he fell in love and married her, even though she was a Christian. Later she bore him a son."

"You?"

Jafar nodded, but his gaze seemed distant, as if he were

sifting through old memories. "I was given the name Jafar, after the pirate who had captured her."

"You were named after a *pirate?*"

His lips curved in a faint smile. "Jafar is what my father called me. My mother called me Nicholas. I was raised to be a Berber warrior, but my mother never allowed me to forget my English heritage."

Jafar was silent for a moment before he added softly, "She was happy here, I know, though she always hoped to return home one day to visit her father. 'When we return to England,' was one of her favorite phrases." Jafar smiled again, this time sadly. "But she wouldn't go without me, and my father would not allow me to leave. I think he feared I would be seduced by the English life of wealth and privilege that had been denied me."

"Did you ever go?"

"Yes." His reply was terse. "After my parents' deaths, when it was learned that I was half English, I was sent home to my noble grandfather. I remained there for ten years."

Ten years that had been an eternity, Alysson suspected, hearing the echo of the young boy's anguish in the man's bleak tone.

"Perhaps you can understand," Jafar said, regarding her intently, surprising her with his direct appeal. "The money and titles my grandfather offered meant nothing to me. I had been raised here, in a different world. I was my father's heir. Here I lacked for nothing—I had only to say 'Do this' and it was done. Here I was among family, friends, familiar customs. In contrast, England was a foreign land, filled with cold, contemptuous strangers."

Alysson returned his intent gaze, her own filled with sympathy. She was not akin to him by class or race, but she had endured similar experiences. She understood very well the kind of prejudice and contempt he would have been subjected to by the haughty British nobility because of his mixed blood. She'd suffered much the same way for her own common origins. "You never fit in."

Jafar shook his head. "No, I never fit in. I could never become the civilized young gentleman my grandfather wanted me to become. One doesn't forget his heritage sim-

ply because he finds himself in a different country. Being
half English does not make him an Englishman.''

No, Alysson thought silently, Jafar could never be an Englishman. Not when the blood of Berber warriors ran so
fiercely in his veins. And yet he was not all Berber, either.
Had she known to look, she would have seen the signs of
his European upbringing in his mannerisms, in his care of
her. He'd kept his past hidden from her, but his rare lapses
into speaking English should have warned her, if nothing
else.

''And later? You gave up your English life to return
here?''

''There was a war being fought here. This is my country,
my home. I had to return. I had just taken leave of my
grandfather the day I came across you up in that tree, throwing acorns at me.''

She thought back, remembering. Now she knew why the
bay stallion in his stables seemed familiar to her. She had
seen it before. It was the same savage-looking beast he had
ridden in England, the same one she had seen in her dreams.
And Jafar—he was the stranger who had comforted her that
long-ago day, the stranger who had made her grief more
bearable.

He was the man who had affected her life so profoundly
seven years ago. Much of her happiness during her awkward
progression from girlhood to womanhood she owed to him.

It would take her a moment to grow accustomed to the
idea.

Her gaze searching, she scrutinized Jafar with new eyes.
The lamp glowed, giving intriguing play to the lean hollows
and planes of his face. It took no effort to see in those hard
features the authority of one born to rule . . . or the determination of a man unflinching in love and hate. But now
that she knew who he was, she understood things that had
always puzzled her, things that his conflicting heredity and
disparate upbringing might explain. Why, for instance, his
conduct and manner of address sometimes seemed European. Why she'd thought he always seemed alone, even
among his own people. He was a man caught between two
cultures, Berber and English. Half of this world, half of a
foreign one, perhaps a true part of neither. Within him

warred the sensual soul of the East and the cool pragmatism of the British aristocrat. And no doubt he had inherited a measure of both pride and arrogance from each side. He might have disavowed his English heritage, but it was still a vital part of him.

"Did you ever see your grandfather again?" she asked finally.

"I visited him once more," Jafar said with a sigh. "In '43, the tide of the war had turned. Abdel Kader's army was facing defeat, and the French government was intent on crushing any final opposition. Not only were they determined to limit the authority of our sheiks and administrators, but they attempted to destroy our very culture. I led an envoy to England on behalf of Abdel Kader, where I petitioned Queen Victoria to enter the war against France on the side of the Arabs . . . to no avail."

Silently Alysson studied him. Thinking back, she remembered the harsh, bitter words Jafar had once flung at her about the sufferings his country had endured at the hands of the French. She'd realized then how powerless he felt about his ability to save his people or prevent them from being ground under the heel of French oppression. Jafar was struggling with his own kind of grief over the French conquest of his country. She could sense his anguish, his silent rage over his helplessness, and it wrung her heart. She longed to comfort him, though she could find no consolation to offer.

But she could thank him for the consolation he had once given her.

"You gave me hope that day," she said quietly. "You told me to make myself indispensable to my uncles, to make them want me, and I did. I still have your handkerchief."

The harsh emotion in Jafar's eyes suddenly abated, his gaze softening as he contemplated her. "I am curious to know how you implemented my advice."

"I became what my uncles wanted most—a traveling companion, a helpmate, a daughter."

"I'm glad that your term in England was not as bad as you feared."

"I wouldn't go so far as to say that." Alysson regarded him with a wry smile. "I was an outcast from the first moment I arrived at boarding school with my Indian servant. Chand prostrated himself to pray to Allah and promptly was branded a heathen. I was considered an unholy terror."

Jafar's lips curved upward. "I can well imagine how you might have shocked some sensibilities. You were rather a contentious young lady, if I recall."

Alysson gave a graceful shrug. She still couldn't look back on that time with equanimity. She'd been a reckless, unruly, inelegant young girl back then, stubbornly determined to flout the disdainful social elite who had scorned her. "I didn't allow their rejection to bother me, not once my uncles came to notice me. I even became accustomed to being a byword."

She said it lightly, but Jafar heard the underlying hurt in that simple admission.

"I wasn't totally without resources," Alysson continued. "A vast fortune can gain one entrée into even the highest circles. I even had a presentation at court. Not that I was keen on the idea, but my Uncle Cedric thought it a great coup that I make my curtsies to the queen."

"A fortune can be an advantage," he agreed quietly.

Alysson fell silent, remembering. She had been raised to elegance and wealth, but money was not a cure for loneliness. Indeed, for her, money had never been the great blessing it was supposed to be. She'd quickly learned what a curse it could be to be so exceedingly rich . . . to be used by impoverished aristocrats and social climbers for their own ends, to pay the price in loneliness, never knowing who you could trust to be a true friend, never knowing who you could love. Yet it was because of that very wealth that society tolerated her. In spite of her wild ways, she could do little wrong.

Shaking herself mentally, Alysson struggled to refocus her thoughts. How had they managed to change the subject? They had been discussing him, not her.

"I wish I had known you were part English," she said finally. "It would have made my captivity easier to bear."

Her wistful tone affected Jafar like a blow, making his soul ache.

Guilt smote him as he thought of the countless wrongs

against Alysson that could be laid at his door. He had taken her captive, terrified her, humiliated her, almost gotten her killed. He had made war on her race and come within a hairsbreadth of slaying the man she loved. He had nearly caused the death of her beloved uncle. He had taken her virtue and destroyed her good name in the eyes of her society, perhaps destroyed her life.

At the time, when he had first embarked on his mission of vengeance, he'd had entirely justifiable reasons for every savage action he'd taken, every uncivilized thing he had done to her. But now, what he wanted most to do was take her in his arms and console her, to beg her forgiveness.

He stared down at Alysson, wondering at the bewildering gentleness she inspired in him. He had never felt that so strongly, not for any woman but her. How easily she could endear herself to him . . . No, she had already done so. She *was* dear to him. But was she so dear that he could put her interests before his own? Was he willing to let her go? Without warning, the word *love* invaded his thoughts. Was it love he felt for her?

The question prodded him like a dagger, as did his next reflection. If he truly loved her, he would value her happiness above his own. If he truly loved her, he would set her free.

But his feelings for his defiant young captive were not something he wanted to scrutinize, just as her freedom was not a subject he wanted to face. He wasn't sorry when Alysson interrupted his musings with a pensive query.

"Your being part English . . . does your tribe hold it against you?"

"In the past they haven't, but some consider my motives suspect for failing to carry out my oath. One member of the council has charged that my heredity caused me to sympathize with the Europeans."

"That," Alysson said emphatically, "is complete nonsense. I've never seen you act the least sympathetic toward Europeans."

He smiled tiredly. "Well, the charge will have to be proven before the council. I will not give up my rule easily."

"Good."

Her obvious partiality warmed him, though her next comment made that warmth fade.

"You said our being here gave you greater bargaining power with the French, but I suppose your tribe would have been outraged at you if you had let us go?"

Jafar hedged. "That influenced my decision to keep you here, yes. I would have had difficulty defending my position if I released you before securing the freedom of as many of our war prisoners as possible."

Aware of his hypocrisy, but not wanting to explain his true reasons for keeping her captive, Jafar rose and went to the doorway. Alysson's next question, however, prevented him from leaving.

"Jafar . . . why didn't you want me to know who you were? Why didn't you tell me?"

Halting, he turned to glance over his shoulder, his expression enigmatic. "If you learned my identity, you would be able to lead your fiancé to me, to my tribe."

"And now you think I won't tell him, that I won't betray you?"

Would you betray me, Ehuresh? he thought silently. Aloud, he gave a different reply. "Now I think it doesn't matter. I have Bourmont's pledge not to come after you, if and when he is released. He gave you up . . . once he had my assurances that you would not be harmed."

Alysson looked down at her hands, but not before Jafar caught the flash of despair in her eyes at the knowledge that her colonel had abandoned her.

"What else could he do?" Jafar said quietly, conscious of the irony in defending his archenemy. "His troops had just suffered a major defeat. He had wounded men who needed medical attention. And I had just spared his life when by all rights I should have killed him."

She raised her head then, her luminous gray eyes troubled and questioning. "Why didn't you kill him?"

Jafar hesitated. "Because of you," he replied softly. "What else could *I* do?"

Alysson had a number of disturbing reflections to ponder during the course of the following week. Jafar's background. The decisions he'd made regarding both herself and his blood enemy. His possible impeachment. His relationship with her.

He had given up his vengeance because of her. Not for Gervase, but for her. She was the reason he had betrayed his oath, and now his rule, his very future was at stake. It made her feel very humble.

As for their relationship, his revelations about his identity had not changed the circumstances between them . . . and yet they had. Knowing he was half English, she felt closer to Jafar, more attune to his thoughts and feelings. Which was absurd, considering that he treated her no differently after their discussion in the library than before. He still spoke French whenever they met in public, and he still played the considerate host, making every effort to entertain and please her.

Yet she was still his captive.

She still had no place in his life, no future. They were nothing like equals. Jafar was a Berber prince, an English nobleman, while her bourgeois blood was common red—its only claim to blue being her aristocratic French grandmother. She was also tainted by the smell of the shop.

And then there was the issue of their disparate backgrounds. Jafar might have spent a great part of his youth in England, but by his own admission, he hadn't fit in. She wouldn't fit in here either, not in this Berber culture, with its different religion and vastly different customs.

No, they had no future together. If she thought about it at all, it was only to scold herself for being a fool. Not in her wildest dreams could she imagine that Jafar would want an Englishwoman for his wife. Not with his aversion to all things European. Not with his tribe already questioning his motives. He would be suspected of siding with the enemy were he even to consider marriage to her.

Besides, Zohra had told her Jafar would wed one of his own kind. When Alysson subtly introduced the subject one afternoon in the kitchens, Tahar only confirmed it.

"Yes, the lord must take a noblewoman to wife. It is his duty."

"A Berber noblewoman?"

"Or Arab."

"Not English?"

Tahar looked surprised at the question. "The lord would not wed a foreign woman."

"But Jafar's mother was a foreigner, was she not? His father married her."

Tahar shrugged fatalistically. "That was before the war."

Alysson heard the finality in that simple statement with an aching heart. *Before the war.*

Of course the war had changed everything. It was the very reason Jafar had disavowed his English heritage. No, he wouldn't want a foreign wife. Foreigners were brutal murderers, the conquerors of his beloved homeland. And even if he could bring himself to overlook that overwhelming obstacle, Alysson reflected, *she* wouldn't be the woman he chose. Culturally he despised everything she represented, but personally, the marks against her were nearly as formidable. She was not at all like the women of Barbary. She could never be submissive and docile, toward Jafar or any other man. She had been too independent and strong-willed for far too long.

No, Jafar might desire her for the moment, but he couldn't possibly come to love her. He would use her body, if she let him, and that would be the end of it.

If she let him. She didn't know if she could bring herself to stay as his mistress, even if she were asked. But so far Jafar hadn't given her the slightest indication that he was considering such a longer-term relationship with her, scandalous or otherwise.

She had begun her third week at Jafar's mountain fortress when Zohra again gave a dance performance for the company. Alysson endured the evening, but was grateful that she had worn her most attractive outfit. Tahar had sewn for her a new djellaba of rich yellow velvet, and the garment gave her a confidence she wasn't aware she was lacking.

Early the following morning, however, even that confidence was shattered. Alysson was strolling in the courtyard while Jafar held audience in his reception hall. There was no sign of the young greyhound who had befriended her. When she came across a wizened old Berber woman sitting on the ground chanting and waving an amulet, Alysson withdrew a discreet distance to give the woman some privacy. Settling herself on one of the marble benches, she turned her face up to the warm sunshine.

Mahmoud found her moments later and startled her with his sudden exclamation. "Come away, *lallah!* Please, you must come away at once!"

Abruptly opening her eyes, Alysson stared at him in bewilderment. His face was pale beneath the vicious red scar and he was wringing his hands in what seemed to be fear. "The old woman," he babbled, "she is a *kahina!* A witch! She commands the djinns—the evil spirits—and will cast a spell on you! You must not stay here!"

Alysson cast a dubious glance across the courtyard at the harmless-looking old woman. The Berbers were highly superstitious, she knew, but she herself did not believe in such nonsense.

Her hesitation sent Mahmoud into a frenzy. In his distress, he totally forgot his place as a servant and grabbed Alysson's hand, giving it a fierce tug as he implored her again to leave.

Just then Zohra stepped from the shadows of a fig tree, her eyes gleaming with malevolence as she fixed them on Mahmoud. "Get you gone!" she demanded in Berber, pointing at the boy.

Alysson leaped to her feet to defend him, but to her surprise, before she could say a word, Mahmoud turned and fled as fast as his limp would allow.

He had not abandoned her, however. Instead he had run to fetch his master. Zohra had only time to turn her virulent gaze on Alysson before Jafar came striding out of the house, his robes swirling fiercely around his ankles as he bore down on them. The harsh fury on his face was visible even at a distance.

When he reached them, the *kahina* stopped chanting and Zohra took an involuntary step backward.

"What is the meaning of this?" Jafar asked the Berber beauty, his low, controlled voice vibrating with rage.

With her limited command of the Berber language, Alysson understood only one word in three of the subsequent discussion, but she comprehended enough to realize what had happened: Zohra had arranged for the Berber sorceress to cast a spell on the "infidel Englishwoman."

Mahmoud, who had returned to the scene, edged closer to Alysson. "I came in time," he whispered anxiously, "before the *kahina* could appeal to the evil spirits and cast *rbat* on you—the great curse. The lord will prevent her, praise Allah." Despite his faith, however, Mahmoud placed his thin crippled body between Alysson and the witch.

At the protective gesture by the young boy, Alysson's heart swelled. She gave his shoulder a gentle squeeze, both in gratitude and because she wanted him to hush so she could try to follow the stormy conversation.

She had never seen Jafar so angry, not even the time she'd threatened to kill herself. Zohra, understandably, looked frightened by his savage temper, yet there was no prostrating herself at the lord's feet. Indeed, more than once Zohra gave a proud toss of her head, her eyes flashing defiance as she railed at her rival.

"She is evil, lord!" Zohra finally cried, pointing at Alysson.

"She is an innocent, and here at my command!"

"She has bewitched you! She is not one of us! You have made her your woman and betrayed your own people. The djinns of madness have seized you."

"Enough!" Jafar's roar echoed resoundingly in the suddenly quiet courtyard. He pointed at Zohra. "You, woman, are no longer welcome here in my home, in this village! Be gone at once, before I banish you from this province entirely."

Zohra's tirade ceased abruptly as apparently she realized she had vastly overstepped the bounds. Her mouth half-open, she stared at Jafar, looking aghast. "Forgive me, lord, for my heedless tongue . . . I meant no disrespect."

"I will not repeat myself," he warned softly, in a deadly voice.

His implacability must have sunk in, for after a long agonized look, Zohra began backing away. Yet when she reached a safe distance—the arched passageway that led to the street—she halted. Clenching her fists, she spat on the ground. "I curse her!" Zohra cried with vehemence, raising her voice so that the crowd that had gathered in the courtyard could hear every word. "I curse the *saiyid*'s infidel woman! May the evil eye look down upon her and destroy all she holds dear!'' Then she spun on her slippered heel and fled.

In the ensuing silence, Alysson found herself shaking—and not just because of Zohra's venom. Rather, because she had again come between Jafar and his tribe.

She sent him an imploring glance and found him watching her. ''I'm sorry, Jafar,'' she said with regret. ''I did not mean to cause trouble for you.''

''You are in no way to blame,'' he retorted grimly.

Breaking contact with Alysson's gaze, Jafar sent the Berber sorceress away with a sharp command, then dismissed his retainers and supplicants with an impatient wave of his hand . . . all except for Mahmoud. Instead he beckoned to the young servant. ''Instruct Saful to prepare the falcons and ready the lady's mount,'' he ordered before turning back to Alysson. ''You will accompany me on the hunt.'' At her quizzical look, Jafar raised a golden eyebrow. ''You once expressed a desire to hunt, did you not?''

''Yes, but . . . you needn't feel obliged to take me—''

''One day, *Ehuresh,*'' he interrupted, ''you will learn that I do as I wish. And at the moment I wish to make amends for the distasteful way you have been treated in my home.'' Suddenly his savage expression softened and he smiled, a tender, exquisitely sensual smile. ''Now go and change your clothing, *chérie,* for something more appropriate for riding.''

Alysson hesitated only a moment before turning to do his bidding. After days of being allowed only ''women's'' activities, she longed to escape the strict confines of her gender.

As she ran upstairs to change, anticipation curled inside her at the promised pleasure of hunting and the greater pleasure of enjoying Jafar's company for a few hours. And for the time being she was even able to banish her disturbing thoughts of Jafar's impending impeachment and the stark foreboding that Zohra had managed to create with her sorcery and her accusations of betrayal.

Chapter 21

I t was a day always to remember, an intimate moment to be stored away and cherished, to be drawn out when youth had gone and the lonely years of old age were upon her.

The sun was bright, the fall air crisp and mingled with the scent of warm horseflesh and the sharp fragrance of cedars. The hunting party was small. Leaving the greyhounds behind, Jafar took only three servants, his falconer, several of his hawks, and Alysson.

She gave a good account of herself. She'd been hawking numerous times before with her Uncle Oliver, and so had no trouble earning Jafar's admiration.

Just as he earned hers.

It was a pleasure simply to watch him, to be near him. As in everything he did, Jafar brought with him his vitality and cool magnetism. The sight of him on his fiery Barb, with a proud, golden-eyed falcon sitting on his wrist, was magnificent to behold. Even more so than the picture of the falcon spreading its wings and soaring, or attacking with talons stretched as it plummeted after small prey and game birds.

Jafar apparently still believed she had led a sheltered life, though, for when they entered a forest of holm oaks and discovered telltale bristles on some of the tree trunks, he commanded Alysson to keep behind him. When shortly they came upon a black boar, Jafar brought it down in one shot, with a bullet positioned behind the ear. Only a Berber could have placed a bullet so well from the saddle, Alysson reflected, marveling.

It was only later, when Jafar sent his adherents home without him, that she realized he hadn't brought her along merely to hunt. Her heart started to race. He smiled at her then, a smile of pure sensuality, and led her mount further from civilization.

Shortly they topped a rocky hillock and descended into a rugged glen, where oleanders, brambles, and hawthorns choked each other in wild confusion, and a bright, pure fountain gushed from the rocks to tumble far below into a small pool.

"How beautiful!" Alysson breathed, seeing the rippling threads of silver that marked the path of the waterfall.

"Yes," Jafar replied in a low voice. At the husky tone, she turned her head to find him regarding her intently, his eyes smoldering like hot gold. She began to tremble, while her heart beat with the heavy thud of anticipation.

Without another word, he dismounted and came to her side, helping her down. Then, holding her hand, he led her up the rocky incline to a shallow cave half-hidden by a thicket.

The rock was warm from the sun, Alysson noted in one part of her dazed mind. The rest of her attention was occupied in watching Jafar. With an economy of motion, he spread his burnous on the hard ground and tossed his turban aside. When he turned back to her, sunlight beamed down on him, gilt-glittering a thousand blond threads of his hair and intensifying the smoldering ardor in his jeweled eyes.

"Will you deny me now, *Ehuresh?*" he asked simply, quietly.

Alysson knew her answer was written in her own eyes; she could no more have denied him than she could have denied her next breath. Just now it didn't matter if she was only his captive and Gervase his prisoner. Just now she couldn't think of the past or the future, of guilt or betrayal, of right or wrong.

There was only this man, this moment, this feeling of heat and hunger and need.

She heard his sharp intake of breath as he read her expression, and only had time to whisper "Jafar" in a breathless plea before he dragged her into his arms and kissed her with such devouring hunger that she felt giddy.

His mouth was hot, his tongue fiercely thrusting as he pulled her haik back from her face to give him better access.

His kiss was savage and unrelenting, desperate, yet strangely Alysson understood that desperation. She felt it herself. She ached to be touched, possessed, filled.

She returned Jafar's embrace with a violence that matched his own, and heard him groan at her response. His arms wrapped tightly around her, forcing her closer, crushing her in a hold that should have hurt but didn't. She could feel the need that shuddered through his body, feel his violent heartbeat merge with hers, feel the heavy, rigid length of his arousal grinding against her.

Wanton pleasure coursed through her. Feverishly she strained to get closer, molding herself against him, her fingers digging into the corded muscles of his shoulders. Hunger was too tame a word for the wildness she was feeling. She hadn't known hunger until now, had never felt this kind of raw need—mindless, relentless, endless. A primitive ache so deep her body throbbed.

Breathing raggedly, Jafar finally dragged his mouth away, but his fingers tangled roughly in her hair, holding her face captive. "Do you know how I've longed to do this?" he whispered hoarsely, "how much I've ached to have you?"

"Yes," she rasped. "I've wanted it, also."

Her answer was all Jafar needed.

He wasn't gentle as he tore at her clothes, stripping away her haik and tunic and the loose pantaloons she'd worn for riding, shoving up the sheer chemise till her breasts were bared to his mouth. With a rough sound of passion, he bent her back over his arm and feasted, his burning lips attending each nipple till it tightened with pleasure so intense it was painful.

"Jafar . . . please . . ." she begged.

He raised his head, heeding her urgent plea. His eyes were fiercely primitive as he divested her of the chemise, then swiftly lifted her in his arms and laid her naked on the makeshift bed. Kneeling beside her, he ripped off his dagger and tunic, but was too impatient to remove his pantaloons. Instead, he joined Alysson on the cave floor, laying his full length against her as his hard mouth covered hers. His tongue plunged deeply while his fingers sought the feminine recess between her thighs. She was all honey, primed for him with a damp, lusciously ready warmth. With a soft groan, Jafar freed his throbbing shaft and pulled her beneath his fully aroused body, his muscled thighs spreading hers wide.

Alysson felt his heaviness, his heat between her legs . . . the swollen flesh, hot and satin-smooth, pressing for entry. Joyously she opened to him, whimpering as he filled her, tears of pleasure welling in her eyes. The hard, pulsing length of him was like a huge fiery spear piercing her, invading her with a white-hot heat. Desperately she wrapped her legs around his flanks, her fingers clutching blindly at his shoulders.

He thrust deeper, burying his rigid fullness as far as possible inside her. The soft, frantic sounds of passion she made deep in her throat nearly drove Jafar mad. Lifting her hips with both hands, he surged into her again, claiming her triumphantly. The burning ache in his loins after the long days and nights of restraint, of being unable to touch her or caress her or drown himself in her silken heat was too great to bear. His body blazed with the maddening need to possess.

His rasping breath choked words against her mouth as he began driving hard, rhythmically into her. Alysson sobbed in awe.

Slowly, Jafar tried to command himself—to no avail. His blood was raging totally out of control. Alysson had often called him savage, and just now he felt that way . . . savage and warlike. But she responded with equal fervor, her hips answering his wild rhythm, mating with his.

Frantic with need, she writhed and arched and strained, trying to match his erratic, uncontrollable pounding. Her head was thrown back, her mouth open as he took her, her nails digging mindlessly into his muscled back.

Then it began, the wrenching, tearing, exquisite release. He heard her frenzied cries, felt her convulsive shudders moments before his own body contracted in hard, racking tremors. Against her open mouth he gave a hoarse shout as with a violent hot pulsing, he poured himself endlessly into her.

He was insensate for many moments while the shudders stilled, as the heavy, sharp-edged need dulled. Finally, he became aware of the chill afternoon breeze wafting against his sweat-slick skin, and that he was crushing Alysson's slender form beneath him.

Slowly, weakly, he dragged himself off her and, nestling her close against him, wrapped them both in his burnous. Her contented sigh echoed the emotion in his heart.

For a long, quiet interval they lay there unmoving, with heartbeats mingling. Jafar absently stroked her bare hip with a casual finger, the same touch that had moments before turned her into a wanton now gentle and caring.

After a time, Alysson slowly opened her eyes to watch the flutes of the waterfall at the edge of the cave entrance. She was aware of an enveloping feeling of warmth, a tenderness as devastating as the wild loving had been.

Unable to help herself, she turned her face to him and pressed her lips against the warm skin of his shoulder. She tasted the salty taste of arousal and satisfaction that lingered on.

"Did you know that you make love to me in English?" she murmured, lifting her curious gaze to Jafar's.

A lazy smile filled his eyes, turning them to sunlit amber. "Do I?"

"Mmmm . . . always. I never consciously realized it until now."

Drawing back slightly, he surveyed her flushed, tousled beauty with a satisfied gleam in his eyes. "I expect I get carried away when I am with you, *Ehuresh.*"

Alysson very much would have liked to believe she affected Jafar enough to make him lose his rigid control. "This morning . . . I understood some of what Zohra said when she accused me of bewitching you," Alysson mused, her tone a bit hesitant. "She called me your woman."

In response, Jafar closed his eyes. He was not pleased that she had brought up Zohra, yet he was too sated to be annoyed. And in fact, the thought of Alysson being jealous of his past affairs was distinctly gratifying.

"Am I your woman, Jafar?"

A curiously passionless frown crossed his face as he reflected on her question. For some time now, he'd known that in many ways Alysson was a kindred spirit, as isolated by fate as he was. But only this morning had he come to realize another truth. The aloneness that had been such an integral part of his existence since the death of his beloved parents faded whenever Alysson was near. She filled an emptiness in his life that he'd never acknowledged until now. As he'd stood there shaking with fury at Zohra's machinations, he'd finally understood the possessiveness he felt for Alysson. He wanted the right to protect her, to share her love, her future. He wanted to father her children. He wanted to become the center of her universe, the way he feared she had become the center of his.

But no man could *take* those rights. They had to be given freely.

"If you were truly my woman," he answered quietly, cryptically, "you would not want to leave here."

"What does that mean?" She searched his face. "Do you expect me to say I *want* to be your captive?"

Jafar sighed. It meant that she would have to make the choice to stay, that he wanted her to come to him willingly, of her own volition. But so far Alysson had shown no indication that she wanted to remain here with him.

When he didn't reply, Alysson bit her lip, still tender from his savage kisses. "Tahar told me that you must marry a noblewoman from another tribe."

"Yes." He sighed again. "I have no alternative but to marry for political reasons. It is my duty as *amghar* to strengthen my tribe's alliances through marriage."

"Oh."

The quiet disappointment he thought he'd heard in her voice made Jafar's heart skip a hopeful beat. But perhaps he was reading too much into her tone. Even strong evidence of a woman's jealousy did not mean she held any deeper feelings. Feelings such as love.

Jafar's jaw tightened. In truth, how could Alysson learn to love him after all he'd done to her? He'd seduced her, taken her innocence. He'd shamelessly tried to rouse her desire and make her forget her love for another man. In the first goal at least he'd been successful. He had a certain power over her, he knew. One that went beyond their captor-captive relationship. The attraction between them, the desire, was too strong for her to deny or resist. Her presence here in his arms just now proved that.

But while he could compel her desire, he couldn't force

her love. She might be drawn to him for the moment. She might be unable to deny the fierce physical attraction between them. But desire was a fleeting, insubstantial basis upon which to build a future.

As for her question, he could not make her his "woman." She would never remain here as his concubine. And he would not insult her by asking it of her.

But what of marriage? His religion allowed him to take up to four wives, and yet he knew Alysson well enough to realize she would never be content with second place.

And he could not offer more. His first wife would of necessity come from a neighboring tribe. He could not put his own wishes, his own needs, ahead of his people's.

Nor could he in good conscience ask Alysson to spend the rest of her life here, with him, in this savage land. Merely the idea was impossible. What could he offer her but war and strife? What future besides a lifetime sentence in a strange land, amid a strange culture? Even if he *could* wed her, there was every possibility that he might be killed in the war. And what then? She would be cut off from all she held dear.

No, the truth was, she would be better off without him, among her own kind, with a man who could offer her a safe, secure future.

With Gervase de Bourmont.

Involuntarily, possessively, Jafar tightened his hold on Alysson. The thought of his blood enemy taking what he'd just been given, of *any* other man enjoying the intensely satisfying ecstasy of making love to her, of unleashing the fascinating energy in her sweet body, the delicious warmth, made Jafar's blood boil. But he had to face that eventuality. He had to force himself to view the circumstances unemotionally.

It was in his power to determine Alysson's fate. He could keep her here indefinitely as his prisoner, or he could give her her freedom. He could put her happiness before his own. He could allow her a future with the man she professed to love. He could send her back to Gervase de Bourmont.

There was little standing in the way now. Yesterday he'd received a message from his chief lieutenant Farhat, reporting that the negotiations with the French government were proceeding satisfactorily. The exchange of prisoners would soon go forth. Once that occurred, there would be no compelling reason to keep Alysson and her uncle as a bargaining advantage.

And the letters he'd written to certain highborn English friends of his grandfather should bear fruit any day now. He was almost positive he could make Alysson's return to Algiers less traumatic, that he could manage to protect her name and reputation enough so that she would not suffer too greatly.

Now it was only the matter of his own selfishness, Jafar reflected caustically. Yet how could he bear to send her back?

"Jafar? Do you . . . have you chosen a bride yet?"

Jafar felt an ache center in his chest. Next to the decision about whether to grant Alysson her freedom, the last thing he wanted to think about was his future bride. He wanted to forget entirely the existence of such duty. At the moment he wanted simply to enjoy the pleasure of having Alysson warm and willing in his embrace.

"I do not wish to discuss it, *chérie*."

"What if I wish to?"

He opened one eye to glare at her in mock menace. "Hush, or I will beat you."

"No, you won't," Alysson retorted at once. He would not hurt her, she was certain. A soft smile curved her mouth as she remembered his tenderness when she had been so ill. No, he would never purposely hurt her.

Jafar saw her smile and raised an eyebrow. "You are taking my displeasure very lightly."

Alysson lowered her eyes demurely, but it was an expression that was patently false. With casual ease, her fingers lifted to his muscular arm, to trace the scar that her bullet had left when she'd wounded him. "And you are taking *mine* lightly. Just remember, if I ever have the opportunity to shoot you again, I do not intend to miss."

He laughed softly. "Now that sounds more like my tigress, scratching and spitting . . . whenever she is not purring in my arms." The smug male confidence in his voice was laced with pride, which pricked her own.

"Tigress . . . *Ehuresh* . . . the names you choose for me are hardly flattering."

Jafar turned slowly in her arms to face her fully. "Is it flattering endearments you want then? How about Rose of Dawn? Or Pearl of Desire?"

His tone was so charming that it could melt stone; Alysson wanted both to laugh and to hit him for dismissing her concern so easily. "I might be impressed if you meant them," she returned wryly.

"Ah, but I do." The look on his face was one of uncompromising masculinity mixed with the ruthless amusement that she was coming to know. "You are a star of paradise, a sultan's treasure—"

"Lover," she interjected with a stab of honesty.

His expression slowly lost its amused look. "Yes, lover."

Her thoughts sobered as well as she realized how much she *wanted* to be Jafar's lover. He was magnificently, undeniably male. A beautiful savage man with a core of gentleness. And yet there was still a harsh reality that kept them from being true lovers.

"And captive," she added softly to the names he had given her.

Jafar stared a moment, then shook his head slowly, his seriousness fading. "Not today, *Ehuresh*. Today I am yours to command."

"Is that so?" she replied skeptically.

"Indeed it is."

The possibilities caught her imagination. She stared at him thoughtfully. "I think I would find it immensely satisfying if *you* were *my* captive."

He smiled then, a slow sexual smile that burned right through her. "Very well, I shall be your slave for the afternoon, *chérie,*" he agreed gallantly.

Alysson was not fooled by the peaceful handsome face, or this unusual show of servility. But she was woman enough to be goaded by his offer. She gave him a bold, direct look, her eyes clear, filled with challenge and desire. "You still have on some of your clothes," she observed in a provocative, commanding tone. "Take them off. I want to see you."

He hesitated only a second before obeying. With a graceful shrug, Jafar untangled himself from her arms and the burnous and sat up to remove his boots. Then, rising, he shed his pantaloons.

Alysson couldn't keep from staring at Jafar as he stood over her, feet planted slightly apart. He was ruthless strength and lithe elegance, and just looking at him made her feel breathless and wild. Ungovernably, the soft heat of her gaze drifted upward over his hard muscular body, traveling along the long elegant stretch of his legs with their golden sun color, to the hard jutting arousal that was the blatant evidence of his desire.

"You see what you do to me, my jewel?" he remarked with hard-edged amusement. "How you make me ache?"

She was startled to see Jafar reach down to hold that swelling sex in his hand, to see his tanned fingers curl around his engorged shaft, around pale skin flushed with red. She was even more startled by his next scandalous comment. "Would you like to ache, too? Do you want to feel this inside you?"

Alysson caught her breath, shocked by the fierce desire that ripped through her at his question. Slowly she lifted her gaze to Jafar's lean, intense face. His features were heavy and drugged with passion.

Their eyes merged, hers hazy, his hot. Alysson shivered at the naked hunger in those heated golden eyes.

Still trapping her gaze, he came to her again, lying beside her and propping himself up on one elbow. Slowly he pushed the burnous aside to bare her naked body.

"I am yours to command, lover," Jafar repeated, his voice a husky rasp. "Tell me what you want."

"Kiss me," Alysson whispered, hardly able to speak.

He sighed as if well-pleased and sank his mouth onto hers. Feverishly her arms closed around him, but soon her hands were roving the heat of his skin, searching, exploring . . . his chest . . . his taut belly . . . his groin. She made him draw a sharp breath as her curious fingers curved over the pulsing crest of his manhood. For a long moment she enjoyed the sensation of touching him wherever she wanted to, until with a soft curse, Jafar grasped her wrists and pinned her arms above her head with one hand.

He held her immobile, making a mockery of his invitation to enslave him, but Alysson was beyond caring who was captive or captor. This dizzying, lazy seduction was all she could focus on.

His lips rubbed hers languorously, delicately sipping. Then plundered in a series of long drugging kisses. Then finally moved down her throat to lavish attention on her breasts.

With a moan, Alysson arched her back in surrender. She felt her nipples swell for his approval, peaking in aching arousal, and at the softest lash of his tongue she shuddered.

Jafar began a tortuous game then, withholding anything but the lightest of caresses, teasing her with his warm breath and delicate nips of his teeth. He seemed determined to make her frantic. Desperately, she kissed the only parts of him she could reach, her own teeth gently biting the flesh of his shoulder, tasting the warm, musky skin. It had no effect on him.

"Jafar . . . please, I can't bear it," she begged finally, pleading for release. When he paid no attention, she pulled her hands free and tangled her fingers in his hair, with a tug making him lift his head. "Jafar, please . . ."

His eyes went dark and passionate as he stared down at her. "You have bewitched me into wanting you," he said softly. "It is only right that I make you want me."

"I do want you!" she insisted breathlessly.

At her answer, he suddenly rolled onto his back and pulled her astride his hips. He watched her face flush with eager pleasure at her dominant position, watched her eyes turn hot and smoky as slowly he guided her down and impaled her on his large arousal, heard her grateful sigh. When he was deep inside her, though, Jafar went totally still. He could feel the shimmering pulses of desire rippling around him, clutching at him. *Her captive,* he thought as his hard flesh swelled further. He had taken her hostage, but he was the one tied with silken chains of desire.

"Jafar!" she said plaintively at his stillness.

Obediently his hips began a slow, upward, surging thrust. "Do I please you, lover?" he demanded on a husky breath.

"Yes . . . you . . . please me!"

"You have muscles you didn't know you had," he mur-

mured hoarsely, reveling in her dazed look of pleasure.
"Use them to hold me."

She obeyed mindlessly, tightening her inner muscles
around him, which made Jafar stiffen and groan in reaction.

But still he did not hasten his movements. He retained
complete control until the final shattering moment of ecstasy. Until then, he was so exquisitely slow that he almost
drove her mad.

For the remainder of the entire golden afternoon, it
seemed as if that were his intention, to drive her insane
with need. He made her body quiver with desire while
showing her how to please him as he was pleased. Over and
over again he had her moving and pulsing with mindless
pleasure.

At other times they played at being lovers . . . sexual,
foolish, erotic games that made Alysson blush to participate. And all the while Jafar proved again and again that he
desired her. He was a sensual animal, his passions never
far from the surface and easily aroused. His passion fed her
woman's hungering heart. But he had no words of love to
give her, only the demands of his body.

That realization was the only harsh note of reality to mar
an otherwise magical day.

Chapter 22

S he had to face that realization when she arrived home
that evening, for her uncle was waiting anxiously for
her. Honoré was lying in his sickbed, fidgeting with the
covers, but to judge by the look on his face, he would have
been pacing the floor had his injuries allowed it. Worry,
disappointment, and sorrow all vied for expression on his
ruddy features.

He knew she had been with Jafar, Alysson realized.

She accepted the intelligence with embarrassment and re-gret. Embarrassment because her body was still warm and glowing with loving, her mind still filled with the heated memory of Jafar moving in a slow, senses-maddening un-dulation within her. Regret because she hadn't wished her uncle to learn about her loss of innocence. Honoré had wanted so badly to pretend that she hadn't suffered from her captivity. For the sake of his peace of mind, she hadn't told him the entire story of her time with Jafar. He would have felt obliged to defend her honor and call Jafar out, or some such foolishness, and no doubt get himself killed in the process.

When Honoré fixed her with his concerned gaze now, though, Alysson gave up the pretense of hiding the truth. Sinking to her knees beside his bed, she took his hand. Her intimacy with Jafar had been her choice, her decision, and she had to make her uncle understand that.

"He didn't force me, Uncle," she said quietly. "I went to him of my own free will."

"*Sacre Dieu . . .*" Honoré stared at her. "How could you, Alysson? The man is a savage, a barbarian."

"He is not. He is as civilized as you or I. In fact he is the son—" Alysson broke off abruptly. She wanted to share her knowledge about Jafar's English heritage, but she didn't have the right, not unless Jafar wanted it known. "He was educated in Europe," she finished lamely.

"What does that matter? He is a heathen and a mur-derer!"

"He is not!"

"He is! He and his savage horde slaughtered scores of French troops! He nearly killed the man you might have taken as a husband! Have you forgotten Gervase?"

"No." She pulled her hand from her uncle's grasp as guilt returned to assail her. "I haven't forgotten."

"Alysson . . ." Honoré waved his hands helplessly. "You know that I love you like my own child. I only want what is best for you. I wish I could dismiss this as simply some wild prank of yours. But this ordeal you have been through has obviously affected your judgment."

Alysson looked away, her throat tight. "I want him. Is that so wrong of me?"

Honoré raised his fist in the air. "Yes and yes and yes! What future is there in it for you?"

"I . . . don't know."

Her uncle shook his head sorrowfully. "You and he are too different. Your ways are too different. It can never be."

For a long moment Alysson didn't answer.

"What a horror this trip has become," Honoré muttered finally. "How I wish we had never come to this heathen country."

Alysson could not wish the same. If she'd never come to Algeria, she never would have met Jafar, never would have fallen in love, never would have known such fulfillment as a woman.

And yet she couldn't simply blithely dismiss her uncle's concern. *Could she have a future with Jafar?*

It was a question she didn't want to face, but one that occupied her thoughts almost to the exclusion of all else during the next few days. She loved Jafar, but she wasn't at all certain he could ever return her love.

So much stood between them. Even if she were willing to give up her own life—her family, her religion, her entire culture—in order to live with him, would Jafar want her, an Englishwoman, in his life? And if so, in what capacity? He would not want an English wife, most certainly. Not when he'd disavowed his English heritage and turned his back on his mother's people. Not when he blamed her fellow Europeans for the murder of his parents and the rape of his country.

Besides, it was presumptuous of her even to think Jafar might take her for his wife. He had never spoken of marriage or even love. And his duty required him to marry a noblewoman of his own country.

What had he meant by his cryptic remark? Alysson wondered. *If you were truly my woman, you would not want to leave here.* Was he saying she had a choice? But no, he would not let her decide whether to stay or go. He was the most possessive man she knew. What belonged to him would never be surrendered easily. He had never once made any mention of her release. That afternoon by the waterfall, Jafar had merely jested about playing her slave for a few hours.

And as satisfying as it had been to have him at her mercy during their erotic lovers' games, she hadn't forgotten that any power she enjoyed over him was totally at his discretion, because he allowed it. Nor could she forget that Jafar had vowed she would call him master someday.

That was not the kind of relationship she wanted with him. She wanted them to be equals, not master and slave. But then, her wishes hardly mattered. In fact, she was slowly, painfully, coming to the realization that her happiness belonged to Jafar, whether she wanted it so or not.

And despite her uncle's warning that she had no future here with Jafar, Alysson feared that it no longer mattered. Lamentably, she had little pride left. She might even have remained with Jafar as his mistress, if only he had asked.

But he didn't ask.

The week following their magical afternoon of lovemaking was a time of torment and confusion for Alysson as she struggled with her feelings for Jafar. Self-respect alone kept her from confessing her love for him. How piteous a figure she would cut if she begged him to allow her to stay and he refused. Or if he grew tired of her and turned to another woman. She couldn't bear his pity or his disinterest. And so she remained silent, as did he.

She would have liked to ride off her frustrations and uncertainties on the back of a swift horse, but the weather turned cold and ugly—the bone-chilling slashing rain of late November. More to the point, Jafar had forbidden her to ride without his accompaniment. It seemed that a lion was stalking the hills, preying on livestock, and Jafar did not want her exposed to such danger. Alysson would have argued, but on the subject of her safety, Jafar was adamant. After her near-death from the scorpion's sting, he was not inclined to risk her life again.

It was nearly the end of November, by her calculations, when she was forcibly reminded that not only her future was at stake, but Jafar's as well. Alysson had gone up to the rooftop to be alone when she spied a large crowd of black-robed men gathering in the village arena. Suddenly uneasy, she hurried downstairs and found Mahmoud.

The boy was nearly the only male present in the house.

The tribal council was meeting to vote on Jafar's impeachment, but Mahmoud was too young to attend.

Alysson turned pale when she heard the news, but she squared her shoulders in determination.

"I mean to attend the council meeting, Mahmoud. Will you accompany me?" Even as she spoke, she turned and strode quickly across the courtyard.

"You? But you are a female, *lallah!*"

"What does that have to say to anything?" she replied impatiently, walking so fast that Mahmoud had to scurry to catch up.

"It is not permitted for a woman to attend without invitation."

Hearing his shuffling gait, Alysson paused to wait for him. "I mean to speak in your lord's defense, with or without an invitation. But I need you to act as my translator. Now, will you come with me or not?"

The boy's scarred features showed an agony of indecision—whether to defy the lord but act in his best interests. "Oh, *lallah,* I dare not," he said finally.

"Then I shall go alone."

That settled it; Mahmoud went.

The warriors guarding Jafar's house allowed her to pass without challenge, but as she approached the crowd, Alysson slowed her pace and drew the hood of her burnous forward to hide her face.

For a short while, her presence went undetected. Nearly all the men of Jafar's tribe were there, Mahmoud explained in a whisper, as well as the ranking officials of all the neighboring tribes, but they had their backs toward her, their attention focused on the speakers in the center of the gathering. She could not see Jafar, but she heard him speak occasionally. And with help from Mahmoud, Alysson was able to follow the line of conversation.

Jafar's prime accuser, it seemed, was a cousin of Zohra's, a *caid* of another tribe, and the prime allegation was one of betrayal of the blood oath.

"You have failed to avenge the death of the late lord, your father," Zohra's cousin charged in a ringing tone.

In response, Jafar began his defense for sparing the life

of his blood enemy. "My lord father's death has been avenged. Blood has been spilled in battle."

The sudden chorus of whispers that suddenly broke out around Alysson made her realize she'd been found out. She felt a hundred pairs of eyes on her.

Then the whispers quieted, while the sea of warriors slowly parted, making a path to the highest-ranking members of the council. She could tell by the severe expressions on the faces of the Berbers around her that they highly disapproved of her interruption. Some, like Zohra's cousin, were incensed by her presence.

As for Jafar himself, she couldn't tell what he was thinking. His eyes narrowed for a moment upon seeing her, but otherwise he showed no sign of surprise. Perhaps he had come to expect such outrageous behavior from her, Alysson thought uneasily.

He stood there waiting imperiously, looking every inch a prince in his flowing scarlet robes, a regal warlord in total command of the moment. Drawn by the power of his golden gaze, she moved forward, while Mahmoud trailed miserably behind.

"I should like permission to address the council," she said finally to Jafar, and was pleased that her voice did not quaver.

"To what purpose, mademoiselle?" His cool tone was devoid of emotion, giving her no encouragement.

Alysson bit her lip. Perhaps she was acting foolishly for daring to intrude on the council's business, but she couldn't stand idly by while Jafar paid such a high price for his act of mercy. "I . . . want to speak in your behalf. Whatever your reasons for sparing Gervase, politically it was a wise move. He is one of the few officials in the French government sympathetic to your cause, and he can help. I think your tribal leaders should consider that before they condemn you."

Jafar's features seemed to soften for a brief instant, but if he was flattered or displeased by her eagerness to defend him, he gave no other sign. "There is no need for you to be here, *Ehuresh.*"

She started to protest, but his next words forestalled her; Jafar raised his voice again to address the crowd. "Gervase de Bourmont is a good man," he said clearly in his own language.

At first Alysson thought she must have misunderstood, even with her growing command of Berber, but Mahmoud's translation into French verified what she'd heard. Her eyes widened in disbelief. Jafar was actually defending his blood enemy?

"This Frenchman is not like the others of his kind," Jafar told the council. "He has used his office to help our people, not to drive us into proverty and submission. The Englishwoman has pleaded on his behalf and sworn his innocence, and I believe her. This man Bourmont is not his father. It is not required that his life be forfeit."

Stunned, Alysson listened with amazement and throat-tightening joy. *This man is not his father*, Jafar had said. Gervase should not die for his father's sins. It was a huge admission for Jafar to make. She watched as he continued his defense.

"Bourmont's capture proved advantageous for our side. His exchange will spare the lives of a score of our sultan's warriors. They will live to fight again."

That point was deliberated in detail, which Mahmoud tried to translate. Then the discussion shifted to Alysson herself.

"The infidel Englishwoman is an evil influence over Sidi Jafar!" Zohra's cousin cried. But Jafar scornfully refused to debate either Alysson's influence over him or her presence in his home.

"She is only a woman," he told his accuser in a lethal tone, "and you insult me by suggesting I could be corrupted or governed by her. She is also my captive to do with as I please. *You* may choose to cast your vote against me, but that is the extent of your power. You will not prescribe my choice of women or dictate what manner of guests I invite into my home. I will step down if you wish another to lead you, but let me be judged on the issue at hand."

At the moment Alysson was too concerned with the seriousness of the charge against Jafar to be incensed by his demeaning dismissal of her. She remained silent, straining to follow the conversation.

The dispute then swung back to the crucial question of

Jafar's clemency for his father's murderer. It was a solemn, black-bearded man who offered another argument by quoting the words of the Prophet Mohammed. "Avert the infliction of prescribed penalties as much as possible, the Prophet says. If there is a way out then let a man go, for it is better for a leader to err in forgiving than to err in punishing."

Caught up in what was being said, Alysson was startled to realize Jafar was addressing her again.

"If you will be so kind as to return to the house, mademoiselle," he said gently, "we have business to attend to."

His quiet tone of command left her no room for argument. Realizing the total irrelevance of her presense, Alysson flushed and ducked her head. Jafar hadn't needed her testimony at all. If anything, she had only provided ammunition for his accusers, the ones who claimed his judgment had been corrupted by an infidel woman.

With a small murmur of apology, she withdrew as gracefully as possible, leaving Mahmoud behind to observe the rest of the proceedings.

She retreated to the courtyard of Jafar's house to await the verdict, but it was nearly two hours later before Mahmoud came running and, despite his limp, began dancing in excited circles around her, exclaiming in rapid Berber. Alysson jumped up in alarm, while the greyhound bitch lying at her feet bared its teeth menacingly at the boy.

"The council has voted!" Mahmoud exclaimed in French. "The lord has been cleared of all charges! He is still *amghar el-barood!*"

Relief, swift and sweet, flooded through Alysson as she stared at the boy. Jafar was still chief of war. He had not been deposed for his act of mercy.

"Thank heaven," she murmured with heartfelt elation, then commanded Mahmoud to sit beside her and tell her the details of what had occurred after her dismissal.

In actuality, her defense of Jafar had made little difference, the boy said. It had been the lord's own argument that had swayed the council—that the exchange of prisoners had benefited the Berber cause more than the shedding of blood would have done. In the end, the vote had been nearly unanimous. Jafar was reaffirmed as *amghar el-barood.*

She thanked Mahmoud for relaying the good news, and sat there after he'd gone, trying to come to terms with the truth.

A short while later, she heard the sound of footsteps and looked up to meet Jafar's eyes. Somehow she forced herself to speak. "I am glad you won, Jafar."

"Thank you. I am also." His expression was half tender, half serious when he commented softly, "I did not need you to defend me, *Ehuresh.*"

"Yes . . . I see that now."

"But I am honored that you made the attempt."

Alysson gazed back at him, not knowing if she could believe him.

When he reached out, laying his palm against her cheek in a caress, she closed her eyes, his recent declaration haunting her. *She is only a woman . . . you insult me by suggesting I could be corrupted or governed by her.* Jafar wouldn't want her love, any more than he'd wanted her interference in his affairs.

When finally he turned away, she didn't prevent him from leaving. And yet watching him go, she felt totally bereft.

No, he hadn't needed her. She'd only been a detriment to him.

The elation she'd felt at his vindication disappeared, to be replaced by aching despondency. The answer to her uncle's question was obvious. She had no future with Jafar. She had been deluding herself for one moment to think otherwise.

No, their parting was inevitable.

Forcibly, Alysson swallowed, blinking back the stinging tears welling in her eyes. She had to be strong. For Jafar's sake, as well as her own, she had to resist the insidious desire to pretend they could build a life together. Their passionate wanting would not be enough. Her love for him would not be enough.

At least she had not been blessed with Jafar's child, Alysson thought bleakly. Her intimacy with Jafar had not resulted in pregnancy. Her monthly courses had begun shortly after their last tryst, an event for which she ought to be grateful. She knew Jafar well enough to realize he would never let her leave carrying his child.

And she had to leave. She had to flee from him while she still had the chance to forget him. She must somehow escape this impossible love that threatened to consume her.

As if sensing her despair, the greyhound raised its sleek head and sniffed Alysson's cold hand, then gave her fingers a sympathetic lick. Absently, Alysson stroked the silken head, but she could draw no comfort from the dog's friendly gesture. It would take a great deal more than that to diminish her sense of raw desolation or ease the fierce ache in her heart.

Chapter 23

Her chance for freedom came in a way she never expected. It was the first of December, a day marked by two disturbing incidents.

The first was news of a tragedy. The lion that had been stalking the hills at night had attacked and savaged a woman from a neighboring tribe. Mahmoud gave Alysson the gory details when he served her breakfast.

"*Ezim ezher*," the boy said with solemnity and awe. "The lion roars."

No longer possessing an appetite, Alysson pushed away her plate while Mahmoud expounded on his subject. The Berbers had the greatest respect for the king of beasts, she learned, calling it *sidi*, which signified ruler or master. But Jafar's tribe had supreme confidence in the lord's ability to track down and kill the savage creature. Jafar was at this very moment making preparations to hunt the lion that was terrorizing the countryside.

Before he could depart, however, an event of a different nature occurred, one that filled Alysson with a stark foreboding. Messengers from the west began streaming into Jafar's reception room, bringing word of their sultan, Abdel

Kader. The noble Berber leader had been betrayed by the Sultan of Morocco, they reported, and Abdel Kader might at any moment be forced to retreat to Algeria.

Alysson greeted this intelligence with dread. Surrounded as she'd been during the past three weeks by the luxury and comfort of Jafar's home, she'd almost forgotten that a war still raged in his country. But hearing of the dismaying turn of events in Morocco brought reality back to her with a vengeance. For Jafar the conflict was not over. Perhaps it never would be.

The messengers were followed shortly by the arrival of Jafar's Arab friend, Khalifa Ben Hamadi. The general was returning from the eastern province after trying to raise support for his sultan, and since Jafar's mountain fortress lay near the direct road to Constantine, Ben Hamadi had called to discuss the fate of their leader, Abdel Kader.

Unable to leave his guest to hunt for the lion, Jafar remained closeted with the general for several hours. Afterward, a feast was held, similar to the one given during Ben Hamadi's last visit to Jafar's camp. Unlike last time, however, Alysson was invited to attend, as was her Uncle Honoré. She was aware of the honor, but Honoré—perhaps because of his pain, perhaps because he held the khalif's army to blame for his injuries—glared at the Arab chieftain during the entire meal and answered any remark with a testiness that bordered on rudeness.

In fact, the entire atmosphere that afternoon was grim, despite the delicious food. Squabs, roast chickens stuffed with olives, and a savory meat pie made up the first courses, followed by couscous mounded with chunks of mutton, eggplant, turnips, and grapes. Yet Alysson barely tasted what she ate.

In direct contrast to her uncle's scowling expression, she smiled graciously at the *khalifa* and responded with deferential respect when he spoke to her, her civility a measure of how much her relationship with Jafar had changed her. Weeks ago during Ben Hamadi's last visit, she had dismissed his gallantry and paid little attention to his ramblings about his Berber commander. This time, however, she listened intently as he told her the news of Abdel Kader's possible banishment from Morocco. Jafar's future and that of his countrymen might very well depend on the Berber leader's fate.

"The traitorous Moroccan sultan has sided with the French," Ben Hamadi explained to her. "The sultan has denied Abdel Kader refuge in Morocco any longer and has even threatened to drive our leader out by force. Abdel Kader must decide whether to fight the Moroccan army as well as the French."

Alysson met Jafar's eyes across the low table. "Do you mean to go to his aid?" she asked, her throat hoarse.

"He has not yet called upon his followers," Jafar said carefully.

"But you will go."

"You know I will."

She fell silent. She wanted to argue, to plead with him to reconsider. But she knew nothing she could say or do could persuade him differently. He would never give up his struggle. Not as long as his sultan needed him. Not as long as his country needed him.

Jafar skillfully changed the subject then—perhaps, Alysson thought despairingly, because he still suspected her of trying to discover the Arab army's plans so she could report back to Gervase.

Her thoughts bleak, she was not aware at first that Ben Hamadi had addressed her. "I am certain you are relieved now that your fiancé, Colonel Bourmont, has been released, Miss Vickery."

Released? Gervase had been released? Shocked, Alysson turned to stare at Jafar. "Gervase is *free?*" she asked in a hoarse whisper.

Jafar gave her an enigmatic glance. "Yes. He was exchanged for some two dozen other prisoners of war last week."

"But you didn't tell me."

"I only just received word. My lieutenant, Farhat, returned yesterday with news of the success."

Alysson regarded him in consternation. "Then you will let us go now?" she asked raggedly.

Jafar's mouth tightened. "As I have said before, you will remain here to allow your uncle's wounds time to heal."

"They have healed well enough for him to travel."

"Indeed," Honoré asserted. "I may not be able to sit a horse, but if you would allow me the use of the litter, I could manage adequately."

Alysson started to agree, but Jafar gave her a quelling look. "We will discuss this later, *Ehuresh.*"

It was a direct command to drop the subject, and she knew argument would be fruitless. The company resumed the meal then, but Alysson's heart and mind were in such turmoil that she couldn't eat.

Eventually the conversation turned to the local tragedy, and how best to kill the lion that roamed the hills. Politely, the general described to Alysson the two usual methods of lion-hunting in Barbary.

"One is to dig a deep pit and cover it with brush, and tie a live kid or calf to a nearby tree. The hunters then watch, concealed, till the sacrificial prey attracts the lion. The second, mademoiselle, is for scores of hunters to form a wide circle around the lion's usual poaching ground, then close in. The footmen advance first, rushing into the thickets with their dogs and spears to flush out the beast, while the horsemen keep a little behind, ready to charge."

Honoré spoke up again, his tone one of derision. "I fail to see why you must make all these elaborate preparations. My niece has hunted tigers in India armed only with a rifle."

Ben Hamadi, a self-professed avid sportsman, gave Alysson a look that was both curious and disbelieving. "Is this true?"

Alysson sent her uncle a distracted glance. She had once killed a Bengal tiger single-handedly, under the direction of her Uncle Oliver, but destroying such a magnificent animal was not something she was particularly proud of. "Yes, Excellency, it is true," she answered with reluctance. "Another uncle of mine is a hunter renowned for his marksmanship. He taught me a great deal about hunting game in the wild."

The expression on Ben Hamadi's dark, sharp-featured face turned admiring. "No woman of my country has such courage or skill."

"But then Miss Vickery is not of our country," Jafar interjected coolly.

Alysson might have retorted that the women of his country were given little opportunity to exhibit either courage or skill, but she bit back the remark. "My skill is meager," she said instead, with an Eastern display of humility.

The *khalifa*, however, seemed intrigued by her revelation. He stared at her thoughtfully while he stroked his beard. After a brief glance at his host that might have been called sly, Ben Hamadi addressed Alysson again. "Perhaps you would care to demonstrate this skill, Miss Vickery. No doubt Jafar el-Saleh would be pleased to be rid of this scourge that is menacing the population. If you could kill the beast, perhaps the *saiyid* would be grateful enough to offer you your freedom."

She couldn't believe Jafar would consider such a proposition. Would he really agree to see her free if she could rid his land of a man-eating lion? She turned to him, her gray eyes questioning. His jaw was set, his expression guarded and watchful, like one of his hawks. She was not surprised when his refusal came.

"I could not allow Miss Vickery to put herself in such danger, Excellency," Jafar replied firmly, holding Alysson's gaze.

"I agree," her Uncle Honoré said more slowly. "Perhaps it would be too dangerous for you, my dear."

Dangerous perhaps, Alysson thought, yet she couldn't allow that to dissuade her. If she could possibly gain their freedom by meeting the challenge the *khalifa* had laid out, she owed it to her uncle to try. If only Jafar would allow her the opportunity.

"Even so, I would like the chance to try and kill the lion," she declared, endeavoring to keep her voice steady.

She saw a muscle in Jafar's jaw flex, before he disciplined his expression into unreadability. "The beast has already killed one woman. The risk would be too great."

Oddly, it was the Khalifa Ben Hamadi who took her side. "But you have heard from her own lips, *sidi,*" the general pressed, "that she is skilled at the hunt. Would you deny her the opportunity to win her freedom?"

Yes! Jafar wanted desperately to answer, even as he admired the *khalifa*'s masterful attempt at forcing his hand. Ben Hamadi did not approve of his holding Alysson and her uncle prisoner, Jafar knew. The general had not said so directly, yet in a veiled accusation just this morning, he'd expressed surprise at Jafar's unusual reticence to resolve the problem of the Englishwoman, especially since there was no longer a need to keep her captive.

Of course Ben Hamadi would not insult him by condemning his action outright, but with the wisdom and cunning that had made the *khalifa* one of Abdel Kader's most trusted lieutenants, Ben Hamadi had now publicly proposed the conditions for Alysson's release—a proposal that would be difficult for him to refuse, Jafar reflected. He had sworn his allegiance to Abdel Kader and thus to his *khalifa*. Besides, what reasonable grounds did he have for continuing to hold Alysson hostage, other than his own selfish desires?

Jafar felt his hand clench involuntarily in a fist. For weeks now, he'd refused to face the tormenting possibility of losing her. But now it was no longer a mere possibility.

With a sickening sense of powerlessness, he recalled an old Berber adage. A wild bird could be caught and placed in a cage, but it would only fly away at the first opportunity, never to return. He could keep Alysson captive for a while longer, perhaps indefinitely. But in the end, the decision whether to stay or to leave belonged to her. The choice had to be hers.

After all he had done to her, he owed her that much. If Alysson were to remain here with him, she had to do so because she truly wished it, not because he forced her.

And it seemed that she did not wish it.

"I would welcome the chance to earn our freedom," she said again quietly.

Deliberately, slowly, Jafar forced himself to uncurl his fist. "Very well," he said at length, his voice low and toneless. "It will be your decision."

Honoré looked at her first with concern, then dawning elation as he realized their chance for freedom was at hand. But Alysson could not share her uncle's delight. She felt as if a giant hand were crushing her heart.

Jafar returned her gaze, his features cold and withdrawn. It was as if they were the only two people in the room, a room that had turned wintry and bleak. Wanting to shiver,

Alysson stared helplessly into his cool amber eyes. Their aloofness was cruel, their indifference chilling.

The Khalifa Ben Hamadi broke the silence between them. "Good," he observed with satisfaction. "Then it is settled. If Miss Vickery can kill the lion, she and her uncle may go free."

They set off within hours to hunt the *ezim,* while it was still daylight. There was no reason to wait. The lion was a nocturnal animal that normally preyed at night, so the principal time for hunting the beast was at night.

By now, Alysson expected, the creature they sought would have retreated to higher ground. But they could use the remaining daylight to locate the vicinity of its mountain lair, and when the full moon rose later, there would be ample light by which to hunt. Then she would take the field alone, with a single attendant to carry ammunition and an extra gun.

She did not underestimate the danger. The lion was man's most fearsome adversary, with a roar like thunder that could petrify its victims with fear. If it perceived itself in danger, it would turn and attack against even fatal odds. According to her Uncle Oliver, a lion rarely preyed on humans unless it was exceedingly hungry, or was provoked, or was weakened by age or illness and was too feeble to hunt stronger game. But this beast had already killed one woman. Alysson was glad for Jafar's company. She would have made the expedition by herself, but Jafar would not hear of her going alone.

She glanced over at him as he rode beside her on his fiery bay stallion. His face was closed and shuttered, his eyes devoid of all emotion but a steely determination. She shivered, whether from the December cold or from Jafar's chilling distance, she wasn't certain.

Behind her, Saful maintained a respectful length with his own mount. To her surprise, Saful had volunteered for the job of accompanying her on the hunt. Perhaps, Alysson suspected, because the young warrior felt it necessary to make up for his lapse in letting her escape several weeks ago. No doubt he was still smarting from shame because he, a man, had been bested by a mere female.

Beside Alysson, Jafar was thinking similar thoughts as he silently wrestled with his own conscience. It went against every masculine principal, every chivalrous nerve in his body, to allow a woman to risk her life. Especially this woman. The thought of Alysson facing such danger made his blood run cold.

Jafar's gaze found the defiant young beauty who was the cause of his torment. What would she say if he professed his love for her, if he begged her to stay? If he asked her to give up her family, her entire way of life? To risk her future with only the promise of uncertainty and war in exchange? What would she say if he asked her to watch him marry another woman first? To have another woman's sons take precedent before her own? That was all he could offer her.

Unless he stepped down. Unless he left his tribe, *his* entire way of life. Unless he gave up everything he had strived for. Only then could he claim her as he wanted to do, as she deserved.

Jafar closed his eyes against the anguish and helplessness inside him. Was he actually thinking such treasonous thoughts?

He gave a silent, bitter laugh, filled with self-mockery. The *khalifa* had seen the danger Alysson presented, a danger that he himself had refused to admit, Jafar realized. She was his weakness, his vulnerability. She alone had the power to make him betray his duty, his people. She could make him forsake everything he had struggled for. All it would take was one word from her and he would actually consider stepping down. He would contemplate sacrificing honor and duty. If Alysson were to show the slightest inclination to stay, he might very well throw away his past, his future, his allegiance to his country.

Except for her physical response to his lovemaking, though, she'd given no indication that she wanted anything more from him. Her physical response at least he was certain of. He'd shown her the kind of blinding passion that poets exalted but that few mortals ever attained. For a brief time he might even have made her forget her love for Bourmont. But when she returned to her own civilization, that love would rekindle. She would find happiness in his ene-my's arms, among her own people.

And he couldn't deny her that chance.

That bleak reflection occupied Jafar's mind to the exclu-sion of nearly all else as the day waned.

None of them spoke as they made their way through a darkening forest of giant cedars. The quiet intensified, bro-ken only by the soft rhythmic thud of the horses' hooves.

Beside him, Alysson began to feel closed in, surrounded as she was by the thick, sharp scent of cedar and the sen-tinel tree trunks, down here so low where the fading sun-light couldn't reach. She was relieved when they finally left the forest. It seemed warmer out in the open, even though the sharp wind penetrated the wool of her burnous and the final rays of the sun were thin and weak.

The terrain immediately became more rugged and for-bidding, and the Barb horses, which had been bred on such rough ground, had to step carefully as they wound in and out of the rocky hills.

Twilight was falling when they reached the area where the woman had been killed. The air was strangely silent—perhaps, Alysson reflected nervously, because the panic-stricken inhabitants of the mountains were hiding in their homes. Her feeling of disquiet intensified, and she wished she could call even the weak sunlight back.

When Saful's mount snorted, Alysson gave a start, and then felt foolish for letting her courage desert her. Self-consciously she glanced at her two companions, who wore their rifles slung on their backs.

"The lair will likely be up there," Jafar said tersely, pointing at the jagged peaks to the northeast.

They began climbing toward the masses of rock above, negotiating scanty ledges and naked slopes. Shortly they reached a narrow ravine where they were again required to ride single file.

"Keep behind me," Jafar commanded Alysson as he took the lead.

Thick shadows reached out to envelop them as they picked their way along the almost nonexistent track. It was only minutes later that Alysson suddenly felt her mount tense beneath her. As the mare sidled, nervously, Alysson uneas-

ily searched the gloom around them. The ridge just above
their heads was surrounded by the skeletal shapes of thorn
thickets, an ideal setting for an ambush.

Foolish or not, she reached for her rifle. Drawing it from
its scabbard, she checked the cartridge, then rested the
weapon in the crook of her arm, feeling reassured by its
weight. She closed her finger around the trigger at precisely
the same instant she heard a low rumbling sound—half purr,
half snarl.

Her heartbeat arrested, Alysson jerked her gaze upward
to find a pair of savage golden eyes glaring down at them
in the dim light.

Part of her dazed mind registered the lioness preparing
to spring, another part the terrified horses that suddenly
went wild with fright. Jafar's stallion reared while her own
mount swerved hard to the left, nearly crushing her leg
against the rocks. Alysson had the flashing impression of a
tawny body and long tail, of razor-sharp teeth and claws
bared for attack, of a great golden weight gathering for the
vault.

Then, with a blood-freezing primordial scream, the beast
exploded into the air, leaping directly at Jafar.

Chapter 24

A lysson had no time to think, no time to take aim, no
time to shake off the paralyzing fear that gripped her
at the lion's unearthly growl. She had only the instinct of
desperation. Raising the muzzle of her rifle, she fired.

The sharp crack of the rifle echoed loudly amid the snarls
and shouts and screams of the horses. At the same moment,
the lion's sleek golden body jerked and twisted in the air,
then fell with a heavy thud to the ground.

Breathing in hard gasps, her heart pounding violently as

she tried to control her terrified mare, Alysson stared down at the result of her marksmanship. The deadly assault was over as suddenly as it had begun. She had hit her target. She had shot the lion in midair.

She raised her gaze to Jafar and caught the glitter of curved steel in his hand. He had managed to draw his dagger to defend himself from the murderous beast, but even armed thus, in the close confines of the ravine he would have stood little chance against the vicious attack. Very likely he had escaped serious injury . . . or even death.

Jafar seemed to know it, for his intent gaze found Alysson's the moment he had brought his plunging stallion under control. The expression in his eyes was impossible to read in the gathering darkness.

"It seems I owe you a debt of gratitude, *Ehuresh,*" Jafar said in a low tone that held a harsh note of regret.

Alysson couldn't find the voice to answer. With surprise she realized she was trembling; the image of Jafar being mauled and savaged would not go away. Weakly, she slid down from her horse, needing the feel of solid ground beneath her.

Saful, who had leaped from his mount, was cautiously approaching the corpse of the lion, in case it had only been wounded. Touching it with his rifle muzzle, gingerly at first, then with more force, he rolled the head to the side. There was no question. The sovereign of the forests was dead. The bullet had taken the beast directly between the eyes.

It was an impossible shot, Alysson realized. If she had tried a hundred times under ordinary circumstances, she could never have been so accurate.

She flinched as another gun report split the silence. In the manner of his people, Saful had raised his rifle triumphantly in the air and fired it over the body of the prostrate foe. Alysson sank to one knee. She couldn't seem to stop shaking.

She was grateful for the strong arms that drew her up and surrounded her. With a sound that was nearly a sob, Alysson buried her face in Jafar's shoulder, trying to draw comfort from his nearness.

He stroked the curve of her spine soothingly and murmured tender, unintelligible words of solace in Berber.

Words that had nothing to do with the tormenting emotions assaulting him.

In one dim corner of his heart he felt a fierce mingling of pride and gratitude . . . Pride in Alysson's skill at defeating a savage foe. Gratitude for her quick action in saving him. But the bleak sense of loss raking at him overwhelmed any sweeter feelings.

There were no options open to him now. He had given his word. Her freedom for killing the lion. He had to let her go.

An ache rose up in him that was so intense, so raw and anguished, that he had to squeeze his eyes closed against it. He wished he could take the words back. He wished . . .

But what good would wishing do? It would not change Alysson's mind about leaving.

Yet how bitter an irony it was to know that her action tonight would have consequences he hadn't foreseen. He knew the Berber mind. When his people learned of what Alysson had done, what courage she'd shown, they would welcome her into their hearts. She would no longer be a hated European. They would be willing to accept her, perhaps not as his first wife, but they would receive her into their tribe, their lives, with gladness.

He gave a silent, hopeless laugh. She would not be here to see the transformation.

It was a long moment before Jafar realized his equerry was standing to one side waiting patiently, respectfully, for his attention. Repressing a bitter sigh, Jafar released Alysson from his embrace, then took a step back and nodded.

Saful stepped forward, holding a bloody, furry object in his outstretched hands which he presented to Alysson.

"This belongs to you, *lallah*," Saful said in a tone that bordered on awe. He had cut the thick padded paws from the corpse of the mountain cat and was offering the right fore to her.

Numbly, Alysson stared at the grisly relic.

"You earned the right to have it, Alysson," Jafar explained softly in English. "Our women hang the paw of a lion or other ferocious beasts of prey around their children's necks as an amulet to inspire force and courage. Young brides present such gifts to their husbands."

Husband. Alysson closed her eyes tightly, Jafar's words ringing hollowly in her ears. She would never have the right to give such a gift to him. She had fulfilled the terms of the bargain. She had killed the lion and was now free to go.

Why, dear God, *why* had she insisted on the opportunity to earn her freedom? How she regretted it now. How she wished now that she had never fired that shot!

Yet she'd really had no choice. She could never have allowed harm to come to Jafar, not while there was a single breath left in her body. Yet the horrible irony was not lost on her. In saving Jafar's life, she had forfeited any final, remote chance for a future with him.

She lifted her anguished gaze to him. It would take only a single word from him and she would have remained here, under any terms he cared to name. But he had said nothing.

Was it because he was convinced, as she was, of the futility of their future together? Or that her continued presence here would prove a further detriment to him?

Did he feel nothing for her at all? Did he *want* her to leave?

"Are you able to ride? We should return."

At Jafar's quiet, dispassionate question Alysson felt the crushing weight of despair settle over her. She wanted nothing more than to curl up in some dark corner and find relief for her aching heart in the oblivion of sleep, but she nodded wearily and accepted Jafar's help in mounting—and tried to keep her agonizing thoughts at bay during the long ride back.

The moon rose shortly, blanketing the rugged mountains in a cold light, allowing them to see their way. A few hours later, they returned home in triumph, bearing the blanketed corpse of the lion. They were greeted by gleeful shouts and bursts of gunfire, by exclamations of universal joy that the tyrant was dead, that young men and maidens need not tremble as they went forth at night.

Neither Alysson nor Jafar shared in that joy. Neither could banish the terrible feeling of despair that assailed them at the thought of the bleak future.

It had never happened before in the memory of Jafar's tribe. A woman had killed a lion!

How brave the infidel woman was! How courageous! How remarkable! She had killed the *ezim* and saved the life of the lord!

The entire next day was spent in celebration and feasting, to honor Alysson's skill and daring, to sing her praises. The woman being honored, however, missed much of the celebration, for she was making preparations to leave with her uncle and her Indian servant on the morrow. The *khalifa* himself was to escort them part of the way to Algiers.

In actuality, there were few preparations to make. Alysson had only her clothing to pack, and most of that was accomplished by an ecstatic Chand. She spent the time, however, seeking out the people who had served her and cared for her during her captivity, those who had come to mean a great deal to her in the past two months . . . Tahar, the gentle young woman who had shared advice and kindness. Saful, her faithful guard. Gastar, the old healing woman who had saved her life. Mahmoud, the crippled, proud young boy whose emotional scars ran deeper than the scars on his poor face.

Of them all, Mahmoud had become most dear to her. Despite his hatred for the European race, Mahmoud had accepted her and made her captivity easier to endure, albeit grudgingly at first. He had been her link to both to the world and to the strange culture into which she'd been thrown. He'd answered her curious questions about his people and volunteered stories on his own. More importantly, he'd fulfilled her longing to hear about his master. He had even tried to protect her from the spells of a Berber sorceress. How could she not feel tenderness toward a child who had come to her defense in the face of threats from a witch?

Or was her fondness for Mahmoud because she saw something of Jafar in him, something of the bitter, angry boy that Jafar once must have been?

Standing before Mahmoud, Alysson could hardly get the words to say good-bye past the ache in her throat. "I would like to thank you for your excellent care of me these past weeks," she told him in an unsteady voice.

Mahmoud wouldn't meet her gaze. "It was nothing. It was my duty to serve you as my lord commanded."

Despite his sullen, muted response, Alysson believed

Mahmoud might miss her almost as much as she would miss him. She held out the lion's paw that Saful had retrieved for her. "Perhaps you would accept this as a token of my appreciation."

The boy stared at the gift with distrust, before his scarred face suddenly came alight with an expression of awe. "Oh, *lallah* . . ."

Almost fearfully, he accepted the amulet and stood regarding it with reverence. Then clutching it to his skinny chest, he gazed up at her. "You do me great honor."

Alysson smiled through a haze of tears. She wanted to take Mahmoud in her arms and hold him, but any young man who considered himself a warrior, as Mahmoud did, would likely be offended and embarrassed by such womanly displays of affection. She settled for giving his shoulder a gentle squeeze.

Afterward, she returned to her room. She tried to sleep for a few hours, but the sounds of revelry coming from the village and the savage pain in her breast kept her awake.

Beneath the mound of quilts of her sleeping mat, Alysson lay curled in a tight ball. God, how could she bear to leave Jafar? How could she endure the agony that was making her heart bleed? She felt as if it were slowly being ripped in two. And it seemed as if there was nothing in this world she could do to mend the torn pieces.

She went to him that night. She couldn't stay away.

The hour was late—well past midnight—and the household was long asleep as Alysson made her way through the darkness toward the lord's quarters. The guards let her pass. She entered Jafar's rooms quietly, through his library. The door to his sleeping chamber was open, and she could see a faint light issuing from within.

The glow was cast from a single, low-burning hanging lamp, Alysson saw as she paused at the threshold. Jafar's bed was a Berber bed, not Arab, with a wooden frame supporting layers of rugs and cushions. It stood in one corner beside a large carved chest of sandalwood inlaid with ivory. A brazier glowed in another corner, warming the room.

Jafar was not asleep. Rather, he was standing near the

high grilled window, staring down at the floor, at nothing. When Alysson took a step toward him, his head turned swiftly, like that of a wild animal sensing danger, his hand automatically stealing to the dagger at his waist.

Alysson caught her breath in a soft gasp at his action. The low sound Jafar made was sharper, harsher, when a moment later she let her burnous fall from her shoulders. She was clad in silk so sheer that the curves and shadows of her body were clearly visible beneath it.

A still, breathless quietude filled the room as they stared at each other.

For a brief instant Alysson thought she'd imagined a look on Jafar's hard features that was almost vulnerable, a vulnerability that sat oddly on that arrogant face. But she was not imagining his fatigue. Seeing Jafar like this, his face drawn and haggard, his eyes weary, Alysson wondered if he might actually be feeling an inkling of the throbbing pain that was savaging her.

There was no indication of it when his voice came softly stealing through the silence. "You shouldn't be here, *Ehuresh*."

"I came . . . to say good-bye . . ." Alysson faltered, hearing the hope and hollowness in her own voice.

He moved toward her then, coming to stand before her. Capturing her face carefully between his palms, he gazed down at her, searching the shadows that made her eyes pools of mystery.

"What is it you want of me?" he asked hoarsely. No longer indifferent, his tone held a note that suggested emotion was crushing each syllable.

Alysson's heart began to pound painfully. What did she want of him? She wanted to love him. She wanted the touch of his mouth so much that she was willing to take the hurt with it. She wanted memories of him to sustain her through the bleak years ahead. She wanted to believe, just for tonight, that things could be right between them.

"I want to remember you . . ." she whispered as she raised her lips for his kiss.

With a harsh groan, Jafar accommodated her. Dragging her into his arms, he brought his mouth crashing down on hers.

It was a kiss of desperation, Alysson realized dimly. She could feel it in the way his mouth ground against hers, in the fierce penetration of his hot tongue, in the thwarted thrust of his hard body—and she could see it in his blazing, searching eyes when abruptly he pulled away.

Those eyes were wild, fierce, naked in intent, as he tore at her diaphanous robes and his own djellaba. They remained wild as he scooped her up and carried her to the bed, then followed her down. Without pause, his hands tangled in her hair as he attacked with his mouth, as he covered her with his body.

There was no gentleness in him. She wanted none. It was a naked moment of truth between them, a moment when need reigned supreme. His need to stamp her with his ownership. Her need to be taken.

His demanding fierceness sparked an answering wildness in Alysson. Blindly her hands sought his thick hair, while her body reacted with animal passion, straining, arching against his powerful loins.

And then she was being filled by him, with his desperation. Her head thrashed from side to side at the heated carnality, at the intensity of desire so searing she thought she might perish from it. When the desperation became too much, she clawed at his back, sobbing his name, pleading for him to end her torment. In response, Jafar caught her hips and pushed deeper, driving harder, until the frantic woman beneath him was shuddering under his deep thrusts. Her sharp cry of passion shattered his ragged control. Jafar went taut and reared back, letting her name burst from his throat in his own hoarse cry.

Afterward they lay gasping, entwined, the fury of heartbeats settling into a less violent rhythm. Eventually, Jafar drew slowly away, as if separating himself from her was like tearing his limbs from his body.

Feeling similarly, Alysson turned weakly on her side so she could watch him. Jafar lay sprawled on his back among the lush cushions, one arm thrown over his forehead, his eyes closed.

Her fearless Berber lover, she thought with mingled anguish and yearning. Slowly, shamelessly, Alysson let her eyes roam over him, drinking in the beauty of his body, his

sleek muscled length dusted with golden hair, gleaming
darkly in the lamplight. He was much like the lion she had
hunted in the mountain, though not as savage. A wild and
tawny beast, only half-tamed.

Purposely her gaze rose to Jafar's shadowed, sensual face.
She wanted the memory of his face engraved in her mind.

She didn't regret coming here to him, Alysson thought
silently. She had made love to him because she wanted to,
because she needed to, because there were too many years
stretching out ahead of her like a barren desert.

Just then Jafar stirred. As if he'd sensed her watching,
his hand flexed into a fist, though his eyes remained shut.
"So, *Ehuresh,* now you may remember me as I am . . . a
cold, heartless brute . . . a savage heathen."

The bitterness in the soft laughter that accompanied his
remark raked at Alysson's heart. "No," she whispered.

Abruptly his arm lowered and he turned his head to look
directly at her. His eyes contained the fierce rebellion of a
caged hawk, she saw, but it was a rebellion that ineffectually
hid other, more powerful emotions. Alysson was startled by
the torment she saw in his eyes. There was no mistaking it.

This was Jafar as he truly was, Alysson knew. A man
torn by conflicts. She could feel the despair in him, the
vulnerability, the bitterness.

"No," Alysson said fiercely, defiantly. "You aren't cold
and heartless . . . you aren't a savage. You are just a man
. . . fighting for what you believe in, against overwhelming
odds."

His lips twisted in the semblance of a smile. *Ah, Ehuresh,* he reflected bleakly. *Even in this you defy me.* Yet an
unwanted ache tightened in Jafar's chest at her passionate
defense of him. She did feel something for him after all, he
was certain. Perhaps a part of her even found this leavetak-
ing a torment as he did—the physical part that he'd taught
to feel passion. But what he wanted from Alysson went far
deeper than mere possession of her body. He wanted her
heart. And that he could never have.

Slowly he reached up to draw a gentle finger along the
delicate line of her jaw. *Stay with me,* he thought silently,
hopelessly.

Ask me to stay, Alysson pleaded just as silently, gazing miserably into his eyes.

Will you marry him when you return?

Why are you letting me go?

Jafar saw her eyes fill with questions, questions he knew she was too proud to ask, but at the remembrance of his blood enemy, he had to look away. He was sending Alysson back to her fiancé, back to the arms of the man he should have killed. The despair that had smoldered in his heart during the long weeks just past clawed at him now with savage force.

Despair. It was not an unfamiliar emotion to him, but he hadn't expected this kind of deep wound, this kind of raw agony. He'd never imagined, either, just how completely his defiant young captive would fill his life, his heart. Yet she had. And now he would be alone and empty again when she left. The agony washed over him again as he wondered how would face the years of stark emptiness ahead.

How could he find the strength to let her go?

And yet how could he not? In the long run, she would be far happier with her own kind. He had to remember that. Once she returned to her own people, she would forget him. In time her ordeal as his captive would fade to nothing more than a bad dream.

Against his will, Jafar's bleak gaze found Alysson's. There had been so much anger between them, so much pain and passion, so many things said and unsaid. But there was no changing the past. It was much too late.

And the dawn was coming too soon.

Wordlessly Jafar reached for her again, drawing Alysson into his embrace. All he could do now was see to it that she never forgot him.

"You will remember me," he promised harshly against her lips. "You'll carry with you the feel of my hands . . . my body on yours . . . the taste of my mouth . . ."

And then there were no more words as Jafar set out to fulfill his vow. Neither he nor Alysson voiced the tormented thoughts that were uppermost in their hearts. But during their fierce lovemaking, they said silently with their bodies what they would not say aloud.

Chapter 25

Alysson was well-protected on the lengthy journey back to Algiers. The khalif himself provided her escort, along with Jafar's chief lieutenant, the red-bearded Farhat il Taib. Jafar would trust no one else with her safety.

The rain fell in torrents as the armed party negotiated the treacherous mountain passes, but Alysson hardly noticed the bone-deep chill. She felt numb all over, except for the awful hollowness where her heart should have been.

The journey took three days, the slow pace in deference to the rain and her Uncle Honoré. Honoré's ribs had not mended well enough for him to ride so he was carried by litter.

The miserable rain had stopped by the time Ben Hamadi left them near the outskirts of Algiers. The bright, cloudless sky once again glowed with a golden clarity particular to the Mediterranean, while the deep verdure of the hills surrounding the city provided a jeweled setting for the dazzling white seaport overlooking the harbor.

In contrast, the steeply sloping streets were dark and narrow. Alysson found it hard to repress a shudder once she had passed through the walled gates and descended into the town. Algiers with its history of treachery and despotism and cruel bondage now seemed oppressed and shut up—far, far different than when she'd first laid eager eyes on it.

It was with great weariness that she drew her mount to a halt before the Moorish house she and her uncle had hired for the season. Numbly, she sat waiting for Chand to help her down. Had it only been a few short months ago that she had set out from here for the desert, in search of passion and adventure? She had found both, much to her sorrow.

So wrapped up in her misery was Alysson that she only vaguely heard a familiar voice shouting at her in English.

"Alysson! Where in the name of God have you been?"

Startled, she raised her gaze to the tall man in European dress who had rushed out of the house. "Uncle Oliver!" she breathed.

The next instant she found herself being dragged from her horse and crushed in a bear hug. Laughing and crying both, Alysson returned her Uncle Oliver's smothering embrace with all the strength she could muster.

A moment later, he abruptly held her away, his penetrating blue eyes searching her face. "Are you well, girl?" he demanded. Not giving her time to answer, he turned to Honoré with a scowl. "What do you mean, allowing her to be abducted by an Arab devil?"

There had never been any love lost between her British and French uncles, Alysson knew, but never had their subtle enmity been less welcome. Wiping the tears from her eyes, she came to Honoré's defense. "It wasn't his fault, Uncle Oliver! He tried to talk me out of going, but I wouldn't listen—just the way you never listen when your mind is set on an expedition."

"It never would have happened if I had been with you, by God."

Honoré, his face flushed, meekly accepted this scolding as he tried to climb out of his litter. Seeing him wince with pain and clutch his ribs, Alysson moved quickly to his side, at the same time throwing a furious glance over her shoulder at Oliver.

"I'm entirely aware of your vaunted skills, Uncle, but the outcome would have been no different had you been there, except that you would likely have gotten yourself killed! As it was, Uncle Honoré did everything in his power to save me—in fact, he was wounded trying to rescue me. The least you could do is help him, instead of ringing a peal over his head."

Oliver's fierce expression relaxed the slightest degree, though he made no apology as he went to Honoré's assistance. "Well, come inside then, you deuced old winemaker. Cedric will want to examine you."

"Uncle Cedric is here, too?" Alysson asked in amazement, her temper cooling.

"Yes, yes, come inside and you can tell us everything."

In short order, Alysson and Honoré were swept into the house, to be greeted by her third uncle, the physician from London. Cedric's embrace was a bit less violent and more reserved than his brother's, but just as loving. Alysson was surprised and humbled that he'd been so worried for her that he traveled all this distance for her sake. Until now nothing could drag him away from his precious hospital.

The new arrivals were given time to wash and refresh themselves before being subjected to an interrogation. An hour later found them all gathered in the long reception chamber—Uncle Honoré lying on a divan, the other two uncles sprawled on cushions. Too agitated to sit down, Alysson remained standing.

As was his commanding nature, Oliver at once took charge of the conversation, asking all the questions. Alysson's answers were evasive, however, providing only the sketchiest details of her captivity and her subsequent visit to her captor's mountain home. Of Jafar, she divulged absolutely nothing.

It was that hole in her story that Oliver attacked first.

"You mean to tell me you learned nothing about this man who abducted you? His name, his appearance?"

"I'm afraid not, Uncle."

"Then tell me where you were taken. I shall go after the devil at once and put a bullet through his black heart."

Alysson went pale. "I don't know where I was taken. Somewhere in the desert, I think."

By now Oliver was staring at her with incredulity. "That won't wash, girl. I myself taught you how to judge distances and recognize landmarks. You must have some idea where you were held . . . how far from here, what direction."

"I'm sorry, Uncle, but I don't."

Apparently deciding to try a more profitable tack, he turned a look of frustration on her French uncle. "Honoré?"

In response, the elderly Frenchman gave Alysson a long searching look, before his shoulders rose in a Gallic shrug. "I know nothing of the man's identity."

Oliver vented an explosive oath. "That is all you mean to say? What is this, a conspiracy to hide the truth? Why, for God's sake?" He turned his scowl on his niece. "I think I deserve an explanation after all the trouble you've put me to, my girl. I postponed an expedition to the Caribbean in order to come here and search for you."

"Well, forgive me for interfering with your pleasure!" Alysson snapped back.

"Alysson, my dear," Cedric put in more calmly, "we have been distraught with fear for you. Of course you will understand if Oliver is impatient to discover just what occurred. He only wants to protect you."

She was immediately contrite, and yet she knew very well her Uncle Oliver's threat to shoot Jafar was deadly serious. She had to do something to persuade Oliver to give up his thoughts of revenge. There had been too much bloodshed and vengeance as it was.

"Uncle Oliver, I know you're concerned for me, and I am grateful, I assure you. But there is no need to drag this out any further. What happened, happened. It's over. He didn't harm me. He even showed us every kindness—"

"Not harm you? By God, girl, how can you stand there and defend that savage Arab?"

"He is not an Arab!" Alysson said through clenched teeth. "Nor is he a savage. He's far more civilized than most Europeans I know, including you, Uncle. In fact, he's a nobleman and the grandson of a duke, besides!"

At her impassioned declaration, Oliver's blue eyes narrowed. Alysson, realizing her mistake, abruptly bit her tongue. She had said far more than she had intended about Jafar—and far too much, if the calculating look on her Uncle Oliver's face was anything to judge by.

He stared at her for a long moment before speaking again. "I don't suppose we would be talking about Nicholas Sterling, would we?"

The look on Alysson's face was proof enough, despite her swift denial. "I'm sure I don't know what you mean."

"I think you do," Oliver said slowly, anger and disappointment vying for expression on his face. "What I don't understand is why you feel you have to lie to me." He shook his head sadly. "You've never lied to me before, girl."

Alysson stared at him mutely, her throat aching with regret.

Oliver shook his head again sorrowfully. "I've been on intimate terms with the Duke of Moreland for years, my girl, and I know enough about his grandson to add two and two. The boy's half English, and he threw away his heritage to come and live here. Moreland told me so himself. You know Moreland . . . we paid him a call that time I first brought you back to England to live."

Oh, yes, Alysson thought. She remembered that day vividly, the day she had first met Nicholas . . . Jafar.

Her uncle evidently did not expect her to reply just then, for he continued to muse aloud. "This Sterling fellow . . . if he's Moreland's grandson . . ." Oliver's look had been pensive, but that look slowly faded as a flush of anger slowly rose in his cheeks. "Then he's fully aware of the nature of the injury he's done you." His narrowed-eyed gaze lifted to spear his niece. "Any Englishman with the slightest pretense to honor who had compromised a young lady would offer her the protection of his name." His tone was stern, his scowl accusing.

"He isn't an Englishman," Alysson replied, her voice barely audible. "And if he had wanted to marry me, he would have asked me."

Oliver surged to his feet. "What he wants is nothing to the point! By God, he'll marry you if I have to drag him to the altar!"

"No!" Alysson's cry was like the sound of a wounded animal, her gray eyes haunted.

Her uncle stared at her in bewilderment. "What is going on here, Alysson? Why do you insist on protecting the man? He's terrorized you . . . wounded Honoré here . . . ruined your good name . . . I cannot understand why you don't want him brought him to justice."

"Because," she faltered, choking on her tears, "the French army will try to find him, and if they find him, they'll *kill* him, that's why!"

Oliver stared at his distressed niece in shock. The tears

running down her face were genuine; Alysson had never been the kind of female to use tears to get her way.

"Please, Uncle . . . promise me you won't say anything . . . *please*. I'm begging you. Let it go."

Moving to stand in front of her, Oliver took her hands in his large, lean ones, holding them tightly. "Very well, girl," he said finally, helplessly. "If it means that much to you, I won't pursue it."

"Yes, it means that much to me."

Her meeting with Gervase de Bourmont was far more difficult, and far more painful.

Alysson sent her Indian servant with a message for Gervase, informing him of her safe return and asking him to call on her at his earliest convenience. Then she dressed for the upcoming interview in her best day gown. After so many weeks of wearing the simple clothing of the East, she felt uncomfortable in the frilled petticoats, chemise, drawers, and constrictive corset that was de rigueur for a well-bred Englishwoman, but she owed it to Gervase to make her best effort.

When he arrived a scant hour later, she was waiting for him in the courtyard. At his approach, she rose from the bench where she'd been seated—but then hesitated, just as Gervase did.

They stood staring at each other for a long moment, in complete silence.

"Alysson . . ." Gervase said finally in a low voice was that was husky, weary.

He looked older, she thought. And tired. There were harsh lines of worry at the corners of his mouth and between his eyes that had not been there before. More than that, he looked . . . sad.

She discarded all the polite responses she might have made and simply spoke from her heart. "I'm so sorry, Gervase."

He shook his head abruptly. "You have no cause to be sorry. You were not to blame for that bloody—" He paused and chose another word. ". . . that man's act of revenge."

"Yet I share some of the blame. You warned me of the danger, you tried to prevent me from going."

"I never suspected that madman would target you. You must believe me."

Alysson refrained from replying that Jafar was not a madman. "I do believe you," she said quietly instead.

As if he couldn't bear to meet her gaze, Gervase looked away. "I am the one who should be asking for your forgiveness."

"No. What happened was not your fault, either."

There was a long pause while the muscles in Gervase's jaw worked in anger. "How much did he tell you?" he finally asked.

She did not intend to disclose the details of her abduction, nor make the same mistake as she had with her uncle by alluding to Jafar's past. "Simply that he had reasons for making me his prisoner, reasons for his vengeance. He told me about the death of his parents at your father's hands."

The momentary grimace that flashed across the Frenchman's face was bitter. "Ah, yes, the great General Bourmont," he murmured. "The conqueror of Algiers. I've spent my entire military career trying to live up to my father's reputation . . . all the while knowing he was little better than a murderer. It is not something for which I'm proud."

"I know." And she did. She had known Gervase for many years. He was a kind man, a caring man. Nothing at all like his father the general. "You are not responsible for your father's sins, Gervase, any more than you are to blame for what happened to me. Besides, you did your best to rescue me. I haven't yet thanked you for that."

"Thank me for failing you? I would prefer that you didn't." The bitterness in his tone was harsher now.

"You did not fail me."

"I agreed to abandon you to him. What do you call that, if not failure?"

"I call it courage for making a difficult choice. I call it concern for the lives of your men. I call it plain, old-fashioned, much-welcomed common sense."

"Ah, Alysson . . ." He moved toward her then, eliminating the distance between them. Drawing her close, he folded her into his arms. She let her cheek rest against the comforting wall of his chest and gave a sigh as she felt him stroke her hair.

"I want you to know," Gervase said in an unsteady voice, "none of this changes what I feel for you. I still love you. I still want more than anything to marry you."

Alysson shut her eyes. He might *look* older than when she'd last seen him, but she *felt* older. So much older. And perhaps she was. She was no longer a mere girl, no longer an innocent in matters of the heart. She knew now the anguish of loving and being unloved in return.

Her newfound knowledge made her view Gervase's dilemma with compassion. And it made her all the more reluctant to say what had to be said.

"I can't marry you, Gervase," she declared softly. "It would not be fair to you. I shared his bed."

There was a long pause. "I suspected as much. *Mon Dieu.* Alysson, I would have given anything if I could have spared you that. It must have been a nightmare, being forced to endure his—" Gervase broke off, incapable or unwilling to complete the thought.

Unable to bear the anguish in his tone, Alysson drew back and raised her fingers to touch his cheek comfortingly, holding his gaze with her troubled one. "He didn't force me, Gervase. I . . . went to him willingly."

There was another long pause while Gervase regarded her in haunted silence.

"So you see . . . I can't marry you."

"You must, Alysson," he said finally, quietly. "You will likely be shunned by society, otherwise."

In response, she stepped back and shook her head. "I am well accustomed to being the subject of gossip and censure. What society says or does has never carried much weight with me. The only people whose good opinion I care about are the ones I love. And those people—my uncles—mean to stand by me."

"As I will. I trust you know that. You will always have my good opinion . . . my love."

Alysson felt her throat tighten with unshed tears. She had not expected Gervase to be so generous, that his love for her ran so very deep. He was still willing to marry her, even after her damning confession that she had acted the wanton with the stranger who had carried her off. Gervase was offering to give her the protection of his name. He was prepared to face the dishonor and disgrace that would surely follow once the scandal of her abduction became known. Despite his apparent willingness, though, she could never allow him to make such a sacrifice.

She reached for his hands and held them in her own smaller ones. "I would be grateful to keep your friendship, Gervase. And I am honored, believe me, that you still want me for your wife. But I cannot accept your proposal."

His face assumed a wounded look. "You *do* hold me to blame, is that it? I can only try to make it up to you—"

"No, of course I don't blame you! Not at all. I told you that."

"I can be a good husband to you, *coquine.*"

"I have no doubts on that score. But I very much fear I could not be a good wife to you . . . not the kind of wife you deserve."

"Zut!" He pulled away from her, breaking the contact between them. In agitation he ran his hand through his dark hair. "I won't accept your refusal! I intend to change your mind. All I need is time to persuade you."

"I won't change my mind, Gervase."

"How can you be certain? You once were willing to give me a chance."

Alysson hesitated. She did not want to say the words that would only cause Gervase more pain, but it was perhaps the only way he would accept her refusal.

"Because I love him," she answered quietly, and was rewarded by the unmistakable, unbearable look of defeat in Gervase's dark eyes.

She loved, and was unloved in return. That was the bitter truth that Alysson tried desperately to ignore during the following days.

Blessedly the self-protective numbness shrouded her heart and dulled her grief somewhat. For several minutes at a time, she managed not to think about Jafar, about the passion they had shared, the intimacy, the rapture, the impossible situation.

She even had hopes that the pain might diminish over time, that someday she might learn to forget her fierce Berber lover. But if she thought this wished-for memory loss might happen any time soon, she was destined for disappointment. Too many events conspired to remind her of Jafar.

The first was the unexpected visit the next morning of the wife of the British Consul in Algiers, Lady Jane Wolverton. The lovely, golden-haired Lady Wolverton was one of the arbiters of European society in the country, and Alysson recalled meeting her at several functions two months before.

When presented with the lady's card, Alysson's first inclination was to have Chand declare her "not at home." But curiosity got the better of her—that, and sheer contrariness. If Lady Wolverton had come to torment her about her scandalous conduct, she would not let the challenge go unanswered.

Apparently, though, condemnation was the last thing on the lady's mind. She had called for the purpose of extending personal invitiations to Alysson and her uncles to a supper and muscale for the following evening.

Expecting something entirely different, Alysson looked at the woman with blank astonishment. "Did Colonel Bourmont put you up to this?" she asked.

Lady Wolverton graciously overlooked the rude bluntness of the question. "Actually, no, my dear. I am not well acquainted with your charming fiancé, but naturally I have included him on my guest list."

"My lady, please forgive me for correcting you, but the colonel is not my fiancé. We are not engaged, nor do we plan to be."

Lady Wolverton raised an eyebrow at this revelation, but blithely let it pass. "I am so looking forward to have you attend my entertainment, Miss Vickery. I long to hear about your exciting adventures—how your party was set upon by bandits, and how you were rescued by an elderly French couple who took you to their homestead, how you enjoyed their hospitality until your Uncle Larousse could come for you. How romantic it must have been!"

Alysson couldn't decide if the lady had gone mad, or if she was simply trying to help—for whatever obscure motives of her own.

"Forgive me again, my lady," Alysson said wryly, "but

with all the tales that are sure to be circulating about me, no one with an ounce of intelligence would believe that rapper."

"Well, if anyone can carry it off, I daresay I can," Lady Wolverton retorted with a warm twinkle dancing in her blue eyes. Her smile faded slightly at Alysson's bewildered silence. "I'm sure I don't need to tell you, my dear, that the best course is to show your face in company as often as possible, and to allow your engagement to Colonel Bourmont to stand for the time being. You can always quietly end it later, once the rumors have died down."

"I suppose," Alysson agreed slowly, "that might indeed be the wisest course."

"Excellent! Hold your head high, I say, and never, never apologize. Well then, it is settled. I shall see you and your uncles tomorrow evening at my party."

She rose then and swept across the room in a rustle of silk, but paused at the arched doorway to glance over her shoulder. "Oh, yes, perhaps I should mention that the Duke of Moreland is a firm friend of my husband, and that we both have known his charming grandson for ages. Good day, Miss Vickery. I look forward to welcoming you in my home."

With another attractive smile, the lady made her exit, leaving Alysson with her mouth hanging open and her thoughts spinning. The oblique reference to Jafar had both startled her and roused painful speculation. Did he have a hand in Lady Wolverton's kind attempt to protect her name and reputation? It would be so like Jafar to act with generosity and refuse to take the credit.

Alysson forced herself to attend the musicale, flanked by all her uncles and Gervase. As it turned out, the ordeal was not as bad as she feared, thanks to Lady Wolverton's skill at manipulation and persuasion of the very society Alysson had once disdained. Just as her hostess had predicted, the ladies veiled their claws and expressed profound exclamations of sympathy for Alysson, while the gentlemen vowed with renewed fervor to protect their womenfolk and rid the land of the scourge of bandits. Alysson would have laughed at the absurdity of it all—if she could have found it in herself to feel anything as light as laughter.

Shortly her scandal was overshadowed by reports from the front lines. The day after the musicale, the news spread like a desert sandstorm through the European and Moorish community alike that the rebel Berber leader, Abdel Kader, had been forced to flee Morocco, driven out by the Moroccan and French troops, back across the river into Algeria.

That, too, served to remind Alysson of Jafar, and arouse her fears. Had Jafar had gone to the defense of the valiant Sultan of the Arabs? Had he joined the defiant Algerines to ride against the superior French forces? Was he even now lying wounded and helpless on some battlefield? Her apprehension mounting daily, she sent Chand to scour the Arab coffee shops and barbershops to discover any scrap of information available about Abdel Kader's movements. And she asked Gervase to keep her informed of events, as well.

Otherwise, Alysson tried to distance herself from the world.

She found herself sitting hour after hour in the courtyard, staring down at the twisted handkerchief in her hands. One corner bore the initials *NJS,* initials she had always wondered about until now.

She knew, of course, that she ought to plan her departure from Algeria, but she couldn't bring herself to consider it. Indecision, passiveness, lethargy—all characteristics normally foreign to Alysson's nature—seemed to be her constant companions now.

Her Uncle Oliver had invited her to sail the Caribbean with him, but she was no longer anxious to travel the world in search of adventure. Nor was she enthusiastic about retreating to London, where her Uncle Cedric meant to return at once. Not only were his services needed at his hospital, but he was only weeks away from completing his treatise on the mode of communication of cholera through contamination of drinking water.

As for her Uncle Honoré, he declared his intention of remaining in Algeria for a time, to Alysson's great surprise. After the ordeal he had been through, she had expected him to rush home at the first opportunity. But he still intended to establish his vineyards. He had experienced and survived the worst this land had to offer, Honoré declared, and furthermore, he felt safe enough, now that he had the protection of one of Barbary's most powerful *amghars*.

When Alysson quizzed him, Honoré said he'd been given letters of safe conduct by Jafar. She couldn't understand why Jafar would countenance a Frenchman settling on Algerian soil, unless perhaps it was his way of making amends for involving Honoré in his affairs. But she was pleased for her uncle. He planned to remain a few more months at least, he said, but she was welcome to accompany him to France when he finally returned.

Yet day after day Alysson put off making any decision about her future. The need to distance herself from the source of her pain, to get away so she could begin forgetting, was not as vital to her as the need to remain near her love.

She said good-bye to her Uncle Cedric with little of her usual regret. And when her Uncle Oliver expressed his desire to leave directly after Christmas, Alysson was almost relieved. Oliver still had not given up his thoughts of vengeance, it seemed.

"He hurt you, girl," Oliver declared one morning, trying to jolt Alysson out of her misery. "I say shooting is too good for him."

In her more defiant moments, Alysson agreed. In those vulnerable moments, she tried to hate Jafar. She tried to tell herself that he didn't deserve her love, that he had abused her body, ravaged her soul, without the slightest consideration for her feelings or her welfare.

Yet there was still a part of her heart that wanted to believe his concern had been real, that he cared for her, that she had meant something to him. She wanted to believe she hadn't imagined the shared torment of that last night in his arms—his eyes blazing with desperation, his kisses tasting of pain as well as passion.

Alysson was again thinking about that night several days before Christmas as she sat in the courtyard. In the distance, she could hear the falsetto voice of a muezzin chanting from the minaret of a nearby mosque, calling the faithful to evening prayer.

Suddenly the peacefulness of the moment was shattered by her Indian servant who came rushing toward her.

Alysson looked up, grateful for any respite from her tormented thoughts.

"I bring you good tidings, memsahib!" Chand exclaimed, forgetting to make his normal respectful salaam. "Abdel Kader has surrendered!"

Part Four

From the desert I come to thee
On a stallion shod with fire,
And the winds are left behind
In the speed of my desire.

BAYARD TAYLOR
"Bedouin Song"

Chapter 26

Abdel Kader had surrendered! The rebel Berber leader had been defeated at last!

From the rumors and reports that flew during the next few days, Alysson managed to piece together the events leading to Abdel Kader's capitulation. After striking a swift counterattack against the Moroccan army, he retreated into Algeria, where more French troops lay in wait. Pursued from the rear, challenged in front, he was required to make a decision—to flee through the mountains into the desert and live to fight another day, or concede victory to the superior forces that had brutally hounded him for so many years.

On December 21st, Abdel Kader had made his submission to General Lamoriciere. Two days later, he formally handed over his sword to the Governor-General of Algeria, His Royal Highness the Duc d'Aumale. Abdel Kader's defeat, it was reputed, was due in part to the independent Berber spirit, since many of the intractable Berber tribes in the mountains had refused to join with the Arabs against the French. But regardless of the reason, Abdel Kader and his armies would no longer be a menace to French forces or civilian settlers.

The excitement and relief that the news roused in the French community were unbounded, but Alysson could not share the triumph of her fellow Europeans. Indeed, she could feel only sympathy and great sorrow at the defeat of the valiant Berber leader who had defied the French invaders for fifteen years. Whatever his crimes against his French conquerors, Abdel Kader was a remarkable man with heroic greatness.

What would happen to him now was the cause of much

speculation. It was said that Abdel Kader would likely be executed as a traitor. Or he would be imprisoned like the meanest criminal. These brutal rumors circulated freely, even though as a condition of surrender the emir had been promised by the French government that he and his family could seek refuge in Palestine or Egypt.

The possibility of either his execution or imprisonment whipped up Alysson's anger and sympathy. Hoping to aid him, she persuaded her Uncle Honoré to accompany her while she paid a visit to Gervase at his offices.

The European quarter of the city was little more than a huddle of French barracks and military headquarters grouped around the harbor. She finally managed to track Gervase down in one of these dreary buildings, but he was so busy that he could only spare a moment of his time. When she pleaded with him to help Abdel Kader if possible, Gervase promised to try, but he had few hopes that he would be able to persuade the ruling powers to show leniency. The best that could be expected would be exile.

When Alysson came out again, she wandered disconsolately across the courtyard. Her uncle had paused inside to speak to an acquaintance, though Chand followed her at a respectful distance.

To her left, set against a background of hills, the city rose in a mass of white walls that glittered in the sun and contrasted richly with the cypress and myrtle and other verdant foliage that grew along the coast. To her right, below the walled fortifications, the azure sea was dotted with fishing boats and merchant vessels. Ordinarily the beauty of the view would have awed her, but at the moment her spirits were too depressed for her to appreciate it.

She had just gathered breath for a deep sigh when she spied a gentleman in the distance, striding purposefully across the court toward another of the buildings. Her heart leapt at the sight of the gleaming golden hair beneath his elegant chapeau. *Jafar,* she thought dazedly, and then berated herself for her absurdity. Her mind was playing tricks on her, obviously. She was so desperate for some word of him, for even the slightest glimpse of him, that she was imagining his presense—here, in this bastion of French au-

thority. Ridiculous to think Jafar would be foolish enough
to set foot in his enemy's sanctum.

She watched as the gentleman disappeared inside, then
turned away, only to have her gaze fall on a cluster of horses.
To one side stood a fiery bay stallion.

Alysson had no doubt that she had seen that horse before.
There was no doubt either that the young boy who held the
reins was Jafar's servant.

Without pausing to think, Alysson picked up her skirts
and almost ran across the courtyard. "Mahmoud! It *is* you!"
she cried, managing to startle both boy and horse. "Whatever are you doing here?" she asked once Mahmoud had
brought Jafar's beloved steed under control. "I never expected to see you again."

"Lallah!" Mahmoud's scarred face lit up momentarily,
before his expression suddenly became guarded. "I do not
know you, *lallah*. You have mistaken me for another."

"Not know me— Of course you know me. What on earth
are you talking about?"

Mahmoud's voice dropped to a murmur. "It is not wise
for you to be here, for us to speak."

Bewildered, Alysson glanced around her to discover they
were drawing curious stares from several passersby, while
a few paces behind her, Chand stood glaring at her. "I will
pretend I am admiring the stallion in your charge. Perhaps
I might wish to purchase him."

"But he is not for sale, *lallah!*"

"I know that, but it will do no harm if I am seen making
inquiries. Now tell me what has happened to bring you
here."

Mahmoud shifted uncomfortably, while his brow took on
a gloomy cast. "Have you not heard of the defeat of our
armies?"

"Yes . . . and I am sorry, Mahmoud. I wish the outcome
could have been different."

"It should have been different! Allah could not have deserted the true believers to side with the French infidels—
those foul offspring of snakes and scorpions!"

Alysson murmured an appropriately soothing sound of
agreement. "But what is your master doing here . . . that
was Jafar I saw just now, was it not?" When the boy didn't

answer at once, Alysson bit her lip, trying to control her impatience. "Mahmoud, please, you have to tell me."

"The lord is here on behalf of the Sultan of the Arabs, Abdel Kader."

"What does that mean?"

"It is not my place to say."

Mahmoud obviously did not want to tell her, but Alysson would not give up. When she continued to press, she learned that Jafar was here to negotiate terms of exile for the vanquished leader. Jafar had presented himself to the French authorities, not as a Berber warlord, but as the Englishman Nicholas Sterling, the grandson of the Duke of Moreland.

Her thoughts racing ahead, Alysson stared at Mahmoud in horror. In hopes of aiding his vanquished sultan, Jafar had given up his Berber identity in exchange for the bargaining power his British nationality and noble family name could give him. But even if he'd adopted English dress and assumed his English name, Gervase would surely recognize him as the Berber warrior who had abducted her, the same one who had nearly killed him. And then Gervase would expose the man she loved as an enemy of the French government, as a traitor.

A shudder of fear ran up Alysson's spine. She had to find Gervase at once and prevent him from setting eyes on Jafar.

With only a brief word to Mahmoud, ordering him to wait, she whirled and reentered the building where her Uncle Honoré was just concluding his conversation. Sweeping past her startled uncle, Alysson pushed her way into Gervase's office, only to discover that he was no longer there. When she demanded to see him, she was told apologetically that the colonel was now closeted in conference with other officials of the French government and could not be disturbed.

She finally gave up when Honoré forcibly took her by the arm and steered her outside. To her further dismay, Mahmoud had disappeared with the horses. Alysson wanted to search for him, but Honoré insisted that enough was enough, and she didn't dare push him further. So far her uncle had acquiesced to her wishes and protected Jafar by remaining silent, but he was not likely to continue if her abductor could easily be brought to justice.

So instead of protesting, Alysson reluctantly, quietly, returned home to wait in a state of nervous dread, wondering if any minute she would hear that her fierce Berber lover had been captured and taken away in chains.

The same concern lay in the back of Jafar's mind.

He had risked recognition in order to participate in the negotiations, but he could not have done otherwise. If there was the slightest possibility that he could impact his sultan's fate, he had to take it. And so he had attended the conference called by His Highness, the Duc d'Aumale, determined to lend whatever weight his family name and position in the European community could bring.

Any moment, though, Jafar expected to be arrested. He was even resigned to that eventuality. He had little doubt that Colonel Bourmont could identify him. And he was prepared to face the consequences—afterward, when the negotiations were completed. The case against him was not particularly strong, he thought. It would be his word against the colonel's, in fact. But Jafar hoped sincerely to delay the moment of reckoning. If it occurred now, the charges would be serious enough to complicate matters and completely destroy his ability to plead his commander's case.

He knew the exact instant the colonel made the linkage between the Englishman Nicholas Sterling and the Berber warlord who had captured an innocent young woman and used her to lure the French army into the desert where they could be slaughtered.

The two of them were sitting at opposite ends of a long table, but Jafar could feel the colonel staring at him during the opening remarks, and later, when, as Nicholas Sterling, he rose to address the gathering.

At his first words, he could see Bourmont's face freeze in a startled expression, then slowly turn dark with anger.

But the colonel did not leap to his feet and point an accusing finger at him. Bourmont made no move at all—probably, Jafar decided, because he preferred not to interrupt the proceedings. Thankful for the reprieve, Jafar forced himself to relax and devote his attentions to the subject at hand, though knowing his conflict with the colonel was not over by any means.

The present discussion over what to do with the vanquished Berber leader was both heated and surprising to Jafar. He had not expected to find himself on the same side of the debate as his blood enemy, arguing for leniency. Like he, Colonel Bourmont favored exile to any of the harsher punishments to which the leader of the Arabs could have been sentenced. The Duc d'Aumale listened with appropriate graveness before making his decision. When it was over, Jafar felt he had achieved the best terms he could have hoped for. Abdel Kader would be escorted to France, where the king would determine his fate.

The gathering of government officials and military men was starting to disperse when Jafar heard a hard voice at his left shoulder.

"Might I have a word with you, m'sieur? In private."

He turned to meet the dark, narrowed eyes of his longtime enemy. With a brief nod, Jafar followed the colonel to his offices, noting the half dozen armed subalterns that accompanied them at a discreet distance. The colonel, it seemed, was taking no chances that his enemy could escape.

But this was to be a civilized discussion, apparently. The colonel offered him a chair and a glass of claret before hesitating thoughtfully. "Or do you drink liquor?"

"Occasionally," Jafar replied, accepting the drink. Bourmont's odd question only confirmed what he already suspected; the colonel knew who he was. Otherwise the Frenchman would not have shown such consideration in asking if his religion allowed him to imbibe alcohol.

Waiting uneasily, Jafar sipped the wine and studied the colonel over the rim of his glass while endeavoring to hide his surprise. He was accustomed to French officials who showed a contemptuous display of superiority and superciliousness when dealing with Muslims, officials who enforced the regulations laid down by the French government with haughtiness and severity.

The colonel, however, seemed only to possess the severity. Jafar watched warily as the other man settled himself in an adjoining wing chair.

"If you are wondering at the chances of my exposing you," Bourmont said then, "you may cease to worry. I did indeed recognize you, but I intend to hold my tongue . . . for two reasons. You spared my life that day in battle, and it is not something I can easily forget. I could not repay such magnanimity by turning you over to a military tribunal, to perhaps face a firing squad.''

Jafar was silent for a long moment while he considered Bourmont's disclosure. ''No one would fault you for enacting such a reprisal,'' he said slowly.

''*I* would fault me. No man of honor could do otherwise. As it is, I shall always be in your debt, m'sieur.''

''The word 'always' does not exist on earth.''

''Perhaps.''

There was another long pause while the two men regarded each other. ''You spoke of two reasons?'' Jafar said finally.

''Yes, but I first should like to ask you a question, if I may. Why did you not kill me when you had the opportunity? You seem to have gone to a good deal of trouble in order to carry out your vendetta against my father. And then to pass up the opportunity to finish it . . . I admit having some curiosity as to why.''

Unwilling to answer, Jafar looked down at his glass. ''My reasons are my own, Colonel. Suffice it to say that I have forsworn vengeance on the Bourmont family.''

''On the contrary,'' Gervase replied softly, sadly. ''I think you have already had your vengeance. You have taken Alysson's love.''

Jafar's head came up like a wolf scenting the wind. He stared at Bourmont, his heart suddenly pounding.

''Alysson is in love with you,'' Gervase said quietly. ''You didn't know?''

Jafar swallowed, suddenly bereft of speech. When he finally spoke, his voice was strangely hoarse. ''Forgive me if I find that hard to accept. She had every opportunity to make her feelings known. The decision to leave was hers. She chose not to stay.''

''Yet it is true, I'm afraid. She told me so herself. It is why she would not accept my offer of marriage.''

''She refused you?'' This time his voice was merely a cracked whisper. ''But I heard no rumors of a broken engagement.''

Gervase's brief smile was one of bitterness. "Perhaps because there never was an engagement. Before she left on her expedition, Alysson had promised to consider my proposal and give me her answer upon her return. Afterward . . . it was wiser to let society assume our engagement had never ended. If I had cried off so soon after her abduction, it would have branded her for life. My only thought was to protect her."

A long pause. "You . . . must love her very much, then."

Again that bitter smile. "I like to believe that I am unselfish enough to put her happiness before my own."

"Then we are more alike than I suspected," Jafar said in a low, tortured voice. "The most difficult thing I've ever done in my life was to let her go."

"Ah," Gervase murmured. "So I was right. She was the reason you spared my life."

"Yes . . . she was the reason."

"Because you love her yourself."

Jafar looked away. "Yes."

"And now? What do you intend to do about her?"

Jafar closed his eyes, remembering the torment of the past weeks when he'd held no hope that Alysson could ever be his. He had gone through the motions of living, but he'd been more like a corpse, a mere ghost of a man, his spirit broken. Perhaps that was why he hadn't hesitated to walk into the stronghold of his mortal enemy, to put himself at the colonel's mercy. The thought of death held no terror for him, compared to the pain of living. "I had not considered yet . . . I thought she was lost to me."

"I don't believe that is so. She has not left Algiers, did you know that?"

"Yes, I knew. But I didn't dare hope that I might be the reason."

Abruptly Gervase leaned forward in his seat, his face searching and intense. "You will take good care of her?"

Jafar met the colonel's gaze directly, his expression a solemn promise. "I would give my life for her."

Apparently believing him, the colonel relaxed somewhat. "I can rest easy, then." Settling back in his chair, he sipped his claret. After a moment he introduced an entirely new subject. "Alysson was not the only reason I asked you here.

I should like to discuss the future of your country with you, if I may."

It was with tremendous effort that Jafar dragged his mind from his half-agonized, half-optimistic thoughts of Alysson, and focused his attention on what the colonel was saying.

"You are aware, are you not, of the responsibilities of the *Bureaux Arabes?*" Bourmont asked.

Jafar thought back, recalling what he knew of the Arab Bureau. It was the system by which the French government ruled the native peoples of the country—a department of the French military staffed with French officers to administer the conquered territories and supervise the native chiefs. The Turkish hierarchy of *khalifas, aghas,* and *caids* had been retained, but at every level a French intelligence officer, acting as advisor, actually did all the governing—raising taxes and administering justice through a docile Muslim nominee.

"I know something of it," Jafar replied. "It is the institution through which the French army maintains domination over Muslim populations by controlling their tribal chiefs and councils."

The colonel stiffened slightly at the veiled contempt in his guest's tone. "Assimilation is the goal of the Bureau, not domination. The native tribes are allowed to govern themselves, with chiefs selected and approved by the Arab Bureau. It is a fair and just system."

"I expect that depends upon one's point of view."

"Perhaps," Gervase agreed. "But regardless, it is the only system we have to work with. As head of the Bureau, my primary job is to protect our settlers. There are some hundred thousand of them now, half of them French, and there will be more to come. Now that the war is over—"

"You will come in ever greater numbers," Jafar said grimly, "all burning with a love of conquest."

This time Bourmont sat up in his chair. "The French presence has not been all bad for your country. Look at the advantages we have provided. When we arrived seventeen years ago, Algiers was suffering from plague and famine and was almost a ruin."

"Is that what you believe, or what you were told?"

The colonel hesitated, angry color rising in his face.

"Your father no doubt used numerous fallacies to justify his rape of the Kingdom of Algiers," Jafar observed, his tone cool. "But I was here seventeen years ago, Colonel, and I can assure you Algiers was in no way suffering the kind of devastation you speak of."

"I had thought," Bourmont said just as coolly, "we had tacitly agreed to allow the past to remain in the past. My father has been dead nearly a decade now, and I would be well satisfied to leave him buried and forgotten."

"Indeed, we did. Forgive me. Please continue, Colonel."

"Yes, well then. As I was saying, the task of protecting the colonists will be easier, now that the war has ended, but there are other aspects of this situation which concern me. I intend to provide justice for the Arab population, if I can. My predecessors . . . lacked what might be called the virtue of the victor. The balance of the spirit and of the heart. The regard for the right of the weak. I hope to do better."

Returning a look of polite restraint, Jafar made no reply.

"If we mean to have a peaceful and effective administration, I believe we must have accurate and comprehensive knowledge of the people we govern—the customs and social organization, the language, the institutions. I want the Bureau staffed with officers well acquainted with the entire way of life of the native population. Which leads me to my point. I would very much like your help."

"Mine?"

"I am prepared to offer you an official position in the *Bureaux Arabes.*" When Jafar's jaw hardened, Gervase held up a hand. "I can see by the look on your face that you mean to reject the idea, but before you decide, consider this. Holding a position of authority in the French government is the best way to influence your country's conquerors and protect your people. You would have the autonomy to govern a major part of your province, maintaining Arab justice while administering French laws. In exchange, you would act in the role of interpreter, judge, tax collector, intelligence officer. More importantly, you would advise me on the effectiveness of our policies and aid me in making appropriate changes and improvements."

Repressing his first inclination to tell Bourmont precisely what he could do with his offer, Jafar remained silent. In fact, he had to admire the colonel, both for the courage to present his plan honestly and without the use of threats, as he might have done, and for the plan itself. Enlisting the aid of the enemy to subjugate itself was clever and quite tenable in this case. Yet the colonel's paternalistic view of his responsibilities struck Jafar as genuine. It was even possible—no, likely—that the colonel's motives were philanthropic, that he truly did want to foster peace between the Arabs and the French.

Jafar forced himself to let out the angry breath he had been holding. Glancing toward the curtained window, he saw the dwindling daylight and thought of Alysson. This was the best time of day, when late afternoon passed into evening, when waning sunlight faded from rose-gold to soothing violet. This was the time of day when he missed her most sharply. Unless one counted the moments when he woke each morning filled with a relentless ache, or when he restlessly sought sleep each night, or when he rode one of his horses, or when he visited any of the places he had been with her, when he walked through his empty house, when he gazed out at his barren courtyard and saw no defiant young Englishwoman sitting among the almond trees, her face lifted to the sun as if she wanted to wring every drop of energy out of life . . . when he simply existed. His sense of bereavement never left him.

But now he was being offered the chance to influence the future of his country. Even more, he was being offered salvation. The chance to have Alysson at his side without betraying his duty. If he were to accept Bourmont's proposal, he would be allying himself with the French. In his people's eyes, his marriage to a European would serve the same purpose as marrying the daughter of a neighboring ruler—the strengthening of tribal alliances. He could make Alysson his first wife . . . his only wife. If she would have him.

Even if that audacious dream were unattainable, he could not pass up the colonel's proposal if Bourmont was sincerely interested in working toward justice for the Algerian people. No matter if it galled him to play the role of the vanquished.

No doubt it galled Bourmont also to ask for aid from the man who had stolen his love and nearly destroyed his forces. They were each in positions that required compromise—although his own position was by far the weaker. The French were the victors for the moment. And like in the negotiations regarding his sultan, he would have to press for the best terms possible and continue from there.

Bowing to fate, Jafar returned his solemn gaze to Bourmont, who was quietly waiting. "I will consult with the other tribal leaders of my province, Colonel," Jafar said finally.

Bourmont eyed him quizzically. "I had assumed you would be able to make such a decision on your own."

Jafar permitted himself a brief smile. "No, the decision is not mine alone. I rule at the will of my people, not at my own whim. It is our way. If you mean what you say, if you intend to allow us to retain our customs and way of governing, you will try to understand."

"Yes . . . of course, I should have realized."

"And," Jafar said mildly, "if you can summon a bit more patience, I can promise you that your offer will be given careful consideration. I will even tell you that I mean to advise our council of the advantages of your proposal and give it my full support."

"Very well." Gervase leaned forward. "Shall we shake on it?"

Jafar's gaze dropped to the hand held out to him.

"It is a Western custom, I know, but if and when you agree to join me, we can celebrate in the Eastern fashion . . . take a meal together and afterwards smoke a pipe."

With genuine acknowledgment this time, Jafar accepted the colonel's hand.

Satisfied, the Frenchman settled back in his seat, swirling the liquid in his glass as he mused out loud. "Algeria will likely remain under military rule for some time to come, but I can envision the day when administration reverts to civil control. I even hope to see the day when Arabs and Berbers live peacefully beside French and other European colonists." Raising his glass in a toast, Bourmont eyed his guest. "Perhaps we might drink to that day."

Slowly, Jafar raised his own glass. "The good manners

which my grandfather drummed into my head compel me to participate," he said agreeably, "but allow me to repeat what the Sultan Abdel Kader has said of the French . . . *You are merely passing guests*, Colonel. *You may stay three hundred years, like the Turks, but in the end you will leave.*"

In response, Gervase de Bourmont returned a smile that was more than a little sad. "To that day then, m'sieur."

Chapter 27

Vengeance had never been satisfied, and yet . . .
Jafar stood on the darkened terrace outside the crowded, brightly lit chamber, watching the man he had once planned to kill. Gervase de Bourmont was present at the victory celebration, very much alive, and very much the cause of the violent jealousy that raged in Jafar's breast.

And yet Jafar was glad he had forsworn his blood oath. Fulfilling his quest for vengeance would not have gained him what he wanted most in life. Rather, it would have been the death blow to all hope. A hope that even now he dared not embrace completely.

Not for the first time, he shifted his gaze to the young woman standing near the colonel, his eyes going soft with yearning. *Alysson.* Flanked by two of her uncles, she burned with a charm and a vivacious energy that gave no hint she was pining away with love for him or any other man.

That radiant, carefree manner of hers had kept Jafar from making an appearance at the celebration ball held at the palatial residence of the Governor-General. That manner and his own fear. He was utterly afraid that Bourmont had been mistaken about the depth of Alysson's feelings. Afraid to the point of cowardice.

Jafar smiled grimly at his silent admission, though he

found little amusement that an ordinarily fearless Berber warlord had such incredible difficulty working up the courage to approach a mere female. But then, Alysson Vickery had never been a mere female. From the very first she had exhibited her independent, passionate nature, her indomitable spirit—challenging him and defying him at every turn, arousing his anger and admiration, as well as his fierce desire. She had captured his heart, his very soul. And now he couldn't face knowing the truth. He couldn't force himself to take the next step, to ask the question that needed to be asked, to learn the answer, that the woman who meant more to him than life spurned his love. And so he waited in the darkness, fear and despair knifing through him in equal measure.

Within the ballroom, Alysson was battling her own fears. Her dread had not diminished during the past twenty-eight hours. Since discovering Jafar's presence in Algiers, she'd lived in constant terror that he would be exposed as a traitor, that he would be arrested and imprisoned, perhaps executed. She'd attended the victory celebration ball that evening only because Gervase had insisted, and because she couldn't remain calmly at home with her tortured thoughts when Jafar might be in mortal danger.

For the benefit of her uncles, she'd pretended enjoyment, while silently praying that her fears were groundless. Surely Jafar would be long gone by now. There was no reason for him to remain in Algiers. The negotiations were complete, the fate of his sultan sealed; Abdel Kader had embarked for France that morning with his family and his closest followers.

From the roof of her rented residence, Alysson had glimpsed the legendary figure, splendid in a scarlet burnous, as he rode through the streets to the deafening cheers of thousands of his people. His departure marked the end of a violent era, yet Alysson could only feel a deep sadness at his defeat. Emir Abdel Kader had proved himself a born leader of men, a great soldier, a capable administrator, a persuasive orator, a chivalrous opponent. For fifteen years, he had led the valiant struggle against French domination, holding at bay half a dozen great French generals and several princes of the blood. And now he'd been made to pay the price for his defiance.

What concerned her most, however, was not the vanquished Arab leader, but Jafar. What would he do now that his commander had surrendered? Would he accept defeat, or would he carry on the war against overwhelming odds? Or was he even now being taken prisoner? Would she even know of his fate? The uncertainty was driving her to distraction.

Oh, would this interminable evening never end? Alysson lamented, clasping her gloved hands together to hide their trembling.

Just then she met Gervase's solemn gaze. Unable to maintain her pretense of equanimity a moment longer, she murmured something to her uncles about needing air and made her way quickly toward the wide doors, pressing through the throngs of faceless people.

When at last she stepped into the coolness of the terrace, Alysson drew in a deep calming breath, which in itself was a mistake. The moonlit courtyard below was filled with masses of scarlet bougainvillea and laurel roses, and countless other flowers that would continue to bloom even in midwinter. The sweet fragrances brought to mind memories of other scents, of other exotic nights when she had lain in Jafar's arms.

Feeling all over again the anguish of her hopeless passion, she leaned against the balustrade and bowed her head, wishing that the numbness that had once shielded her would return to deaden her pain.

It might have been an eternity later when Jafar stepped out of the shadows, her name on his lips. With a start, her heart pounding, Alysson turned to find him standing merely inches away. Like that first time nearly three months ago, he was dressed in elegant evening clothes, tailored in the European style.

"Jafar . . ." Her whisper was barely audible, the quiver in her voice betraying the trembling, uncertain joy she felt at the sight of him. Hardly daring to believe he was truly here, she drank in the reality of his presence. He filled up her vision, his eyes deep and quiet and searching, his face still and intense.

They stared at each other for a long moment before Jafar finally broke the silence. "I had thought by now you would be gone from Algiers, *Ehuresh*."

Vaguely realizing he had spoken in English, Alysson shook her head. She couldn't think about that or anything else when his life was at risk. "Jafar, please . . . you shouldn't be here. The danger is too great. You have to leave."

"What is this, *chérie?* Is it possible I detect a note of concern in your tone?"

"Yes! Yes, I am concerned for you. If Gervase discovers you here—"

"Ease your fears, Alysson. The colonel himself invited me to attend the celebration."

She looked at him, bewildered. "I don't understand . . . You've spoken to him?"

"At length. He considers himself to be repaying the debt he feels he owes me."

Again Alysson shook her head, not understanding. But no explanation was forthcoming from Jafar. Instead, there was a longer pause, while he seemed to struggle with his choice of words.

"There is something I must ask you, *Ehuresh*," he said finally. "The colonel seems to think . . . that you love me. I desperately want to know if it is true."

She returned Jafar's searching gaze, unable to look away. His amber eyes were grave and vulnerable, not at all like the man who had once professed hatred for his father's murderer and vowed revenge.

"And if it is?" she whispered.

In that moment his eyes filled—with tenderness, hunger, longing, and more than a hint of uncertainty. She read each emotion as clearly as if it was her own—because it *was* her own.

"If it is true," he replied hoarsely, "then I would have to confess my own love . . . for a woman I have long since come to admire and respect."

Alysson parted her lips soundlessly. Wild hope was bubbling in her, but her throat was too constricted to speak. Helpless to respond verbally, she answered in the only other way possible, with her heart; she moved into Jafar's embrace. As his arms folded around her, she leaned weakly against him, shutting her eyes and burying her face in his shoulder.

Jafar could feel her trembling as he bent close, could feel the wetness on her face against his cheek. For a moment, though, he simply held her tightly against him, his cheek pressed to hers. Then, drawing back, he gathered her face in his hands, his hard palms curving to fit the delicate contours.

"Only you can ease the storm raging in my heart, Alysson. Tell me you don't hate me . . . Give me hope that one day you could come to love me."

"Yes . . . Oh, Jafar, yes—"

Before she could complete the words, his lips were suddenly raining soft, desperate kisses on her chin, her cheeks, the moistness seeping under her eyes. She clung to him, sobbing, laughing, until finally he raised his head, his expression all seriousness.

"Marry me, Alysson."

"M-marry you? You want me to *marry* you?"

"Yes, my heart. I want your hand in marriage. I'm asking you to be my wife, Alysson, to share my life and my home, to bear my children, to grow old at my side."

She stared at him in shock, before a sudden bleakness replaced the incredulity in her eyes. "But your tribe, Jafar . . . they'll never accept me . . . an infidel, an English-woman."

"That is not so, Alysson. They will accept you without question. Because of your bravery, your courage. A woman who can vanquish a lion is a bride fit to carry the children of a Berber *amghar* in her womb. That is what is being said about you among my people."

The knowledge that the members of his tribe had been discussing her fitness as wife to their lord should have disturbed Alysson, at the very least annoyed her, but all she could feel was relief. Immense relief. And happiness. The thought of bearing Jafar's children made her weak with joy.

He must have misunderstood her hesitation, though, for his voice went low and quiet. "If you say you cannot live here with me, in my country, I will understand. We can live wherever you wish . . . England, France . . . India. It matters not to me, as long as I have you.''

Her eyes filled again with tears. It did matter to him, greatly, she knew, but he was prepared to leave his homeland, to give up his entire life, his country, his struggle, simply for her sake.

"Do not weep, beloved," he pleaded in his own language. "I cannot bear to see you cry."

"I'm not crying," she replied shakily in English. "And yes, we can live here, Jafar."

"Then . . . you will marry me?"

"Yes. Yes, I'll marry you."

He still didn't seem convinced. Gently, almost tentatively, he stroked the wetness under her eyes with his thumbs, brushing away her tears. "It won't be as disagreeable as you think, Alysson. I don't want to take away your independence or your freedom. I won't try to change your passionate nature to fit our culture. Your spirit is one of the things I love most about you. Nor would I ever ask you to give up your religion. It is not against the Koran for a Muslim man to marry a Christian woman. We can be married in a Christian ceremony as well as a Muslim one, in order to satisfy your uncles and my English grandfather." He stopped, searching her face intently.

Her tremulous smile must have encouraged him, for his intensity relaxed the slightest degree. "As for our future children, we can strike a fair compromise, I think. They will be raised in the Islamic faith, but will study Christianity as well, so that when they are old enough they may choose for themselves. Would that be agreeable to you?"

"Yes, I'm sure that would be fair, but . . . are you truly certain you want an English wife?"

Jafar's mouth curved in a wry twist as, for the first time, he allowed a trace of amusement into his expression. "If I have sunk so low as to consort with the French, especially the man against whom I once swore vengeance, I can take an English wife."

"What do you mean, 'consort with the French'? Are you speaking of Gervase?"

"It seems your colonel wants me to join the *Bureaux Arabes.*"

Leading her to a marble bench then, Jafar sat beside her and told her of Bourmont's proposal, and of his own growing conviction that accepting the offer was the right decision. He was certain he could gain the council's support when he put the question before them.

"So, what do you think?" he concluded. "Would that please you, my heart?"

In response, Alysson reached up to stroke the lean curve of his cheek. She still could hardly believe she wasn't dreaming, that he was truly here, telling her this. "Yes, it would please me . . . it would please me very much. You could do so much good for your people, Jafar, if you occupied a position of authority in the French government. For their sake, perhaps you could put your differences aside."

He gave a soft sigh that held perhaps a trace of bitterness. "It isn't easy to stomach, making peace with one's enemy."

She knew he must be thinking of Gervase. "Do you hate him so much, then?"

"Not so much any longer. And if I am honest, I can admit that much of my hatred stemmed from jealousy." Jafar's gaze probed hers. "All this time I thought you loved him."

"No . . . I just didn't want to see him hurt. It . . . it is you I love."

A moment of silence stretched between them, before Jafar took her hand and drew it to his breast, directly covering his heart. She could feel its steady pulse beating strong and sure. "And I love you, Alysson, so much that I ache with it."

She gave him a long searching glance, a question lingering in her eyes. "If you love me," she asked at last, "then why did you let me go?"

"I thought you would be happier with Bourmont," Jafar said simply. "And in any case," he added quietly, "I had to allow you the choice. You had to come to me freely, of your own accord. If I had forced you to remain, I would have been no better than the savage heathen you thought me. Yet I hoped . . . I told myself that if you loved me enough, you would make the decision to stay."

"I wanted to stay, Jafar, but I was afraid—for your sake.

I didn't want to come between you and your tribe, to cause more trouble for you. I saw how you were tried for showing mercy to Gervase, and I couldn't bear the thought of harming you further. I still can't. Are you certain your tribe won't object if you marry me? I thought you had to marry for political reasons."

"I still do. But you must understand the Berber concept of politics. Until now I couldn't offer you the marriage you deserved without betraying my duty. But if I ally myself with Bourmont, then my taking you to wife would not be compromising my responsibility as *amghar* to strengthen our tribal alliances. By Berber law, it is permissible for an *amghar* to marry outside tribal affiliations, even with an enemy, in order to extend the range of possible allies. Not only permissible, but encouraged. In this case, it would be highly advantageous for me to form an alliance with you, a foreigner who has the ear of the head of the Arab Bureau."

She hesitated. "Is that why you want to marry me, to use me as an *alliance?*"

She said it lightly, with a hint of exasperation, but Jafar caught the uncertain note in her voice and smiled grimly. "Come here," he commanded brusquely, not waiting for Alysson to obey before pulling her into his arms.

He lowered his head then, taking her lips with a determination that left her reeling and totally reassured. His mouth retained the same possessiveness, the same hot fierceness it always had whenever he kissed her.

By the time he finally ended the kiss and allowed Alysson to draw breath, her cheeks were flushed and her lips swollen and tender. Yet she didn't care. She wanted his fierceness, his jealous passion. Indeed, she hoped the savage nature of his lovemaking never changed.

Jafar smiled in satisfaction as he surveyed her dazed expression, his own eyes gleaming hot and dangerous. "I do not kiss my allies like that, *Ehuresh,* or take them as lovers."

"I should hope not," she said with a small, shaky laugh. "That was . . . very persuasive."

Making a futile attempt to regain her composure, she smoothed the disheveled folds of her gown. Abruptly Jafar's gaze dropped to the neckline of her bodice which demurely covered the swell of her breasts but left a tantalizing display of silken skin naked to his view. Desire flared up in him swiftly, uncontrollably, as he remembered the taste of those taut peaks, that sweet flesh.

Yet when the increased volume of revelry from the crowded ballroom finally registered, Jafar shook himself. Releasing Alysson entirely—if reluctantly—he eased away so he wouldn't have to touch her and face such temptation.

"I would like nothing more than to carry you away from here, *Ehuresh*," he said huskily, "to undress your exquisite body and make love to you all night long . . . but I expect it would be best if I first sought out your uncles and gained their permission to wed you."

Having focused on the opening part of his provocative comment, Alysson had difficulty finding the voice to contradict him. "That isn't necessary, Jafar. I don't need my uncles' permission to marry."

"Even so, I would prefer their blessing."

"I expect they will be glad to give it. Their biggest concern is for my happiness. I imagine if you give your word that you won't abduct me again or make me your prisoner of war, they will be willing to accept you as my husband and welcome you into the family."

The lightness of her tone seemed to lift a great burden from Jafar's heart. "I suppose," he returned dryly, "I could swear to behave in a civilized fashion."

"Not too civilized, I hope," Alysson murmured. She didn't want Jafar to change. He was a man as proud and as fierce as the lions that roamed his mountain retreat, untamed and unlikely ever to be tamed. And she wanted him to remain that way. No doubt in the future she would frequently find him arrogant, difficult, possessive, dominating, and entirely infuriating, as she had in the past, but she wouldn't trade that future for all the riches in the world.

"Still," he was saying, "I want to assure them I intend to care for you to the best of my abilities." Jafar hesitated again, his amber eyes showing that vulnerability that so touched her heart. "I cannot promise you anything but an uncertain future, Alysson. I can only swear that I will do everything in my power to make you happy."

Finally allowing herself to believe in his sincerity, that

Jafar loved her, that this moment was truly real, Alysson raised her lips again to touch his briefly, tenderly. "That is more than enough," she vowed softly. "I don't want empty promises for the future. I only want you."

The love reflected in her eyes, shining clear in the moonlight, filled him with a tenderness that threatened to shatter him. It took every ounce of willpower Jafar possessed to direct his thoughts back to the present.

"I must go and find your uncles," he repeated in a husky rasp, "so that we may discuss the bride price. Which one will drive the hardest bargain, do you think?"

Alysson shook her head, not understanding his insistence. "Jafar, you don't have to pay for me to become your wife, I tell you."

"Ah, but I do, *Ehuresh*. It is our custom . . . and I don't want your uncles thinking I want you only for your fortune."

She laughed softly again, this time with genuine amusement. "I'm certain they'll realize it is no such thing. As much as you despise foreigners, your marrying me could only be because of love."

"What is important to me is that you realize it."

Her eyebrows rose in surprise at his quiet tone. This humility was quite unlike him. She'd never known Jafar to lack that overwhelming confidence bred into him by generations of fierce rulers. Yet, after considering, she thought perhaps it might be wise to take advantage of the unprecedented moment.

"I do have one misgiving of my own," Alysson remarked slowly. Despite the casualness of her tone, she was immediately aware of Jafar's sudden tenseness. "I think," she explained, tilting her head to one side as she looked up at him, "I could perhaps learn to address you as 'my lord,' but I honestly don't know if I could ever bring myself to call you 'master.' "

His tension fading, Jafar gave her a smile that was one part tenderness and three parts seduction. "That was a foolish declaration that never should have been made—besides which there's not an ounce of truth in it. By Berber custom, I may be your master, but you rule my heart, *Ehuresh*."

"Is that so?"

"Indeed, and I intend to spend the rest of our lives proving it to you."

Her throat suddenly tight, Alysson gazed back at him with desire glimmering in her eyes. At her melting expression, Jafar inhaled a sharp breath. When she looked at him like that, with such naked longing, his blood quickened with such a rush of hunger that he wanted to take her right then and there. He wanted to bury himself so deeply inside her that neither of them could tell where the other began or ended.

Helplessly, despite his stated intentions, Jafar reached for her again, his fingers closing possessively on her arms. "Ah, *Ehuresh*," he whispered, his warm breath caressing her mouth, "can you not see how very much I love you? What power you hold over me? You can conquer me with a glance, vanquish me with a smile from your sweet lips, crush me with the merest frown—"

"Jafar, do you mean to shower me with meaningless flattery, or will you behave like a man of action and kiss me again?"

At her challenge, he laughed, and the laughter stayed inside him as he lowered his head once more.

It was a long time before either of them remembered their initial intentions of gaining a familial blessing for their passion, and a longer time still before they rose together and, hand in hand, went in search of Alysson's uncles.

Epilogue

Paris
1852

Following his wife into their plush hotel suite, Jafar tossed his chapeau on a side table and began peeling off his gloves. With fond tolerance he watched as Alysson shed her own outer garments and restlessly threw open the windows to look out over the vibrant French metropolis. It was obvious she was still excited and keyed up after the day's revelry. Yet he himself was feeling the exhilaration of the moment after so many years of striving fruitlessly to negotiate his sultan's release.

Events after the war had not gone as he'd hoped. Abdel Kader's surrender had been followed within a few weeks by a revolution in France and the end of King Louis-Philippe's reign. The new French government, in violation of the promise to allow Abdel Kader to seek refuge in a Muslim country, instead had imprisoned him and his family in France for nearly five years. During the entire interval, Jafar had spared no effort to free the emir, efforts which included persuading his ducal grandfather to petition the French emperor.

But now Abdel Kader's treacherous detention on French soil was finally at an end. At the invitation of Napoleon III, Jafar and Alysson had journeyed to Paris for the celebrations and to pay their respects to the Arab leader. Alysson claimed to be enjoying herself, yet this was only the third day of parades and ceremonies, and already she was professing an eagerness to return to Algeria.

"How stuffy this room is," she exclaimed now, drinking in the crisp fall air. "I hadn't realized how much I've grown accustomed to fresh air. Or how much I would miss home."

Jafar smiled to watch her, his heart too full to vouchsafe a reply just then. He'd grown to love her more deeply with each passing day, if that were possible. In the intervening years of their spirited marriage, Alysson had presented him with two beautiful children—a son and a daughter—whom they'd left behind in England with his delighted grandfather. Both had inherited their mother's passion and independence, and Jafar loved them all the more for it.

"But I'm pleased we came," his wife was saying. "Otherwise, I might never have met your sultan. You never told me what a compelling man he is, Jafar. Or how humble. I felt so . . . special in his presence, like I was the only woman in the world."

"Perhaps because you are so special, my heart."

Alysson glanced absently over her shoulder, her thoughts still on the events of that morning. She'd finally had the opportunity to meet the charismatic Berber chieftain, Abdel Kader. A handsome and intelligent man, he was surprisingly young—in his mid-forties—with an incomparable grace and a fascinating smile that reminded her somewhat of Jafar. Alysson could very well see why her husband had been willing to follow him into battle, and why the French officials paid him such deference and attention now. Even Uncle Honoré had been impressed. She'd felt inordinately proud when Abdel Kader had called Jafar "brother."

She would have expected Jafar's thoughts to be similarly occupied, but he seemed more inclined to study her than to discuss the day's events.

"What are you thinking?" she asked curiously.

His intent expression softening, he gave her a smile that was slow and seductive. "I imagine you know."

Yes, Alysson realized, seeing his eyes haze with a possessive look. She knew. After nearly five years of marriage, she recognized very well that heated look which still had the power to make her breath quicken and her heart beat faster. He intended to make love to her.

A quiver of anticipation ran through her as she returned his regard. For a moment neither spoke except with hungry eyes, while passion and desire flowed strong and vibrant between them. Then, slowly, Jafar came to stand directly behind her.

Feeling his lips softly brush her temple, Alysson leaned back against her husband, heedless of crushing the full skirts of her promenade dress. "Have you forgotten we are expected at the opera this evening?" she asked a bit breathlessly.

"It is fashionable to be late."

"It isn't fashionable to spend the evening in bed with your wife. In most circles it would be considered quite scandalous."

"Indeed. But then when have you ever cared about scandal, my dove?"

Alysson gave a throaty laugh and capitulated. "Will you help me with the hooks?"

"I am yours to command."

He took his time, though. Almost lazily he removed her gown and crinoline petticoat, then muslin petticoats and corset, until finally only her lace undergarments—pantalettes and chemise—remained. Required to submit passively to his ministrations, Alysson found herself thinking back over the past years of her marriage and counting her blessings.

Those years had been good ones. As Jafar had wanted, they'd been married twice, first in a civil ceremony by the Bishop of Algiers, then in a lavish, week-long Berber celebration at Jafar's mountain fortress. She had never adopted her husband's religion, but she'd tried to observe his tribe's customs and traditions.

She had also done everything in her power to aid their cause and to support her husband in his role of keeping an uneasy peace between the French and the Algerines, the conquerors and the conquered. The decision Jafar had made to ally himself with Gervase de Bourmont had been the right one. Gervase had lived up to his promise to strive for a better future for the country. The native Arab and Berber tribes had at least one voice in the French government to support their cause, while the European settlers met a solid resistance to their ever-increasing greed. And for the most part, the bloodshed had ceased. Her Uncle Honoré was able to tend his thriving vineyards without fear of attack. Gervase, too, was satisfied with his life, having married a young Frenchwoman who properly adored him. Even Chand had found happiness in Algeria. Refusing to desert Alysson after her marriage, he'd gone with her to live among the Beni Abess. Eventually he'd taken a wife, a cousin of Tahar's, and now had several lively children of his own.

As for herself, Alysson remembered, the Beni Abess had accepted her completely, just as Jafar had predicted. Unlike her own peers. She was not "received" by some European families. But then, she had never cared about such things. Jafar was all she wanted or needed. He had eased the wild ache of wanderlust in her blood. No longer did she feel compelled to travel the globe searching for adventure, for some nebulous, elusive sense of fulfillment, of belonging. She had found her home in Jafar, and he in her.

"So many layers of clothing," she heard him say with amusement as he bent to press a kiss on the bare swell of breast above the neckline of her chemise.

The feeling was decadent, delicious, Alysson thought distractedly; she was nearly naked, while Jafar still wore his elegant frock coat and starched black cravat, with not a single hair out of place. Impatiently, she threaded her fingers through those sun-lightened locks that seemed more golden in the half-light of early evening. But Jafar refused to do more than tease her with a brief tantalizing kiss on her upturned mouth.

"There is no rush," he scolded mildly. "I want to enjoy you."

That promise alone served to arouse her blood to a fever pitch, but Alysson obeyed without protest as her husband led her to the bed and made her sit on the edge.

He then proceeded to increase her frustration level with his unhurried movements, pulling off her slippers one by one, slowly massaging each slender foot, making a production out of drawing off her garters and embroidered stockings. Only then did he finally push her back gently onto the bed.

Feeling herself sinking into the feather mattress, Alysson realized that a soft bed was another amenity she was no longer accustomed to. This one was entirely too soft after the mats and carpets at home, and not nearly as satisfying without her husband's hard muscular body beside her.

She tried to reach for him, but Jafar captured her hands and pinned them to her side while he knelt before her. Her breath caught in a soft gasp as he kissed her through the soft cambric of her pantalettes, his tongue hot and moist.

"Jafar . . ." she murmured, stirring restlessly.

"Not yet, *Ehuresh.*"

Ehuresh. Defiant one. His endearments had become more lavish and varied over the years . . . pride of my heart, sunshine of my life, my adored one . . . but her favorite one was *Ehuresh.* She occasionally still gave him reason to call her that, but in general, she rarely defied him these days. Perhaps because he rarely gave her cause. No man could have been more considerate of her wishes. No man could have been a more wonderful husband, a more loving father, a more magnificent lover.

Then again, she had mellowed somewhat herself. Not enough to call him "master," perhaps, but she had upon occasion kissed Jafar's hands in public, which was a Berber woman's way of paying her husband a high compliment.

She would have kissed his hands now—those skillful, magical hands—but he wouldn't allow her to move. Forced to lie still, she could only whimper and grip the counterpane as Jafar indulged in his favorite form of torment—seeing how many ways he could arouse her.

He was the ultimate sensualist, savoring her, inundating her senses with pleasure, driving her half mad with his exquisite attentions. Shortly he had her arching against his mouth while her soft cries filled the room.

Only then did Jafar smile in satisfaction and continue with his undressing of her, drawing off her chemise and pantalettes before stepping back to remove his own clothing.

Still quivering in the aftermath, Alysson lay there languidly, watching her husband undress, admiring the sculpted lines of his hard, lean, beautiful body, and thinking of the ecstasy to come. He would take her with all the sweet savagery in him, and she would respond to him with all the passion she could summon. It was always like that, wild and intense and free.

When finally he stood naked before her in all his proud magnificence, she held out her arms to him eagerly. And when he joined her in the bed, settling with familiar ease in the cradle of her femininity, Alysson gave a breathless sigh of contentment. Locking her legs around his hips, she drew him more fully into her body, receiving the gift of his vital maleness, her damp softness gripping him.

"Mistress of my heart," Jafar whispered, his golden eyes hot and intense as he began the sweet urgent rhythm that would carry them to paradise and beyond.

"Yes . . ." she murmured in return, responding with the love of a passionate, giving woman for her chosen mate. "Yes . . ." she cried again moments later, welcoming him with all the joy within her.

Author's Note

Many historians consider the Berbers to be descendants of the Vandals, which would explain the predominance of fair hair and blue eyes among the Berber tribes of modern-day Barbary. There is no doubt that the Berbers occupied North Africa long before the Arabs and the Islamic religion swept across the continent in the seventh and eighth centuries A.D.

The Abdel Kader in my story is a true historical figure who led a Holy War against French domination for fifteen long years. In the end he was forced to surrender, in part because he failed to unite the factious tribes of Berbers and Arabs. After being imprisoned in France until 1852, Abdel Kader settled in Damascus, where he wrote, among other things, a philosophical treatise and a book about the splendid horses of the Sahara. A deeply devout Muslim, he was nevertheless credited with saving the lives of thousands of Christians during a Muslim uprising there.

He is also credited with saying to his French conquerors, "You are merely passing guests. You may stay three hundred years, like the Turks, but in the end you will leave."

It was more than a century later, in 1962, that Abdel Kader's prophecy of Algerian independence at last came true.

Avon Romances—
the best in exceptional authors and unforgettable novels!

HIGHLAND MOON Judith E. French
76104-1/$4.50 US/$5.50 Can

SCOUNDREL'S CAPTIVE JoAnn DeLazzari
76420-2/$4.50 US/$5.50 Can

FIRE LILY Deborah Camp
76394-X/$4.50 US/$5.50 Can

SURRENDER IN SCARLET Patricia Camden
76262-5/$4.50 US/$5.50 Can

TIGER DANCE Jillian Hunter
76095-9/$4.50 US/$5.50 Can

LOVE ME WITH FURY Cara Miles
76450-4/$4.50 US/$5.50 Can

DIAMONDS AND DREAMS Rebecca Paisley
76564-0/$4.50 US/$5.50 Can

WILD CARD BRIDE Joy Tucker
76445-8/$4.50 US/$5.50 Can

ROGUE'S MISTRESS Eugenia Riley
76474-1/$4.50 US/$5.50 Can

CONQUEROR'S KISS Hannah Howell
76503-9/$4.50 US/$5.50 Can